ACCLAIM FOR
THE 13TH TRIBE

"The author of *Comes a Horseman* ushers in an exciting new series with this action-packed and intricately plotted spiritual thriller that should appeal to fans of Frank Peretti and Oliver North."

— *Library Journal*

"Liparulo opens the Immortal Files series with a bang . . . A fast-moving, imaginative narrative that examines moral questions . . . Every reader is in for roller-coaster action . . ."

— *Publishers Weekly*

"Drawn from scripture and history, these characters are walking mysteries thrust into situations where trouble is bound to happen. A great read!"

— Frank Peretti, best-selling author of
This Present Darkness

"In *The 13th Tribe*, Robert Liparulo plunges deep into the pages of scripture to find intriguing what-if's and stunning revelations—all woven into a tale that is both skin-tinglingly supernatural and thought-provokingly real. And with all the high-tech, action, and heart that has always made his books a blast to read. Liparulo is a phenomenal storyteller, and *The 13th Tribe* is a phenomenal story. Read this novel! Seriously!"

— Ted Dekker, *New York Times* best-
selling author of *Forbidden* and the
Circle series

"*The 13th Tribe* is a work of sweeping imagination and high-octane action that grabbed me, intrigued me, and wouldn't let me go. The best Liparulo novel I've read yet."

— Steven James, best-selling author of
The Queen

WITHDRAWN

"One of those rare books where cliché descriptions like 'riveting, page-turner, couldn't put it down' must be used, because they're all absolutely true. With *The 13th Tribe*, Robert Liparulo has crafted the start of what is sure to be an epic series."

— James L. Rubart, best-selling
author of *Rooms*

"A rousing, imaginative thriller. I was mesmerized from the opening page. Robert Liparulo does it again!"

— James Scott Bell, best-selling
author of *Deceived* and *Die Trying*

"Cutting-edge technology and ancient vendetta come together in an adrenaline-laced cocktail of intrigue, action, and the hope for redemption. Thrill-master Liparulo's most riveting story yet. An electrifying supernatural ride that will leave you tearing through the pages and thinking long after you've closed the cover."

— Tosca Lee, *New York Times* best-
selling author of *Demon* and the
Books of Mortals series

"No one mixes fascinating characters, cutting-edge technology, biblically based speculative fiction, and can't-put-it-down suspense better than Robert Liparulo. The premise of *The 13th Tribe* is such a great idea that I wish I'd thought of it first! I was riveted, turning the pages as fast as I could, racing toward the nail-biting climax (which is set in an inspired location that's way too good to spoil). With one mind-blowing twist after another, *The 13th Tribe* is Liparulo at his very best."

— Robin Parrish, author of *Corridor*
and *Vigilante*

"In *The 13th Tribe*, Robert Liparulo dives into Biblical history, raises tough questions about the nature and goodness of God, adds in his trademark dash of futuristic technology, and does it all in the context of a pulse-pounding, page-turning story."

— LifeIsStory.com

THE
JUDGMENT
STONE

ROBERT LIPARULO

THE JUDGMENT STONE

THE IMMORTAL FILES

BOOK TWO

THOMAS NELSON
Since 1798

NASHVILLE   DALLAS   MEXICO CITY   RIO DE JANEIRO

© 2013 by Robert Liparulo

Published in Nashville, Tennessee, by Thomas Nelson. Thomas Nelson is a registered trademark of Thomas Nelson, Inc.

Thomas Nelson, Inc., books may be purchased in bulk for educational, business, fundraising, or sales promotional use. For information, please e-mail SpecialMarkets@ ThomasNelson.com.

Scripture quotations are taken from the following: THE HOLY BIBLE, NEW INTERNATIONAL VERSION®, NIV®. Copyright © 1973, 1978, 1984, 2010 by Biblica, Inc.™ Used by permission. All rights reserved worldwide. www.zondervan.com

THE NEW KING JAMES VERSION © 1982 by Thomas Nelson, Inc. Used by permission. All rights reserved.

The Message by Eugene H. Peterson. © 1993, 1994, 1995, 1996, 2000. Used by permission of NavPress Publishing Group. All rights reserved.

Publisher's Note: This novel is a work of fiction. Names, characters, places, and incidents are either products of the author's imagination or used fictitiously.

Library of Congress Cataloging-in-Publication Data

Liparulo, Robert.
  The judgment stone / by Robert Liparulo.
    pages cm.—(An Immortal Files Novel ; 2)
  ISBN 978-1-59554-172-7 (trade paper)
  1. Immortalism—Fiction. 2. Christian fiction. I. Title.
  PS3612.I63J83 2013
  813'.6—dc23   2012051411

Printed in the United States of America

13 14 15 16 17 RRD 6 5 4 3 2 1

To Amanda Bostic—

Thank you for sharing your story
brilliance and your friendship with me.

"Hell is empty and all the devils are here."
—WILLIAM SHAKESPEARE, *THE TEMPEST*

And I heard a man's voice from the Ulai calling,
"Gabriel, tell this man the meaning of the vision."
—DANIEL 8:16 (NIV)

"Your eye is a lamp, lighting up your whole body.
If you live wide-eyed in wonder and belief, your
body fills up with light. If you live squinty-eyed in
greed and distrust, your body is a dank cellar."
—LUKE 11:34 (THE MESSAGE)

[1]

The surface-to-air missile blasted out of a rocket launcher resting on the monk's shoulder and streaked toward the hovering helicopter. Fire plumed from the rear of the bazooka-like weapon, bright in the nighttime gloominess of St. Catherine's courtyard, momentarily blinding Jagger Baird, who stood behind it and off to one side. Through the haze of bleached retinas he saw the 'copter rise and whirl around with the aerial agility of a hawk and the rocket sail past it. Seeming confused, the projectile corkscrewed toward the moon and exploded. The helicopter moved beyond the compound's west wall, over the monastery's gardens, and vanished.

Jagger watched for a few more seconds. When it didn't reappear, he stepped closer to Father Leo. The youthful monk's splotchy beard, flowing black cassock, and—mostly—the smoking weapon still perched on his shoulder made him look more like a Taliban fighter than a man of God.

Jagger said, "Where'd you get that?"

Leo turned a big grin on him. "If only the rocket had been heat-seeking."

"Any more?"

Leo let the launcher slide off his shoulder and fall to the stone ground. "I wish." He reached inside his cassock and pulled out a black shotgun. He pumped the forestock, chambering a shell.

"I need a gun," Jagger told him.

Leo's forehead creased. "Where's yours?"

As head of security for the archeological dig outside the east wall of the monastery, Jagger should have been armed to the teeth—at least better equipped than the monks—but Egypt enforced strict

1

gun restrictions, especially among foreigners. Still, he had petitioned Gheronda, the monastery's abbot, for a firearm, and the old man had reluctantly given him a Ruger Super Redhawk Alaskan, a short-barreled .44 magnum revolver with a wicked recoil. "All the brothers are afraid of it," Gheronda had explained with a slight smile. It was Jagger's under one condition: he had to keep it locked in a pistol safe in his apartment. Far from ideal—how many bad guys waited around while you ran for your gun?—but it was better than nothing. Or maybe not. Not when you were making your rounds when the action started, as he had been just as someone tried to blow open the compound's main gate.

Jagger looked up to his third-floor apartment, where he hoped his wife and son were holed up in a makeshift panic room: a small closet with a bolted metal door, which Jagger had installed after the last attack on the monastery. "Beth has it," he told Father Leo, picturing his wife pointing the weapon at the door in a two-handed grip. *Don't mess with Beth.*

Leo reached into his cassock again and produced a semiautomatic Glock, a model 17 9mm. He handed it to Jagger, who ejected the magazine, checked it for bullets, shoved it back into the grip, and chambered a round. That done, the two of them turned toward the gate. The inner iron door—one of three that blocked the entrance—bulged inward. Smoke seeped through the edges and streamed up the wall like a waterfall in reverse. Five other monks—Fathers Bardas, Luca, Antoine, Mattieu, and Corban—stood or crouched in a thirty-foot semicircle around it. Three of them wore black cassocks and caps. Luca, obviously rousted from bed, had on a gray flannel nightshirt that fell to his knees; all he needed was a cloth nightcap—and thirty more years—to be Ebenezer Scrooge awakened by a ghost. Corban wore a brown bathrobe cinched tight around his waist; a silver pectoral cross hung over his chest. Each of them was pointing either a rifle or a handgun at the gate. They looked as incongruous and awkward as Clint Eastwood competing in the Miss USA pageant.

"Back away!" Jagger yelled. He gestured with RoboHand, his

prosthetic forearm and clamping hook. "Hurry! Move!" The only way anyone was coming through would be if they detonated another explosive, which would most likely send the doors and surrounding stone walls hurling toward the monks.

Apparently, when the first explosion failed to breach the gate, the attackers had decided to use the helicopter to get in. Having encountered Leo's rocket, and with no way of knowing the one shot had exhausted his supply, their next move was anyone's guess.

"Only *six* of you?" Jagger said to Leo. "Where're the rest?"

"Not all of us are fighters. Not the kind you're used to."

"What kind are they?"

"Prayer warriors," Leo said. "You can bet they're engaging the enemy at this very moment."

"Wonderful," Jagger said. He scanned the grounds. The courtyard was wedge-shaped, about thirty feet at its widest point. It was formed by the front wall; the long basilica, which angled diagonally from the back of the courtyard toward the wall; and a structure built around the Well of Moses. No Disney-cute names here: supposedly it was the very well at which Moses met his future wife, Zipporah. Radiating out from the courtyard was a crazy jumble of buildings—constructed at odd angles, in various shapes and sizes and materials over the course of seventeen centuries—honeycombed by alleys, stairs, walkways, terraces, and tunnels. All of it was crammed into an area the size of a city block, hemmed in by ancient walls sixty feet high and nine feet thick.

Over the multileveled rooftops and terraces he could see the top floor of the Southwest Range Building at the far back of the compound. It stretched the entire length of the rear wall and, situated on high ground—the entire monastery was built on the sloping base of Mount Sinai—it appeared even larger than it was. In addition to a hospice, chapel, and monk cells, it housed a library and icon gallery, second only to the Vatican's in historic importance and monetary value. Whatever the attackers wanted, chances were it was there.

Behind the Southwest Range Building, the mountain on which

Moses had received the Ten Commandments rose like a watchful presence, a charcoal silhouette against a slate sky. Jagger was thankful for the moon, which here in the Sinai always seemed closer to Earth than it did back in Virginia. Even in its current half-lit state, its radiance washed away many of the compound's shadows and gave the surfaces a silvery luminosity.

He turned in a circle and stopped when he was facing Father Leo. The monk held the shotgun in one hand, its muzzle pointed up. Feet apart, spine straight, eyes slowly scanning the top of the front wall, he looked ready for anything. No fear, just vigilance. Jagger wondered how many times the man had defended the monastery and if he'd known what he was getting into when he joined the order.

Jagger asked, "What are they after?"

Continuing his visual sweep across the wall's ramparts, Leo shook his head. "I don't know."

In the still air Jagger could hear the blades of the helicopter slowing, its engine dropping to a purr, then cutting off. It had landed in front of the gardens, on the opposite side of the monastery from the archaeological dig. He ran toward the compound's northwest corner, bounded up a long flight of stone stairs, and came to a patio in front of a row of unused monk cells. He climbed onto a railing and hoisted himself onto the porch's steeply sloping roof. After twice almost losing his footing, he reached the flat roof of the monk cells. It was only about eight feet from the porch roof to the exterior wall; "small" didn't even begin to describe the private living space the monks allowed themselves. Crossing it, he reached the compound's outer wall, the top of which came to his chest. He climbed up and crawled to the outside edge.

The helicopter sat in the faded edge of the light from lamps mounted on the outside wall. It was canted on the slope leading to the mountain opposite Mount Sinai, its blades turning as slowly as a rotisserie. The things scrambling out of its wide side door and running toward the monastery made Jagger's breath stop in his lungs.

A single word gripped his mind, momentarily paralyzing him: *monsters.*

[2]

Beth sat on the floor of the bedroom-closet-turned-panic-room, knees bent up in front of her, back to a side wall. By the light of a battery-powered, pull-chain light, she smiled assurances at Tyler, sitting against the opposite wall, frightened eyes, brave smile.

She said, "Everything's all right."

"How do you know?"

"Your father's out there. That's good enough for me." But she didn't blame him for being scared. The last time there was trouble at the monastery, the boy had been shot. That time the attackers had been the Tribe, a small remnant of the original forty who'd been cursed with immortality for their transgressions with the golden calf. They sought redemption by killing sinners, but through millennia of secrecy and violence, their motives and methods had twisted into behavior Beth believed God could never condone. Together the family had discovered that Jagger was like them, an Immortal—a revelation even he had found as startling as the existence of Immortals in the first place. A car crash nearly two years earlier had fragmented his memories, making them neither complete nor reliable. It had also killed a family beloved by the Bairds and taken Jagger's left arm.

Hearing the blasts outside, Beth wondered if the Tribe had returned.

Tyler was now fully recovered from the gunshot wound, largely thanks to possessing a bit of Jagger's incredible healing ability, but he'd almost died and the whole ordeal had been traumatic for everyone. On the bright side, Tyler had snapped out of his need to regress to an age when things were less complicated and scary, when he found comfort in a blankie and his thumb. It amazed her that an event that

5

should have thrown him further into fearfulness and insecurity had instead made him one amazingly courageous and independent ten-year-old. He even wore around his neck the bullet they took out of him. She was proud of him for using it as a reminder of his victory over forces that had tried to kill him. She looked for it now, but his pajama top covered it.

"If everything's fine," Tyler said, "why do we have to be in here?"

"Because we promised Dad," she said. "Remember?"

Rolling his eyes, he made his voice deep and mimicked his father: "'Anything weird happens—gunshots, screams, little green men falling from the sky—get in there and bolt the door. Don't come out until you hear me on the other side.'"

She nodded and glanced at the rectangular metal door set flush to the wall above Tyler's head—the gun safe, just large enough to hold one handgun and a box of ammo. The lock was biometric: to open it, she or Jagger needed only to press a thumb on a square of black glass beside the door. She could get to it in seconds. Jagger wanted her to arm herself whenever she used the closet as a panic room—"*If* ever," she'd corrected him, truly believing he was being overcautious but loving him for it. She had also told him she'd wait until she needed the gun. Despite his teaching her and Tyler how to handle it safely, she didn't want to accidentally shoot herself or Tyler if something startled her while she was holding it in that tight space.

It was *such* a tight space, in fact, that if all three of them used it at once, Tyler would have to sit on one of their laps. She tried to imagine a situation in which Jagger ever would join them instead of fighting the threat, and she couldn't.

What had turned the closet into a panic room were a metal door, a special door-length hinge, four commercial-grade deadbolts, the gun safe, a light, and a bunch of supplies like batteries, a first-aid kit, freeze-dried food, two gallon jugs of water, and blankets.

She wished they'd invested in a satellite phone, though she didn't know whom she'd call. She didn't even know what the danger was. She had been washing the dinner dishes, Tyler had been brushing his teeth, and Jagger had been out making his evening rounds when they'd heard an explosion, and a tremor had run through the floor. Both her and Tyler's first inclination was to rush outside to see what happened, but she'd restrained herself and grabbed Tyler's arm. Then they'd heard shouting and doors slamming; that's when she'd guided her son into the panic room and locked the door. Since then, she thought she'd heard a helicopter, gunshots, and another explosion, this one farther off.

On the way into the closet she'd grabbed her Bible. She cracked it open now and turned to the book of John. It reminded her of God's active involvement in their lives, and she felt a tinge of hope. The Bible had been given to them by John the Apostle—also an Immortal and now using the name Owen Letois—who'd appeared at the monastery in time to save Tyler's life. And it was Owen who'd crashed his jet into the Tribe's drone control center, terminating their attack on Las Vegas. That he walked the earth was wondrous and miraculous; that she could call him friend was God bestowing a blessing on her family.

She read aloud: "Peace I leave with you, My peace I give to you; not as the world gives do I give to you. Let not your heart be troubled, neither let it be afraid."

Tyler smiled, and his face visually calmed. What she wouldn't give to have the faith of a child. The Bible says it, so it must be true. She believed that too, but her adult mind had a propensity to overcomplicate, to put a *but* after every sentence: *But bad things do happen . . . but my husband is out there, no doubt right in the thick of whatever's happening . . . but I'm still afraid.*

"Read more," Tyler said, so she did.

[3]

As the assault team came more fully into the light, Jagger realized they weren't monsters, only men—wildly dressed and cosmetically made up. One, two, three, all of them gripping assault rifles, two with big packs bouncing on their backs. They seemed a ragtag bunch, no uniformity.

One was bald with a mustache and long, pointed goatee; black raccoon makeup over his eyes; no shirt, showing off layers of bulging muscles. Another, tall, maybe six five, six six, wore jungle commando garb: an olive flak vest, matching long-sleeved shirt, and many-pocketed pants. Long black hair flowed out from under a camo hat, the soft brim pinned up on the sides. Two dark lines ran diagonally over each cheek from the bridge of his nose: war paint. The massive gun he carried easily, as if it weighed nothing, appeared to be a .50-cal Browning machine gun—BMG—the kind meant to be mounted in the rear of a Jeep. An ammo belt ran from the weapon and looped over his shoulders.

And one, he realized, was a woman. Jagger's stomach tightened, but then he realized she wasn't Nevaeh, leader of the Tribe. Where Nevaeh was catlike, smooth, this woman moved in sharp, fast jerks, twitchy. She could have fronted a rock band: shiny leather vest fastened in front with studs—bare arms and cleavage suggested nothing underneath—studded wrist bands, leather pants.

A fourth attacker fast-walked into the brighter light, arms swinging like upside-down metronomes, and Jagger decided "ragtag" didn't cut it; *insane* fit the bill better. The guy was a character straight out of a steampunk graphic novel. A tight leather mask covered his face and head, stitches everywhere; round brass-framed goggles; where his mouth should have been, a ribbed gas-mask hose dangled, ending in a canister bouncing against his sternum. He wore a leather trench coat, buttoned from collar to midthigh. The material itself went all the way to his ankles. He was carrying a crossbow, a quiver of arrows on his back.

Movement caught Jagger's eye, and he saw a man standing on the opposite slope in line with the main gate. He seemed to have been there awhile, watching. He wore all black: a tee under a sport coat, snappy slacks, and gleaming dress boots with pointed toes. A fedora angled slightly over a movie star face, dark features, evening shadow, close-cropped mustache, and soul patch. One hand hovered over his chest, a smoldering cigarette between two fingers. The other hand rested on his hip. All casual, just waiting for the show to begin.

Which it did, with an overture of machine-gun fire. Bullets chipped away the stone edge in front of Jagger. Fragments pelted his forehead and cheeks. He scrambled back and jumped down to the roof. Going from there to the porch's roof, in the darkness he misjudged the distance and slope and tumbled forward. He twisted himself around, continued to roll, and felt the roof vanish under him. His right hand grabbed the edge, lost it. RoboHand shot to an upright patio-roof support and clamped it with vise-like strength. He snapped to a stop, dangling fifty feet above a stone walkway.

He hefted himself up and over the railing and clambered down the stairs. He found Leo and the other monks just off the courtyard, huddled together between the Well of Moses and the basilica. They'd heard him coming, and every gun was pointed his way.

"What was that?" Leo asked. "The shooting."

"I guess they wanted me off the wall."

"And?"

"I got off."

"The Tribe?"

Jagger shook his head. "Not this time." He took in the monks, all with frightened eyes, none of them as composed as Leo. "They're coming," he said. "Four, heavily armed. There's a fifth, but he seems to be just watching."

Leo said, "You think they're going to try blowing the gate again?"

"They're heading toward it."

At that, two monks pressed their backs against the building; three crouched and took aim at the gate. Jagger listened, but no sounds came from the other side of the wall. A breeze whipped at the smoke pouring from the damaged gate and blew it across the courtyard at the men. Bardas coughed, trying not to, throwing a worried glance at Jagger. He was a twenty-something, nerdy-looking guy, whose soft, Hellenic-accented words belied a fierce competitiveness Jagger had witnessed during the monks' soccer matches in the gardens. Jagger smiled and nodded, trying to convey confidence.

He crouched beside Luca and patted his back. The monk turned his face to him—squinty eyes, hawkish nose. He reminded Jagger of Lee Van Cleef from *The Good, the Bad, and the Ugly*; he hoped now the guy was as good a shot.

Seconds passed . . . ten . . . twenty . . . and Jagger felt his heart beating. He wanted to look behind him, up at his apartment, just to see the light in the window and know Beth and Tyler were safe, but he didn't dare take his eyes off the gate: he expected everything to happen fast now.

Something clattered up high, on top of the wall, then *rrrrrrrrrrrrr*: an electric motor. Another clatter.

"They're coming over!" Luca shouted and sprang forward.

"Wait!" Jagger said, grabbing for Luca's nightshirt. He missed, and the monk darted into the courtyard, then backed to the basilica wall, eyes and pistol panning the top of the front wall.

"Luca!" Jagger had been an Army Ranger and a personal protection specialist, and he wanted to tell him that one of the worst battle situations was engaging an enemy who occupied higher ground. But he might as well have been addressing a tree; the monk was too keyed up to listen.

Bardas spun around the corner and ran to the front wall, directly under the sounds. He flattened himself against it, glaring straight up, pointing his rifle. Not a bad move, less likely the attackers could get a clean shot at him.

Two objects, each the size of a fruit crate, dropped off the top of the wall. They banged down hard on the stones and began humming and clattering, jittering like beetles on their backs. They appeared to be black metal boxes with tracked wheels, and judging from the positions of the wheels, one was upside down, the other on its side. Metal rods like insect legs swung across their bodies and pushed against the ground. Within seconds of landing they had righted themselves, revealing barrels mounted to their tops.

"Run!" Jagger yelled, but too late. The robots whirled toward the two exposed monks and began firing.

[4]

The chatter of machine-gun fire erupted from the monastery again, surprisingly loud in the still night air—even 1,500 feet up Mount Sinai, where Toby stood on an outcropping. He trained binoculars on the compound but couldn't pinpoint the location of all the action. Too many buildings in the way. He sidestepped until his foot felt the edge of the razorback. Still, he could see nothing but the dark shapes of buildings, amber lights here and there.

"Come on!" he said, almost throwing the binocs down.

The boy thought, acted, and looked like the fifteen-year-old he had been when God had apparently switched on his telomerase genes—that's what Ben had said—rendering him incapable of aging and accelerating his healing abilities. That had been 3,500 years ago: enough already. Which was why Nevaeh had sent him here again, to spy on Jagger's mortal wife, Beth.

For the last six months Nevaeh had been obsessed with the woman, feeling she held some secret that could lead them all to salvation, heaven, God . . . as Beth had done for Ben, the Tribe's previous leader. He had died after Beth had spoken to him at length.

Toby wasn't so sure: What could a single person say, simply say, that would rattle a soul from the flesh in which it had been stuck for so long? What could she say that all of them hadn't thought of a thousand times? Ben had stumbled onto something or eased into a realization over who-knew-how-long—he'd always been poring over theological and philosophical tomes, looking for a word or line or idea like a passkey into heaven. That it came together for him when they were holding the woman captive was pure coincidence. Had to be.

But there was no deterring Nevaeh from an obsession. She wasn't so much like a dog with a bone. That implied she could let go if she wanted to. No, she was more like a fish on a hook. Over the years most of her obsessions had been rooted in her belief that they would bring her closer to redemption: fasting with the monks at Germany's Säckingen Abbey (she twice consecutively repeated the monks' forty-day fast and would have gone longer if they hadn't threatened to expel her unless she ate); for a year, becoming a hermit in what she claimed was Elijah's grotto on Mount Carmel (this was before the Order of the Carmelites turned the cave into a crypt and shrine in the twelfth century); destroying pagan temples alongside Martin of Tours, who'd become so alarmed by her zealotry he banished her to the Eberbach Convent.

So now it was with Beth. Nevaeh wanted to get her alone, find out what she'd told Ben. Not just pick her brain, but excavate it until something happened—a revelation . . . *something*. Toby hoped for the woman's sake that whatever it was happened fast; knowing Nevaeh, she would keep Beth for however long it took—for the rest of her life, Beth's or Nevaeh's, whichever came first.

After securing a new home/headquarters for the Tribe's remaining seven members, Nevaeh had declared it was time to pursue her new obsession and had dispatched Toby to St. Catherine's. So far, he had determined Beth was still there and had identified patterns in her daily schedule—grocery shopping in the village, strolls through the gardens—that provided kidnapping opportunities.

But now this, an attack.

He'd better inform Nevaeh. She'd have questions he couldn't answer, but if he didn't tell her and something happened to Beth, she'd blame him. Never mind there was nothing he could do; she'd twist the facts to make it look like it was his fault.

He dropped the binocs, letting them dangle by a strap around his neck, and stepped to the rear edge of the outcropping. He lifted his T-shirt, squinting against the darkness to see the mesh, wire-laced belt around his waist. He toggled a switch near the buckle, turning on a green LED light. The high-pitched whine of charging capacitors came from the battery pack at the small of his back. His heavy carbon-fiber boots issued a series of metal-clunking sounds. He felt them stiffen around his feet, ankles, and calves; the braces running up the outside of his legs rattled slightly, and the two C-shaped clamps over his hip bones tightened. He rotated his hips to make sure the clamps weren't gripping too much to prevent easy movement. Magnetorheological fluid—a suspension of tiny iron particles in silicon oil—under the boots' insoles hardened and loosened in a ripple from heel to toe as electrical currents passed through it and turned off, testing its functionality and preparing the boots for use.

Called Austin boots, after TV's *Bionic Man* Steve Austin, the lower-limb exoskeleton was part of a Future Warrior System developed by DARPA—the government's research and development arm—to augment human performance on the battlefield. Super-fast microprocessors sensed movement in the hips, legs, and feet to determine the wearer's intentions to walk, run, or jump, then instructed the boots to assist the action. Versions currently being field-tested allowed twenty-foot leaps and fifteen mile-per-hour sprints. The ones Toby wore were several generations beyond those, capable of propelling a person fifty feet in the air and across terrain as fast as twenty-five miles per hour.

Nevaeh had found them in a crate that arrived at a warehouse in London, which the Tribe used for such deliveries. Ben had arranged their acquisition prior to his death. She didn't have the same connections at DARPA he'd had—cultivated by years of exchanging his vast know-how for early prototypes—but she was working on it. "This may be the last technology we see from them for a while," she'd said. "Let's make good use of them . . . and not destroy them," she'd added, referring to the invisibility suits that had vaporized in the plane crash that had ended their last mission.

DARPA had shipped five pairs of the boots—Toby couldn't imagine what Ben had promised or threatened to get even one, let alone enough for nearly the whole Tribe. With Ben and Creed gone, even Jordan had secured his own; Sebastian had shortened the braces, tightened the hip clamps, and used water booties to make them fit the seemingly eleven-year-old boy. So now the Tribe's usual strike team—Nevaeh, Phin, Elias, Toby, and Jordan—were all the fastest soldiers on two feet. They'd practiced with them in the open, rugged terrain of Alia, thirty-five miles outside Palermo. They weren't easy to learn. Putting them on the first time, Toby had stomped his feet and done a backward flip out of his chair into the wall behind him, the first of many bangs and bruises earned in mastering the Austin boots.

Now he jumped off the outcropping to the ground twelve feet below. The boots sensed the fall, and the system prepared to absorb the landing, extending its pistons in the soles and using its braces to force Toby to bend a bit at the knees. Upon impact the pistons retracted; shock absorbers at the knees defused downward momentum, and the hip clamps squeezed in, easing him down like a daddy helping his son jump out of a tree. Not that Toby knew what that was like; he hadn't seen his father in 3,500 years. But he did watch movies, so he could imagine.

He landed in a circular clearing mostly surrounded by cliff walls and felt a hot wire of pain shoot from hip to tailbone. Not the fault of the Austin boots or even the leap from the outcropping: this was an injury left over from Owen's successful effort to stop the Tribe from wiping out Las Vegas with weaponized drones. Six months ago—on the same day Ben had knelt to pray for the last time—the nut had flown his jet into their command post. Toby, Phin, Cabot, and Nevaeh had suffered injuries that truly challenged their healing powers. Broken bones, torn away and burned flesh, internal injuries. Besides the hitch in his hip, Toby still felt an ache deep inside and wondered if this was what it was like growing old. Maybe something had mended incorrectly and his body would never feel quite right again. He didn't like the idea of spending another few months, let alone centuries, feeling this way.

Ignoring the pain, defying it, he hurried to the small cave he was using to sleep and store his supplies. It was the same cave in which Jagger—that's what he called himself these days—found him when Toby was watching the monastery for Creed. He didn't think Jagger would come looking for him again, and it was too good a vantage point to give up. He reached into the cave and grabbed the satphone from the top of his sleeping bag. He stood and looked at the phone, thinking about what he would tell Nevaeh.

When he'd seen the helicopter fly in and then heard the explosion, it'd struck him that maybe she had changed her plans. It would be just like her to scrap the idea of a quiet kidnapping for a no-holds-barred, get-it-done assault. Then he thought: *Nah, she would have told me. Wouldn't she?*

But who else wanted to attack the place?

Maybe she'd decided to go for more than the woman. Maybe it was payback time: Owen may have been at the controls, but it had been he *and* Jagger who'd caused the airplane crash that'd hurt them so badly and stopped them from fulfilling their mission of wiping out that city of sinners.

What happens in Vegas stays in Vegas . . . Man, if that wasn't an invitation to sin, Toby didn't know what was.

Nevaeh had talked about how taking Beth would be like spearing two bodies with one thrust: she'd get to debrief Beth while nailing Jagger with a retaliatory blow where it would hurt him the most. She may have decided that wasn't enough, that she wanted to make him bleed.

Toby carried the phone to where the outcropping ended, leaving an opening from which he could look down a rocky slope at the monastery.

She's going to want to know who's attacking, he thought. *And what am I going to say? Gee, I thought it was you.*

He had to get a closer look, do everything possible to have answers for her questions. He looked down at his boots. Why not? He slipped the phone into a pants pocket and buttoned the flap. He leaped onto the slope, scree sliding out from under him. The boots adjusted instantly to stabilize him, at the same time boosting his efforts, springing him forward. He could barely feel the impact of each step as the magnetorheological fluid cushioned his feet, then nanoseconds later hardened over the firing pistons.

He bounded down the mountain in eight-foot strides. He jumped to a boulder and sprang from it, putting twenty feet of treacherous terrain behind him before touching ground again, heading for the rear wall of the compound.

It was breathtaking. He wanted to whoop, but he held it in and concentrated on not tumbling ahead of the boots. He thought about what would happen if they suddenly lost power or a leg brace seized up. It'd be like spilling out of a speeding car onto razor-sharp rocks.

The wall was coming up fast, a flat blackness before him, and he had to decide where to make his leap. The Southwest Range Building rose above the entire length of wall, except on the ends, where it stepped down to lower buildings that were almost even with the top of the wall. So there, one of the ends. He saw a large boulder close to the left edge of the wall and aimed for it.

He leaped onto it with both feet and sprang up, feeling the boots' pistons blasting down to shoot him up. Right away he realized his mistake: by leaning forward, the boots gave the pistons in his heels a little more oomph, putting him on an upward and forward trajectory—great for hurdling cars and fences, not so hot for reaching the top of a wall.

He slammed into the wall halfway up, smacking his knees, arms, and head. He dropped straight down, instinctively keeping his feet under him so the boots would cushion his fall. It still hurt, and he crumpled on the ground. Rubbing his fresh bruises, he got himself up and started back up the mountain. Another great thing about the boots was their ability to power uphill treks without taxing your muscles.

A dozen long strides later he turned and made another run at the wall, bounding onto the boulder with flat feet. He shot nearly straight up, but not quite high enough to land cleanly on the wall. He punched into the edge with his stomach, leaned his upper torso onto the top, and pulled himself up.

He rolled onto his back and breathed hard. He stared at the stars for a few minutes, listening to gunfire reverberate off the compound's buildings and walls. Then he stood to see what he could see.

[5]

The robots didn't pause after mowing down Luca and Bardas. They spun, looking for more targets. The smoking barrels of their machine guns turned past the alley where Jagger, Leo, and the other three monks hid, peering out. The bots pivoted back toward them. Their wheel systems, miniature versions of a tank's, propelled them forward. Jagger and the others pulled back.

Jagger had read about these things—technically called Unmanned Ground Combat Vehicles, UGCVs. Human operators, probably just outside the wall, directed them remotely, using video-game-like controllers equipped with monitors. He poked his head around the corner, and both robots fired. He jumped back, knocking into Leo. The monks were scrambling to get away. The wall on the other side of their position erupted in dust, chunks of stone, and ricocheting bullets.

The gunfire stopped. *Rrrrrrrrrrrrrr*—growing closer.

He'd have thought these mini-Terminators would have come out of DARPA, the US military's invention division, responsible for everything from the computer mouse to aerial combat drones. But if these buggers were the ones Jagger had heard about—appropriately called Cobras—they were Israeli made, armed with modified Uzis—nine millimeter, rapid-fire killing machines. They were equipped with night vision lenses and infrared, letting their controllers track the heat of their prey's footsteps. They could slip through two-foot-wide openings, climb flights of stairs, and accelerate up to ten miles per hour, faster than the average man could run.

"Go! Go!" Jagger yelled, shoving his hands into Leo's back. He glanced over his shoulder, a futile move: no doubt the Cobras would start firing as soon as their targets were in sight. *Rrrrrrrrr*. Their shadows slid into view along the stones.

"Into the tunnel, the tunnel!"

The monks jabbered in Italian, Greek, and something else, in panic each reverting to his native tongue. They bounded into the black opening of a tunnel that would bend and turn, preventing the Cobras from getting a straight shot at them—at least for the next ten seconds or so.

The monastery was such a jumbled mess of buildings on top of buildings, tunnels, cubbies, and walls—Jagger didn't know if the chaos would help them escape or pin them in a maze that guaranteed capture.

The monastery was nearly square. The apartments—where Jagger's family lived on the third floor—were pressed against the back half of the "garden wall," on the other side of which bloomed an oasis of trees and lush plants. Administrative buildings clung to much of the front wall, which also hosted the main gate. Chapels and monk cells lined the east wall, beyond which lay the archeological dig. And running the entire length of the back wall was the impressive Southwest Range Building. Directly inside the front gates were the bell tower and the basilica. Behind the basilica, as near the northeast corner as the rectory and monk quarters would allow, was the burning bush, supposedly the very bush through which God spoke to Moses. Packed into the rest of the interior were storage buildings, monk cells, the mosque—near the garden gate—and other structures, forming a warren of walkways, terraces, and tunnels. Scattered throughout were a myriad of small courtyards formed by buildings or walls on all sides.

Jagger knew how to get from his apartment to the front gate. He could also make a circuit around the interior for security purposes. But the details of the place still eluded him. Tyler, who'd spent long days exploring, knew the layout best and had once presented his parents with a detailed map of his own making. Jagger wished he had it now.

He suspected their assailants would not be content to merely chase them away—why stop there? If they gunned down the men guarding the compound, the attackers could waltz in and take whatever they wanted at their leisure. Or worse: what if the plan was to wipe out everyone inside? It wouldn't be so difficult; besides the five of them scrambling through the tunnel and the two downed monks in the courtyard, the monastery housed only thirteen more people: Beth and Tyler, the lead archaeologist Oliver, the abbot Gheronda, and nine other monks. Jagger wouldn't be surprised if the Cobras were capable of battering or blasting their way through doors.

"Wait, wait," Jagger said. The group stopped where a dim bulb illuminated a Y-split in the tunnel. The right branch wound toward the back corner of the compound, where the Southwest Range Building met the main apartment building; the left branch would take them to the burning bush. "We have to get around them, come at them from behind," Jagger said.

"And then what?" Leo asked.

Jagger shook his head. "Jump on them . . . shoot their engines." He grabbed Leo's arm. "We can't just run from them. Or hide. They'll catch us, find us . . . or someone else." He was thinking of Beth and Tyler, coming out of the apartment to find out what was going on, running into those things.

The Cobras' humming engines and whirling tracks echoed from the blackness behind them, close.

"All right then," Leo said. He brushed past his monastic brethren, headed toward the burning bush, and was engulfed by blackness, as though he'd plunged into a pool of oil. The others followed. Jagger grabbed the strip of leather around Father Mattieu's waist and let himself be guided as he fast-walked backward and watched the lighted intersection behind them. When the group rounded a bend, cutting off his view of the intersection, he released Mattieu's belt and edged back until he could see the intersection again.

He extended the gun, using RoboHand to steady his aim. The first Cobra rolled into the pool of light, turning toward the tunnel, and he pulled the trigger. Again, again, again. His bullets sparked against a

dome above the Cobra's gun—what Jagger took to be a camera hous-
ing—but nothing shattered, nothing broke.

The Cobra let rip with return fire, loud, echoing in the tunnel.

Jagger pushed against the wall, slid around the bend. The stream
of bullets blasted against the opposite wall, chest high. Chips of stone
slapped his cheek. He dropped to the ground, shifted his gun into
RoboHand, and thrust it around the bend. He fired blindly. Before
his second shot, the chaos on the opposite wall lowered and he felt a
bullet ping against his pistol. Another knocked it out of his hand. The
Glock clattered on the stones, spinning, and stopped in the center of
the tunnel. He reached for it, and a bullet slammed into his hook, like
a club. He yanked his arm in, pulled it close to his chest, and watched
the stone floor spark and kick up dust as bullets pelted it.

He glanced at RoboHand. The bullet had dimpled the metal
where the thumb-like hook pivoted to form a grip against the larger
hook, which formed a T at the tip to provide a larger point of contact. He flexed his arm and back muscles to operate the smaller hook.
Instead of its typically smooth opening and closing, it popped and
stuttered, stopping a quarter inch from the larger hook.

He pushed away from the bend and stood. The bullets kept coming. The sound of gunfire grew louder; the Cobra was advancing, firing
as it came. He calculated: an Uzi's rate of fire was about 600 rounds
a minute. One Cobra could easily carry at least that many rounds,
giving it a full minute of firepower. Assuming he could retrieve his
gun, he wouldn't have a chance to shoot at it again before it reached
him. Not that he believed his bullets would stop it, even if he could hit
it. He waited another few seconds—trying to think if there was any
reason to stay, listening to the deafening roar of the constant barrage
getting louder.

He pushed off the wall and ran to catch up with the monks.

[6]

Nevaeh parked her rented car on the cobblestoned street in front of the Sana Sesimbra Hotel. As soon as she opened the door, the smell of cooking fish—grilled, sautéed, *en papillote*, with butter, saffron, garlic, *lots* of garlic—engulfed her. She looked up the street at all the restaurants, most with outdoor seating, still bustling at half past eight. She locked the car and crossed Av. 25 de Abril to the beach. The sand was yellow and soft; she could have been walking on a foam pillow. It would be warm, she knew, if she stripped off her boots and socks, but she wasn't here as a tourist to stroll through the surf, bask in the sun. It was too late anyway: the sun was nearly touching the wet horizon, turning the Atlantic into undulating black velvet.

Heading northwest, the ocean on her left, she pulled her mobile phone from a pocket, switched off the ringer, and dropped it back in. People were still on the beach, mostly families whose kids refused to call it a day and couples who hadn't yet started the transition from sand and waves to cocktails and dubstep in the many clubs that filled the town.

As she walked toward the harbor she realized the music had already started. She looked back across the street; past a palm tree-lined promenade was a glass-and-steel building wedged between older, stuccoed facades. Blue and red light pulsed against the inside of the windows, in time with the thumping of a bass beat.

She shook her head. Things had changed a lot in the century since she'd last set foot in Sesimbra—anywhere in Portugal, for that matter, except for the occasional refueling stop in Lisbon on the Tribe's way to mete out justice wherever in the world it needed meting out. Sesimbra was once a small fishing village, where it was easy to forget that the rest of the world was rushing to find new ways to destroy itself, physically and spiritually. Now it was a resort destination for the young and rich: at least half the beachfront buildings were dance clubs or white-tablecloth restaurants; mud mask-treated faces had replaced the old toothless and weathered ones; condos, apartments, and hotels—one, stark white with a grid of terraces, looked like a grounded cruise ship—fanned out from the ancient town center. They climbed the foothills of the Serra da Arrábida mountains, almost to the old walls of the Castle of Sesimbra.

Her eyes lingered on the castle, its tall, perfectly square keep and matching watchtower. During the Middle Ages it had defended and fallen to a succession of invading Moors and Castilians. Epic battles—in one of which Nevaeh herself and the entire Tribe, twenty-eight strong at the time, had fought atop those high ramparts. She missed those times, the camaraderie of armies united for a just cause, the intimacy of death, the clarity of right and wrong. Modern "civility," under the flags of tolerance and politeness and humility, clouded moral confidence, making men weak. Just once she'd like to see a modern preacher hack apart a sinner the way Samuel did Agog, king of the Amalekites. But no, it would never happen. People turned a blind eye to sin, or expected authorities to step in . . . or left it for the Tribe to do their dirty—albeit godly—work for them. *Spineless sissies.*

Nevaeh slipped her hand beneath her calf-length leather trench coat—fashion in complete contrast with the location, as were her S.W.A.T. boots and jumpsuit, all black, but what did she care? She touched the material over her outer thigh and felt the hilt of the short sword in the special pocket stitched there. She imagined a day when everyone carried one, ready to slay sinners in the name of God. No trial, no evidence but one's own eyes and knowledge of God's word. It would be a slaughter, until all sinners were wiped from the face of the earth.

Keep dreaming, she thought and continued walking. She approached the Fortaleza de Santiago, a stone fort built right on the beach in the seventeenth century as a first line of defense, then later to keep pirates from pillaging the surrounding communities. What made the village ideal for fishermen and their families—deep water, an inlet that kept the sea calm, a crescent of mountains that protected the land from winds and wanderers—also appealed to invaders.

The fort was so near the surf that high tide brought the water up to its foundation, severing the beach in two. But the tide had come and gone, leaving a swath of moist, patted-down sand. Nevaeh ran her fingers over the fort's rough stone as she strode past. Last time she'd seen the place, it had been a prison.

Memories rushed her like lunatics out for blood, howling and frantic, and she slammed a mental door on them. If she tried hard enough, she could luxuriate in the pleasant memories of her time here—the last time she thought maybe, just maybe she could live somewhat normally, with an abundance of sunshine and a dearth of slaughter, at least for a while. But the malice of the world and the burden of who she was—*what* she was—shattered that dream too quickly and too abruptly, as they always did. Would she never learn?

A beach ball bounced against the wall, and Nevaeh caught it before it pelted her in the face. A boy was running toward her. She smiled and tossed it to him. He caught it and stared at her over the ball, certainly dumbfounded by her attire. If he were half a dozen years older, he'd be staring at her for an entirely different reason, trying to hit on her despite her costume. She winked at him and walked on.

As she approached the harbor, she was pleased to see it full of small fishing boats, rising and falling slowly on swells she couldn't see, their flamboyant colors dim in the twilight. She'd been afraid the fish sizzling for out-of-town diners were themselves from out of town, Setúbal or Azoia maybe. But apparently the yuppies or preppies or whatever they were had not yet pushed away all the rugged men who pulled their livelihood from Sesimbran waters. Somewhere among the expensive villas and resort buildings were the vestiges of the small village she had once loved. She wished she could stay till the morning, when the nightclubs had closed and the tourists were fast asleep; that's when the true residents would appear, shuffling out from the glitter and glam to mend nets, splice lines, fill their bait boxes. They would be the great-grandchildren of her onetime friends and neighbors, but she knew in her heart they would bear the same scruffy appearance and laid-back attitude—not lazy, not slackers, just—she searched for the right word—*philosophical*, wise about what mattered in life and content with their station.

Her visit, however, was intended to be quick, in and out. Any longer would be dangerous.

She traversed the beach beside the harbor and moored boats, first the glistening yachts, then the fishing boats—poised and pedigreed show dogs and junkyard mongrels sharing the same pen.

She was away from the nightclubs and fancy restaurants now. The odor of raw fish guts and the milling about of the men who'd gutted them acted as a natural defense mechanism to repel predatory developers. Only a few low-end souvenir and beach paraphernalia shops on this end of town. And a little farther on, where the sand met the foliage as it began its climb up the hills, was the villa she was looking for. Salmon-colored stucco with a partially covered flagstone patio. Three gray columns delineated the end of the roof and added to the place's Mediterranean feel. It was small but appealing; situated by itself on the edge of a popular beach resort, it could probably fetch a million euros or more.

Children scampered around on the patio, laughing and chattering in Portuguese. The boys wore tattered cutoffs and colored tees, the girls bright sun dresses trimmed with lace. Local kids.

Nevaeh spotted what had drawn them: *pastéis de nata*, palm-sized pies of baked egg custard, half eaten in their hands, a few left on a platter that rested on a round glass-topped table.

Two little girls stood talking to an old man seated at the table. Slightly hunched, mostly bald but for short white patches above his ears and wispy strands arching over the spotted crown of his skull; his face was gaunt, his skin like a salvaged piece of crumpled parchment, but his nose was straight and regal, his eyes bright as they darted between the girls and the other children. He flashed a set of teeth that seemed too large for his shrunken face, and he laughed, a hacking sound that couldn't quite compete—in volume or level of merriment—with the children's voices.

She had found the man she had come for.

[7]

Jagger caught up with the monks in the courtyard of the burning bush, between the back of the basilica and the refectory. The massive bush itself billowed up from an eight-foot-high, semicircular stone planter built into the back of a building. Its leafy stems hung over half the courtyard like a shabby weeping willow. Standing upright on the stone ground beside the burning bush, in a gesture that Jagger had never figured out whether it was meant to be humorous or serious, was a fire extinguisher. A bulb cast jaundiced light over the area, making everyone look sick.

Leo stared at Jagger, who was holding RoboHand as if it were injured flesh and blood.

"It's nothing," Jagger said, releasing his hook. "They're tough buggers, these Cobras—I think that's what they're called. I shot one of them at least four times. It didn't even pause." He turned toward the short flight of stairs he'd descended to reach the court. At the landing on top, another flight led down to the tunnel. "The stairs might slow them down, but not for long."

Rrrrrrrrrrrr—behind them. The men spun, guns coming up. Not yet visible, a Cobra was heading toward them from the alley between the basilica and the front wall, where the monks had been killed.

The sound of another motor reached them, this one reverberating off the walls of the alley on the other side of the basilica. The burning bush courtyard had three entrances, one on each side of the basilica and a third the way they'd reached it, down the stairs. The Cobras had all three covered.

"They must've backtracked," Leo said. "We have to go back through the tunnel."

"No way the one in the tunnel could have gotten out of there so fast," Jagger said. "They must have sent in another."

"*At least* one more," Antoine said.

"The rooftops," Corban said in a thick Irish accent and darted for the stairs. When he passed the alley, three quick shots rang out, the bullets striking the wall of the refectory. The monk bounded up the steps, and Jagger realized what he was doing: at the landing, one flight went down to the tunnel, another went up to the rooftops and terraces. Getting there would buy them a little time and give them the high ground.

"Come on," he said, pulling at Leo's arm. A second later he froze.

Corban reached the landing, and machine gun fire threw him into a wall. He tumbled down into the court. He rose, holding his shoulder, blood spilling out between his fingers. "It's coming . . . up the stairs," he said, groaning. "From the tunnel." He staggered toward them.

"No!" Jagger said, raising his hand.

Gunfire from the alley ripped the night open, and Corban jerked and twitched as bullets sliced through him. He stumbled back and fell onto the stairs. He lay there motionless, gazing at the moon, bleeding from a dozen wounds. Two seconds, that's all it had taken.

The monks yelled out, began mumbling, weeping.

"Shhhh . . . shhhh," Leo said, raising his hands.

The Cobras' motors churned, all of them still out of sight. From the stairs . . . the back alley . . . Leo turned toward the loudest, closest of the three and ran toward the front alley.

"Leo!" Jagger said.

Leo stopped inches from the corner and pressed himself against the wall. To his credit, he didn't take a peek, just listened.

He's going to grab it, Jagger thought. *Just grab the thing, lift it, and point the barrel in any safe direction.* He knew it could be done—he felt sure the attackers had carried them in backpacks. They couldn't be *that* heavy.

He considered positioning himself at the other corner, doing the same with the Cobra that had killed Corban. But then there was the

Cobra coming up the stairs. If they didn't get out of the courtyard fast, it would wipe them all out. No, it would be better to join Leo, go around the corner when he grabbed it, figure out what to do with it and the others after they were out of the kill zone.

"Let's go," he said to the two monks standing on either side of him. They ran to the wall beside Leo and crouched.

The Cobra's engine was loud now. Where was it?

Come on, come on, Jagger thought, eyeing the stairs. A semicircle jutting from the basilica's back wall kept him from seeing the other corner.

A shadow stretched out from the alley nearest them. Leo leapt before Jagger could see the Cobra, but it was there—he saw it now—spinning toward them. Leo grabbed the barrel and the rear of its chassis, rose with it in his hands. It spat out a half-second burst of bullets, shattering a window three floors up. Leo began shaking it violently, as though trying to rattle it out of commission. Then Jagger saw blue lightning bolts, thin as wires, streaking over the Cobra's body: it was electrified.

Leo spasmed and turned toward Jagger, eyes pinched shut, lips curled back from gritting teeth, cords of muscles in his neck bulging, quivering.

Jagger heaved his shoulder into Leo's ribs, knocking him down, falling on top of him. The Cobra clattered over the stones and crashed against the front wall, resting on its side. The wheels began turning and it rotated, the barrel coming around.

Jagger scrambled up, grabbed the barrel with RoboHand. He couldn't squeeze the hooks into a strong grip, but it was enough to lift the Cobra. Electricity licked at the stub of his arm, just below the elbow, where the prosthetic forearm cupped his flesh. He felt it jittering up his biceps into his shoulder, but he was sure that, filtered through the artificial limb, it was static electricity compared to the lightning storm that had hit Leo.

Gunfire erupted, bullets slammed into the front wall. He jerked his head away from the muzzle but realized the firing didn't come from the Cobra he was holding. He turned and saw starbursts of flame erupting from a Cobra on the landing.

"Grab Leo!" he yelled.

The monk was pressing a hand against the wall, trying to stand. Father Mattieu ran to him, helped him up. Jagger carried the Cobra into the alley toward the main courtyard. He braced his other hand under the fake forearm, taking some of the weight off the muscles on his left side. The barrel began sliding through his grip, the Cobra slipping closer to the ground. His knees banged into it. The tank tracks spun, and the Cobra began firing. Bullets caused little explosions at the top of the wall; spent shells zinged out of an ejection port by his face.

The firing stopped, but another sound right on its heels froze Jagger in his tracks. A loud *crack!* Then another: gunshots. They came from the other side of the compound, near the apartments—

Beth! Tyler!

Someone screamed, a man.

The Cobras had been a ruse, a feint. The attackers had used them to push the monastery's defenders away from their real objective.

"Go! Go!" Jagger said, running into the front courtyard. The bodies of Bardas and Luca lay sprawled near opposite walls, horrific bundles of bleeding brown cloth. He glanced up at the top of the wall, where the Cobras had come over, expecting a line of snipers waiting to pick them off, but it was clear. He used his head to gesture at the structure directly ahead of them. "There! Go!"

Father Antoine sprinted ahead.

Jagger tried to get a look at his apartment, but there were too many buildings in the way.

Be safe, he thought. *Please.*

He reached Antoine, who was swinging open large barn doors.

"The cover!" Jagger yelled, and Antoine brushed past him and hoisted open a hatch-like lid.

Jagger strained to lift the Cobra, moved forward, and dropped it into the Well of Moses.

[8]

The old man was Vasco de Sousa.

Nevaeh couldn't approach him now, not with the kids all around. It wouldn't be right. But standing on the beach, only thirty yards and a barrier of low hedges between them, she was exposed. She decided her best option was to walk to the surf, stare out at the water and sunset, just another tourist happy to be away from her workaday life—*now* Nevaeh wished she'd dressed the part. As she turned, the man's eyes caught her. She paused, only a second, to gaze back. She took a step toward the ocean and heard a metallic crash behind her. She looked again, and the man was standing, hunched, gripping the table edge. His chair was lying on its back behind him. His eyes had widened, old skin stretching taut around them.

"*Você,*" he said, too quietly to hear, but she read his lips. *You.*

She nodded and headed for him.

He watched her come, touching his fingers to a gold cross hanging around his neck. He waved a hand at the children. "*Funcione ausente agora, crianças. Funcione ausente.*"

Run along now, children. Run along.

They *awwwed* but maintained the momentum of their joy, some of them spinning in tight circles, others grabbing the remaining *pastéis*, then running and skipping away, vanishing around the corner of the villa like fairies surprised by discovery. Their laughter and giggling voices left with them, a void the sound of the surf rushed in to fill.

Nevaeh found an opening in the hedge, stepped onto the patio, and paused. The old man, Vasco, was trembling: his twiggy arms, coming out of the openings of short sleeves too large for them; his bony hips, making his black slacks quiver down to his sandals; his chin.

She approached him slowly, taking him in.

Speaking Portuguese, he said, "I knew you would come."

She stopped a step away. "I'm sorry it's taken me so long."

He shrugged with one shoulder. "What's a hundred and three years to one who lives forever?"

"Too long."

Vasco released the table and reached out for her. She stepped into his arms and he embraced her, all bones, so little meat. He whispered, *"Mamãe."*

Mommy, not "mother," as she'd expected, if he called her anything at all. *Mommy*, and it broke her heart. It told her he remembered her, had wanted her, needed her. Time had not soured him on her; age and independence had not made him bitter by her absence. She squeezed him, as firmly as she dared, as she had done when he was a baby. His clutching arms loosened and he nearly collapsed. She held him, righted his chair, and eased him into it. She pulled out the one next to his, angled it toward him, and sat.

His eyes were wet, and he made no attempt to wipe away the tears that didn't so much slide over his cheeks as they did fill the wrinkles and trickle slowly through them.

"All these years . . . ," she said. "I didn't think you'd recognize me."

"No child ever forgets his mother's face." His eyes lingered, and he chuckled. "Especially when that face never changes."

She'd told him since he was old enough to listen about her immortality, as she'd done with all her children—not as many as you'd think, given her three and half millennia of existence. She'd planned on playing the role of wife and mother until Vasco's father, her beautiful Reinaldo, grew old and died. But with Reinaldo by her side, she had meddled in Lisbon's politics—how could she not, with an antichristian dictator trying to take power? It had ultimately led to Reinaldo's imprisonment, torture, and death. She would have been next, along with her young son, so she'd kissed him one last time, gathered the Tribe—living in the village, waiting out her distraction—and left.

She lowered her eyes, said, "After the king and his son were killed, the country was in chaos . . ."

Vasco stretched to cup his hand over hers on the table.

She focused on it, long fingers, yellow nails, a cosmic explosion of liver spots. "We, your father and I, thought we could help, we got involved. We offered our counsel, our . . . our . . ."

What had she offered? What had she pulled poor Reinaldo into? They had tracked down the king's and prince's assassins, killed them, used stealthy violence to keep the rebels and their irreligious leaders from overthrowing the monarchy. They'd succeeded for two years until . . .

"The Revolution of 1910," she said. "It was wicked, bloody. More so than anyone knows."

"History books are written by the victors," Vasco said.

She looked at him, wiped away a tear that had formed at the corner of her eye. This was the danger she wanted to avoid: the ache of missing his life. Beyond his old-man face she saw the eleven-year-old she'd left, round cheeks, laughing eyes. "I *couldn't* take you with me." She shook her head. "The things I do . . ."

"There's no need to explain," he said, patting her hand.

She smiled, and was surprised to realize it was genuine. It was just so good to see him, to know any grudges he'd felt toward her he'd worked out. He'd forgiven her. She turned her head away. If only God would forgive as readily.

"Would you like a *pastel de nata*?" he asked. "I have a few more inside." He started to rise, and she stopped him.

"I'm fine."

"They're *your* recipe," he said. "Best in Portugal, better even than the Casa Pastéis de Belém's." The insanely popular bakery in Lisbon that, since 1837, claimed to use the original recipe created by the Catholic monks at the Jerónimos Monastery of Belém.

"The children certainly appreciate them," she said.

He grinned, and she saw that those big teeth were too imperfect—stained and a bit crooked—to be anything but his own. He said, "The *pastéis* are my bait. I love their company, the kids. Their energy and enthusiasm, the way they move so gracefully, not a single aching joint or tired muscle, their optimism, their hope. You know what they say: children are proof God hasn't given up on us yet."

Blessings, she thought. The few times she'd found true happiness—in a man's arms, becoming a mother—she thought they were signs of God's approval, His love for her, His forgiveness. But then she'd remember that "He causes His sun to rise on the evil and the good, and sends rain on the righteous and the unrighteous." And sure enough, God would take away His blessings; husbands and children would die, and even their headstones would age, crack, and crumble. And she'd live on, apparently still unrighteous in His eyes, despite her eternal quest for forgiveness.

She realized Vasco had said something. "I'm sorry?"

"You came along the beach."

"I wanted to see the place." *Needed to*, she thought. Since losing Ben, she'd felt a bit . . . *unhinged*. She had grown weary—of life, of trying to please God, of everything. She'd become distracted, short-tempered, and more willing to pronounce death sentences on apparent sinners without studying all the evidence, without praying. Sometimes she was afraid she was losing her mind. She needed touchstones of better times to keep her steady. Touchstones like Sesimbra . . . and Vasco.

She said, "It's like the Disneyland version of the old village." She glanced around at the villa. "You kept it."

"The land, anyway. Had the old cottage torn down and this one put up. My son designed it. He . . . passed last year. He was eighty-nine, an architect." He smiled and seemed to get lost in the memory for a moment. "When I was in Lisbon, at the university—did you know I was a professor there? Philosophy. Fifty-two years."

She nodded. "I kept tabs." But not enough. It was too painful, what she'd lost.

"I wondered," he said. "Even thought about tracking you down."

"You would have failed."

His eyes flicked around as he thought, and she knew he believed she was wrong about that. She wasn't.

"I was saying," he said, "when I lived in Lisbon, I'd come here on weekends, bring the family. So many times I'd sit here, watch the waves and wonder about you, where you were, what you were doing. I wondered if what you told me about your living forever, if it was only a story, a fable like the Easter bunny. Then I saw—"

He held up his hands, remembering something. He rose, patting the air now to keep her in her seat. He shuffled toward an open French door.

"Vasco?"

He held up his index finger and disappeared into the villa.

She leaned back in the metal chair, feeling her muscles relax, not realizing until then that she'd been so tense. She sighed, at once happy and heavyhearted to see her son. He had received a taste of the activated telomerase genes that made her immortal, just enough to give him a long, healthy life. But he wouldn't be around much longer. She hoped she wouldn't be either.

She fished her mobile phone out of a coat pocket. Six missed calls, all within the last fifteen minutes. She checked the call list: four from Toby, two from the Tribe's main satphone. She was about to listen to one of the voice mail messages when Vasco emerged from the villa. She flipped the ringer on and set the phone on the table's glass top.

He shuffled over, holding a magazine. He sat and placed it on the table. An aged, torn copy of *Avanta!*, a Portuguese magazine comparable to the former *Life* in the United States. He leaned over it and used his fingernail to hook a page flagged with a yellowing bookmark advertising Joseph Heller's novel *Catch-22*. She instantly recognized the photo on the page—it had been syndicated seemingly everywhere: a glow coming from behind the photographer illuminated a crowd of people, their arms raised in victory, their faces showing expressions of elation and empowerment. It was night, and they filled a residential city street. Another, smaller photograph revealed the object of their attention: a smoking, burning building. It had been occupied by a group of thugs who ran an operation dealing drugs, pimping prostitutes, extorting businesses, and generally terrorizing and corrupting a good chunk of the Bronx. Someone had firebombed it.

Almost dead center of the crowd shot, several people were walking away from the photographer, cutting through the mob. One of them was looking back over her shoulder, looking right into the camera.

Vasco pointed at her. "That's you, isn't it?"

She showed him a weak smile.

"8 October 1968," he said. "That's when I knew for sure you'd told me the truth."

"Vasco—"

They both jumped when the phone rang.

[9]

Deep in the well, the Cobra hit water. Blue lightning bolts, orange sparks lit up the black hole, reaching up with diminishing strength . . . flashing bursts of white light . . . fading . . .

Antoine slammed the cover down over the well. Leo limped up, Mattieu's arm around him. He saw what they had done and nodded.

Jagger turned to run to the apartments when he saw Antoine lay his forearm on the well cover and lean over it. Jagger threw up his hand. "Don't—"

Muted, echoing gunfire sounded from the well, and a barrage of bullets ripped through the cover, spraying splinters into the air and turning the wood-board ceiling above it into a colander. Antoine jumped back, stumbled into the wall. Wide-eyed, he examined himself, patting his chest and stomach. He looked at the others. "I'm all right."

"We've gotta find out what those shots were," Jagger said. But he wasn't going to do it without a gun; he'd left his in the tunnel. He rushed back into the main court, glancing up at the front wall's top edge, the night sky beyond it. He picked up Luca's pistol and paused. Over the sound of his own heavy breathing and the blood rushing in his head, he heard the whirling of a Cobra's engine coming at him from the alley that ended at the burning bush. It had come around and was following them. The sound of another Cobra joined the first. He couldn't see them yet, seconds away.

He returned to the others. "Two Cobras heading this way."

He shifted hid gaze toward his apartment, seeing only the roof-tops and spires that blocked it.

You need to check on them, "Leo said. "Go, I'll take care of tthe cobras."

"How?"

"I'll think of something."

But it was Jagger who did: "Their ejector ports . . . that's where the spent shells came out. Jam something into them . . ."

"Got it," Leo said, pushing him.

"A pen . . . a . . . a . . ." Jagger said, thinking.

"Go!"

Jagger brushed past Antoine and said to him, "Come with me."

They ran past the bell tower, heading for the stairs that would take them up to the apartments. They reached the Fatimid mosque: built within the monastery during the thirteenth century to appease Muslim rulers, it had never been used because its *qibla* wall was not properly oriented toward Mecca; Jagger had wondered how intentional that mistake had been. They were rushing along the side of the mosque, almost to the Garden Gate—*Past the mosque, around the storage building, straight to the stairs . . . is this gun loaded? Has to be . . . up the stairs*—when a figure darted in front of them, left to right. It was the attacker in the steampunk outfit, his trench coat flapping behind him. He was coming from the direction of the apartments, beelining toward the northwest corner of the monastery.

Jagger raised his pistol and squeezed off a shot, hitting the wall behind the intruder, who disappeared behind a building.

Jagger quickly backed away from the side of the mosque to give himself a perspective of the apartments' top floor. He could see his door—closed—and window, illuminated from the inside. It made him believe all was well up there, that Beth and Tyler were safe. The pressure in his chest eased, just a little.

Antoine started after Steampunk, but Jagger grabbed his arm, pointed. "Check where he came from, the apartments. I heard gunshots and someone scream." Then he went after the man himself.

First he could hear him on the stairs leading to the second-floor monk cells, where he had lain when he observed the assault team exiting the helicopter. He wondered if his being there had alerted the bad guys to an easy place to breach the compound.

He rounded a corner and got a visual: a dark figure almost to the top. The silhouette of the crossbow rose up from his back, its limbs like a stickman's umbrella. Jagger hit the stairs just as Steampunk was pulling himself onto the steep porch roof.

Jagger stopped and aimed—hard to pinpoint his target against the blackness of the porch and roof. "Freeze!"

The man kept moving, a shifting shadow among deeper shadows.

Jagger fired. The shadow continued its climb. He pulled the trigger again, but the weapon didn't fire. He grabbed the slide to yank it back and eject any shell that might be jammed; it wouldn't move. This was the reason professional shooters avoided using another person's gun: you never knew if it was functioning properly, how often or recently it had been cleaned. Jagger was willing to bet firearm maintenance wasn't high on the monks' priority list. With a growl of frustration, he threw it down.

He bolted up the remaining steps, swung around a support post, and jumped onto the railing. A loud thump told him Steampunk had slipped and fallen. Jagger pulled himself onto the roof as the guy was reclaiming his feet and stepping onto the flat roof. Jagger got to the same place without slipping and sprang for Steampunk, who had climbed onto the top of the wall, four feet higher than the roof, and was beginning to stand. Jagger grabbed the hem of the trench coat and yanked.

Steampunk jerked backward. He spun and came down on one knee, facing Jagger—that leather mask, those brass-framed goggles, the gas-mask tube and canister swinging like an elephant's trunk. His right arm rose high, crossing over his face. Jagger caught the glint of a sword, which Steampunk swung in a diagonal slice that would cleave Jagger's head like a pineapple.

Jagger ducked, felt the blade brush over his hair.

As Steampunk's sword swooped in a rising arc, his body twisted with it, and his left arm, acting as a counterbalance, swung in front of Jagger's face. Jagger grabbed at it, seizing his wrist. Without missing a beat, Steampunk's sword came down again. Jagger raised his prosthetic arm, and the blade struck it hard. Jagger twisted his fake arm around and clamped RoboHand on his opponent's other wrist. He tried to squeeze it, to break the bones—RoboHand had the power to do it . . . when it was working.

Steampunk wrenched his wrist out of the malfunctioning hook and raised the sword again. He tugged with his other arm, trying to free it from Jagger's real hand.

Jagger pulled at it and heaved his body back. He had to change the dynamic of the fight, and the first thing he thought to do was yank Steampunk off his perch, get him on the roof, maybe throw him off it.

It didn't work out that way.

[10]

Balanced on the fortress's wall four feet above Jagger, Steampunk must have realized Jagger's intentions to pull him off. He threw his whole body back.

Jagger's grip slid to Steampunk's gloved hand, to something he was holding. About the size of a soda bottle, but rough and rectangular—a shard of stone. As the men fell away from each other, Jagger's fingers clutched at it, gripped it, ripped it out of Steampunk's hand.

Jagger landed on his back, and his head cracked hard against the flat roof. White light popped in his vision like a camera flash. He squeezed his eyes closed, opened them. He was seeing stars, literally: millions of them in the night sky above him, seeming brighter than ever, larger, closer. And they were moving, swirling and zipping. He viewed them through a patina of rippling, translucent colors: green, orange, purple. It was much like the aurora borealis, but more see-through, almost invisible, and instead of a mere ribbon across the sky, this filled the firmament from horizon to horizon.

All this he grasped in seconds, and while he felt an urge, like the first tugs of a developing appetite, to take it all in, study it for a time, his mind snapped back to the urgency of his situation. He focused on Steampunk, rising to his feet on the wall above him—and the man wasn't alone. Another attacker stood at his side, nearly clinging to him.

The second man's gruesome minotaur face was too perfect, too animated to be anything but professionally applied makeup and the kind of prosthetic appliances they use in movies. His broad nose wrinkled when he snarled; his mouth opened obscenely wide, revealing lion fangs, dripping thick saliva; his eyes were black orbs. Shaggy black hair flowed over twisted bat ears and hung past his shoulders.

His arms were disproportionately long—gorilla arms—and one of them was draped over Steampunk's shoulders. His pants appeared to be made out of animal pelts. No shirt, muscles that made the other muscular attacker look malnourished. Dust or ashes floated off him, as though he'd rolled in soot.

It occurred to Jagger that he might be hallucinating; like the stars, this beast's appearance was a result of cracking his head. Or . . . Steampunk wore a gas mask. The man had sprayed him with a hallucinogen. That had to be it.

No, there'd been no spray. A slight concussion, then, nothing serious.

Then a monkey appeared. It was small and emaciated, with mangy fur clinging in spots to greasy gray skin. It skittered up the beast's body, mounted his head, then leapt to Steampunk's shoulder. It looked at Jagger with human eyes and showed him a mouth full of needle teeth. It shrieked, a chattering, laugh-like sound.

The beast glared at Jagger, appearing to smile wickedly, perversely. His head rotated on a tree trunk of a neck, and he whispered in Steampunk's ear.

Steampunk reached over his shoulder and brought back the crossbow. He checked the weapon, already loaded with a two-foot arrow, the tip a thick metal stud shaped like the bottom two inches of an ice-cream cone. He raised the stock to his shoulder and aimed it like a rifle.

This is going to hurt, Jagger thought. For the first time since rediscovering his immortality, he was glad about it. He wasn't ready to leave Beth and Tyler.

Steampunk's hulking, Halloween-happy friend whispered in his ear again, and Steampunk grinned. He lowered the crossbow to look over it at Jagger.

A voice emanated from the canister at the end of the gas-mask tube, sounding like the scratchy, unreal voices coming out of an old-time radio. "This will pin you down. I'll use the sword to send you home."

He knows, Jagger thought. *He knows I'm immortal. He's going to cut my head off.* Panic pulsed through him like atomic bombs, matching the pounding of his heart. And each one carried with it a single thought—

Beat: *Lord, take care of my family.*

Steampunk raised his weapon.

Beat: *I'm sorry I doubted You.*

Steampunk thumbed off the safety.

Beat: *God, forgive me.*

Light blinded him, and his first thought was that the crossbow's arrow struck without his witnessing its flight, the pain so great his mind turned the sensation into light on his brain's way to shutting down.

No, Steampunk hadn't fired. A helicopter, then. Its spotlight just switched on.

As suddenly as the light had appeared, it was gone.

A man was standing over Jagger, a foot on either side of his chest, and he was on fire. Jagger saw no flames, but glowing orange embers fell off of him. Correction: they didn't really *fall* as much as they *swirled*, billowing away from him, then flowing back toward him. Moving, dancing, the sparks from a raging fire caught in a turbulent, chaotic wind.

The man rushed toward Steampunk, visible to Jagger beyond the man's right hip.

Steampunk fired.

As the arrow left the bow, the man's hand moved faster than Jagger could track it—not there, then there—and touched the flying arrow. It thunked into the roof beside Jagger's ear. The man laid a finger to the tip of one of the crossbow's lathes. The string snapped, whipped up, and fell, dangling from the end of the other lathe.

Steampunk's goggles aimed at the broken string, at the arrow protruding from the roof, then at Jagger. "Lucky you," he said through the canister. To the man who had deflected the arrow and broken the string, he paid no attention at all.

But his beastly compatriots did. The monkey-thing shrieked at him, turned in a circle on Steampunk's shoulder, then jumped down and scrambled away.

The beast roared, drew a battle axe with a head the size of a guillotine blade, and swung it at the man. The sparkling embers swirling around the man sailed forward on their side of him and came together in front, in a blink forming a sort of shield—it looked to Jagger like a force field in a big-budget science fiction movie, shimmering orange translucence. The blade clanged against it, skated off.

The shield broke apart, once again becoming embers flying around the man. They whipped around him to come together behind him, two columns at his shoulder blades, like dual scuba tanks extending from waist to head. They unraveled outward and upward, appearing to form—Jagger could think of no other word—*wings*. They fluttered, and the man jumped/flew to the top of the wall, five, six feet to Steampunk's side.

The beast—behind Steampunk now—was hoisting his axe over his head, turning to aim it at the man, who thrust out his foot in a linear forward kick to the beast's stomach. The beast staggered back, out of Jagger's sight. The man—embers zipping around him, *fluttering* around him—drew a sword that shone with scarlet light, making Jagger think of rubies. Pursuing the beast, the man dashed forward, disappearing beyond the edge of the wall.

Steampunk picked up his own sword and jumped down to the roof. His canister said, "We'll do it the hard way."

Jagger started to rise. Steampunk planted a booted foot on his chest and pushed him down. The sword was already over his head, arcing down.

Jagger raised RoboHand, and in the chaotic muddle of his panicked brain he remembered a term he'd always thought was achingly sad: *defensive wounds*. He imagined the blade severing his prosthetic midforearm on its way to his neck. He wondered if the coroner would label his sliced fake arm a defensive wound.

A shot rang out, and a spark sprang from the sword's handle. The weapon clattered to the roof. Steampunk stumbled back, holding his right hand in his left. He dropped onto all fours at Jagger's feet and scrambled over Jagger's legs and torso, a wild animal going for the throat. He stopped when his face was over Jagger's, Jagger's twin reflections staring back at him from the black glass of the goggles. The gas canister rested on Jagger's chest, and Steampunk's voice came out of it: "Like I said, lucky you." He sprang up, and as he did he grabbed the thing Jagger had taken from him and yanked it out of his hand. Jagger's vision blurred and his eyes filled with tears. When he blinked them away, Steampunk was gone.

"Jagger!"

Jagger craned his head around. He was closer to the edge of the roof than he'd realized. He could see over it, down the sloping porch roof to Mattieu, whose head, shoulders, and chest rose up from that roof's far edge, his forearms bracing him there. One hand was tilted up. It held a gun.

Jagger's mouth dropped open. Beside Mattieu, a man was perched on the edge the roof, crouching there with both hands over the monk's, helping him hold the gun. The glowing embers Jagger had seen swirling around the first man also danced in the air over this one. They had formed into huge wings extending from the man's back, slowly moving in unison, beating the air, like hands treading water.

"Are you okay?" Mattieu said. "Are you hurt?"

Jagger blinked. "Who's that?"

"Mattieu."

"No, the man with you."

"What?" Mattieu said. "Are you all right?"

The man stood, and Jagger realized he was translucent. He could see the domed top of the mosque's minaret through him.

"Who are you?" Jagger said.

"It's *me*, Mattieu! Jag, don't move, okay? I think you're injured."

"No . . ." Jagger rolled over and got on his hands and knees. When he raised his head, the man had disappeared.

[11]

Nevaeh stepped through the opening in the hedge and onto the beach before answering.

"Where are you?" Toby said in a rush.

"Busy." She glanced back at Vasco, who was leaning over the magazine, staring at the picture. She turned toward the water, saw a couple walking hand in hand through the surf, the sun showing only a sliver of shimmering light behind them, as though the ocean were on fire out there. "What is it?"

"You're not at St. C's, are you?"

"You know I'm not. Why would you think—?"

"Someone's attacking it."

"What? The monastery? When?"

"Right now! It started about a half hour ago. A helicopter came in, then there was an explosion, smoke coming from the gate. Looked like the copter tried to get inside the walls, but someone shot a missile at it."

"At the monastery?"

"At the *helicopter*. It came from inside St. C's."

"A missile?"

"Yes! It missed. It went streaking up into the sky and exploded. Freaked the helicopter pilot out. The copter did loopty-loops and got out of there."

"It's gone? The attackers left?" The sun dropped completely below the horizon. Nevaeh felt colder already.

"The copter landed. I'm on the *roof* of the Southwest Range Building, jumped right up the back wall. These boots are *sick*. But I still can't see anything."

Gunfire sounded in the distance. Sounded like a war.

The whos and whys of the situation—answers to which Toby was obviously clueless—pushed the blood harder into her brain, making it throb.

"What about Beth?" she said. "Where's Jagger's wife?"

"I think she's still in the apartment with the boy."

It dawned on her that other Immortals—Tribe defectors—might have heard of Ben's death and Beth's part in it and wanted her for themselves. She said, "Are they after her, you think?"

"Why would they be? How would they even know about her?"

Nevaeh put on a smile and turned toward the patio again. Vasco was not in his chair or anywhere on the patio. Yellow lights mounted toward the top of each column came on, and the old man appeared in the doorway, stepping out with a bottle of wine and two glasses. She closed her eyes.

"Okay, listen," she said. "We're on our way. It'll be a few hours before I can get the others, then a few more to reach you. We'll be there in the morning sometime. If it looks like someone's trying to take Beth, stop them."

"Stop them?" he said. "How?"

"Figure it out."

"These guys have machine guns, and somebody down there has a rocket launcher!"

If she pushed, Toby would try. She pictured him rushing the helicopter, getting cut down by bullets or blown up. She said, "You're right, you're right. Don't do anything. Stay safe. Can you get the tail number?"

"Yeah, sure," Toby said, sounding relieved.

He may have been 3,500 years old, but he had the mind of a fifteen-year-old. She had to remember that sometimes. "Toby," she said, "good job. Thanks for trying so hard to reach me."

"Yeah. When you didn't answer, I called Sebastian. Elias answered, said Sebastian had gone shark fishing. He said he was going to call you, but I thought—"

"Toby, I have to go. Good job." She ended the call and slipped the phone into her pocket. She watched Vasco finish pouring her drink, then glance up at her. She went to him and said, "Vasco . . . son, I have to go. An emergency."

Gesturing to the wine, he said, "I thought we could . . ." His voice trailed off. "I understand," he said and stood.

"I'm sorry." Nevaeh wrapped her arms around him and held him close. She felt his spindly arms encircle her, and they stayed that way for a while. When they parted, she said, "I'll try . . ."

He was trembling again, his lips especially. His eyes were glistening with tears.

She continued: "I really will try to visit you again."

He nodded. "I wish you could have met them," he said. "My Maria, the kids. All gone now. I've had a full, good life." He paused. "But I'm ready, ready to join them." He blinked, sending the tears into his wrinkles. "I don't know how you do it. I don't know how you do forever."

"I don't have a choice," she said, feeling her face muscles tighten, unable to conceal her anger and frustration.

He took her hand. "Don't you realize how patient God is being with you?"

She smiled, sure it appeared more sad than reassuring. She ran her fingers down his cheek and headed for the beach. At the hedge she turned and walked back. "Would you mind," she said, "if I took some of those *pastéis de nata* with me?"

She thought she would always remember the smile he gave her.

[12]

Jagger stared at the spot where the man had crouched, helping Mattieu aim his pistol. Mattieu was watching him with concern. Jagger glanced around. Blue lights streaked straight up into the dark sky from the roofs of the basilica and apartment building, nothing to explain them. He thought: *Gotta be a concussion, but did I really hit my head that hard?* That, or Steampunk was the Houdini of hallucinogens, able to administer it without seeming to.

"Jagger . . . ?"

He sat back on his heels, rubbed his hand over his face, and said, "I . . . hit my head . . ."

"Stay there." Mattieu began pulling himself onto the porch's sloping roof.

Outside the compound someone yelled and the helicopter's engine started, rising in pitch like a tortured scream. Jagger crawled toward the outside edge of the wall. He felt dizzy and paused to close his eyes. He had been knocked silly—or drugged—splayed before a crossbow-wielding psychopath: How had he survived? Who was the man who'd saved him? *Was* he a man? If not, what was he? Assuming he'd hallucinated the whole thing seemed easier than pursuing that line of questioning. He had banged his head, seen stars, and Steampunk's crossbow had broken a string, causing the arrow to miss. That's all.

But he didn't think so.

He shook his head, trying to dislodge all the questions. Right now all he wanted was to know what was going on: were the attackers leaving, and did they get what they came for? He thought of the stone shard Steampunk had been holding; it'd appeared "archeological" to Jagger, a relic or an artifact.

He continued along the rooftop toward a big grappling hook biting the edge. A black nylon rope trailed from it down the front wall. Edging up beside it, he saw the attackers on the valley floor below, caught in the illumination of the bright lamps mounted to the outside wall. They were heading for the helicopter, walking, talking to each other, in no hurry.

All around them chaos whirled like a wildfire as two groups engaged in combat. Eight or ten were monsters like the ones he'd seen with Steampunk. They were obviously protecting the humans who'd attacked the monastery, keeping their backs to them, moving slowly toward the helicopter as they fought.

Some of them were tall and lanky, others muscular and bulky, all of them with hideously misshapen faces, monster faces. The beast from the wall was among them, snarling and swinging that guillotine blade—which was nearly lost among the many flashes of slicing swords, knives, and axes aimed at an advancing horde of warriors.

These other combatants were like the men he'd seen, though he realized now they were taller and more muscular than humans. Their toga-like gowns fluttered around them, blurring their bodies. They were so brightly white they appeared to be caught in the radiance of theatrical spotlights. Glowing embers swirled around them, forming shields just in time to parry a blow or converging into swords even as they struck at an opponent. The pulsing orange bits would swoop back, becoming wings that lifted them off the ground, propelling them away from a lunging enemy and shooting them forward to strike from an elevated position.

The monsters they fought were engulfed by a black cloud of . . . *something*. At first Jagger thought they were flies, swarming as they do around rotting meat. But they were flakier, billowing away before whirling into tighter formations to become swords and weapons. They seemed a counterpart to the glowing embers whirling around the bright creatures, as though they'd once been bright and alive but were now only ashes, black and gray, not quite as quick.

As he watched, a cloud of ashes billowing around a monstrosity coalesced behind the creature, becoming fluttering bat wings. The thing propelled itself into the air, then crashed down into one of the ember-men, crushing him to the ground. Glowing embers snapped and slapped at the attacker. Another ember-man flashed over, kicked the enemy off, hacking at it with a sword. He helped his comrade up, and they both spun back into battle. Their weapons struck sword and shield, kicking up eruptions of sparks and ashes. The violent scene could have been taking place on the floor of a foundry, for all the exploding sparks that filled the air.

The battle went on, and Jagger realized the combatants were becoming harder to see as the seconds passed; it was as though each shadow they moved through stole a little of their bodies, so when an arm, a leg, a torso reappeared in the moonlight or lamplight, less of it was there to see. The sound, too, began fading away, the clanging blades barely audible now.

Jagger noticed the movie-star-looking guy on the slope at the bottom of the opposite mountain, still there, watching his team retreat to the helicopter, his arms now crossed over his chest. Something was moving on his back. It showed its face over his shoulder: a lizard-like creature, blacker than the night. It pressed a reptilian hand on the side of the man's face, looked around. Ashy wings fluttered behind it, occasionally wrapping one around the man's arm, as if hugging him. The lizard-beast looked straight at Jagger, then the man also turned his gaze on Jagger and smiled.

A hand grabbed Jagger's calf, and he jumped, pivoting onto a hip, ready to kick.

"It's me," Mattieu whispered. He crawled along the rooftop to the edge. "What's happening?"

"They're—" Jagger started, then changed course. "What do *you* see?"

Mattieu said, "They're all on the helicopter, but they haven't closed the side door yet. I see . . . they're waiting for that guy." He nodded toward Mr. Movie Star, now walking in and out of the shadows toward the copter, walking *through* the fading combatants. Jagger saw Mattieu's eyes tracking the man, clearly not seeing anything else but him.

Mattieu brought his pistol forward and braced it with his other hand. He dipped his head to sight over the barrel. He closed one eye and squeezed off two quick shots.

A monster—a skeletal-looking thing with papery flesh peeling away from its bones—jumped and stretched out a sword. Moving almost too fast for Jagger to see, it deflected the bullets, which kicked up little plumes of dust five feet beyond the target.

The man glanced up at them and continued striding toward the helicopter.

An ember-enshrouded warrior looked over his shoulder at Jagger and Mattieu, then spiraled into the air, zipping toward them as a streak of light. In an instant he was on the wall, crouching beside Mattieu. He gripped the pistol, leaned in, and whispered: "Again."

Mattieu took aim and pulled the trigger.

As the monster moved to block the bullet, an ember-man tackled it in midair. They spun and crashed to the ground. The man's left shoulder jerked forward, and he grabbed it. He stumbled sideways and dropped to one knee.

Commotion at the helicopter: the commando with war paint jumped out with his .50-cal machine gun. Right behind him came the rock-star woman. She darted toward the injured man, who was standing now, walking again. The fingers of the hand clutching his shoulder were smeared with blood. The commando pointed the muzzle at Jagger and Mattieu, and the machine gun began rattling, flames sputtering out of its barrel. Embers sailed over the warrior beside Mattieu and shrouding them in a dome of sparking translucence. Chunks of the wall exploded in front of them.

Both men pushed back from the edge, rolled, and converged at the opposite, inside edge of the wall, their faces nearly touching. Mattieu was smiling. "I got him."

Jagger looked back where they'd lain, the edge coming apart under a barrage of bullets.

The man with the sparkling aura had vanished.

[13]

Jagger swung down off the porch's roof onto the railing, then onto the porch itself. He helped Mattieu climb down, and as they descended the stairs he heard the helicopter wind up and take off.

"Guess they're not coming back for revenge," Mattieu said, trying to see the departing aircraft; the wall was too high and too close.

"They got their blood," Jagger said, thinking of the three monks cut down by the unmanned ground combat vehicles. "What about the other Cobras?"

"We jammed their ejector ports, like you said."

Jagger stopped to look at him. "With what?"

Mattieu smiled. "What do monks always have with them?"

Jagger thought. "Crosses," he said, noticing Mattieu was missing his.

"Then Leo shoved a broom handle into their barrels, and we carried them to the well."

"They're in the Well of Moses?"

"Soaking," the monk confirmed.

Jagger reached the bottom and picked up the defective gun he'd thrown down. He said, "The guy I chased, he came from the direction of the apartments. Antoine went to check it out. Has he—?" He couldn't finish. Dizziness engulfed him, and he pressed a hand against the wall to steady himself. Shadows shifted everywhere, as if moving of their own accord, adjusting themselves into different positions.

His eyes settled on the basilica across a small courtyard, past a storage building and the mosque. Bright threads of blue light rose from its roof into the sky. As they climbed they came together, twisting into a thicker beam that went deep into the dark sky, seemingly forever.

He started walking toward the basilica—officially, the Church of the Transfiguration—and Mattieu stopped him. "Jagger, are you all right? What is it?"

He couldn't take his eyes off the glowing threads. "Do you see them, the lights?"

"Jag, I think you better—"

"I have to see." He pushed past Mattieu's hand and continued toward the church.

He didn't know what was going on inside his head, whether cracking it against the roof had given him a concussion or he was caught in some tide of chemicals Steampunk had administered. But he didn't believe the warriors he saw were real. It was all too dreamlike: the over-bright, too-close stars, the colors in the sky, the way the ember-men became more and more see-through.

And he didn't believe these lights coming out of the basilica were real either. Something, however, drew him to them, and he couldn't let go of the idea that everything he'd witnessed—hallucinations or not—meant *something*. A premonition, maybe? An important but long-lost memory? Had he fought here at the monastery before, ages ago, and forgotten? Were the translucent warriors people he'd known then? Why were they coming back now? He was vaguely aware of the absurdity of his conviction that the hallucinations had meaning: didn't every LSD-tripping addict feel the same thing about their talking dogs, Salvador Dali surroundings, morphing body parts? But he was also aware that even hallucinations drew from the well of an individual's experiences, memories, fears. If he *was* hallucinating, he wanted to know not only how it came about but why his mind was showing him these particular things.

He walked, aware of the mechanical quality of his movements, his trance-like fixation on the lights, his need to know more. Mattieu was following close, probably afraid Jagger would faint or fall. As he drew near, the basilica's facade cut off his view of the lights, and he faltered. Mattieu gripped his shoulder, said nothing. Jagger felt the desire to step backward so he could see them again, something about them beautiful, enticing. He reminded himself of his mission to find their source, and he climbed the stairs to the basilica's big wooden doors, above which was the Greek inscription Tyler recited in English whenever he entered: "This is the gate to the Lord; the righteous shall enter into it."

Jagger pulled open a door and stepped inside.

Immediately he sensed an urgency to turn and bolt from this place—and an equally strong, conflicting desire to be embraced by it. On each side of the nave was a row of granite-columned arches, beyond which were doors to small chapels. Between these arches, the nave itself: ancient tiles turning its floor into patterns of geometric art; overhead, a hanging forest of golden, ornamental chandeliers sparkling with each flutter of flame from the candles they held; short pews, each a king's throne, lining one side. At the front, past a huge crucifix mounted high on a beam, a gilded screen—an *iconostasis*—was decorated with priceless art and artifacts and separated the main body of the church from the altar. If the best that man could do to honor God—outside of his own desire to love Him and keep His commandments—was to expend his talents and time, his worldly wealth, into a palace of worship, this place represented man's best.

Yet all of it dimmed, became insignificant, compared to what Jagger saw on the nave floor before him: seven monks on their knees, facing the crucifix, heads bowed or lifted in prayer. Extending from their heads, rising to and through the flat, beamed ceiling high above, were the glowing threads of blue light. Several disappeared into the ornamental limbs of chandeliers, then continued on the other side.

Beside each monk stood or knelt a warrior, his hands clasped in prayer. Bright embers swirled around them, forming on each an arm-like appendage that embraced the monk or a shroud over him. Each ember pulsed brightly, dimmed, brightened again. It seemed to Jagger that the rhythm was familiar, everyone knew it: the beating of a human heart. He wondered if it was the heartbeats of the monks.

Though earlier it had crossed his mind, there and gone, he could no longer deny it—these beings were angels. Whether it was their presence in this holy place or their postures of humility, worship, and protection, or simply their ember-cloaked forms outside the context of battle, he didn't know, but he was suddenly certain. They were semitransparent, and through their bodies he could see the patterned floor in front of them, the iconostasis, the monks they embraced.

An angel turned his head and gazed over his shoulder at Jagger. His face at first appeared tanned, then Jagger amended that thought: it was as though a soft light was shining on it, like reflected gold. It was as flawless as the Carrara marble from which Michelangelo had chiseled his *David*. In fact, this being reminded him of the statue in other ways: the wavy hair, the strong brow and nose, the youthfulness and confident stature. His irises were blue sapphires.

He realized that from the angel's body came an undulating white light, so bright, even in its semitransparent state, it was hard to look at. What he thought was a flowing white garment could be the pulsing of this light, and he wondered if the angels were clothed at all. But he could see how anyone who saw them would think they were—and with the Roman-era garments so many angels were depicted wearing.

Jagger's gaze returned to the angel's eyes, and he saw recognition there, and compassion. It was the way a loving father looked upon his child. Jagger understood the angel was mirroring the feelings of his Creator, perhaps the way humans were meant to do but rarely did. He felt a calm penetrate him, a sense of peace he hadn't felt since the crash that had taken the Bransfords, his arm, and his faith—if he'd ever really experienced peace like this at all. As a fire warms the flesh, the angel's gaze soothed his soul.

But I'm cursed, he thought, and felt again the conflicting urges to flee and to fall before this being and ask God to take away his confusion, his sins, his curse.

Then someone beside him spoke. The words didn't register, but the human voice seemed foreign and wrong in this place of quiet prayer and miraculous wonder. Intuitively, Jagger knew this vision before him was fragile, hard to find and easily lost. He was gazing into a bubble reflecting God's world—and the voice was the finger that would rupture it.

The angel smiled and turned his face away.

[14]

Standing in the archway between narthex and nave, as if between two worlds, Jagger felt himself pulled back into his own reality. Awareness of his surroundings returned to him, though he hadn't realized it had ever left, like waking after a brief catnap in a chair on a sun-warmed porch. He blinked, became aware of the floor beneath his feet, gravity holding him to it, the coolness of the air on his skin. He smelled incense, flowery, herbal.

The angels were still there—even more ethereal than when he'd entered—and the threads of light: dimmer, as though they were hot wires cooling off. Jagger ached at their passing, at their leaving his world or his leaving theirs.

Someone touched his arm, said again, "What's wrong? What's happened?"

He rotated his head toward a man standing near him, out of focus. Jagger ran two fingers over his eyelids, surprised to find tears there. He squeegeed them away.

Father Augustus watched him with concern. One hand rested on Jagger's forearm, the other held a shotgun.

"We heard gunfire, lots of it," a man said from the other side of him. Father Stephan, sitting in a chair just inside the nave on the right. It occurred to Jagger that these men had been positioned just inside the basilica's door to protect the praying monks.

From behind him Mattieu described the carnage outside, the loss of their brothers.

Stephan's mouth dropped open. Augustus clasped a cross hanging over his chest and fell to his knees on the spot. He bowed his head, and Jagger reeled back when the blue light appeared, too fast to tell if it had come up out of the man or down into him. Then something like golden smoke streaked down from the ceiling, spiraling rapidly around the thread of light. In a flash it flowed over Augustus's head, spilled to the floor, and piled up beside him. Before Jagger could comprehend it happening, the smoke-like substance had become an angel, kneeling with one knee on the ground, a hand on Augustus's head. Embers broke free from him, as if flaking off of his skin, forming the wings he had seen on the other angels.

He knew humans throughout history had seen angels, both in human form and as they really were—or at least in an angelic form made compatible to the human eye and mind. It was no wonder so many people thought angels had wings, even though very few in Scripture did. The embers apparently could be formed into any shape, and when they came together around back, they did appear wing-like.

He stepped back into Mattieu, who moved to his side and wrapped an arm around him. As he watched, the angel beside Stephan faded, faded, and disappeared, along with the blue light. He took in the nave: all of the angels and threads of light were gone, at least to Jagger's eyes. He wondered if they were still there, if they'd left . . . or if they'd ever been there at all. The monks remained, praying, and Jagger saw Gheronda, St. Catherine's abbot, at the lectern, chanting softly in Greek. Without the glow of the blue lights, the church was dark, the candles doing little more than pushing the shadows away from the nave's central aisle.

Jagger passed his hand over Augustus's head, then through the spot where the angel had knelt, thinking he'd feel something, a chill or a warmth, a tinge of emotion, happiness or peace, but there was nothing.

●　●　●

After leaving the basilica together, Jagger and Father Mattieu split off in the courtyard at the base of the apartment stairs. Leo went off to find Father Antoine and the man who'd screamed; Jagger bounded up the stairs, thinking now only of Beth and Tyler. Relief washed over him when he found their apartment door locked and nothing disturbed inside.

He knocked on the panic room's door, said, "It's me."

"Dad!" Tyler said. The first bolt thunked open, and Tyler called out: "What's the password?"

"What?"

"The password." Another bolt disengaged.

"Spaghetti," Jagger said. As anxious as he was to squeeze the living daylights out of his wife and son, he couldn't help but mess with the kid.

"No!" The third lock clicked.

"Uh . . . macaroni?"

The last bolt slid away and the door burst open. Tyler rushed into his arms, all teeth and sparkling eyes and flying hair. "Ravioli!" he said.

"Oh yeah." He hugged his son, then reached past him to help Beth stand and pull her into the embrace.

Beth leaned her head into his chest, now turning her face up for a kiss.

"What happened?" Tyler asked. "We heard shooting and a helicopter and *explosions!*"

Jagger let his lips linger on Beth's before answering. "You sure it wasn't just television?" he teased.

"We don't *have* TV here." Thankfully, the boy didn't launch into the topic of how deprived he was, which he did on a weekly basis, just said, "Are you okay? Was it scary? What happened?"

"I'm fine." He kissed Beth's forehead and brushed the hair off Tyler's. He took their hands and led them into the living room/dining room/kitchenette—with this room, two bedrooms, and a bathroom, it was the largest apartment in the complex, which wasn't saying much. Beth had commandeered the tiny eating table for her writing project, an anthology of vignettes about pilgrims to the monastery and what they'd discovered here. A manual typewriter—she felt it helped her get into the mood of the book's old-time stories—and stacks of paper and notes forced the family to use the living room area to eat, read, relax, and just about everything else. Jagger sat them down on the sofa and knelt in front of them. "Some men broke in. They were heavily armed. I think they took something, but I don't know what yet. The monks, some of them, are trained for this sort of thing. They . . . fought well . . ."

He looked from Tyler to Beth, who read him perfectly. She covered her mouth, said, "Jagger . . . what happened?"

"Three of them were killed."

Beth gasped. Her eyes moistened.

"Father Bardas and Father Luca and Father Corban."

Beth dropped her face into her hands and began sobbing.

After a moment of shock, Tyler pushed himself forward on the cushion, enough to get both arms around Jagger's shoulders, and buried his face in the crook of his neck. He began not only to cry but to wail, loud wrenching sobs. He knew all the monks in the monastery, and every one of them—except Father Kostya, a seventy-something block of Russian ice and the monastery's token curmudgeon—treated Tyler like family. Especially Luca, who had let Tyler help him tend to the gardens and regaled him with stories of his childhood spent manning his family's fishing boat off the small Greek village of Gerolimenas—stories that had made Jagger ponder the distinction between exaggeration and lying. Jagger suspected that friendship contributed only a little to Tyler's grief; the boy had a tender spirit and most likely would be crying just as hard if "Kostya the Cold" had been the attackers' sole victim.

"I know," he said, feeling like he should fall back on the old standards—*they're with God now; they're in a better place*—but Beth and Tyler knew that as much as he did. And as true as the statements may be, God put in everyone a strong instinct to survive, to appreciate the breath of life and the world He built for them. Even if you were at peace with your own mortality, utterly comfortable with letting God choose the time and place, being murdered was no way to go. Saying *They're in a better place* was just a way of trying to feel a little less terrible about something that was a big pile of stink any way you cut it, same as getting excited about a sliver of sunlight in the distance after a hurricane had already picked you up and whipped you around while deciding how far to throw you.

Beth reached out and ran her fingers over the back of his head. In her eyes he saw more sorrow. The attack, the deaths brought back the anguish she'd felt when Tyler had been shot, coupled with that shaky, light-headed terror of realizing how bad it could have been: Jagger had been out there; it could have been him lying dead on the stone ground right now.

If she knew how truly close he'd come, she'd probably have an anxiety attack.

No, he thought. *Not Beth.* She'd be out in the compound picking up a shotgun, planning to track down Jagger's killer if she had to cross the desert on foot to do it.

Tyler leaned back. "Bet you tried to save them," he said with a trembling smile.

"You know it, Ty. But it all happened really fast, not a lot I could do."

"You gonna get them, the people who killed them? Make them pay?"

"There are people whose job it is to find them and bring them to justice. It's not mine."

"But—" Tyler stopped, and Jagger turned his head to listen: someone was stomping up the stairs outside, in a hurry. He felt his son's muscles tighten and he told him, "The bad guys are gone, don't worry."

The footsteps stopped outside their door and someone pounded.

"Come in," Jagger called.

The door opened, and Leo leaned in with it. "Ollie's hurt," he said.

"Shot?"

"With an arrow." He touched his chest, indicating the wound's location.

Jagger looked at Beth, gave her thigh a squeeze, and stood.

Tyler rose and grabbed him. "I want to come, please!"

Of everyone they knew in Egypt, outside his own family Tyler was most fond of Oliver Hoffmann, the lead archeologist and director of the excavation outside the compound's east wall. Because of him, Tyler said he wanted to be an archeologist, and Ollie had taken it upon himself to nurture that interest.

"Not now, son," Jagger said. "I'll let you know how he is." He turned and followed Leo down the stairs.

[15]

Jagger had gotten ahead of Leo on the stairs, anxious to see Ollie. He pulled a flashlight off his belt and entered the tunnel formed on one side by the apartment building's bottom floor. He paused at the first door, an empty guest room. The door was canted on one hinge and the jamb was splintered where the latch belonged. Someone—Steampunk, of course—had smashed it open. He went to the next door, broken open as well. The room had been converted into a storage area for the excavation's artifacts, organized on metal shelves by dig unit—Ollie had named the two holes Annabelle and Bertha—and by date of the find. A lighted bulb in the ceiling showed that many of the finds for Bertha during the last week had been swept to the floor, mostly pottery shards and what looked to Jagger like dirt clods.

Leo brushed past him, said, "He's in his apartment."

Jagger hurried to the next room. A lamp was glowing on a table beside a couch—cluttered with books, journals, and papers, except for one empty spot by the arm where Ollie would sit when he was reading.

Father Pietr stood in the entrance to the bedroom, his back to Jagger. He turned when he heard Jagger's footsteps and moved out of the way.

Ollie lay wheezing on his bed, head propped on a pillow, blankets pulled up to his chest, where an arrow jutted up from the left side. His work shirt had been torn away from the wound, which to Jagger looked devastating. Thin cuts in Ollie's flesh fanned out from the arrow's shaft, where the broadhead's plus-sign razors went in. His left hand was clenched into a fist, resting on the blanket over his stomach. His eyes were half lidded, and he was stretching his lips over those horrendous teeth of his that Jagger had always thought were somehow endearing, humanizing.

Gheronda knelt near the foot of the bed, praying. Father Jeffrey crouched close to Ollie's head, patting it with a cloth.

Behind him Antoine leaned against Jagger's arm. He whispered, "He was on the floor when I found him." He pointed at the safe in which Ollie kept important documents relating to the excavation. Its door was open, and papers were lying on the floor in front of it. Some of them partially covered a handgun, only its grip and hammer visible. "They were looking for something."

The rock, Jagger thought. Or was there something else?

"Brother Ramón went for the first-aid kit and to call for a medevac," Antoine said. "I didn't want to try to remove it."

"No, that's right," Jagger said over his shoulder. "Let the doctors take it out." Common sense that wasn't so common. He'd read of a hunter who'd pierced his thigh with a broad-headed arrow while climbing over a fence. In a panic, he'd yanked it out and bled to death from a lacerated femoral artery. The article said the man probably would have lived if he hadn't removed the arrow, which was effectively sealing the wound.

But Jagger understood the impulse: looking at the arrow in Ollie's chest, wavering like a tachometer needle with each breath, he wanted it gone, out of his friend.

Ollie's eyes opened wider, and his scowl turned into a grin. He raised his hand, as if reaching for something, and said, "They're beautiful! The sparks!"

Jagger felt as though he'd been slapped. "What?" he said. "What'd he say?"

Ollie lifted his head from the pillow. "Jagger?" he said.

"You said sparks—"

"They're beautiful," Ollie said. "All around, so bright. They're smiling at me."

Jagger knelt beside the bed. "What do you see, Ollie? Are they angels?"

"Angels! So . . . *lovely* . . . strong and glowing. The sparks, like stars all around them!"

Jagger realized Ollie was gazing beyond him and turned to look. Leo was walking toward the bed.

"You—" Ollie said. "So beautiful."

Leo grinned. "Thank you," he said, and bent to whisper in Jagger's ear. "He's delirious."

Jagger eyed him. "Obviously."

"But . . . but . . . but . . . ," Ollie said, reaching out to Leo, who took the cloth from Jeffrey and pressed it against the spot where the arrow entered his chest. Ollie groaned, closed his eyes, and tilted his head back on the pillow.

Leo dabbed at the spot, then handed the bloody cloth back to Jeffrey. Jagger saw that the wound wasn't as bad as it had first looked. The broadhead slices were gone, trickles of blood, not lacerations.

Leo stood, patted Jagger on the shoulder, and left the room.

Jagger leaned in. "Ollie," he said. "Tell me about the sparkles. How—"

Someone gripped his shoulder. Gheronda leaned close, said, "Come with me, Jagger. We need to talk."

"But . . . wait a minute. Ollie—"

Gheronda gave his shoulder a shake. "Now," he said firmly. "Please."

Jagger rose and backed away from Ollie's bed. Gheronda grabbed his arm and led him out of the room, pushing past Pietr and Antoine, still in the doorway.

Ollie called, "Do you see them, Jag? Aren't they beautiful?"

Gheronda released Jagger and went back to the bedroom door. "Brother Pietr," he said, "please go find out what's taking Brother Ramón so long. Brother Antoine, Oliver needs your prayers." When the monks departed, Gheronda turned to Jagger. He said, "I've seen it before, people on their deathbeds seeing angels."

"I don't think that's what's happening," Jagger said. "What he's saying, what he sees . . . I . . ." He didn't finish. He wasn't ready to talk about his vision, not yet. But if Ollie was having the same vision, that changed everything. He just wasn't sure how. "It doesn't look like he's ready to die. I mean, he doesn't look that close to death. He's so animated . . . and the air ambulance is coming."

The old man nodded. "I'm praying God will let Oliver live to dig another day. But that's not what I wanted to talk to you about." He stepped closer. "Father Leo tells me you saw who did this terrible thing."

"He was wearing a mask," Jagger said. "A tight-fitting leather thing with stitches and zippers and black goggles."

"The other attackers, you saw them?"

"One of them had dark hair, good-looking, snappy dresser. The others—" He shook his head. "They looked like a group of trick-or-treaters, all dressed up differently. A muscle man with black makeup streaked over his eyes, a guy who looked like a jungle commando, a punk rock girl. And the one with the mask. If it weren't for their fire-power—and homicidal tendencies—I'd almost laugh."

The bushy whiskers of Gheronda's beard bristled as the muscles in his jaw tightened. His brow scrunched in the center. He said, "If they're who I think they are, there's nothing to laugh about."

"Well, no, they killed three monks." But Jagger knew what the man meant.

"Come," Gheronda said. He strode out through the open apartment door.

"Who do you think they are?" Jagger called, starting after him.

"Come and see!"

[16]

Jagger caught up with him as Gheronda was unlocking the door to the library on the second floor of the Southwest Range Building. Jagger turned to look across the rooftops and walkways to his apartment. A light was still glowing in the window. He hoped Tyler wasn't waiting up, but Jagger knew he was.

"Shut the door behind you, please," Gheronda called from inside.

They walked down the long central aisle of the library, and as they reached each square, white-painted column positioned at the border of the aisle and the shelves of books, Gheronda flipped a switch. Florescent lights two stories overhead sputtered on, illuminating their path to the next column.

The air smelled grassy and musty. It wasn't a bad smell—it was soothing, actually—but it seemed at odds with Jagger's emotions, which at the moment might have given off the odors of gun oil and blood.

At the far end of the hall, Gheronda made a ninety-degree turn into a shorter corridor and stopped at a wooden desk set in the middle of it. He crouched, keys rattling in his hand, then the abbot rose with a set of white cotton gloves, into which he worked his hands. From a drawer he withdrew a book the size of a briefcase, which he thunked down on the desktop.

The book looked to Jagger like an antique scrapbook, no real spine, just pages sandwiched between leather-covered boards and stitched on one side with a long strip of leather.

Gheronda cracked it open a few inches and peered in from the side. He thumbed down through the pages, then hinged it all the way over until both covers lay flat. The book was open to a page about three-fourths to the end. It was the color of creamed coffee, appeared water-stained on one side, and had a slightly bumpy texture, like onionskin paper. Mounted to it, at odds with the book's apparent antiquity, were color photographs, two columns of three.

Jagger pointed. "That's the handsome one. He just stood there, watching the others."

"Bale," Gheronda said, and made a disgusted sound with his mouth. "This makes two times in less than half a year," he said. "First the Tribe attacked the monastery, this place of God and a supposed Haven for any Immortal who needs it. Now Bale and his ruffians."

Not long ago Jagger had whittled Gheronda's face into a piece of wood, looking for something to challenge the new skill a physical therapist had suggested he learn to get used to his hook. While doing so, he'd realized the old man had a cartoonish mug—bulbous nose, pronounced cheekbones, deep-set eyes, sloppy gray beard. He'd made the mistake of telling Beth that within Tyler's earshot.

"Grumpy!" the boy had exclaimed. "You know, one of the seven dwarfs." And he had pegged it perfectly. Gheronda's disposition was far from grumpy, but you'd never know it looking at him. Now that cartoon-character face became a thing of utter ferocity.

Gheronda slammed his fist on the desk.

Jagger had never seen him this riled. In fact, he'd been such a model of even temperament that whenever Jagger felt himself back-sliding into his hate-everything mood he'd think about Gheronda, just taking everything in stride, believing everything would be all right. And if it weren't, well, that was all right too. All in God's plan.

"Hold on," Jagger said, remembering. "Bale. Owen said something about him. Leader of a group of Immortals who broke away from the Tribe?"

"They were never a part of the Tribe, not really. They became immortal at the golden calf, like the others, but they never cared about redemption. They embraced immortality, and since they'd never answer for their sins—their thinking, anyway—why not rack up as many as possible? Nasty bunch. All they want to do is destroy and kill, and they don't care who: men, women, children. Call themselves the *Clan*." He said the word as though it tasted bad in his mouth. "Sort of a jab at the Tribe."

As an Immortal himself, Jagger should have had personal knowledge of Bale and his Clan, but they were simply more memories that had slipped between the cracks.

He returned his attention to the photographs. Each bore the image of a single person, four men and two women. They all appeared to be angled marginally away from the camera, as though they were unaware of the photographer.

"These are candid shots?" he asked.

"The Clan doesn't pose for pictures," Gheronda said. "In fact, they don't like their photos taken at all. But as host of a Haven, one of three sanctuaries around the world where any of the Immortals can go for protection—or *used to* be able to go—we need to know whom to allow in and whom to keep out, if they pose a threat to someone we're protecting. He waved a hand over the page. "Owen took these for us a few years ago."

"Owen?" Jagger said. Owen had left the Tribe when he became one of Christ's apostles. Since then he'd been trying to convince the Tribe that their goal of regaining God's favor by killing sinners would never work. He believed his purpose on earth, the reason for his continued immortality, was to help others. When Jagger had met him six months ago, he'd just come from a war zone in the Democratic Republic of the Congo, working with Médecins Sans Frontières—Doctors Without Borders. And had he not shown up with his medical skills and helicopter when he did—a few minutes after Nevaeh shot Tyler—his son would be dead now. He loved Owen for that, but he believed that had they met under less trying circumstances they still would have become dear friends. Owen was just that way; it was hard not to appreciate him. Jagger had spoken with him only once since then.

He looked down at the photographs. Where had he seen Bale

before? Then it dawned on him. "That's Bale," he said, pointing at a painting on the twin doors of a wooden cabinet across the aisle from where they stood. Tyler had described it as a zombie coming out of a grave. In it a man—Bale—was pushing himself out of the earth, dirt falling from his hair and face and mouth. Strokes of black paint, almost imperceptible against the blackness of the painted sky, radiated out from behind him. They could have represented the faintest of mist—or huge bat-like wings. Jagger felt his skin grow cold.

"Nevaeh painted that," Gheronda said. "In 1609."

"That's the triptych you showed Beth and Tyler, isn't it?" he asked. "Inside is a painting of the Israelites worshiping the golden calf, right? I'd like to see it."

Gheronda smiled and laid his hand on Jagger's shoulder. "Perhaps another time," he said. "Do you recognize any of the others on this page?"

There was the muscular guy, complete with raccoon eyes. "Him," Jagger said.

"Therion," Gheronda said.

"And him." The tall commando who'd lugged the .50-cal machine gun, sans war paint in the photo.

"Artimus."

And there was the rock'n'roll girl.

"Lilit."

Jagger leaned closer to inspect the photos of the other man and woman. "Not these two," he said.

"The woman is Hester," Gheronda said. "The studious-looking man with the glasses, that's Cillian."

"I didn't see him tonight."

"He's their pilot."

"He must have stayed in the helicopter." He remembered the way the copter had maneuvered to avoid Leo's missile. The guy had chops.

They looked at all the photos together. The Clan. It was clear Gheronda regarded them as worse than the Tribe, and yes, they had just killed three monks and severely wounded Ollie. But the Tribe had kidnapped Beth, shot Tyler, and tried to destroy a major city—killing 312, the news said, before Owen stopped them. He shook his head.

How could the Clan be *worse*?

[17]

The helicopter zipped low over the Sinai's Colored Canyon on its way to Taba Airport, one hundred miles northeast of St. Catherine's. The airport was perfect for the Clan's needs: its one runway was long enough to accommodate their big Bombardier Global 7000 jet, small enough that its officials could be bribed into losing records of their landing and takeoff, and only forty minutes to the monastery by helicopter, which they'd been able to rent from a tour operator. Cillian was at the controls.

From his backward-facing seat behind the unoccupied copilot's chair, Bale struggled to get his jacket off. His black T-shirt was torn near the sleeve seam and glistened with blood. He inserted his fingers, ripped the material away.

Beside him, Lilit leaned over a tackle box on the floor between her feet. She rummaged through an assortment of medical supplies. "How bad?" she asked without looking up.

"Tore a chunk of meat away," Bale said. "No bone. Nothing to worry about."

She handed him a plastic bottle with a bent tube on top. He aimed the tip of the tube at the wound and squeezed the bottle. A stream of saline washed the blood away. He watched her fill a syringe from a rubber-topped vial, then took it from her and jabbed the needle into the wound. The local analgesic would dull the pain without affecting his mind; he wanted to stay clearheaded at least until they were on the jet heading out of the country. No telling how the Egyptians would respond to their attack on the monastery or how quickly they'd move to apprehend the perpetrators. He dressed his shoulder with gauze, taped it down, and leaned back. He glanced out the window, but it was too dark to see any of the landscape's famously contorted and colorful rock formations, canyons, and plateaus.

The others were laughing it up and congratulating themselves on a successful mission, like high school football players after winning a big game. At least they'd waited until he reported on his injury.

Lilit closed the tackle box and picked up something from her lap: the controller she'd used to operate the Cobra that had taken out the first two monks. Normally Bale would have operated a drone himself, but they'd had only three, and sometimes being leader meant letting others have all the fun. Therion—facing Lilit across the aisle that separated the cabin's two bench seats—said something nasty about her letting them drop her Cobra down a well, and she hurled the controller at him.

"They *all* got thrown in the well," she reminded them.

"Only after you showed them it could be done," Therion said. He ripped the controller in half and tossed the pieces on the floor among their machine guns, rifles, and swords. As if the man's layers of bulging muscles weren't intimidating enough, he got off on tearing things apart that seemed impossible to tear apart with bare hands: furniture, trees, the human body. Bale had once seen him dismantle a 1968 Cadillac with nothing but brawn and fury.

Waving his bulky arms around, Therion elbowed Artimus, seated beside him. Artimus promptly punched him in the face, making a sound like a baseball bat striking a tree. Therion gave him a wild look, his crazy eyes seeming that much crazier set in the black raccoon stripe tattooed across his face. Both men started laughing, then Artimus pulled a knife from his boot—a nine-inch blade, wide as a cowboy's belt, with a serrated spine—and flicked it over one of Therion's pectorals.

Therion looked down at his bleeding chest and scowled at Artimus. "Keep the cutting to yourself," he warned, and Artimus did, dragging the tip along the length of his own forearm, as he'd done a thousand times, watching it bleed.

Bale eyed the person seated directly opposite him, still clad in a leather mask with opaque black-lensed goggles, brass-framed, and a gas mask tube in place of a mouth. One arm was draped over a knee, gloved fingers dangling. He watched as a drop of blood grew fat on the tip of a finger and fell, plopping into a small pool on the floor.

"You're injured," he said.

The unbloodied hand came up, found a zipper in the back of the mask, and ran it up to the crown. Watching it come off was like witnessing someone peeling off his face. Hester dropped the mask into her lap and ran the gloved fingertips of one hand over her close-cropped blond hair, scratching the scalp. She raised her wounded hand and inspected both sides.

"More damage to the glove than to me," she said. She shrugged and said, "Flesh wound."

"We were both lucky tonight."

They gazed at each other for a few moments, unable to hold eye contact with the way the helicopter jostled them.

Bale said, "Well?"

Hester smiled and reached into an inside pocket of her leather duster. She produced a shard of stone, roughly the length of a railroad spike and twice as thick. One end was broken into a blunt point. It could have been a heavy stone-aged spearhead, but Bale knew better.

He held out his hand, and Hester dropped the shard into it. A flash of white consumed his vision. A second later he could see again. Oh, could he see. In the cabin with them were creatures, the most majestic and gorgeous beings imaginable, a variety of them, but all powerful in form, with claws and fangs; quivering, ragged, and veinous wings; sheathed blades; fidgety arms; gaping grins. Black eyes that darted around as though expecting an assault at any moment from any direction, but always coming back to him, watching him. One with a scaly black hide stood in front of Artimus, looking from Bale to Artimus, using a finger to push the tip of the knife along the man's forearm. Another, as small as a child, sat on Therion's lap. It boasted a chest nearly as muscular as Therion's, but the rest of its body was right out of the Holocaust: from the rib cage its stomach collapsed in, seemingly to its spine; sharp, protruding hip bones; limbs like cloth-covered bones. It rested its misshapen head on Therion's chest and caressed Therion's face with twig-like fingers. As solid and substantial as the creature appeared to Bale, Therion's waving arms passed through it, neither of them noticing.

Beautiful.

A monkey-looking thing with a human face and tiny flapping wings leapt from Hester's head to Therion's to Artimus's and back again, making a game of it.

A large creature occupied the empty seat next to Lilit, who was between Bale and it. Bale leaned forward to get a good look. Its body bore human proportions, more or less—its arms were longer, each hinged with an extra elbow—but its face was that of a dragon's, long snout under which its jaw opened and closed like an alligator's; almond eyes, solid red.

Beyond it, a face peered in through the window. The beast seemed to be clinging to the outside of the helicopter.

Bale turned to look out his own window, focusing beyond his reflection. More creatures were flying through the night sky—he counted five, eight, twelve of them. They were twisting, weaving, soaring up and dipping down, like dolphins in the wake of a ship; all of them pretty much staying with the helicopter.

And what's this . . . ?

In the distance, lights ran in perfectly vertical lines from the earth into the heavens. They were scattered around a vast area, no beginning or end in either direction, some thicker and brighter than others, a single beam here, a cluster of them there. He wondered about them, then something poked his side and he turned.

Hester was leaning out from her seat, a crossbow arrow in hand, ready to jab him again. She said, "You there?"

He grinned. "Better than ever."

"Have you heard a word I said?" The monkey thing appeared to be picking something out of her hair.

"About what?"

"I asked what you were doing, glaring around like a druggie, talking to yourself."

Ignoring her, he scanned the cabin, making eye contact with each grinning creature, then looked at the stone shard in his hand. When he looked up again, the Clan had fallen silent, all eyes on him. As he had done with the creatures, he stared at each of his human companions in turn, stopping on Lilit. He said, "Are you ready?"

"For what?"

He addressed all of them. "Are you *ready*?"

Therion yelled, "Yeah!"

"Good," Bale said, "because I have a feeling things are about to get a whole lot more exciting."

[18]

Gheronda started to close the book, but Jagger stopped him.

"Wait a minute," he said. He was leaning in to examine the picture of the woman Gheronda called Hester. She was striding along a crowded sidewalk. "That slicker . . . and those boots. Steampunk was wearing—" He turned to Gheronda. "Steampunk's a woman."

"She's Clan," the old man said, as if that's all that mattered. He flipped the page, then another, moving toward the front of the book. "It's in chronological order," he said. As he continued back in time, the photos became faded, then black-and-white . . . then sepia, tiny cracks forming. A few more pages and the photos gave way to drawings, rendered in exquisite detail. Hairstyles and fashions changed. People coming and going, but a core remained the same: Bale, Therion, Lilit, the one called Cillian. He stopped on a drawing of a boy. Dressed in a toga, the child looked about twelve. As drawn, nothing about his face differentiated him from any other boy that age, no scowl or wicked smile, just a boy.

"So young," Jagger said. There were children in the Tribe and that was difficult enough to think about, but in the *Clan*—Jagger couldn't believe it.

Gheronda said, "He's on a few pages, so he might have been with the Clan twenty or fifty years, maybe longer. Then he disappeared. No word of what happened."

"They ate him." The voice came from behind them, and they both jumped. Father Leo stood there, a slight smile, hands on hips.

"They did *what*?" Jagger said.

Leo shrugged. "I don't know that they did. I'm just saying they're the type who would."

"Did you come just to give us a scare?" Gheronda asked.

Leo nodded toward Jagger. "I stopped by your apartment. Beth and Tyler are wondering about Ollie's condition . . . and where you are. They're pretty upset. I said I'd hunt you down."

"Thank you. I'll head over in a few minutes." He nodded at the book and said to Gheronda, "Turn to the first page." When the old man did, Jagger's heart leapt into his throat. Attached to the page was a swath of animal skin. On it was the etching of a single man, Bale. He was on his knees, arms and face raised, mouth open, as if screaming at God. He wore something like a skirt, his upper body bare. Faint wings stretched out behind him. From the side of his face another face emerged, twisted and hideous, with bulging eyes and a nose so short and so dominated by nostrils it appeared almost nonexistent, like the sinus cavities on a skull. Fat lips stretched over a mouthful of fangs. Arms—corded with veins and muscles— branched out of Bale's forearms, also straining toward the sky, clawed fingers splayed.

Jagger realized he had raised RoboHand and was holding it between the etching and his face, as if protecting himself from the image. He scratched his cheek with the hook.

"Nevaeh etched this one too," Gheronda said. "Pre-Christ."

Jagger snapped his head toward him. "Nevaeh? Where did she come up with the idea?"

The old man sighed. "You don't have to know Bale long to think of him as demonic."

"Demonic?"

"Oh, he's human enough. Immortal, but human."

"And evil," Leo said, and Jagger and Gheronda looked at him. "Owen says Bale was the instigator of what happened at the golden calf. He threw the first rock at Hur, and everyone joined in. He called for a human sacrifice, a baby."

Jagger felt sick. No way he could have been part of that. He'd say not in a million years, but it had been only 3,500.

Gheronda reached across Jagger's field of vision and closed the book. Jagger watched him put it away and lock the drawer. "So we know it was the Clan who attacked," Jagger said. "Now what?"

"Before Ollie started rambling about angels," Gheronda said, "he said the person who attacked him took something, a stone."

Jagger nodded. "I saw Steampunk with it. I grabbed it from her, but she took it back."

"Well, we don't know why they wanted it, but they have it now. That's where I'm stuck. I don't know what to do."

"Call Owen," Leo said.

"Why?" Jagger asked. "What can he do?"

"He's much wiser than I am," Gheronda said, stripping off his gloves. He walked away, heading for the front door, saying, "He knows Bale. He's tracked the Clan. If anyone knows what we should do, he will."

"But—" Jagger started, then reconsidered. He and Leo walked after Gheronda, who flipped the lights off over each section of hallway as they vacated it. "Look," Jagger said, trailing behind the abbot, "if we have to get Owen involved, let me call him. I was there when the monks died, I saw the—"

Gheronda was holding something over his shoulder for Jagger to take.

A satphone.

[19]

"Where to?" Cillian asked, seated in the pilot's seat of the Clan's Bombardier, a computer screen and keyboard on an articulated arm in front of him.

Bale sat in the copilot seat, head back, eyes closed. The vision of the demons, lovely as they were, and all that came with them—rippling lights in the sky; spotlight-bright stars; the orchestral voices, too faint to understand, but painful to his ears; the feeling of a *presence*—had finally faded and disappeared. Odd how releasing the Stone didn't immediately release you of the vision. It was like a bad smell, a noxious chemical, and it had given him a headache. His human mind couldn't comprehend it all. Yet. He assumed it was something he'd get used it, having the eyes of God. And oh, what he could do with those eyes.

"Bale?" Cillian said. "Where to?"

"Stockholm."

"Bronson Radcliff?"

Bale nodded.

"Thought we got what we wanted from him. Finally."

"And that's why we don't need him anymore." The Clan had helped the man for years, making him rich in exchange for his playing front man in their quest for relics and icons that would aid in their mission to be as destructive to God's world as possible. Now that he had the Stone, Bale didn't care what else was out there to find. It was too much work, cost too much, and left them too exposed to continue. And nothing could possibly be as powerful as the Stone. It was perfect that it'd come into his possession. Who else could put it to such effective use? The spiritual world would open up to others and they'd ooh and ahh or feel a warm fuzzy or argue that it was a trick or wasn't from God, it proved nothing. He, on the other hand, accepted its source, marveled at its power, and would do something with it—and the world would ooh and ahh at *him* . . . after it was finished screaming.

"We're going to need refueling," Cillian said. "Didn't do it earlier because you said you wanted the plane out of sight, and—"

"We were in a hurry, I know."

"We can do it now, here."

"After what we left behind at the monastery? I don't think so. We better get out of here before they close the airport."

Cillian looked at him over the top of his glasses. "You think times have changed that much, that anyone cares about St. Catherine's?"

"Only if they think it was a terrorist attack."

"No reason for anyone to think that."

"Because people are stupid," Bale said. "They don't realize how big of a terrorist attack it was."

Like stealing all the nuclear bombs in Russia. Too bad they didn't know, the entire population of the world on edge, terrified, wondering where he'd strike and how bad it would be. Bad, he thought. Apocalypse bad. But they would figure it out soon enough, and they would pray, and the more they prayed, the worse it would get. Then one day, maybe soon, maybe not—he had all the time in the world— they would figure it out, and stop praying.

Cue the scary music.

"We have enough fuel to get to another country?"

"Oh yeah. Fifteen hundred miles or so."

"So where, you think?"

Cillian studied the screen. He ran his fingers over the keyboard, which drew flight paths on a map. "Varna?"

"Bulgaria?" Bale remembered some good times there. "Why not?" He rolled out of the chair, patted Cillian on the shoulder, and said, "Wake me when we're there." He started into the cabin, then turned back. "Hey, Cillian?"

"Yeah?"

"Who discovered DNA?"

"What?" Looking over his shoulder.

"Who discovered DNA?" Bale repeated.

"I don't know. Uh . . . Watson and Cricket, I think. Why?"

"Just asking."

"Why do you always do that?" Cillian said, taking off his glasses.

"What?"

"Ask me weird trivia for no reason."

"No reason." Bale went into the cabin. The first section was their living room/theater: seventy-inch plasma, chairs as comfortable as your bed, bar. The lights were dim, and Therion was clicking a controller at the screen. Lilit sat in another chair, leg bent over the arm, bottle of wine in hand.

"What's on?" Bale asked.

"Thinking about *Sodom and Gomorrah*," Therion said. He shifted his bulk in the chair, finding a position that accommodated his muscles.

"Is that the snuff film?" Bale didn't watch movies. He funded a few he thought were appropriately corrupting, PG-13 fare to reach those impressionable teens, but he never partook himself. Too many better things to do.

"No, this one's based on the writings of the Marquis de Sade."

"Wonderful," Bale said. "Enjoy."

"I've seen it five times."

"That good?"

"That disgusting," Lilit said.

Bale nodded. "Training film, huh?"

Lilit snorted. Bale knew no artist's imagination in any media, no matter how depraved or vile, could come close to the Clan's exploits. One reason movies bored him: why watch a film about an old man using a walker to get up a hill when you climbed Everest on a regular basis?

He left them to it and walked through the kitchen—no galley on this plane; they had a kitchen chefs would die for—into the area of the cabin that housed their bedrooms. Artimus's and Hester's doors were closed. Artimus was no doubt reading; he loved popular novels. Bale tapped on his door and opened it. Well, surprise, he was sitting on the bed, wiping a silicone cloth over the barrel of his .50-cal.

Bale asked, "Who discovered DNA?"

"Johannes Friedrich Miescher. At the University of Tübingen, Germany, in 1869. But he was Swiss."

Bale grinned, shook his head. "I love it." He started to shut the door, then asked, "Did Watson and Cricket have anything to do with it?"

"James Watson and Francis *Crick*. They discovered the molecular structure of DNA in 1953."

"I guess Cillian gets one point for coming close," Bale said. He laughed and took in the man's machismo: the big honking gun, the Indian hair, war paint—still on. "Thanks," he said and continued down the corridor. Cillian looked the part, and no doubt he was an intelligent guy, but Artimus . . . ? Bale laughed again, went into his bedroom, and shut the door.

[20]

The little girl sitting on her mother's lap started crying before Owen picked up the syringe. He reached under a table into a large cardboard box and pulled out a stuffed blue monkey. He peeled away its plastic wrapping and jiggled it in front of her. In as squeaky a voice as his vocal cords would allow, he said, "Privet, Taisia! Ya Adeen gōd. Skolko vam let?" *Hi, Taisia! I'm one year old. How old are you?*

Taisia blinked and brushed the hair away from her face. She smiled, showing a big gap where her two upper central incisors used to be, and said, *"Syem." Seven.*

Continuing in Russian, the monkey said, "Ooh, you're a big girl. Will you let Dr. Letois give you an itsy bitsy shot? It will make sure you don't get sick, and then I can come home with you."

Taisia looked suspiciously at Owen . . . for a long time.

"Taisia?" the monkey said.

Slowly the girl nodded.

"Oh, goody!"

Taisia grabbed the monkey and gripped it tightly to her chest, burying her face into the top of its head. Her mother nodded.

Owen raised the girl's sleeve and swabbed a spot with a water-moistened wipe. Taisia pulled away. Her mother whispered something to her, and she turned her arm back to Owen. He opened a syringe and filled it with BCG tuberculosis vaccine. He laid the syringe nearly parallel to the girl's arm and gently slipped the needle two millimeters into the superficial layers of the dermis. Injecting the vaccine slowly, he frowned at the bruises on the girl's forearm and the ones extending out from under the hem of her dress on her thigh.

Taisia was the fourth child—out of twenty-two so far—on whom he'd witnessed bruises. He knew better than to question her mother; the other parents he'd spoken to had become instantly and aggressively defensive, yanking their children away before he'd finished examining and vaccinating them. If word got out that he was asking the wrong kind of questions, chances were high he'd find his long queue of patients suddenly much shorter. He'd have to find another way to uncover the truth.

He had come to Tabashino in the heavily forested region of Mari El Republic, Russia, to give the children physicals, vaccinations, and any other medical care he could provide; in addition, he'd brought boxes of much needed supplies and pharmaceuticals, which he intended to leave with the area's general practitioner nearly thirty miles away. He hoped to inspire other Western physicians to follow his lead. He'd expected to find all kinds of medical issues—a recent study by the Russian Health Ministry suggested that nearly eight million children were in need of medical attention, most of them in backwoods towns like Tabashino, where the likelihood of receiving care was infinitesimal.

What he hadn't expected were these signs of abuse.

"All done," he said in Russian. The injection had caused swelling similar to a mosquito bite. He told Taisia's mom it should go away in fifteen minutes, to return if it didn't. He grabbed a handful of *Iris Kis-Kis* treats, little squares of caramel, from his medical bag and handed them to the little girl. Telling the blue monkey that the shot didn't hurt at all, she and her mother disappeared around the fabric screen that blocked the patient area from the rest of the basketball-court-sized community center Tabashino's mayor had provided for Owen's visit.

He was typing notes into a tablet computer—later, he'd print them and leave the hard copies for each parent to pick up—when his next patient appeared, a boy about ten. Without a word he handed Owen a folded note, which identified him as Dima Morozov and gave Owen permission to examine him and "inject any medicines to make him good."

"Is this from your mother?" Owen asked.

Dima nodded. From his pants pocket he produced a card and handed it to Owen. It was a prayer card featuring a reproduction of *Theotokos of Vladimir*—Mary holding a baby Jesus, painted by the Apostle Luke. Owen had seen the original, freshly painted, and smiled at the card.

"Thank you," he said, and placed it on the pile of other cards he had received today.

"Can I have a monkey?"

"Of course. Take off your shirt and have a seat." Owen dug into his box of toys and said, "Would you like blue or green?" He turned to show them to the boy. "Personally, I like the—"

Beside bruised biceps, Dima's stomach bore a fist-sized black-and-blue mark; red welts swelled on both shoulders.

"Dima . . ."

The boy frowned and dropped his head. Owen opened both stuffed animals and handed them to him. "Both monkeys want to be your friend," Owen said. "Can you handle two?"

Dima embraced the stuffed animals. His grin alone was worth the trip to Russia, as far as Owen was concerned. Then the boy spotted something over Owen's shoulder and stiffened. His eyes grew wide, his lips trembled . . . then he dropped his face again.

Owen turned and saw a man standing in a short hallway leading to the back door. A mousy-looking fellow, his expression went from glaring malice to smiling welcome when he saw Owen looking at him. The man nodded, then pushed through the door.

"Who is that man?" Owen said, standing. Dima was frozen, staring down at the monkeys in his lap. "Dima? Stay here." He ran to the door and went through. An alleyway stretched in both directions. It was empty.

He returned to the examination area and sat across from Dima. The boy looked up, and Owen locked eyes with him. Owen hoped the love and compassion he felt for the child came through. "Dima," he said, "you have to tell me about the bruises."

• • •

That had been eight hours ago.

Now, Owen's fist made contact with the Russian schoolteacher's face. Fyodor Titov fell to the street in front of the closed school and lifted his knees and arms to protect himself.

The satphone in Owen's backpack started ringing.

Owen straddled the little man, grabbed a handful of his wool coat, and lifted him a foot off the ground. His fist was pulled back, ready to strike again.

The phone kept ringing.

Owen shook with anger, his breath forming visible clouds of vapor in the cold air, chugging it out like a steam locomotive. He released Titov and stood, pointed at him, and said in the man's native tongue, "Don't move." He walked to the concrete steps leading to the school's front doors, fished the phone out of his pack, and answered it.

"Owen, it's Jagger."

He smiled despite himself. "Jagger! I'd say it's always good to hear from you, but since it's"—he pushed up the cuff of his down jacket and checked his watch—"one o'clock in the morning here, it must be eleven at night for you. I'm guessing there's trouble?"

He heard shoes scuff the pavement behind him and turned to see Titov getting to his feet.

"Ey!" Owen said. *Hey!*

The man took off running.

"Ostanovis!" Stop! Owen said into the phone, "Hold on a sec," and tore after Titov. It took him a block to catch up. He tackled him in the center of the street, blocked his pathetic slaps, and got a grip on his thinning hair. He jabbed a finger at his nose, gave him a serious look, and stood. He planted his boot on the man's chest and lifted the phone. "Sorry about that, Jag."

"I caught you at a bad time."

"No." He looked up and down the deserted street, just a smattering of dilapidated storefronts, a single parked car, no lights; only the moon kept it from being as black as a cave. The town might have been pleasant once—a tailor, a cobbler, a florist, what looked like an ice-cream shop, boarded over now because the whole place was suffering from economic starvation. Trash rustled along the curbs, paper signs announcing long-over sales flapped on the windows of stores whose owners couldn't work up the motivation to peel them off, defoliated bushes grew untended from wide cracks between the curbs and side-walks, their scraggy limbs mirroring the town's desperation. Over the tops of the stores he could make out the silver onion domes of the local church. "I'm up here in Tabashino. Know it?"

"Never heard of it."

"Beautiful, forests and rivers everywhere. But horrendous medical care, especially for the children." He gave Jagger the short version of what brought him to that part of the world and the evidence of the abuse he'd seen. "I found out a schoolteacher's been sexually abusing them, taking their pictures."

"Oh man," Jagger said.

Owen scowled at Titov, pushed his boot harder into his chest. "He was selling the pictures to a porn distributor in St. Petersburg. Even more terrible, the parents know about it. The teacher pays them to look the other way. As impoverished as this area is, I think it's the only way they can put food on the table."

"There's gotta be a better way. So what are you doing about it?"

"I'm having a word with the teacher now."

And that's all he had intended to do, until the guy ran from him when Owen approached him in a general store. Owen had found him in a *pivnaya*—a pub—and decided to wait for him elsewhere, not get into it with all his buddies around. He'd sat on the school steps—between the pub and where some townsfolk said the teacher lived—for six hours, at first chatting with passersby. Then, when they'd rolled up the sidewalks and everyone vanished into their homes, he'd sat alone, thinking about the kids, how they'd come to him with the sweetest smiles, bearing gifts like the prayer cards and a few things they'd made themselves, how they beamed when he gave them hand-fuls of candy and little toys. Stewing over the abuse they'd endured.

Growing angrier and angrier—even through prayer. When the guy came stumbling down the street, listened to Owen's accusations, and dismissed him with a curt Russian phrase meaning "mind your own business"—but not as nice—Owen had lost it.

Or found it: what the guy had coming to him.

"I see," Jagger said. "Give him a word from me too."

"Back to your trouble. What's up?"

Jagger explained: the attack, the monks' deaths, Ollie's injury.

"What did they want?" Owen asked.

He said he didn't know, but told him about an attacker he'd dubbed "Steampunk" and the rock she had stolen.

Owen said, "And you're sure it was the Clan?"

"Gheronda showed me a scrapbook with pictures of them. He said you'd taken some of the shots. They were the same people."

"Okay." Owen felt as though his stomach had been filled with molten iron.

"I wasn't sure I should call," Jagger said.

"I'm glad you did."

"But what can you do? What should *we* do?"

"Just hold down the fort," Owen said. He calculated: an hour to reach his jet at the Yoshkar-Ola Airport, roughly 1,800 miles to Sharm-el-Sheikh—four and a half hours—add an hour to refuel at, say, Erzurum—no sense risking trouble in one of the paranoid Arab countries—then another hour to get a helicopter to St. Cath's. "I can be there in seven and a half, eight hours."

"Are you sure you need to get here that quickly?" Jagger asked. "I'm not even sure—"

"It's *crucial*, Jagger!" He fairly screamed it, then said, "I'm sorry." He took a deep breath. "If the Clan's involved, I need to be. I'll explain when I get there."

He disconnected, pushed the phone into a pocket, and stood staring at the domes of the church, like candle flames pointing to heaven. *Lord, give me the strength to stop Bale and his cohorts. Give me wisdom and help me do Your will . . .*

Fyodor Titov squirmed under his foot, pulled at his pant leg. Owen removed his foot and sat on the man's stomach, hard. Titov *oomphed* and looked terrified—so much so that tears were rolling down his temples—all of which lightened Owen's mood. Just a little.

He leaned over, pinning the teacher's arms with his hands. In Russian he said, "No more children. No touching, no photographs. I'll be back, and if I find out you've been up to your old ways . . . well, let's just say I know some people who would love to get their hands on you. 'If anyone causes one of these little ones—those who believe in me—to stumble, it would be better for them to have a large millstone hung around their neck and to be drowned in the depths of the sea.' Matthew 18. Look it up. It's one of their favorite ways of disposing of people like you. Understand?"

Titov nodded vigorously, rambled assurances.

"And all of the parents you've paid?" Owen said. "I think it's only fair that you should continue paying them."

The teacher looked shocked, started babbling about how impossible it was, about his lack of funds.

Owen simply glared.

Finally the man nodded, said he'd find a way.

"I'm sure you will." Owen climbed off and walked back to the school to retrieve his backpack. As he continued down the street toward the rented Jeep he'd left at the edge of town, he made a mental note to have a millstone delivered to the schoolteacher's door.

[21]

Jagger lowered the phone and stared out at the compound from the Southwest Range Building's third-floor portico. Past the mishmash of buildings, smoke drifted off the front wall opposite his position, the courtyard light giving it a spectral appearance. He watched it as he would flames in a fireplace, curious about what form it would take next, awed by its ethereal nature, momentarily distracted from the jumble of thoughts clambering for attention in his head. But the delicateness of the smoke—translucent, wispy—made him think of the suddenly-there, suddenly-gone beings who'd helped him on the rooftop and the similar ones he'd witnessed in the basilica. Were they really angels? He'd come to that conclusion, and apparently so had Ollie.

"They're beautiful," Ollie had said. *"The sparks!"*

They'd both had contact with Steampunk, which strengthened his theory that the woman had sprayed or somehow emitted some sort of hallucinogen. But how could any drug cause two people to hallucinate the same thing? And why did the effects wear off quicker with Jagger than Ollie? Had Ollie received a stronger dose?

And what about the way he'd felt while seeing the things? Real or imagined, the vision had stirred sensations he'd never felt before: elation, peace . . . and unease, apprehension. How could those conflicting emotions coexist? Not going from one to the other, even instantly, but feeling them simultaneously. It didn't seem possible.

But as big as that event had been, other things needed his attention, not the least of which was the murder of three monks. It wasn't fair to them, or right, that he should be distracted from mourning their loss—or analyzing how they died. What had gone wrong? Could he have done something to prevent it? What could he do to make sure it never happened again?

He could barely see the smoke now, just a wisp catching some light every few seconds.

Then there was the matter of the attack. Had they come for the rock Steampunk had? If so, why? What was its value?

Something else was nagging at him as well—as if his mind was too overwhelmed to try managing any of it: *What else can I worry about? Bring it on! World hunger? Okay! Global peace? Got it!* But this concern was more immediate, more personal: Ollie's condition. The monks were already tending to him, the air ambulance had been called. Should Jagger be there with him too? There was something he should be doing regarding Ollie. He knew it, but couldn't get his mind around it.

He needed Beth. She would help him sort things out; she had the ability to see the big picture *and* the details. He had a feeling that all the things he needed to spew out would overwhelm her as well. But he couldn't think of any better way to be overwhelmed and confused than to be overwhelmed and confused with the woman he loved.

He started toward the end of the walkway, toward the corner where the Southwest Range Building met the structure that housed their apartment. He was thinking about all the things he would tell Beth when the roof above him creaked. He was on the top level, and unlike most of the other buildings in the compound, the flat roof of the Southwest Range Building did not double as a walkway or terrace. He leaned over the railing and looked up, listening. Another creak, quieter. Probably some settling, or the wind giving the building a nudge.

He heard footsteps and realized they were coming from the stairs at the far end. Someone in a rush. He stepped into a strip of darker shadow from one of the portico's columns and pressed himself against the wall. He dropped the phone into his pocket and put his hand on the hilt of his collapsible baton.

A figure appeared, hurrying along the walkway. It stopped. "Jagger?"

Father Antoine.

Jagger stepped out from the shadow. "What is it?"

"Ollie—he's insisting on speaking with you."

Jagger started toward him. "Is he all right?"

"He's not looking good. He's lost a lot of blood. The medevac should be here any minute."

Jagger hurried past the monk and started down the stairs. "What's he saying?"

"Besides that there are angels all around him?" Antoine said. "Just that he needs to talk to you before they take him away."

"The *angels*?"

"I think he's referring to the medevac."

Jagger hoped so.

When he entered Ollie's bedroom, Ramón was hunched over him, one knee on the bed. He was taping gauze onto Ollie's chest, where the arrow protruded. Jagger held back, waiting for the man to finish.

In his midtwenties, Ramón had received combat medicine training as a *sabo segundo*—the equivalent of a private first class—in the Paraguayan army. He'd been at the monastery only a little longer than Jagger, making him Brother Ramón instead of Father Ramón.

It was unclear to Jagger at what point *brothers* became *fathers*. Leo was only a few years older than Ramón, but he was a *father*, and Brother Daniel was older than Leo. But then, Jagger didn't get the titles and positions of the monastery. He'd called Gheronda *Father Gheronda* for months before Beth pointed out that Gheronda was an honorary title or name, so it was just "Gheronda." The old man was the monastery's abbot as well as archbishop of the Orthodox Church of Mount Sinai. To make matters more confusing, the monks called each other brother, regardless of brother or father status. It gave Jagger a headache.

Beth said it was because he didn't care, which was true: titles didn't mean anything to him. When he was in the army, he'd seen corporals with more leadership ability and battlefield savvy than some of the majors and colonels, and he knew teenagers with more compassion and people skills than the pastors he knew. Forget titles: what kind of *person* are you?

Father Jeffrey was still at the head of the bed, still patting Ollie's forehead with a cloth. And Gheronda had made it back, kneeling again at the foot of the bed, praying. Just then, the old monk turned his head to look at Jagger. He mouthed Owen's name, and Jagger nodded.

Ramón leaned back and sat on the edge of the bed. "How you feeling, Dr. Hoffmann?" Ollie's eyes were closed and he didn't answer. "Hey!" Ramón said. "Stay with us, now!"

Ollie rolled his head, opened his eyes. "I'm here." Slurring a little. He looked around. "So's everyone. Hey, guys."

Jagger had the feeling he wasn't addressing the monks or anyone else visible to the average person.

Leo whispered in Jagger's ear: "Ramón shot him up with painkillers."

"'Zat Jag?" Ollie said. "I want to talk to Jagger. Everyone else out!"

No one moved.

"Come on," Ollie said. "I'm not going to die . . . this minute. Out!"

Ramón stood and walked past Jagger. He said, "Keep him talking."

"I don't think that's going to be a problem."

Jeffrey handed Jagger the cloth as he walked out. Gheronda patted him on the shoulder, went into the living room, and closed the door.

"Jag," Ollie said, holding out his hand. Jagger moved in, gripped his hand, and sat on the edge of the bed. "He took it. I tried . . ." He wheezed in a breath. "I tried to stop him."

Jagger noticed flecks of blood on Ollie's lips and dabbed at them with the cloth.

"I tried to stop him," Ollie said again. He looked beyond Jagger. "Sorry, guys."

Jagger looked at the open safe, the papers and gun strewn in front of it. He said, "What'd he take, Ollie?" He wasn't about to correct him on the gender of his attacker.

Ollie's eyes found Jagger's, and for a moment the fog seemed to clear. He said, "The Judgment Stone."

[22]

"The Judgment Stone?" Jagger recalled the thing in Steampunk's hand. "That's what he took? What is it?"

Ollie tried to laugh. It was airy, weak. More blood peppered on his lips. He said, "Something only briefly mentioned in a few ancient texts, hearsay some monk or scholar inserted in passing. A stone that revealed the nature of your heart by showing what surrounds you, angels or demons . . . that unveiled the connection each person has with God."

"The blue lights?"

Ollie grinned. "Some people guessed it was one of the twelve stones Joshua used to commemorate the Israelites' crossing the Jordan into the Promised Land. Others said it was the stone David used to slay Goliath, or even the stone that blocked the entrance to Jesus' tomb." Ollie tried to laugh again, but it came out as a cough. "They were wrong."

"So what is it?" Jagger asked. "What did they take?"

"A piece of the first tablets . . . the first Ten Commandments."

Jagger stopped breathing. The actual tablets, the first ones God made and Moses destroyed upon finding the Israelites worshiping a golden calf. A piece of them had been Ollie's quest, an impossible dream; he had called it his holy grail.

"I thought . . . ," Jagger started, searching for the words that would express his incredulity. "I thought the pieces were put in the ark of the covenant, along with the second set of tablets."

"No, no." Ollie coughed, depositing more flecks of blood, this time on his chin as well. Jagger blotted them up. "Some people think that." He panted, three quick breaths. "They just assume that's what happened to them, or they . . . misinterpret some passages. But 1 Kings says, 'There was nothing in the ark except the two stone tablets that Moses had placed in it at Horeb.' That's what I held on to, that's what I always believed." Cough, then a whisper: "I was right. I was right."

"When did you find it, Ollie? You didn't tell me."

"This morning. I uncovered the piece of stone and started working to uncover the rest." He paused to breathe and remember, his gaze turning toward the ceiling. "It looked like granite, but then it . . . it shimmered. I took off my glove to rub it. And that's when it happened. At first I thought the crew had jumped into the pit with me, all these people. Then I thought, 'These aren't people, they're on fire, they have wings'—ha, wings—'their skin, it's glowing.' The angels had come to watch me discover it." He breathed, smiled. "I was so shocked . . . and scared . . . the most incredible discovery of mankind. I wrapped it up and brought it back here, to my apartment." He shook his head. "I know, I know, it's against all the rules of archaeology. But this was no ordinary discovery. This was more about . . . about *God* than history or archaeology." He flashed his grin again, blood on his teeth. "So sue me."

Jagger pressed the back of his fingers to the man's cheek. The fever seemed to be subsiding.

"Jagger, the angels, they're *magnificent*."

"I know, Ollie."

The archaeologist's eyes grew wide, and Jagger nodded.

"I've seen them too."

"Oh! Oh! Then you know!" He grabbed Jagger's arm, lifted himself a few inches off the bed. Jagger tried to ease him back down. "But how?" Ollie said. "How?"

Jagger explained about Steampunk, his getting the Stone and losing it again. "I thought I'd just hit my head too hard or Steampunk had gassed me with a hallucinogen. It wasn't until the basilica that I started thinking angels and . . ." He turned his head, looked at Ollie from the corner of his eyes. "Ollie, are angels all you see?"

"No . . . no." Shaking his head, terror crossing over his face.

"There are . . . others . . . demons. That's what you're saying, isn't it? You saw them too."

"A lot of them."

"When I was digging it up," he said, "the Stone . . . I thought I saw them, things . . . glaring at me from the edge of the hole. As I carried it here, under my jacket . . . they were all around me, but the angels stood in their way. I could barely see the demons through the sparks around the angels." His eyes darted around the room, stopping for a second at specific points. "Thank you," he whispered. "Thank you."

That got Jagger thinking, and he said, "Where were the angels when you were attacked, when Steampunk shot you?"

"They got overpowered, demons everywhere, all over them. One of the angels knocked away the first arrow that guy fired at me." He pointed, and Jagger saw it: in the wall a foot out from the safe and four inches above the floor, a divot of plaster had been chipped out. Pieces of plaster lay on the floor under it.

"I'd had the Stone with me. When I heard the gunfire, I went to put the Stone in the safe. That's when he came in. I pulled out my pistol—I keep it in the safe—and got a few shots off, but he moved like a cat." Ollie's eyes seemed to vibrate as he remembered the scene. "And you know what? A demon helped him. I saw it. The guy jumped out of my aim, and the demon—a big ugly thing—was shoving him."

Jagger wondered if the demon's shove physically helped Steampunk move, or if it acted like intuition, telling her to move a second before she otherwise would have. He knew they had the power to affect the physical world: he'd seen them deflect Antoine's bullet, and angels had deflected the arrow aimed at him, broken the crossbow string, helped Antoine aim when Steampunk had her sword poised over him. But the thought of demons with that sort of physical control over humans frightened him as much as anything else had in the past two hours.

He looked at the arrow beside the safe, and his gaze fell on something on the floor. The excavation's satphone. He said, "Who did you tell, Ollie? Who did you call about the rock?"

"The Judgment Stone," he corrected, as though it was suddenly important to use the name he or someone in history had termed it.

Ollie was looking around the room again. *"Glorious."*

"Ollie, who did you tell? The people who took it, they knew you'd found it."

Ollie stared at him, his lips slack. "I told Bronson Radcliff. Only Bronson, not even any of his people."

"From the Ice Temple Foundation?" Bronson was the director of the foundation funding the Mount Sinai excavation. It was the nonprofit arm of Ice Temple Enterprises, the conglomerate of media companies and retail stores that had made Bronson a billionaire.

Ollie continued: "He said if I found anything extraordinary— that's the word he used, *extraordinary*—I should contact him and only him immediately." He coughed, causing the arrow to shake wildly. "I couldn't *not* tell him. What if something happened to it? What if word got out and . . ."

"And someone stole it," Jagger finished, letting the irony hang on his sentence.

"Besides," Ollie said, "I promised."

Jagger knew Ollie enough to know his word wasn't something he gave lightly; unless he were dead, he'd keep it. Even a find as incredible as the Judgment Stone couldn't keep him from fulfilling his promise. Considering what the fragment was, what it represented, perhaps it was even more important than ever that he kept his word about it.

"What'd he say," Jagger asked, "when you told him about it?"

"He said . . . he said . . ." Ollie squeezed his eyes shut, gritted his teeth in pain.

Ramón hadn't given him enough painkillers, or the excitement of talking about the Stone had burned it off, adrenaline counteracting it.

Groaning, Ollie said, "He said he'd send a team to fetch it, that it was safer at their headquarters. I was going to go with it." He raised his hand and moved it around slowly in the air. "Those sparkles . . . so beautiful."

"Ollie," Jagger said, "after I let go of the Stone, I could still see the . . . the spiritual world for a while."

"Like something hot, yes. When you step away from a heater on a cold day, you don't get cold right away. The warmth fades."

"But the vision *did* fade. I lost it after about ten minutes."

"I put the Stone under my pillow. When its power wore off, I'd touch it again. I couldn't help it."

Jagger remembered the aching sense of longing he felt as he watched the angels in the basilica fade and disappear.

"Are you seeing them now, the angels?"

"Oh, yes."

"How? It's been at least an hour since Steampunk stole the Stone."

Ollie's expression grew serious. "That's what I wanted to talk to you about." He looked at his fist, still resting over his stomach. He turned it over and opened his fingers. In his palm lay a fragment of stone. It was about an inch wide and two inches long, thin as a piece of cardboard.

"I didn't do it," Ollie said. "It broke off while I was handling the Stone, just touching it."

Jagger couldn't stop staring at it. Gray, with specks of white and black. It did look like granite.

"It's not as strong. The angels are more . . ." Searching for a word. "See-through. Like after they start to fade, before they're gone. But they're still . . ." Looking around the room. "So beautiful." He lifted his hand, bringing the piece of stone closer. "Take it."

Jagger threw him a puzzled look.

"I don't know if I'm going to pull through . . ."

"You will."

"I don't know; you don't know. I need to give this to someone I trust, someone who will take care of it. I trust you, Jag. Do with it what you think is best. Pray about it."

"Ollie—"

Feet pounded outside the bedroom door, then it opened. Ramón rushed in, followed by two EMTs in flight suits. One carried a big case with a red cross on it, the other a wood stretcher. "They're here," Ramón said. "It's time to go."

"Jagger!" Ollie said, pushing the edge of his open hand into Jagger's ribs. "Take it!"

Jagger dropped the cloth he'd used to dab Ollie's face over the Stone and scooped it up, pinching it between the folds.

Ramón pulled on the back of Jagger's shirt to get him out of the way. "Come on, they're here."

Jagger rose, pushed the cloth into his pocket, and stepped to the foot of the bed.

The EMTs gave Ollie the once-over, Ramón saying, "I told you he's ready to go. Go!" They slipped the stretcher under him, strapped him down, and started carrying him through the door.

Ollie groaned.

"You'll be all right, Ollie," Jagger said, needing to say something. "You'll see."

Ollie said, "Hurts like a son of a—"

And he was out the door.

[23]

Jagger stopped outside the apartment door before entering, hand on the knob. Tonight had conjured monsters. For his fallen brothers, it was the cloaked skeleton of Death, shrieking with hunger as its foul breath blew over them. For Ollie, it was a beast of Pain, possibly leading Death to him, possibly not, but tearing and shredding either way. And for his family, it was a hideous creature with the prickly quills of Fear, the claws of Grief, the snapping teeth of Worry. He felt as though it was in with them now, snapping and digging, rooting into their spirits. He wanted more than anything to be the White Knight, the hero who'd magically appear, slay the creature, and make everything better. But he wasn't. He was as vulnerable as they were, probably more so, already injured with doubt and frustration.

The knob turned under his hand and the door opened. Beth stood there, eyes red, lines in her brow and around her mouth showing her concern. She threw her arms around him and whispered, "How's Ollie?"

"It doesn't look good," he said.

She squeezed him tight, pushed her face into his chest. She gripped his shirt and looked up at him. "I feel so bad . . ."

He nodded. "Ollie's a good man, and the monks—"

She nodded, but said, "That's not what I mean." Her face was pained, and what he saw there wasn't only grief and worry. It was guilt. "Those monks . . . ," she said. "They shouldn't have died like that. Ollie, that man's been so kind to us. Such a gentle soul. Tyler loves him." She lowered her eyes and appeared to be speaking to his chin. "I hurt for them, but I'm more grateful that you're all right. I can't get it out of my head that you could be dead too, and that you're not . . ." She shook her head. "I want to praise God." She showed him a sad smile. "I want to dance and sing. I'm . . . *elated*." She pressed her face into his chest again and began to cry, not the sobbing or weeping of sorrow, not now; hers were tears of relief and thankfulness.

"That's normal, Beth," he said, rubbing her back. "If the whole world were wiped out tomorrow, but somehow you and Tyler and I survived, the only ones, my joy would wash away my sadness. That's . . ." How to say what he was feeling? "That's the way love works. That's the way it's supposed to be."

And he realized something: it worked both ways. If every living being suddenly became happy and healthy and death-free, but the price of that was Beth's and Tyler's lives, his grief would be boundless. It would be deep and dark, a black hole that threatened to suck everything in and end it all.

She took him by the hand and led him into the living room. They sat on the couch and she shifted to face him, one leg tucked under her. She held his hand in both of hers. "Will you pray with me?"

"Of course."

She lowered her head and asked God to take the monks into His arms, to ease the grief of the other monks, to make Ollie all right and bless the hands of the surgeons working on him. She thanked God for Jagger's safety and for protecting everyone else in the compound who'd survived that night's attack. When she was finished, she squeezed his hand and waited.

Jagger was still uncomfortable praying, though he did it in private sometimes. His anger at God for letting the crash happen had diminished, while a new sort of fury had swelled up inside him, a fury at God for making him what he was, destined to outlive his family, to witness their deaths. Threaded through his anger was shame . . . for having committed the atrocities that condemned him to immortality and for being part of the Tribe for as long as he had been, perpetrating the very sins he hated them for. He couldn't blame God for turning His back. Between the anger and shame, praying seemed . . . what? Pathetic? Hypocritical? Insincere? All of the above.

His only hope was that God would change His mind about him, Jagger. Praying was his way of reminding God he was here, an outcast tapping on the window.

"Lord, thank You for sending Your angels to save me," he said. "Please show me what You want me to do with the piece of stone Ollie gave me. In Jesus' name we pray. Amen."

Beth looked at him, wiping her cheeks. "What? What piece of stone?"

"Well . . . ," he said, and went on to describe the events of the evening.

"You saw angels?"

"And demons."

"What did they look like?" She waved her hand at him. "The angels. I don't care about the demons."

"If you saw them, you would."

She ignored that and said, "Did they have wings?"

"You believe me?"

"Yeah!" Said it with two syllables, as in *of course*.

"I'm not sure *I* believe it yet."

She slapped his shoulder. "Jagger Baird! You of all people. What don't you believe?"

He shifted, pushing himself farther into the back cushion, and took a deep breath. "Well, for starters . . . all of it."

"Was something, a *being*, standing over you?"

"That's what I *think* I saw."

"And you saw them in the chapel?"

"Yeah."

"And Ollie saw them too?"

"That's what he said."

"What don't you believe?" she asked again.

"I don't know," he said. "I mean, angels? Demons? Fighting each other, helping people?"

"But you believed in angels, right? Before tonight?"

"Yeah, but—"

"Where did you *think* they were? What did you *think* they were doing?"

"I guess I never really thought about it."

"But you didn't think they were *visible* before. They're invisible because they're spiritual, right? Or did you think they're always visible to us, and the reason no one sees them is because they don't come around? Because they spend all their time in heaven?"

"Uh . . . no. I've always thought they were active in people's lives."

"Okay," she said, feeling like she was getting somewhere; he'd heard the tone before. "So it's not the angels you find unbelievable. Is it the demons?"

"No, I believe in them." *More now than ever*, he thought.

"So." She should have been a lawyer. "It's not the angels or demons you can't believe. It's that you *saw* them."

He thought about it. "Yeah, that I saw them."

"But it didn't just happen. You touched that stone, the one Ollie thinks is a piece of the first tablets on which God wrote the Ten Commandments, the ones Moses broke." She stretched to reach the Bible on the coffee table and flipped through it, searching. "Listen to this. 'Now Moabite raiders used to enter the country every spring. Once while some Israelites were burying a man, suddenly they saw a band of raiders; so they threw the man's body into Elisha's tomb. When the body touched Elisha's bones, the man came to life and stood up on his feet.'"

She smiled at him, and at that moment he would have accepted anything she said: Jesus left a message for you in the sesame seeds on a hamburger bun? Yeah! Wow!

"It's right here," she said, poking the Bible passage with her finger. "God can put incredible power in *things*, make miracles happen through *things*. If He did it with bones, why not a stone, especially *that* stone?"

"Yeah. Wow."

"I'm being serious."

"I know. So am I. It's just . . ."

"What? It happened in the Bible, but it can never happen to you?"

He shrugged. "And what did you mean, 'you of all people'?"

"You're immortal, sweetheart. You've come to accept that, right?"

"I don't *like* it."

"I mean, you know you are. You've seen the evidence: pictures, the things Owen told you, the way you healed when Owen shot you." Which Owen had done to prove the very point Beth was making.

"Yes, I believe that some people in this world are immortal. I happen to be one of them."

"So God can and does do things that science can't explain?"

He nodded.

"Jagger, how did you become immortal?"

He frowned.

"Not why," she said softly, rubbing his hand. "And we know it was God, but what was the instrument He used to change you into an Immortal? The first tablets Moses brought down the mountain! Jagger! The stone you're talking about now, the Judgment Stone. You *know* it had power once. You experienced it. Why can't God's power still be in it? I don't know why He does things like that, but He does. I don't know why it lets us see the spiritual world, but I believe it." She squeezed his hand. "Don't you?"

He didn't say anything for a few moments, then: "I guess I do."

She lifted herself up to kiss him, pausing before their lips touched so they could taste each other's breath, their essence. Then she planted her lips on his.

When they parted, she said, "Now, tell me all about it. I want to know everything. What did the angels look like? Did they have wings? Were they male or female? Or neither? Did they speak? Did you feel different while you were having the vision? Was it wonderful?"

He smiled at her excitement. He leaned to one side so he could reach into his pocket and pull out the cloth he'd put there in Ollie's room. He said, "I can do you one better."

[24]

"What is it?" Beth asked, looking at the piece of stone lying on the cloth. "That's not the Judgment Stone, is it? You said that woman dressed all Steampunky took it."

"She did," Jagger said. "It's a piece that broke off. Ollie gave it to me."

"It's a piece of a piece of the first tablets."

"Call it a fragment. Go ahead, touch it."

"Should I pick it up?"

"Just touch it," he said. "I think it'll be enough, and I'm still kind of unsure about it."

"What do you mean?"

"As you said, it has power. What if there are side effects?"

"Like what? You don't think it'll make me immortal, do you?"

That made his stomach clench up. He hadn't thought of that, but this *was* a fragment of the rock God used to make *him* immortal. As much as he'd cherish having her with him forever, he'd rather die right on the spot than curse her the way he was cursed. He folded the cloth over the fragment and pulled his hand back.

"No, wait," she said. "I was kidding. God was punishing the Tribe when He made them immortal. I don't think He'd punish everyone who just *touches* the Stone. He doesn't work that way. Or at least He would have warned us. Moses would have said don't touch that, and it'd be in the Bible." She gripped her hands together and raised them to her chin. "Please?"

"I still don't know about possible side effects. Maybe we'll get headaches or go blind."

"Go blind?" She gave him an exasperated look. *"Really?"*

"Who knows?"

"You're okay."

"For now."

"Come on."

He uncovered the fragment again.

She scanned the room. "You think they're in here?"

Considering Beth's faith—if not his own—and that David says in Psalms that angels encamp around believers, he said, "I hope so."

"I'm scared."

He shrugged. "Don't do it."

Her hand shot out, and she laid the tip of her index finger on the Stone. She screamed, at once grabbing Jagger and trying to push herself back through the couch, sliding up onto the back cushion. Half-dollar eyes, trembling lips—she was terrified.

"J-J-Jag! Jagger!"

"Beth, it's okay." But he wasn't sure it was, not with her response. He brought his other hand around to touch the Stone and remembered he didn't have another hand. He dumped the fragment onto his thigh, tossed away the cloth, slapped his palm over the Stone.

White light burst in his eyes, and then he saw: a demon with lion-like features was coming through the front wall of their apartment. Not the powerful-but-somehow-attractive Aslanian lion, but a Chinese shishi: flaring nostrils, oversized mouth and teeth, exaggerated brow furled in fury. Instead of fur, it was covered in scaly, reptilian skin, hued in reds and yellows. Its mane was a congregation of writhing, snapping snakes. For a nanosecond Jagger feared that it wielded Medusa's power of turning anyone who laid eyes on it into stone; but the boulder that had formed in his gut notwithstanding, he and Beth hadn't become statues. The thing was twice the size of any lion he'd ever seen. It apparently walked on all fours, though at the moment its front paws were off the floor and it was swinging kitchen-knife-sized claws at an angel.

Just as the earlier angels had done, this one glowed with an impossibly bright body that rippled and undulated, giving the impression of flowing robes. Its embers swirled around it, primarily in front, instantly coming together to form a shield against the demon's slashing claws, then breaking apart and snapping out like a whip at the beast, which flinched away, ducked its head, twisted to come in low at the angel. The angel swung a sword through its own embers, which parted for its passing. The blade sliced a gash in the beast's scaly hide. Ashes billowed out, floated away.

Only the front half of the demonic creature was inside their apartment. The rest went through the wall and must have been standing on the walkway outside. Moving fluidly, it didn't seemed burdened or hindered by the physical structure of the building. Jagger realized that no movie magic could mimic the sight: there was no line or blur, no demarcation on any kind between the wall and the beast; it was simply there, occupying the same space as the wall.

The angel was as tall as the ceiling, and when he—for it seemed male to Jagger, perhaps because of its muscular build or its fierceness in battle—jumped away from the sweeping sets of claws, his head disappeared into the whitewashed, plaster-covered ceiling. Only boards lay beyond, then the sky, and he wondered if the angel's head could be seen from the outside, bobbing out of the roof, to anyone with the Stone-induced vision to see.

The beast snarled and growled and snapped, spewing flakes of ash. More ash swirled in from the wall, whipped around, pulled back into the wall. It lunged, and the angel kicked its snout.

Jagger crossed his arm over Beth's chest, protecting her. He said, "Beth, it's okay. They were there before we could see them." Movement caught his eyes, and he noticed another angel standing in front of Tyler's bedroom door. He was doing nothing to help his comrade, but watched intently, seeming ready to join the fray. His embers sailed around him, seeming agitated to Jagger. They came together like a force field in front of him, then came apart to form two big spike-like weapons aimed at the beast. They broke apart again, flew behind him—looking wing-like for a few seconds, before flattening out into a vertical pane over Tyler's door.

Jagger realized the angel was specifically protecting Tyler. He didn't know how he knew. He might have come to the conclusion

THE JUDGMENT STONE | 109

simply by the angel's position and posture, but he knew it with a certainty that went beyond that; he *sensed* it.

"Beth, it's all right," he said.

Another flash of brilliant light appeared, this one sapphire and appearing as a beam coming out of Beth's head going straight up into the ceiling. He saw that Beth had lowered her head, clamped her eyes shut, and was praying silently, her lips moving fast. This close, he saw that the blue light was veined like marble with sparkling gold cracks. Gold light came from the cracks, instantly intense and blinding. Embers spiraled out of the ceiling, spiraling down the beam and washing over Beth. They flowed off of her and formed an angel.

All of this—from the appearance of the beam to the manifestation of the angel—happened in maybe a second, no more than two.

This new angel's millions of glowing orange embers formed wings, a shield, a weapon, one after the other in the span of the blink of an eye. They became a sword and stayed that way, looking to Jagger as though it was forged from molten lava. Holding it in an upraised fist, the angel charged forward.

The new angel joined the first, swinging at the beast, snapping at it with the instant confluence of their embers. The demon lurched toward one, then the other, its huge jaws opening and shutting like a shark at seals. It pulled back away from the angels, less of its body coming through the wall now.

The angels and demon were fading—Jagger realized they had been for ten, fifteen seconds. They drove the beast back until it completely disappeared beyond the wall. The two spiritual beings continued slashing with their swords, moving forward. And before they walked through the wall in pursuit of the retreating beast, they faded away.

Jagger blinked. Nothing there but a wall. The framed photograph of Beth's parents that she had hung there when they first arrived. Closer, the window, its curtains hanging on either side, undisturbed. Not even the slightest ripple. He looked at Tyler's door. Nothing there either. Looking at the spot where Tyler's protective angel had stood, he whispered, "Thank you." Then: "Beth, you can open your eyes."

Lips moving, she shook her head.

"The vision's gone. It wore off." He hoped it had for her as well.

She opened one eye, then the other. She stared at the wall, the front door, around the room. She clutched Jagger's shoulder. "Jagger—"

"Honey, I'm so sorry . . ." Searching for something to say. "Did you at least see the angel?"

"For about two seconds. I couldn't take my eyes off that . . . *thing.* Why, Jag? Why was it here, trying to get in?"

"I think that's what they do." He remembered something from Scripture, one of Peter's letters, he thought: *Your enemy the devil prowls around like a roaring lion looking for someone to devour.*

"Are they all like . . . *that*?"

"They're all different, as far as I've seen. All of them hideous, but that . . ." He shook his head. "It was like a Chinese lion, but a lot worse. The fangs and claws, reptile scales . . . did you see that brow? Looked like the edge of a cliff . . . What?"

She was scowling at him, puzzled. "Where were the scales?"

"All over," he said. "Instead of fur. Over its face and legs . . ."

"The thing I saw was lion-like, definitely, but it was skeletal. It didn't have fur *or* scales or a covering of any kind. It was like a big lion's skeleton, but . . . burnt. And there was no brow. A ridge over the eyes, which were set in big, gaping holes. Black . . . I don't know, sludge, kept pouring out of its nostrils, or holes in its skeleton-face, and its mouth. It was all over the floor. Things like maggots with faces were squirming around in it." She closed her eyes, lowered her forehead to his bicep. "It was the worst thing I've ever seen."

The two of them had seen a similar demon. No, it was the same demon, but what each had seen was *different*. The one Beth had witnessed was obviously more grotesque. The difference went beyond opinion, the way one person might call a mountain range majestic and beautiful while another called it forlorn and ugly. This went to matters of fact, as if one person said a mountain range had three peaks, while the other said it had six.

Jagger didn't know what to say . . . or think.

[25]

It was just after midnight local time when Nevaeh landed the Tribe's corporate jet at Palermo's Falcone-Borsellino Airport. Named after two judges who were murdered by the Mafia, it seemed to her a subtle way of reminding people of the city's most famous export: organized crime. She taxied into their private hangar and drove out in the white panel van Sebastian had secured for shuttling them around the city. She cranked up her favorite "going on a mission" playlist—fast-paced orchestral music, the kind used in action movie trailers and video games to get the blood pumping—and got on the A29.

She drove automatically, thinking of getting to St. Catherine's, grabbing Jagger's wife, hoping it wasn't already too late. Who were the people attacking the place? Were they after Beth? Even if they weren't, their assault could easily foil Nevaeh's plans: it could be the impetus that drove Jagger to hustle his family away, or implement tighter security that would make kidnapping her next to impossible. Or worse, she could be killed. Then how would Nevaeh know what Beth had told Ben that ended his punishment, that finally earned him God's forgiveness? It couldn't be that the situation was as the others suggested, that Beth's presence at the time Ben went home was merely a coincidence. God didn't do coincidences. God must have put in the woman the gift of drawing souls to Him; it was an elixir Nevaeh wanted, *needed* to taste.

Twenty minutes later she exited onto Via Calatafimi. She could see the pyramidal, majolica-tiled roof of la Porta Nuova, which in the sixteenth century marked the city's entrance, before turning and driving under its tunnel-like arch. She wound through still-bustling streets and into the quieter Kalsa quarter, then took Via Pindemonte to the Piazza Cappuccini, where she parked.

The square's dominant structure, painted the color of a fall leaf, looked more like a dilapidated apartment building than what it was: a monastery for the Capuchin monks. A sign over one door read *Ingresso Catacombe.* That was the tourists' entrance to the macabre crypts beneath the monastery. Instead, Nevaeh slipped through the gates behind the building into a cemetery, disused for centuries. She entered a mausoleum, pushed aside a stone sarcophagus, and descended a long flight of narrow steps hiding beneath it.

She used the flashlight on her phone to navigate several long, sloping tunnels, barely wide enough to accommodate a human, and turned into a gloomy corridor. Bare bulbs, newly tacked to the ceiling, did little to dispel the ancient darkness. Forty yards away, in the brighter light coming through their bedroom door, Jordan and Alexa appeared to be trying to lift something. She realized they were stuffing a corpse into a recess carved into the wall.

"Don't mess with that," she called.

They snapped guilty faces toward her.

"Jordan pulled it out!" Alexa said, her six-year-old voice sounding like a cartoon character's.

"It was an accident!"

"I'm sure," Nevaeh said.

Jordan was forever stuck in that curious-playful-mischievous stage of an eleven-year-old boy. Most times Nevaeh found this refreshing and sweet.

Alexa dropped the skeletal feet, causing Jordan to loose his grip on the upper half. The body fell, and the head—nothing more than a leathery skin-covered skull—snapped off and rolled down the hall. Jordan pushed Alexa and called her stupid.

Sometimes it wasn't so sweet.

Nevaeh proceeded toward them, her rubber-soled boots crunching bits of rock and plaster into the marble tile of their new home. They had already tapped into the electricity of the buildings above and rigged the necessary cables, transponders, and routers for Sebastian's computers, but they were still sweeping and scrubbing away four centuries of disuse. She said to Jordan, "Why are you still in your pajamas? We have to go."

"Where?" Jordan said.

"Elias didn't tell you? I called him from—"

Ahead of her, Elias stepped into the doorway of his room and leaned against the jamb. A three-inch cylinder of ash clung to the ever-present cigarette dangling from the corner of his mouth. He bore no trace of the bullet that had put him out of commission in Paris. It had entered his head right above his left eyebrow, but in the course of three weeks the wound had scabbed over, scarred, become a small pock, and then vanished completely. Now that area wrinkled as he squinted at her.

"Elias," she said, "why isn't he ready?"

"What's the rush?" he said, his pleasant voice at odds with his appearance—long, scraggly hair, mustache and goatee, three-day growth on his cheeks, all of it forever gray, with hints of the brown all of it was eons ago. The ash dropped off, and he caught it expertly in the palm of his hand, which he then rubbed on his jeans-clad thigh.

She stopped in her tracks, spread her palms. "Someone attacked St. Catherine's."

"So?"

"You *know* I need the woman. I'd think you'd be as interested in getting hold of her as I am."

He watched her with impassive eyes. His mellowness about drove her nuts.

"Think about it," he said. He plucked the stub of his cigarette out of his mouth, seemed to talk to it. "If she was their target, she's already gone. If not, shouldn't we go in at night? We'll get there too early if we leave now."

"We can go in anytime," she said, and he looked at her, one eyebrow raised.

Nighttime *would* be better, fewer witnesses, scant or no security—except Jagger—the element of surprise, the cover of darkness. But she was more anxious than ever to grab Beth. The attack had made Nevaeh realize that anything could happen before she had a chance. She said, "Toby said he used the boots to go straight up the back wall, so we can get in without a lot of eyes on us." She tilted her head and conceded, "Better after closing, when the monks are less watchful."

"And after the bulk of the tourists have come off the mountain," he said. The rear of the monastery was in plain view of the two trails leading from the peak.

She nodded. "Okay, anytime after two or three, then."

"We'll leave in the morning." He nodded toward Jordan. "Give the boy a chance to catch some shut-eye. You too."

"Can I go too?" Alexa said, hopeful.

"Not this time, honey. It's going to be real quick, there and gone."

Alexa made an exaggerated frown, big pouty lips. She said, "It's always that way."

"Maybe next time. Now get to bed, both of you."

"But—" Jordan said, pointing at the corpse at his feet.

"Leave it."

Heads lowered, they skulked into their room and shut the door, plunging the corridor back into twilight. Immediately their laughs and giggles reached her, and Nevaeh couldn't help but smile. Elias clicked his lighter and dipped his head, touching a fresh cigarette to the flame.

"Sebastian back?" she asked.

He squinted against the smoke and nodded. "Got himself a hammerhead. Went to bed a couple hours ago. Phin's out."

"Where?"

"He heard about some dude round Ballarò mugging tourists. Went to talk to him."

"Talk or kill?"

Elias shrugged.

"In Palermo." Killing in their home city was against their rules.

But who was she to complain? She had been guilty of it as well. It was probably how Jagger and Owen had tracked them to Paris six months ago. And the urge was stronger now than ever. She, Phin, Sebastian, and Toby and been severely injured in the plane crash Owen had orchestrated to stop them. Concussions, broken bones, ripped flesh. It had taken them a long time to recover, and now that they were well, everyone was itching to catch up on their kill quota. She hoped it didn't make them sloppy, and she wondered how Ben would have handled it. He'd always been the restrained, rational one. She was more devil-may-care. She supposed she'd have to adjust to make up for his absence, but how did you change your personality after millennia?

You didn't. You simply made do, and that's what she was doing. It might mean not having Ben counterbalancing her impulsiveness, that the Tribe's collective behavior would shift to be more like hers, but what was so wrong with that? Maybe he'd been holding them back all this time, not allowing them to achieve forgiveness as quickly as they would have without him. Guess they'd find out.

Elias blew out a stream of smoke and smiled at her, making her suspect he knew her thoughts. He had that way about him. It reminded her of something Mark Twain had said: it is better to keep your mouth closed and let people think you are a fool than to open it and remove all doubt. She returned the smile, expecting him to say something. But he stepped back into his room and shut the door.

[26]

Nevaeh went to the kids' door and opened it, holding the handle and letting her body swing in with it. Having left all but their most meaningful toys in Paris, they were rebuilding their supply here. Empty toy boxes were scattered among the actual products, and at the moment Jordan seemed to be checking Alexa's ability to be stuffed into one. The little girl's laughter signaled her consent, so all Nevaeh said was, "I'll be back in ten minutes to tuck you in. Brush your teeth."

Jordan nodded, and Nevaeh shut the door. She continued toward the end of the corridor, considering the bedrooms as she passed each door. Toby's. Phin's. Hers. She'd worked herself up so much about going after Beth, there was no way she could sleep. She'd try to catch a few winks later.

She stopped in front of Sebastian's door. He'd stay here tomorrow, using his computer and connections to line up the Tribe's needs: a helicopter and a discreet pilot for the trip from Sharm El Sheikh to the monastery and back; jet refueling; any interference necessary with Egyptian police or aviation authorities; medical care, if it came to that. Through decades of acting as a one-man operational support team, he'd become as essential as the boots on the ground. More times than she could remember, he'd anticipated their needs before they did, saving a mission or preventing their capture.

With Alexa and Sebastian here, that left her, Elias, Phin, Toby, and Jordan in the hot zone. More than enough under normal circumstances. But this wasn't normal. They would be breaching a fortified position with armed defenders—on high alert because of tonight's assault—to kidnap the wife of one of the few men in the world who stood a chance against them. Not only was Jagger—that stupid new name of his—one of them, an Immortal, but he possessed an almost supernaturally fierce determination to protect his family at all costs. Nevaeh had learned that the hard way.

She continued walking, reached the end of the corridor, turned left, and found herself facing the reason she had chosen this place: corpses, hundreds of them in this hall alone. On the floor along each wall, the bodies lay reposed in glass-topped coffins. Upon many of them was another body, using the coffin lid as an eternal bed. Above them, the mummified remains had been mounted vertically, like rows of floating soldiers. Some wore what was once their finest clothes, suits and dresses; others came to rest wearing their workaday outfits, pants and shirts, skirts and blouses, habits and vestments. All the clothes, like their wearers, showed varying signs of decay, from near disintegration to off-the-rack perfection—not many of those.

In the Paris catacombs she'd had miles of skulls and long bones to feed her fascination with—her craving for—death. Here she had whole bodies, most of them still in possession of their hair and skin—dry, leathery stuff clinging in patches to bone; the Capuchin monks were famous for the effectiveness of their embalming and mummification techniques. The catacombs—or *necropolis*, as the Sicilians preferred— were a major tourist attraction. Fortunately for the Tribe, only the top level, in the basement of the Capuchin monastery, was open to the public. As far as Nevaeh could tell, no one, not even the monks, knew about the lower depths. In fact, many puzzled over the discrepancy between the eight thousand recorded interments and the considerably fewer bodies on display. The Tribe now resided in that discrepancy.

She paused in front of a body lying prone on a coffin. Her fingers ran over what was left of the flesh on its cheeks, traced the oval of its gaping mouth. Nevaeh slipped her fingernail under a patch of paperthin skin on the mummy's forehead and peeled off a piece. Rubbing it between finger and thumb, she continued along the hallway.

She stopped again to look at a corpse mounted vertically on the wall. It was dressed in the tattered remains of a monk's habit and hood. He had been from the Capuchin order, designated by the habit's brown coloring, from which *cappuccino* gets its name. His nose was gone, but not his eyes: they looked like dehydrated olives glaring out from slits in skin that seemed to have melted over the sockets. His mouth was a black Edvard Munch scream. It was funny how so many of the corpses down here had frozen expressions of surprise, as if eternally shocked to find themselves dead—or hanging on walls for the amusement of those still living.

Farther on, she stopped to stare at another body on the wall, the only one she had put here herself. Despite a dazed expression—the unfocused eyes, the slack jaw—he looked good, Ben did. His skin had taken on a mottled sheen, but it hadn't turned gray, not yet. She'd wired his thumbs together in front, and that along with his bowed head gave his corpse an air of humility he had never displayed in life.

But what really made him look snazzy was his attire. She had dressed him in clothes from the time he'd said was his favorite for men's fashion: coat made of velvet, silk, and satin, long and flared in back; white shirt with ruffles at the cuffs and chest; a finely embroidered waistcoat, adorned with gold buttons; knee breeches, stockings, and high-heeled shoes. A white wig with curls in all the right places hid his bald head. A regular Georgian-era gentleman, Mozart or King George II.

He had often complained that masculine style had gone downhill from the turn of the nineteenth century, culminating in T-shirts and jeans. No imagination, no creativity or flare.

"So there you go," she said, bowing her head. "I hope you're happy."

In her mind, Ben answered: Eternally, my dear.

Nevaeh: Don't rub it in.

Ben: You sound bitter.

Nevaeh: Why shouldn't I be? God forgave you, *you*. We lived the same lives, did the same things for millennia. So why you?

Ben didn't answer.

Nevaeh: It was Beth, wasn't it? Something she said?

Ben: You mean, a secret?

Nevaeh: Yes, a key we've overlooked all these years.

Ben: There is no secret, dear. God has spelled it all out for us.

Nevaeh: So, what? You were smart enough to finally understand. And I'm not?

More silence from Ben.

Nevaeh: Don't look so smug. Well, we'll see what Beth has to say.

Ben: What are you planning?

It was Nevaeh's turn to hold her tongue.

Ben: Don't do anything stupid.

Nevaeh: You're just trying to keep it for yourself.

Ben: What?

Nevaeh: Salvation. But I know Beth had something to do with your going home, and I'm going to find out what it was.

Ben: Nevaeh, don't—!

But she was already walking away. He could just hang there and rot, jabbering to his heart's content. She had things to do.

[27]

From the Varna Airport, the Clan hired two taxis to take them to the docks.

"What for?" Bale's cabbie asked in Bulgarian. "There are no hotels there."

"Shut up and drive," Therion said behind him. Crammed into the tiny Toyota Yaris, he sat with his head tilted sideways, pinned between the roof and his massive shoulder. Skinny Lilit occupied the space next to him. His bulk pushed her into the door.

Seated in the front passenger seat, Bale said, "We're looking for a little excitement."

The cabbie looked at his watch. "Almost three. All the nightclubs are closed."

"You must be a family man."

The cabbie flashed rotting teeth at him. "My wife's name is Bisera," he said. "It means pearl, you know, and she is." He shrugged. "A big pearl, but a pearl nonetheless. Three beautiful daughters and a handsome—" Therion slapped him in the back of his head.

The way it flew forward and almost struck the steering wheel made Bale laugh. But he pulled a wad of euros from his jacket pocket, making sure the cabbie—rubbing his head now—saw it before he could start yelling at them to get out. He peeled off a twenty and handed it the driver, who wrinkled his nose at it and continued rubbing, casting icy glances into the rearview. Bale handed him another. "Listen, Family Man, why don't you leave the excitement to us, huh?" He raised an eyebrow. "The docks."

"We're the maritime capital of Bulgaria, we have lots of—"

"Port of Varna," Bale instructed.

The cabbie activated the meter, clunked the shifter into drive, and pulled away from the curb. Behind them, the taxi containing Artimus, Hester, and Cillian followed.

Bale touched the outside of his jacket pocket, felt the Stone through the material. He was itching to hold it again, see what kind of wild creatures were roaming about, if there was anyone nearby worth paying a visit. But sorting out his world from theirs gave him a headache. He would have to use it sparingly and make those times count.

In anticipation of eventually finding the Stone—or one of a dozen other relics on his list—he'd investigated claims of miracles associated with relics: the point of the lance that had pierce Christ's side, making Adhémar de Monteil, the bishop of Puy-en-Velay, undefeatable in battle during the First Crusade; a piece of the staff of Moses doing the same for Hannibal; a baby tooth of Jesus giving Napoleon Bonaparte glimpses of the future, which he used to strategize his military expansion of the French empire; Marc Antony using a thorn from Christ's crown to resurrect his beloved Cleopatra, if only for a night. By the time Bale had arrived on the scene, each relic had been gone, lost or stolen, or—in the case of the thorn—disintegrated upon its use.

The powers of resurrection and invincibility were attractive, but nothing like what he'd found the Stone could do. He couldn't wait to use it.

He hitched his arm over the seat and twisted to grin at Therion. "Remember that ship we blew up here?"

"Crimean War," Therion said, nodding. "A sixty-gun frigate. French, I think. That was something."

The cabbie glanced over, said nothing.

Bale looked at Lilit. "Dracula's ship was from here. The *Demeter*. The one that takes him to England? It runs aground, and the entire crew is missing, except the captain, whose corpse is tied to the helm."

Therion said, "Seriously?"

Lilit elbowed him. "In the novel." She glared out the window. "Idiot."

Half an hour later they were rolling along Bulevard Primorski:

closed restaurants, grocery stores, pawnshops, and convenience stores on their right, warehouses on their left. Beyond the warehouses, the harbor was crowded with container ships and freighters. Towering above them, barely visible in the glow of security lights, the skeletal arms of cranes looked like a city under construction, all girders and no walls or floors.

"Go slow," Bale said. He rolled down the window and leaned his head out. After five minutes he said, "There." He turned to the driver. "Hear it?"

The driver shook his head.

"Music. Stop here." He got out, tossed two more bills through the window, and started following his ears. They led him down an alley to a metal door with a wicket door set in the larger one—about ten inches square at face level. A disco beat pulsed into the alley. He turned to the Clan, coming up behind him, Hester tugging on her leather mask. "There's one in every city," he said. "Just gotta know where to look."

He pounded on the door and held his wad of cash in front of the wicket, which opened, releasing a stream of music and smoke. A moment later a hand snaked through. Bale pulled away the money. He stuck a single bill in the hand, which disappeared back inside. The entry door opened.

As soon as they were in, four of the six Clan members produced weapons from beneath their jackets: Therion, a shotgun; Artimus, a PP-19 Bizon—a Russian-made submachine gun as small as Artimus's preferred but unconcealable BMG .50-cal was big; Lilit, a curved katana sword; and Hester, a crossbow with collapsible limbs, which she now snapped into place. Therion cracked the doorman in the head with the shotgun stock, and Artimus let loose with a three-second burst of machine-gun fire into the high ceiling.

Several women screamed.

Moving deeper into the club with his Clan forming a semicircle around him, Bale looked around, disappointed. The space was huge, able to accommodate a good-sized rave party—it even boasted squiggly neon lights running around the wall just above reach, flashing multicolored spots, and earsplitting electronic dance music. But the place was dead. He counted five women, six men—all of them sitting at small round tables near the bar, no one dancing—and a bartender.

"*Kakvo e tova?*" he yelled. *What is this?* "Where's the party?"

The bartender raised his hands. "It's on Friday, man," he said.

Bale laughed. "That's all right! We can still have fun, can't we?" He stepped closer to a man in his twenties, sitting with a woman at a table. "Can't we?"

When the man didn't answer, Bale raised his hands as if to say, *What's the deal?* He turned to Hester, her goggles and leather mask making her look robotic. He said, "The man won't answer me."

She shot the patron in the leg with her crossbow. The arrow pierced his shin and protruded from his calf, eight inches on either side, give or take. He screamed and tumbled to the floor, holding his leg and rocking back and forth, getting blood everywhere. His girlfriend shot up and staggered back, knocking her chair over. She covered her mouth but didn't scream.

Bale liked her already. He gestured for her to come to him. Nodding up and down, she took a backward step, which puzzled Bale until he remembered Bulgarians nodded *no* and shook their heads *yes*.

"*Ella tyk,*" he said. "*Njama strashno.*" *Come here. I won't hurt you.*

She moved in tiny steps, a few at a time, until she was close enough for Bale to drape his arm around her shoulders. He started kissing her neck. She pushed him away, and he yanked her back.

Lilit and Artimus circled around the small group of people. Artimus abruptly raised the Bizon and fired past Bale, at the entrance. The doorman was up, opening the door, slipping out. Artimus's rounds chipped away the brick beside the jamb, kicking up a plume of dust.

Therion bolted for the door, reached it just as it slammed shut. He grabbed the handle and tugged. It opened a few inches, closed. "He's out there holding it," Therion said.

Artimus came up behind him with the machine gun. "Move," he

said, but Therion said, "It's metal, stupid." Therion opened the wicket door and reached through. A scream sounded from the other side. He pulled his arm in, revealing his fist entangled in the man's hair. The doorman began screaming.

Bale said, "Ah, the music of the night." He waved his hand at the bartender. "Turn that other garbage off." A few seconds later the electronic dance music snapped off, leaving only the doorman's bellowing pain and the gasps and cries of the patrons.

Bale's new girlfriend glared past him at the door—where the screams had become heaving cries—and tried to pull away, but he held her firm. Her streaming eyes, wide as silver dollars, watched the events at the door with horror. "Don't look, baby," Bale said.

"Bale!" Lilit cried out, raising her sword and starting for the bar.

Bale turned to see the bartender hefting a shotgun, taking aim at Therion. Bale pushed his girlfriend into Cillian, who'd been casually observing the goings-on, and leaped toward the bar. He swatted the shotgun's barrel as it fired, blowing out a chunk of bar top. Bale grabbed the bartender's collar and slammed his face into the bar, simultaneously twisting the gun from his hands. He tossed the weapon to the floor, released the man's collar, and seized his wrist. Holding the man's arm flat against the bar, he nodded—no—and said, "Shame on you."

"Tell him to stop," the bartender said, mumbling it through his hand. Blood coated his chin. He glanced at Therion and back at Bale.

Bale cocked his head as the doorman's cries fell silent. "I think it's too late," he told the bartender, then told Therion, "Don't leave him like that," indicating the thing half-wedged through the wicket, hanging down the inside of the door.

Therion nodded and shifted around the hanging body, apparently figuring a way to get the hips through.

The bartender was probing the gap where a front tooth was gone. Bale pointed to it on the bar, being helpful, then he fetched his girlfriend from Cillian's embrace. The patrons were staring at one of the Clan or another, or had their faces cupped within their palms.

He spotted a sign above a door: стълбище—rooms to let.

"Let's go," Bale said, pulling his girlfriend toward the door. He snapped his fingers at another woman. "You too. Come on."

Behind him, Artimus yelled, "Everyone else! Up against the wall!"

[28]

In the dream, Jagger was hiding in an alcove behind a heavy curtain, among coats and robes on hooks. He peered through the curtain at the marble floors, walls, and columns of an opulent residence. Children laughed somewhere in the house and flashed by as they darted around. He'd been waiting hours, and when the Greek magistrate finally arrived home, he'd unexpectedly brought his family with him. From the sounds, his children had invited their friends.

The magistrate, a rotund figure with an impeccably trimmed beard, came into view and headed for Jagger's hiding place. His face was flushed with exertion, a grin pushing his cheeks into half globes under his eyes. Holding his robes up over his ankles, the magistrate trotted forward, casting quick glances over his shoulder.

Jagger backed into the darkness and pushed himself into the folds of the hanging clothes. A few seconds later sunlight flashed into the alcove and disappeared again as the magistrate entered and closed the curtain behind him. Jagger looked through the folds to see the man standing with his back toward him, peeking through the curtain as Jagger had done. The man was trying to restrain his labored breathing with little success, the breaths forming hushed laughter as he watched the house through the curtain.

And Jagger had thought he'd have to wait until the family went to bed. He took this fortunate turn as a sign that God wanted this to happen. He was always looking for signs, as did the others in the Tribe. Scattered among four additional homes in Athens, the others were waiting for their own targets or making their escapes, having finished their deeds. Five magistrates total, all of them colluding with Greece's Ottoman invaders, betraying their country and their countrymen by relaying troop movements and the names of spies to the Sultan's people. The Tribe had decided that the magistrates' reward would not be the retainment of power—or at least their worldly goods—that they hoped for after the inevitable conquer of Athens, but God's swift justice . . . and a dark tomb.

Anxious to be done with it, Jagger stepped forward. He covered the magistrate's mouth, simultaneously pushing his head back and slicing his neck from ear to ear. The magistrate kicked and spasmed. Blood sprayed onto the curtain and through its opening. He sheathed the knife and covered the wound with his palm. The blood was hot, as copious as wine from a broken jug. He felt the pulse growing weaker under his hand.

Sunlight washed over him again. Jagger saw a little girl standing outside the alcove, holding the curtain aside. Her huge eyes took in the scene, and she began to scream.

Jagger startled awake, sitting up in bed. His breath came short and fast; drops of sweat ran over his face and chest. He looked over at Beth's sleeping form.

Another dream.

But he knew it was more than that. He had no memory of the events, but he was certain he had been there and done that. It was merely the most recent of a series of such nightmares, coming more frequently, always a different situation, time in history, and victim, and always ending in blood.

He lowered his head back onto the pillow and placed his hand on his chest, feeling the wetness, the rise and fall of his lungs, his stampeding heart. He closed his eyes, certain he wouldn't get another wink of sleep that night.

●　　●　　●

Gunshots woke him and he bolted up in bed, disoriented, frightened. He reached for his gun on the nightstand, grabbed his prosthetic arm instead.

That's right, the gun's in the safe in the panic room.

It came to him that he'd never kept a gun on or in a nightstand, not since Tyler was born. Maybe sometime long ago he had.

"Jag?" Beside him, Beth propped herself up and rubbed his back. Sunlight filtered through the curtains, making the room bright. "What is it?"

A knock came from the apartment door, and he realized that's what had awakened him, not gunshots. He pressed his hand over his eyes, squeezed his temples, and groaned. "I must have been in a deep sleep, but it feels like I didn't sleep at all." He remembered the nightmare and wished he didn't.

"It's the stress, the grief," she said, pulling his pillow over her face. "Feels like I ran twenty miles last night."

"Or it was the vision," he said. "I think it takes a lot out of you. Maybe the mental strain of processing so much new information."

More knocking.

Beth flipped the covers off, started to rise. He stopped her, saying, "I'll get it." He looked at his watch. "Seven thirty. We overslept." At least two days a week they woke at four to attend matins, the monastery's first service of the day. Other days they woke at six, in time for him to be at the dig by the time it got going at seven. But not today, not with Ollie in Sharm El Sheikh, at the same hospital Tyler had gone to after being shot. Tragedy here had become too common.

"Owen said he'd be here about this time," Jagger said. He pulled on his pants and selected a khaki shirt.

It *was* Owen, as disheveled as Jagger remembered him. Unruly hair, bushy beard, flannel shirt with pushed-up sleeves—the gold tattoo of the burning bush, which all the Immortals had on the inside of their left forearms, showing—blue jeans, a tattered canvas satchel on a strap over his shoulder. He stood there sporting a cautious smile, inquisitive eyes.

"Did I wake you?" he asked.

Jagger stepped forward and gave the man a one-armed hug, which Owen returned. Remaining in the embrace, he said, "It's good to see you." He and Owen had spent only three days together, but to Jagger he felt like a brother. High emotion, intense shared experience will do that to people. Never mind that Owen's sincerity and genuine concern for people made him instantly likeable. Never mind that he was a physician who volunteered his services in war-torn territories and where he was needed the most. Never mind that he was really John the Apostle, had walked with Jesus Christ, and had written five books of the New Testament—as if one could put *that* out of one's mind. But to Jagger, Owen was the man who had saved Tyler's life. And probably Jagger's and Beth's as well, by snatching Nevaeh away as he flew his jet into the Tribe's drone control center—which, just saying, also saved untold hundreds of thousands, if not millions of lives. All of this wrapped up in the man Jagger now hugged, but it wasn't until Jagger sniffed that he realized he was crying.

Owen whispered, "If you genuflect, I'll beat the living tar out of you."

"What?" Jagger said, stepping back and wiping at his eyes like flicking away flies. "Sun got in my eyes." He smiled. "Get your butt in here."

Owen stepped in, held up a brown paper sack and a molded cardboard tray with four cups, and said, "Breakfast and coffee. From the hotel in the village, so I don't know how good any of it is." He set the goodies down on the coffee table. "I got here about an hour ago. Gheronda let me in the side door by the gardens. That front gate is truly messed up. He said they weren't making bread today, so I went into town. The hotel's going to bring up enough to feed everyone, though I don't think anyone here's hungry."

Jagger looked at the bag and shook his head. "I don't think I could eat."

"John . . . Owen . . . what do I call you?" Beth stood in the bedroom doorway, clad in a terry-cloth robe. She stretched out her arms, walked to him, and gave him a long hug.

Owen said, "I've been Owen so long, I might not know who you're talking to if you call me anything else."

Tyler's door opened and he peered out. "Dad?"

"Tyler, come here, son." Jagger waved him over.

The boy padded out in his pajamas, grabbed hold of his father's arm, all the while keeping his eyes on Owen.

"This is Owen," Jagger said. "We told you about him. He patched you up when you got shot. We used his helicopter to get you to the hospital."

Tyler stepped forward and offered his hand. "Nice to meet you, sir."

"Your mother and father gave me hugs," Owen said. "Can I get one from you? Or are you too old for silly stuff like that?"

Tyler grinned and moved in for a hug.

Owen said, "It's good seeing you so healthy. A lot better than the last time I saw you."

Tyler pulled on the chain around his neck until the bullet popped free from his pj top. "They pulled this out of me," he said.

"Wow," Owen said, raising his eyebrows. "You know, I've had quite a few of those pulled out of me, but I never thought about wearing one around my neck. That's cool."

"How many times have you been shot?" Tyler was completely fascinated now.

"Enough to wear them as earrings and make a whole necklace out of them and a ring . . . for every finger." He waggled his fingers in front of him.

"Man!" Tyler said.

Owen stooped to picked up two cups, which he handed to Jagger and Beth. He said, "Tyler, I got coffee for your mom and dad." He picked up another cup and held it out to Tyler. "I figured you'd rather have hot chocolate."

"Thank you!" He grabbed it, peeled off the lid, and drank.

"Made it from scratch myself," Owen continued, retrieving his own cup. He walked around the table, placed his satchel on the couch, and sat beside it. "The hotel didn't have hot chocolate. I guess there aren't too many requests for it here in the desert. But I showed them how to make it with a Hershey bar and milk. How'd I do?"

Tyler nodded, cup to mouth.

Jagger placed a hand on Tyler's head. "Why don't you go get dressed, buddy."

At the bedroom door, Tyler turned to grin at Owen. The chocolate on his upper lip had run down both sides of his mouth, turning it into a Fu Manchu mustache. He said, "My favorite verse is John 4:50."

Owen looked surprised. "'Go,' Jesus replied, 'your son will live.' The man took Jesus at his word and departed"?

Tyler's eyes flicked to his mother. "Mom says it shows that you don't have to *see* God for Him to help you. The boy never saw Jesus, but he was healed. She says people believe too much in what they can see, and not enough in what they can't."

Owen nodded. "You have a smart mother."

"Yeah," Tyler said.

Jagger raised his left arm, causing the sleeve below the elbow to flop down. "I feel naked without RoboHand. I'll be right back."

He went into the bedroom and shut the door.

[29]

"Sweet boy," Owen said, taking a sip from his cup.

Beth felt herself blushing. She sat in a chair beside the couch and said, "I don't even know if my interpretation of that passage is right."

"It is for you," Owen said, smiling. "Scripture is layered with meanings. Like seeing different colors when we look into a prism, depending on the light and angle. That's the magic of God's Word."

"But you wrote it."

"No more than you and Jagger *made* Tyler," Owen said. "Just as God knit him together in your womb, He knit the words I wrote in my head." He set his cup on the table and touched her arm. "Whatever the Holy Spirit led you to believe about that verse, it's the lesson you—or Tyler—needed to learn at that moment. But I remember that event as a testament to the power of prayer. When that official pleaded with Jesus to save his son, he was praying." Owen shrugged. "It's almost incidental that God happened to be standing there in the flesh at the time. He begged for his son's healing"—Owen pushed the coffee table away and knelt in front of it—"on his knees, clutching Jesus' garments." He brought his fists together, close to his chin, and leaned his head back. Beth could see the man gazing into Jesus' face. In a heartbreaking tone, Owen said, "Please heal my son, Lord. Without You, he will die." He looked at Beth. "I fail to see the difference between that man then and us now."

Beth's heart ached. She felt her lip quiver and tears ready to come. Not only because Owen was right, but because she had prayed those very words in much the same way when Tyler was fighting for his life. And just as God had answered the official's prayer, He had answered hers.

Jagger came out of the bedroom, buttoning his shirt, flexing his hook open and closed. He stopped, his gaze moving between Owen on his knees and Beth near tears. "I . . . uh . . . ," he said, hitching his thumb toward the bedroom. "Let me know when you're done."

"No," Beth said, "it's okay . . ."

Owen rose and plopped down on the couch. He chuckled. "I was just acting out the scene Tyler said was his favorite verse."

Jagger half smiled at Beth. He walked around the table and sat beside Owen. "Do that for Tyler. He'll love it."

"Do it for everyone," Beth said, wiping her eyes, laughing a little as she did. "Change the world."

Jagger shifted to face Owen. "When Tyler told you his favorite verse, you looked surprised."

"Only because I could tell he knows who I am."

"We decided that we wouldn't keep anything from him," Beth said. "We told him about the Tribe, the Immortals—"

"About . . . ," Owen started, gesturing toward Jagger.

"About Jagger being one, yes," Beth finished for him.

"We told him he couldn't tell anyone," Jagger said.

"We—Jagger and I—are trying to work through it," Beth said. "We couldn't do that and keep it from Tyler at the same time."

"It affects him as much as it does us," Jagger said.

"How's he taking it?" Owen asked.

"He doesn't understand the implications," Beth said, thinking about all it might mean . . . moving around so people wouldn't notice Jagger's perpetual youth; how one day Tyler would look the same age as his father, then older, then a lot older; having to explain that to his wife and kids; Jagger being there at Tyler's deathbed, Tyler old and worn out while Jagger was still young and vital . . . so many problems to overcome. But they'd have years to figure them out. Most important, they were a family, and families did what they had to do; they accommodated one another no matter what.

Owen clamped his hand on the back of Jagger's neck, brotherly. "And how are *you* holding up?"

Jagger shook his head. "Still trying to get my head around it. The crash got me thinking of God as an ogre, someone who couldn't care less about the people He created. Being here, surrounded by so much love for Him, His saving Tyler . . . I think I was coming around. But now . . ." He shook his head. "It seems so . . . so . . ." He looked at Beth for help.

"Pointless," she said, then rushed to say: "That's Jagger's thinking, not mine."

"Hey," Jagger said. "Apparently I've been on a quest for God's forgiveness for thirty-five hundred years. Why would He give it to me now?"

"He took Ben," Beth said. "I believe He forgave him."

"And others as well," Owen said. "Not many, but some. You've changed, Jagger. You got off the path of the Tribe, trying to *earn* His grace."

"I feel like praying, going to service, doing what He wants me to do is just a different way of doing the same thing, of earning my way into heaven."

"Depends what's in your heart, what your motives are," Owen said. "Do you love Him because He's given you things—Beth and Tyler, for example. Or do you love Him simply because He's God? *Despite* the bad things. Big difference." He squinted at Jagger, thinking. "If your love for God is pure, no matter what, then the God I know will open His arms to you."

Jagger frowned, looked at his lap, where his fingers were absently rubbing the hook that used to be his other hand.

"What?" Owen asked.

"I just don't know if such love exists."

"It does," Owen said definitively.

Tyler's door opened. He came out rubbing his stomach. "Something smells good."

Owen reached out for the bag he'd brought and tossed it to Tyler. "Libbah," he said. Bedouin bread made with dark wheat, water, and vinegar, rolled flat, buried in sand on which hot coals were placed. Somehow sand never stuck to it.

"Yum," Tyler said, reaching in and biting into one while digging in the bag for another.

Watching Tyler chow down, Beth realized she was starving, despite her aching grief for the monks who'd died last night. "Ty," she said, holding out her hand. He tossed her one, then one to Owen and another to Jagger.

"There are honey packets and a carton of diced fruit on the bottom," Owen said.

"I'm fine," Tyler said around a mouthful of bread.

Owen nudged Jagger. "We need to talk business," he said.

[30]

Jagger and Owen sat in the two heavy wooden chairs on the balcony outside the apartment watching Beth and Tyler wend their way through a small courtyard two floors below.

"Amazing child, Tyler," Owen said.

"I think so," Jagger said, working a jeweler's screwdriver into a hinge on RoboHand. He thought the few spare parts he kept would make the prosthetic right again.

"And Beth . . . I see now why you were so adamant about cutting all ties to your past, willing yourself to forget it in order to be with her."

The car crash that had taken his arm had also damaged his *parahippocampal gyrus*, the brain's memory banks. Owen had theorized that Jagger's ten years of trying to forget 3,500 years of wrongful living, his wishing so badly that he were normal, coupled with the rapidity of his healing—specifically his brain—had resulted in a wish come true: a true loss of memory of his life before meeting Beth. What Jagger hadn't told Owen was that since learning of his immortality some of those memories were coming back, and they disgusted him. If Jagger were God, he wouldn't forgive himself.

He looked away from the confused scattering of buildings splayed out in the compound before them to look at Owen: the man's wild splash of auburn hair and beard, strong jawline, muscular build, and eyes that had seen so much and gave back nothing but compassion. Jagger had no idea how Owen had witnessed a hundred lifetimes of sorrow and maliciousness without becoming bitter.

He said, "You told me before that you used to visit me, but I asked you not to come by anymore after I met Beth."

"You wanted to rid yourself of all reminders of your past."

"Before that, we'd gone parachuting together?"

Owen grinned at the memory and nodded. "The last time in Taupo, New Zealand, 1985."

"So we were friends?" Jagger was thinking about the feeling he had upon seeing Owen this morning, and wondered if some of that stemmed from a relationship they shared a long time ago. If the terrible images he was having were indeed memories, why couldn't good things come back too, nice feelings, eventually happy memories? Certainly he couldn't have been miserable—or thoroughly corrupted—for all that time?

"After you left the Tribe," Owen said, "we became friends, yes."

"And I knew who you were? That you were the Apostle John?"

"All the Immortals know."

Jagger shook his head. "Hard to imagine I'd turn my back on you."

"I understood, even more now that I've met Beth." He took a bite of the libbah he was holding, then opened the satchel in his lap. He pulled out a tablet computer, tapped a button, and let his fingers dance over the screen.

"You have an iPad?" Jagger said.

"Just keeping up with the times. Here." He handed it to Jagger.

On the screen was an array of photos: Bale, the big guy with raccoon eyes, the woman he'd identified as Steampunk, a man with glasses he had seen among the others. These photos were different from the ones Gheronda had shown him—crisper, newer.

"Those are the ones who attacked last night." Jagger handed back the iPad. "The Clan."

"And this stone they took . . . you say after you touched it you saw angels?"

"I didn't know what they were at first, but then I saw them in the chapel. They were coming down on beams of light, standing over the praying monks." He looked Owen squarely in the face. "I think an angel helped me. Steampunk had me dead to rights, shot an arrow from a crossbow at me, maybe ten feet away. The angel reached its hand out, and the arrow missed. Then the angel touched the crossbow, and the string broke." Jagger rose from his chair. "Hold on."

He went into the apartment to his nightstand, picked up a folded washcloth, and returned to the balcony. Laying the washcloth in the palm of his hand, he used RoboHand to open it up and reveal the fragment of stone Ollie had given him.

"Ollie said this broke off the larger stone."

"Does it . . . work like the other?"

"Touch it."

Owen looked at him, then down at the fragment. After a few moments, he moved his index finger toward it. He touched the fragment, twitched, but kept his finger on it. He looked around, a dazed expression on his face. "Whoa . . ." His eyes settled on something below and stayed there.

Jagger followed his gaze to Beth, Tyler, and Gheronda coming back through the courtyard, probably heading outside through the garden entrance to see the real destruction of the main gate. Jagger felt the pressure in his palm lessen, and saw that Owen had removed his finger and was now sitting back in his chair.

He was still gazing around, and he raised his hands as if to catch a ball. "I'm still seeing them," he said.

"The vision will fade pretty quickly after you stop touching the fragment, a few minutes or so. Longer with the big stone. That's how I was able to see the angels in the chapel. They faded before my eyes about ten minutes after Steampunk took the Stone from me."

"Angels," Owen said. "They're everywhere. I saw four walking with Beth and Tyler and Gheronda. They're on the roofs, on the terraces. Just seem to be strolling around."

Jagger felt a strong urge to pick up the fragment. The word *reenter* came to mind. He wanted to reenter that world, as though what happened when you touched it wasn't that the spiritual realm became visible as much as it was that you entered it, became a part of it. He wondered if that was simply a failing of his humanity. As Beth had told Tyler, we believe what we can see and not what we can't. Was

Jagger subconsciously unwilling to accept that the spiritual realm was all around him—whether he saw it or not?

He flipped the washcloth back over the fragment, trying to lessen the temptation to touch it. He didn't know why it seemed like he shouldn't, but the urge felt too needy, too much like he imagined a drug addict felt about getting a fix.

"Do you," Jagger asked, "see . . . *other* beings?"

"Demons?" Owen said. "They're here too. But not many. Ugly things, aren't they?"

"Last night Beth and I saw a demon, and it seemed like she saw something slightly different from what I saw—more grotesque."

Owen thought about it, nodded. "Anthony the Great claimed to have seen angels and demons," he said. "He was from around these parts, actually. He's called Father of All Monks. His journals record that as he became closer to God, more holy, if you will, the demons grew more hideous. He believed the holier you were, the more terrible the demons appear."

"What if you were just plain evil?"

"Well then, the demons would seem like beautiful creatures to you. I guess it correlates with sin. To a righteous person, child abuse is vile, repulsive. But to a pedophile it's not so awful, maybe even attractive."

After a minute Jagger said, "You don't suppose Anthony the Great got his hands on a piece of the Judgment Stone? And that's why he saw angels and demons?"

Owen's eyebrows went up. "I hadn't thought of that." He squinted, thinking. "That would explain the visions he describes in his journals." His brow furled. "It's fading," he said. His eyes and head moved slowly around, as though he were watching dust drifting in the sunlight.

Jagger flipped the sides of the cloth over onto the top. He returned it to the nightstand drawer, and when he came back, Owen was blinking his eyes.

"Wow," he said, and smiled. "I like that about God. Most of the time when He reveals something to me, it's a wow experience." He opened his eyes as big as they could get, shook his open hands on either side of his face, and said, "Woooooow!" He closed his eyes and his lips moved, but nothing came out. A private prayer, just him and God.

Jagger looked for Beth and Tyler, but they were gone. No doubt Tyler was climbing on the rubble that had shattered away from the wall around the three iron doors that protected the main entrance. And Beth was telling him to be careful, and Gheronda was giving her an earful about how this made twice in six months that the sanctity of the Haven had been violated. Which Jagger wondered about: did whatever treaty the Immortals and keepers—mortals sworn to help them and keep their secret—had agreed to way back when, a thousand years ago, he'd heard—did it prohibit attacks on Immortals who were in Havens, or attacks on Havens themselves? Because as far as he could tell, the Clan hadn't come to harm an Immortal. Ollie and the monks had gotten in their way, but the Clan had not come for any human; they had come for the Judgment Stone.

"Whew," Owen said, finished with his prayer.

"Is that the first time you've seen anything like that?" Jagger asked.

"I've seen angels before, some in human form, some . . ." He nodded, pointing around at nothing. "Like *them*." He scooted to the edge of his seat, looked around, squinting, as if trying to see through the veil again. "When an angel comes to you—me anyway," he said, "that's what you see, only an angel. This . . . this was different. There were more lights, more . . . I don't know, as though you can see the *air*, the spiritual air around them, everywhere. Before, it was like seeing a fish out of water—not that they're uncomfortable or in danger when they come to visit, you understand. But this time it was like seeing fish in their natural environment, swimming around, zipping here and there, totally at home and free. It's not just seeing angels, it's seeing the whole spiritual world, God's world." He shook his head. "Over the years, I'd heard rumors of something called the Judgment Stone. But that name doesn't really fit."

"That's what Ollie called it."

"But it's not judging."

"It reflects a judgment," Jagger said. "Whether a person has a relationship to God or not."

"It's more than that. It shows His presence on earth, how active He is here."

Jagger waited while Owen thought about it.

Finally Owen said, "The *God* Stone." He smiled at Jagger. "The God Stone, right?"

"I like it," Jagger said.

"And you said the big one, the one they took, caused something different?"

"More powerful," Jagger said. "I don't know if it revealed different things, but everything was more vivid, more solid."

Owen placed his palms on the wide arms of the chair. He sat still like that, eyes slowly taking in the monastery, but Jagger suspected he wasn't seeing anything other than whatever his mind was mulling over. Sitting there, broad-shouldered, stiff, contemplative, he reminded Jagger of a *Star Trek* captain, Picard with more hair.

Owen stood up suddenly, slinging the satchel over his shoulder. "Come on."

Jagger didn't move. "Where are we going?"

"To get the God Stone back."

[31]

"Wait, wait," Jagger said, grabbing Owen's wrist. "Why? So what if the Clan can see the spiritual world? Maybe it'll scare them into giving their lives over to God. Except for the religious icon value of it, what's it matter who has it? Look around this place." He pointed down. "The burning bush." Then up. "Mount Sinai." Over at the Southwest Range Building. "There's an entire library of artifacts and relics right there. From what I've seen, they don't do anything except maybe get people thinking more about God . . . until they get back to their Sharm El Sheikh hotel, where they can lie out on the beach and order drinks with little umbrellas."

Owen turned to face him. He leaned against the railing, resting his hands on the top rail behind him. "You're really comparing the top of that mountain and the burning bush to that stone? Has anyone ever had visions from touching the bush?"

"One woman plucked a leaf off and claimed to see Moses standing next to her."

Owen cocked his head, narrowed his eyes.

Jagger shrugged. "No, but—"

"But nothing. That stone peels back the veil between us and the spiritual realm."

"Visually," Jagger added.

"In this world, that's a lot. Granted, it's not a doorway to heaven—as far as we know. It probably won't make people more spiritual. But I can tell you this: if Bale wanted it, he's planning on doing something terrible with it."

"But what? What can he do?"

"Let me tell you something about the Clan. They hate God. They hate Him with a burning fury that may just frighten Satan himself. And the way they show how much they hate God is by grieving Him every chance they get. What God loves, they not only hate, they defile. They've murdered and raped." He lowered his eyes, shook his head. "Women, children, nuns, priests . . . the more innocent their victims, the more pleasure they take in it. They assist the wicked, corrupt the good, drive godly men to hate God by the atrocious things they do to their loved ones. Are you hearing me?" He pointed back to the terrace where Tyler had been shot. "Nevaeh shot your son, but you know what? I bet she felt bad about that, would take it back if she could. But if that had been Bale or any of the Clan, he would have slit your throat and dragged Tyler off to do things to him that would make you tear open your chest with your fingernails and yank out your heart. If you weren't already dead."

He scowled at Jagger, breathing hard, his face etched with an anger that could only have come from experience. Jagger realized that to Owen the Clan was not some distant entity; they had personally harmed him, killed someone he loved. But still Jagger was stunned.

More quietly Owen said, "I'm sorry." He sighed heavily. "Shakespeare's *Titus Andronicus*, you know it?"

Jagger shook his head.

"Shakespeare paints Aaron the Moor as being as wicked as a person can be. In one scene Aaron recalls the evil things he's done countless times: devised deadly enmity between two friends, burned down the barns of poor people just to see them weep . . ." Owen donned the persona of a Shakespearian actor to say with gravelly voice and sharp tones:

"Oft have I digg'd up dead men from their graves,
And set them upright at their dear friends' door
Even when their sorrow almost was forgot,
And on their skins, as on the bark of trees,
Have with my knife carved in Roman letters
'Let not your sorrow die, though I am dead.'"

He looked at Jagger with an expression that asked, *You understand?*

"That's the Clan," Jagger said.

"They make Aaron look like a Boy Scout."

Jagger felt sick to his stomach. He felt dirty just hearing about them. Still he said, "But I don't understand what this has to do with the God Stone."

"I don't know what they'd use it for," Owen said. "What if simply exposing it to the world bears consequences we can't foresee: mass suicides by people who want to get to that realm faster, or people who think they've done things that could never be forgiven by a Higher Being they never believed in. And by *mass*, I mean in the hundreds of millions; wars, as different religions stake their own claims on the spiritual world." Agitated again, he spun off the railing and sat in his chair. "Thing is, Jag, we can't know for sure about the ultimate outcome, but we do know that in Bale's hands nothing good can come from it."

His eyes bore into Jagger's; gazing back, Jagger saw in Owen worry, anguish, desperation. "I believe you," Jagger said.

"Then help me get it back from them before they figure out how to use it for evil."

"I'm not going with you," Jagger said, firm about it.

"We make a good team," Owen said, grinning now. "You know what we're up against. You're one of us. I'd take you over ten other men."

"Maybe you should find twenty other men then," Jagger said. "We're just starting to recover from what happened last time. Beth would say you're crazy for asking me and I'm crazy for even listening to you. She'd say, 'Jagger, you belong here.'"

"You know Beth better than that," Owen said. "*I* know her better than that. If she had heard everything I just told you? About the *possibility* that the God Stone could further the Clan's agenda of causing heartache and chaos?"

"I seem to recall our having this conversation before," Jagger said. "You trying to convince me to join you on an impossible mission."

"Turned out to be not so impossible."

"If you say, 'With God, all things are possible,' I'm going to walk away."

"Why?"

"You have a habit of quoting Scripture."

"I have a habit of living Scripture." Owen leaned forward. "I talked you into combating the Tribe with me, and God saved millions through us . . . because you stepped up. I was right then, I'm right now. You know we have to get the Stone away from Bale. I don't care if it ends up on the ocean floor or destroyed into dust, Bale just can't have it. You don't want to go because you don't want to leave your family. I get that. But be honest . . . what would Beth say?"

[32]

"Go," Beth said, having listened to Owen repeat what he'd told Jagger—except the part about what would have happened if it had been Bale they confronted six months ago instead of Nevaeh. Thankfully, he skipped that, though Jagger was sure he was right.

They were standing outside the west wall near the gardens, an oasis of trees and bushes that produced figs, apricots, plums, strawberries, blackberries, and more kinds of vegetables than Tyler would sample in a lifetime. Between the wall and the trees they were shielded from the blistering sun. Tyler had run off to see how the carrots were coming along—a task Father Luca had assigned him.

"Jagger," Beth said, gripping his arms, "we'll be okay. We'll be safe. Gheronda said they've closed the monastery to visitors, and even the checkpoints on the road from Darpa to here are turning people away."

"What are they saying, that the mountain's closed?"

"That St. Catherine's is, and they strongly advise coming back next month."

It would be a hearty soul who'd continue past a checkpoint against the advice of the gruff Egyptian police manning it. On a good day those guys were as unpleasant as Dobermans with hemorrhoids. They must be thinking Allah was smiling on them, getting to turn away all those rude tourists.

"For how long?" Jagger asked.

"At least two weeks, Gheronda said. The monks need time to get the gate repaired." She frowned. "And mourn. He said the Egyptians were more than happy to help them keep people away."

"I'm sure. Did he say what the police are doing about the

murders?" Jagger knew they had come to the monastery last night and this morning, but they hadn't bothered to take a statement from him.

"Going through the motions," Beth said. "But it happened inside the monastery and the victims were residents there, so they're acting like it's a church problem." She smiled up at him. "So, see, we'll be fine."

But he saw the worry in her eyes. "I'm not going to lie to you," he said, wanting to lie very badly. "These guys are bad. They could easily kill—"

Beth touched her fingers to his mouth. She stroked his cheek. "If the Clan really can use the Stone to"—she looked at Owen—"how'd you put it, 'grieve God by hurting what He loves, His children here on earth,' then isn't trying to stop them worth dying for?"

Leave it to Beth: bottom line. He thought of their discussion about grief. He would grieve more if Beth or Tyler died than if everyone else in the world did. But how much would he grieve if people died and he could have stopped it but hadn't?

Her face got firm, and she said, "We'll be okay, and I believe you will be too."

• • •

Jagger squeezed Tyler until it seemed the boy would pop. He ran his hand through his son's hair and kissed him on his cheek, tasting Tyler's tears.

"You stay in the monastery and obey your mother," Jagger said. "I'll be home as soon as I can."

"But why?" Tyler said, sniffing. "Why do you have to go?"

"I told you, we think the people who attacked the monastery are going to do even worse things, and we have to stop them."

"But why *you*?"

He looked into his son's eyes. They were blue like Beth's, the first thing he'd noticed about her, because he remembered thinking they were deep blue lakes that he'd fallen into, plunging fast with no desire to save himself. He ached for the pain he was causing Tyler, and it made him all the more angry at the Clan.

He said, "Because I can."

•   •   •

Tyler helped him pack his backpack, and they all prayed, each of them taking a turn. Owen's was sincere and confident, without affectation. He was a guy comfortable with prayer and intimate with God, which resulted in simple words and sentences that were weighted with meaning, a casual conversation that simultaneously conveyed respect and utter awe for his Creator. Jagger remembered that from before, the way Owen prayed. He'd tried to imitate it, but either it didn't come naturally to him or it was a quality it took longer than a few months to acquire. He suspected it was both. Tyler's prayer was short, but— punctuated by sobs and sniffles—it impacted Jagger's heart the most.

More hugs and kisses and they were out the door, Tyler clinging to Jagger's arm all the way to the side gate, Beth trailing behind. As the helicopter lifted up, Jagger waved. The copter started rotating toward the south, and Jagger saw Tyler drop his arm to hug Beth and push his face into her. Then Owen completed the turn, rising steeply out of the valley, and his family passed out of view.

[33]

Jagger stood shaking his head at Owen's jet. It was a white Cessna 501, exactly the same as the one he'd crashed, right down to the gold and green stripes. He remembered thinking of it as a bullet with wings.

He said, "Didn't feel like trading up?"

Owen swung open the door and looked back at him. "I'm sentimental. I did change a few things around, though."

Like adding the Roman numeral *II* after the plane's name, Jagger saw. It was stenciled in script under the cockpit's side window: *Boanerges II*. It meant Sons of Thunder, a term of endearment Jesus had called John and his brother James, a reference to their habit of letting enthusiasm trump caution. Jagger hoped Owen wasn't doing that now.

When he climbed inside he understood what Owen meant. Gone were the hundreds of photographs, notes, and news clippings that had lined the walls of the first *Boanerges*. Only one thing was now tacked to the wall, a huge map of the world marked with dots and scribbled words in a variety of highlighters. The aisle was clear—none of the old jet's piles of books, magazines, and papers. A desk, similar to the old one, sat in the center of the cabin, left of the aisle. This time, however, there were two computer monitors bolted to it, big plasma screens. Opposite the desk was a bed, unmade, with clothes strewn over it. *That* was the Owen abode Jagger remembered; it made him feel more comfortable.

"You haven't had a chance to mess it up too much," Jagger said.

"I lost so much research in the crash," Owen replied from the cockpit, "I'm trying to do everything digitally now. Backing up to a cloud server."

What had Judas sung to Jesus in *Jesus Christ Superstar*? Something about if He'd come today He could have reached the whole nation, referring to the era of mass communication. Well, He did anyway, and Jagger was glad He'd done it when and how He did. The thought of Jesus having a Facebook page—two billion fans!—and His miracles getting ten million hits on YouTube just made him queasy. John uploading the book of Revelation to a cloud server from his exile on Patmos. Oh man.

Jagger dropped his backpack on the bed and sat facing the twin screens. He tapped the keyboard's space button and the screens lit up. One displayed a flight path from Yoshkar-Ola, Russia, to Sharm El Sheikh. The other was opened to a photo-organizing app with a grid of pictures of the Clan, a few of which Jagger had seen in Gheronda's scrapbook.

Owen came out of the cockpit. Seeing Jagger at the screens, he said, "I had some DVD backups in a safe deposit box in Zurich. I was able to retrieve about 10 percent of what I had on the Clan and the Tribe before the crash. I lost a lot of current stuff, like the IDs and whereabouts of some loners."

"Immortals?"

"There are a few out there trying to make a go of it on their own. You were one. I'm trying to reconstruct my files from memory." He shook his head. "No easy task. We may be immortal and have better healing abilities than normal people, but we're still human. I can barely remember what I had for breakfast yesterday, let alone whom I was tracking four years ago." He stopped on his walk down the aisle. "I take that back. Yesterday one of the mothers in Tabashino brought me *kasha*, a porridge made from oats, wheat, rice, barley, and rye flakes. Delicious. But you know what I mean."

Jagger considered it. He said, "I kind of thought of them, the ones whose memories didn't get scrambled—I thought they remembered everything. All the places they've been, the people they've met, the things they've done."

"Thirty-five hundred years of memories?" Owen said, sitting down next to him. "No way. Important things, yeah. I remember every day, every minute I spent with Jesus."

No kidding, Jagger thought, thinking that time spend with God would be like a brand upon the brain. He said. "So, like, what . . . the year 413 is just a blur?"

Owen made a face, looking at the ceiling. "Actually," he said, "I spent much of that year in Hippo Regius—Annaba, Algeria, now—with Augustine and—"

"*Saint* Augustine?"

"I knew him as Augoustinos Aurelius, yes. And Jerome—Saint Jerome now. We'd ramble all night about everything from the sufficiency of Scripture to which of us made the best tea." He smiled at the memory.

"Yeah, it sounds like you've totally forgotten everything." Jagger wondered if Owen ever remembered himself as a member of the Tribe, before he'd met Jesus. Did he have the kind of nightmares Jagger was having? If anyone on earth truly understood the breadth and depth of God's forgiveness, it had to be Owen. But did being forgiven mean being completely free of the ghost of past sins?

"Trust me, there's plenty I can't remember . . . and plenty more I'd *like* to forget." For a moment his face took on a melancholic expression. Then he seemed to shake it off, patted Jagger on the back, and stood. He stepped to the map on the wall, scanning it with his hands on his hips. "So, where to?"

Owen was chomping at the bit to retrieve the God Stone, sure, but Jagger wondered if he'd just changed the subject because he knew what was on Jagger's mind. Thirty-five hundred years of dealing with people had made him scary-good at reading people's minds. He'd said the Tribe was like that: experts at human behavior, able to know what people would do before the people themselves did. They've seen it all before, a thousand times.

At one time Jagger must have had that ability as well. How much of it was still in there, acting like intuition? He'd made an efficient Army Ranger, sniffing out dangers before the rest of his squad, and a top executive protector, sensing when to change itineraries and routes to keep his alphas—the people he was protecting—safe.

So what could he read into Owen's deflecting his question before he'd asked it? That even the Apostle John was still haunted by his past? Or that he wasn't, which meant Jagger's terrible memories would forever be a reminder that his name was not in God's Book of Life?

"Jagger—?"

He snapped his head up. Owen was turned away from the map, watching him.

"Where to?" Owen said.

[34]

Jagger blinked, pushing away his thoughts to get back into the here and now. He shook his head. "I thought you'd know," he said. "You've been tracking these guys, Bale and the Clan. You were so anxious to go after them. I thought you had a plan."

"I do," Owen said. "Get the God Stone away from the Clan."

"That's a goal, not a plan. Where's their base?" He was thinking of the Tribe's home in the Paris catacombs—at least where it used to be; he supposed they'd found a new place by now. He wasn't sure of the vernacular. The dark, bone-filled catacombs—how could anyone call that "home"?

"The Clan doesn't have one," Owen said. "They're nomads, vagabonds. They travel from place to place, wreaking havoc wherever they go. Their strategy for not being caught is twofold: their violence is wanton and random, but typically not so excessive that it becomes an international incident. I think if they had their way they'd kill everyone they meet, but they restrain themselves. They travel from country to country. Police departments have enough trouble communicating, comparing notes with other departments within their own countries, let alone across borders. The Clan uses time and distance to avoid detection."

"So, what, they stay in hotels?" That fit a vague notion he had of the people who'd attacked the monastery. A rock band with no roots. The anything-goes sort who hit the road and never stop. Bale, the charismatic and Adonis-handsome leader, letting his wild band pursue any debauchery their hearts desired as long as they performed.

"Sometimes," Owen said. "But by and large they live in their plane. This is a small business jet. Their Bombardier is more like a commercial airline's. It has more cabin space than the average single-family home, more than twenty-six hundred square feet. There're six Clan members, and they each have their own bedroom. There's a kitchen—a galley, like mine"—he gestured toward the rear of the cabin, at a closed door—"but larger, more decked out. A library and computer room, a storeroom and armory. A bathroom, of course, but theirs has a Jacuzzi tub instead of a tiny shower."

"How do you know all this?"

"As you said, I've tracked them, studied them as much as possible. In the case of their jet, I got a hold of the plans from the company that built it out for them."

"If they're as nasty as you say, why haven't you stopped them?"

"I've tried," Owen said, his shoulders slumping a little. "They're always one step ahead of me. There's no pattern, no planning . . . nothing I can plot in order to anticipate where they're going to be. And they never stay in one place for long."

"You've taken their pictures," Jagger said, waving his hand at the monitor displaying the evidence. "The camera could just have easily been a sniper rifle."

"Those pictures were taken over many months, one snap at time, in different locales. Sometimes I just happened to see one of them. Other times I was there investigating one of their crimes and spotted one of them before they'd left. About ten years ago I did manage to take one member out. Saw him on the street and got ahead of him, confronted him in an alley. I was going to talk to him, as I try to do with all Immortals—as I did with you before you finally left the Tribe. But there's no talking to anyone in the Clan. They're as corrupt as any demon. Pure evil. Before I even opened my mouth, this one attacked. He was like a wild animal, swinging, biting. Pulled a gun, then a knife. I was able to turn the knife on him and he went down, but not before he'd shot me twice, tore my ear half off, sliced and stabbed me in a dozen places. At one point he was sawing on my neck."

He rubbed the side of his neck, obviously thinking about it. Then he continued: "After that, the rest of the Clan came after *me*. I was wounded, needed time to heal, so I ran. Took a year to shake them. Besides, I might be able to stand up to one of them at a time, but I'm no match for any number of them together."

"And this is who you want us to go after?" Jagger shook his head.

"You said that about the Tribe when we went after them."

"We survived, but just barely." What Jagger didn't say was that his motivation for going after the Tribe was greater then than it was now: they had kidnapped Beth, and he would have fought all the demons of hell to get her back. Nevaeh had also shot Tyler, and he'd wanted revenge—a compulsion he wasn't proud of. He was aware it put him in their camp, justifying violence by calling it justice. But it was true, and he'd have to work it out in time, between himself and God. When he was on better terms with the Big Guy. Owen's motivation had been to stop the Tribe from destroying a city. Jagger had never pretended that was more compelling than rescuing Beth.

This time Jagger was having a hard time working himself up to go after the Clan. They'd killed three monks, injured Ollie. They were bad dudes, no doubt. But was it really his job to stop them? He didn't even know how the Stone could help the Clan in their mission to— Owen's words—*grieve God*. Why did they have to go after them now?

He said, "You say these guys are exponentially worse than the Tribe, more vicious, harder to track. What makes you think we can do it this time?"

"All I want to do is get the God Stone out of their hands," Owen said. "That's different from killing them."

"Maybe."

Owen dipped his head, conceding the point. He said, "As far as finding them, whatever they're going to do with the Stone, it's *something*. Instead of following their whims, they're going to be guided by the Stone, somehow, some way. We have a piece of the Stone. If we can see what they're seeing, maybe we can figure out what they're doing."

"That's a big maybe."

"It's something," he said again. "And in regards to confronting them"—he grinned—"I have you."

"Oh yeah, a one-armed man—cursed by God—who doesn't even know what he's doing here."

Owen returned from the map to sit next to Jagger and pat him on the back again. "Have faith, my friend. There's a reason you're with me. Now . . ." He leaned forward to get his hands on the keyboard. He pushed a button, clearing the old flight plan, and said, "Where should we go?"

Jagger told him what Ollie had said about calling Bronson Radcliff from the Ice Temple Foundation, and finished with: "I'm guessing Radcliff sent the team he promised Ollie to fetch the artifact."

Owen was nodding, but said, "You think it was the man who funds the excavation who told the Clan?"

"Who else? He was the only one who knew about the Stone."

"You don't look too sure."

"I just can't see Ollie being in bed with someone who'd know the Clan, who'd be so ruthless, so corrupt."

"You don't know much about archaeological funding, do you?"

"It's corrupt?"

Owen shook his head. "I'm not saying that. But archaeologists are passionate about digging in dirt, not about money. If a foundation offers to fund a dig, few dirt diggers are going to question it. Not that they don't care. They just don't think about it. This foundation, do you know anything about it?"

"I saw a brochure," Jagger said. "It's backed digs at Petra, in Mexico—Xochicalco, I think—"

"There you go," Owen interrupted. "If Radcliff is dirty, chances are he's covered his tracks. Even if Ollie did look into him, I doubt he would've found anything suspicious." He pulled at his beard, thinking. "Okay, let's say this Radcliff guy has some connection with the Clan—they threatened him to help them find the Stone, or any artifacts, who knows? Or he's working with them because he wants to, for whatever reason. Why would he tell them before he had it in hand? Ollie was prepared to give it to him."

"Yeah, but only if he could go with it. Maybe Bronson didn't like that. Or he was afraid Ollie would disappear with it once he realized how valuable it was or decided he couldn't live without it." Jagger threw up his arms. "I don't know, but if Radcliff was the only one who knew . . ."

"Maybe he told the Clan it had been found, not knowing Bale would go after it the way he did."

"Whatever happened, he's our only lead," Jagger said.

"And where is he?"

"The Ice Temple Foundation is based in Stockholm. I think that's where Ollie reached him."

Owen typed it in, then their current location. The computer showed an image of the globe. It rotated and stopped when Sharm El Sheikh was in the five o'clock position and Stockholm at eleven. It seemed a long distance away.

Jagger said, "Why would Bale go there?"

"As you said, he's our only lead. If they're not heading there, Radcliff knows how to reach them."

"And he's going to tell us how?"

Owen gave him a serious look. "Yes."

He switched his gaze to the second monitor and called up a program. It looked like a form with lots of blank text boxes. He started filling them in: Rape. Murder. Homicide. Mayhem. Kidnapping. Abduction. Gang. Multiple suspects. Multiple perpetrators.

"What's that?"

"Essentially, it's a scanner. It'll monitor the police channels along our route." He clicked a tab on the screen, and a new group of boxes appeared. He glanced at the flight route and typed: Egypt, Cyprus, Turkey . . . all the countries they would fly over. Another tab, another screen of text boxes, into which he entered Egyptian, Greek, Turkish . . . "The program will listen for the keywords I've entered in all of these languages."

"And you think they'll stop to commit murder, rape, kidnapping?"

"Hard to imagine they'd pass up the opportunity to pop into countries they haven't visited in a while. It's what they do. But now that they have the God Stone, who knows?" He shrugged. "Can't hurt, looking as we go."

"This scanner thing works?"

"Seems to, from a few tests I've run. Part of my new high-tech arsenal."

Owen stood and headed for the cockpit. He called back, "Think of some more keywords, anything that might identify our guys. Then hit the Run button. I'm going to get us in the air."

[35]

It was after noon, the sun hot overhead, when Bale pulled open the nightclub door—pushing the body of the doorman along the floor—and stepped into the alleyway. The others followed, and Lilit was locking the door with a key she'd taken off the bartender's belt when Bale stopped her. He backhanded Therion's bicep. "Clean that up," he said, nodding toward the slick of blood running down the door from the wicket set in it. "We need some time to get out of here."

Nightclubs made excellent accommodations for the Clan. Besides the obvious—what Bale called "booze, broads, and bodies"—and the fact that they were typically well insulated to muffle loud noises— music, gunshots, screams—they were also nocturnal businesses; no one expected them to be open until late afternoon, giving the Clan time to sleep in and make a leisurely exit. It was only good luck that no one had yet reported the blood on the door. Either no one had seen it, or they'd figured it was part of the décor. No need to keep tempting fate.

He hit the big man again and said, "There's a bucket and rag behind the bar."

Therion sighed and went back into the club.

Stretching his back and limbs, Bale looked down the alley in both directions. One way, warehouses, the Black Sea beyond, cargo cranes pivoting and dipping in the harbor; the other way, shops, restaurants, people.

"I'm hungry," he said, looking around at his group. Lilit and Hester were leaning against each other, whispering; Artimus and Cillian were holding up the wall on the other side of the alley. Everyone was still tired, hungover, despite the copious amounts of alcohol needed for any one of them to get drunk. "Who's with me?"

They all nodded, unenthusiastic.

Therion came out and started scrubbing. Bale told him, "Find us that way when you're done. Make sure you lock it." Lilit gave him the keys.

Forty minutes later they were all leaning back in metal patio chairs around a table on the sidewalk. The café they'd chosen was a few blocks east of the nightclub, where the harbor pushed farther inland and there was no warehouse to block their view of the water. Therion was pushing another *banitsa* into his mouth—his seventh or eighth by Bale's count. Just one of the croissant-like pastries had filled *his* stomach. The women had ordered *tarator*, a cold yogurt and cucumber soup, which caused Artimus to make gagging sounds. How the man could have seen all the things the world offered and be as cool in a firefight as he was, yet still be so childish, Bale would never know.

Lilit, Hester, and Cillian were now sipping *airian*, a mix of yogurt and water—Bulgarians loved their curds—while Bale finished his coffee.

"So," Cillian said. "Stockholm?"

Bale stood. "Let's do it." He walked across a wide plaza to a concrete wall and looked out at the ships coming into and leaving the harbor. He wondered what the spirits did around boats. Did they fly overhead, ride along on the decks, swim in the water around them, the way some had stayed close to the helicopter last night? He reached into his coat pocket and touched the Stone. Light flashed in his eyes, and he saw the glorious creatures in their myriad forms doing a bit of all of it—flying, swimming, standing on decks and cabin roofs—as well as a few things he hadn't considered. Some spidery fellows—long, spindly legs, but a beautiful shade of white, like mother-of-pearl, and the most fascinating, charming faces—were clinging to the hulls as the ships moved through the water; a few more human-shaped things were actually walking on the water, jumping playfully over wakes. One was skipping over the surface like a rock, heading directly for Bale. The thing leaped up, landed on the top of the wall, not three feet from Bale, and started laughing. Bale laughed back.

It had huge round eyes, a beak-like nose, and canine fangs, but still it was adorable. It was *different*, no denying it, but so were otters and cats and polar bears—each lovely in its own way. Bale wondered how these beings could be so feared, why they were so often depicted as hideous by artists. Michelangelo, Hieronymus Bosch, and their ilk—ignoramuses who painted what they thought demons should look like, thinking, Bale was sure, *Why, these evil beasts must certainly be physically as despicable as their wicked intentions.* Or, if they'd had special insight of the spiritual realm, as many people—including Bale—thought they must because of their extraordinary talent and creativity, and because their artwork resonated as only truth does—if they did know better but painted lies, they must have done so thinking, *I will paint them ugly and gross, so my brethren are not tempted to give in to their schemes. Never mind truth, never mind how wonderfully glorious demons really are!*

Bale wished he could go back in time—or had known the truth sooner. He'd have sought out each one of these so-called masters and slapped them silly. *Paint the truth!* he'd tell them. *Beautiful demons, enticing and gorgeous—the way you depict the angels!*

But Bale had to admit, angels were stunning as well. They were out there too, standing on decks, moving through the sky, hanging around those blue beams streaking into the sky from a half dozen ships—as brilliant and visible in the sunlight as they had been at night. Yes, the angels—with their fiery sparks and glowing bodies—were nearly as beautiful as the demons. But their attitudes! They barely gave Bale a second glance, and when they did it was to glare at him—with contempt, Bale thought, and wariness, as villagers might look across a river at a tiger that had been eating their children.

The thought made Bale smile. Apparently he had been achieving his goal of harming God all along. He thought he had been, but there had never been proof outside the grief he could witness in the tears of the people he'd corrupted, the families of those he'd killed. Now he could also see it in the eyes of the angels, the ones closest to God, who knew Him best and reflected His will. He'd gotten to them, so he'd gotten to God.

If the Stone did nothing else for him, letting him see the contempt in the angels' eyes was enough. But that's not all it would do. It hadn't taken him long to figure out what those blue beams were—if not what they were, exactly, then what they signified, who they pointed out. And that was going to make his job so much easier.

That lovely creature was still poised on the wall before him, blinking at him, tilting its head curiously. Bale laughed again, loud and unrestrained. The creature snapped back, startled, then laughed with him.

He heard the others coming up behind him. He looked around over his shoulder at them, thinking he couldn't keep the Stone to himself for long. It was too wonderful not to share. The creatures were all around them, the ones from the helicopter, a few others. Once again they were fidgeting, agitated. The big one was pacing back and forth behind them. The little monkey creature hopped from Lilit's shoulder to Artimus's to Hester's. Another was wringing its hands, staring at Bale as though it expected him to toss him a scrap of meat.

He started to say, *Wait till you see the company we have*, but got only the first word out when the rest caught in his throat. Over the Clan's heads, over the roofs of the nearest buildings, a sapphire beam was piercing the clouds. He could see it continuing up high, high above them. It was *thick*, that's what got him. Thicker than any he'd seen so far. It shimmered and pulsed and seemed to extend forever. He had no doubt that if he were able see into space, there'd be that beam, shooting past planets and stars.

He pointed at it. "That's where we're going," he said.

The others looked, turning back to him with puzzled expressions. "Where?" Cillian said.

"Right there, over there, beyond the city." Bale felt like an explorer after the pot of gold at the end of the rainbow, but knowing it would not move away from him the closer he got to it. Knowing it would be there when he arrived.

"Bale," Hester said, "I don't see anything."

"You will," Bale said, removing the Stone from his pocket.

[36]

Bale stopped, the Stone in his hand. Someone had joined their party, an old man in raggedy clothes—his belt was a length of rope, for crying out loud. Bale turned to him. *"Kakvo?" What?*

The old man wrung a cloth cap in his hands. He smiled toothlessly, glancing at each of the Clan in turn, then fixed a soft expression on Bale. "Please, sir," he said in Bulgarian. "A few Euros?"

Bale stared. An angel accompanied the old man. It stood beside him, the sparks flying around the two. Protecting the old geezer, he thought, and wondered what would happen if he pulled out a gun and blasted the bum away. Could the angel actually prevent the bullets from tearing the old guy apart? A whole magazine of bullets? Would his gun jam? Would the man start dodging them, dancing away like a rapper, the angel moving him as if he were a puppet?

The man said, "My wife and I have not eaten in two days. All we have goes into our grandchildren's mouths, so little for them too."

Therion stepped forward, a creature nudging him from behind. "I'll take care of the little grandrats for you," he said. "Where are they?"

Lilit said, "We'll even bring you back some grandrat steaks. Eat like kings."

The man tried smiling at them, but it wouldn't hold.

"Get out of here, old man," Bale said with a dismissive wave of his hand. He looked into the angel's eyes. "You too."

"Just a few Euros, kind sir." Persistent bugger.

"Go!" Bale took a step toward him. The man backed up, turned, and walked away, glancing back every few steps. The angel walked beside him, a hand on his shoulder.

Bale watched them for a few moments longer, then looked over the roofs. The beam was still there. Given what he knew about it, it could disappear at any moment. He pointed, said, "It's still there, but we have to hurry. If I show you this, let you experience it—" He held the Stone up in his palm. He eyed the demons milling around the Clan. "Don't get caught up in what you see. There'll be plenty of time for—"

"Sir?" The old man and his creepy angel were back, not five feet from Bale.

You've got to be kidding me.

"Ne!" Bale said. *No!* "You can't possibly be this stupid."

Therion moved in, arms extended. "Over the wall with you, Pops. Hope you can swim."

In a flash, the angel moved around the man to insert itself between him and Therion. Its sparks became wings, which folded backward, encasing the man. Bale watched, fascinated. As Therion approached, the angel held up its hand in a stop gesture, pressing it against Therion's forehead. At the same time, one of the wings broke apart, flew forward, and became a long narrow blade. The point of the blade pressed against the neck of the big demon who'd been walking beside Therion. It stopped, but Therion kept walking, noticeably slower. For a moment the angel's hand went *into* Therion's head, and Therion appeared to be walking through the angel. Then the angel shifted and was standing now beside Therion, right at the old man's shoulder.

Instead of seizing the guy and tossing him over the wall, Therion merely gripped the man's shoulder and shook it. "Look at this guy," he said. "Ninety pounds of nothing. Not worth my time." He waved his hand dismissively and walked back to the group.

"I got something for you," Bale said, stepping toward him. He held out the Stone, moving it toward the old man's face.

The angel swung around, its sparks shooting toward Bale's hand, passing through it. Bale felt his fingers go weak, the weight of the Stone pressing against them, tilting out. He gripped tighter and touched the point of the Stone to the man's cheek.

The old man's eyes opened wide, darted around. Bale knew he was taking in the creatures. As beautiful as they were, their sudden appearance had to be startling. But the beggar's reaction was several levels above what Bale had expected. The man shrieked and shielded his face with his hands. He stumbled back, tripped and fell, scrambled backward twenty feet, glaring and screaming. *"Ne! Ne! Ne! Martas!"*

Bale looked at the creatures. How could anyone call them monsters?

With the angel's assistance—the man hardly noticed it, just glanced at it once before looking back at the creatures—he turned onto his hands and knees, crawled a ways, got his feet under him, and ran. His arms alternately waved over his head and shot behind him, as if warding off any pursuing demons.

But none of the creatures followed him. They remained with the Clan, grinning, wiggling their bodies, looking at each other in obvious mirth.

The angel flew beside the man, touching him, stroking his head with one sparkle-wing, apparently talking to him. The old man ran up a side street and disappeared behind a building, only his screams coming back to Bale's ears.

Bale turned to the Clan. They were all too stunned to smile or laugh. Bale wished he had let them touch the Stone before giving the beggar a dose. "Trust me," he said. "That was funny."

"Was it the rock?" Hester asked.

Cillian said, "Did it drive him crazy?"

"Only for a time," Bale said. "I think." He had a feeling that if the old guy's own constitution couldn't do it, the angel would help him find his sanity again. "But don't fear it." He held the Stone out to them. "It will open your eyes."

One by one they stepped up to touch it, each reeling away, stammering about the things they saw. Bale felt like a priest, administering Holy Communion to his children for the first time.

[37]

Toby watched the helicopter come into the valley. He was standing in the mouth of the cave in which St. Onuphrius had lived as a hermit for seventy years during the fourth and fifth centuries. It was said that Onuphrius was the prototypical hermit-monk, becoming a wild man in the desert—long, shaggy hair, and wearing only a loin cloth made of leaves. To the few people who stumbled upon him, he described visions of angels "like all the stars of heaven coming together to form a single celestial being." Toby wondered whether it was true or the crazy old coot had been off his rocker. One visitor told of angels delivering bread and water to the cave every morning when he awoke.

Hiking here from the clearing above the monastery, Toby had wished that one was true and that the angels were still providing room service. He'd gone through his supply of meal bars, candy, and trail mix. He was famished and down to his last few sips of water.

The valley spread out before him—called Wadi el Arbain—was three miles south of St. C's, Mount Sinai between them. It was an oasis of olive groves and cypress trees, watered by a natural spring from which Toby refused to drink. He'd heard Montezuma's revenge was nothing compared to Onuphrius's, and a mission was no time for *that* problem.

He emerged from the cave and headed down a slope toward the disused Monastery of the Forty Martyrs. The small grouping of stone structures was built in the sixth century to honor forty Christian soldiers of the Roman army who were put to death in Sebaste—in modern-day Turkey—for not disavowing Jesus Christ as their Lord. Everywhere you looked, it seemed to Toby, people were dying for God—and here they were, the Tribe, *wanting* to die but not being allowed to.

Though abandoned four hundred years ago, the buildings still provided shelter and were a lot more comfortable than a cave. In fact, monks from St. C's occasionally stayed there. It was a shame the place was too far from the monastery for Toby to sleep in and still do his job.

The helicopter's downdraft whipped the trees around, sending leaves into the air like confetti. It set down on a flat spot near the buildings, and Nevaeh was out before its blades started to slow. Ducking, holding the crown of her head while her hair snapped round her face, she strode toward Toby.

"What's the word?" she said from thirty feet away. "Is Beth still there?"

"She was when I left. But Jagger's gone."

"Where? When?" They reached each other, and she leaned in to give him a quick hug—part of the role she'd taken on eons ago as foster mother of the younger Tribe members. Toby liked it as often as he hated it, so he never complained.

"This morning, right before I left to come here. Owen was with him."

"Owen?" Nevaeh said, thinking. "Those two have become quite the buds. Any idea where they went?"

"Took off in Owen's copter. He came in around seven, left with Jagger tenish. I'm thinking they went after whoever attacked them."

"What makes you think that?"

Toby shrugged. "A hunch. That's what they do."

"Vengeance?" She smiled.

"Maybe. I heard some chatter on the satphone's radio band before it went out. Three monks were killed last night."

"Those hypocrites," Nevaeh said. "They give us grief for doing what we do, and they're doing the same thing."

"Unless whatever the attackers were after they got, and Jagger and Owen want it back."

"That's more like them," she conceded. "But it's more satisfying to think they're starting to see things our way."

"Again," Toby reminded her.

"Again." She looked over her shoulder at the others unloading packs and duffel bags and cases from the copter. She turned back. "I was expecting to face Jagger," she said. "Total overkill now, the personnel and equipment we brought just to grab the woman."

"The monks will be protecting her," Toby said, and when Nevaeh rolled her eyes, added, "Last night they had shotguns and rocket launchers."

She nodded. These were no ordinary monks. "Any word about what the attack team was after?"

"Nothing. I was on the Southwest Range Building roof last night when Jagger placed a call. I think he was talking to Owen, but I couldn't get close enough to hear anything." He stuck out a foot, showing her an Austin boot. "Sometimes these things beep or squeak at the worst possible times."

She looked at it, running her gaze along the leg brackets and hip clamps. "Otherwise, no problems with them?" This was the technology's first use on an actual mission.

"Battery seems to be draining faster than we expected. I used them to get here but turn them off whenever I can." He lifted his shirt and tipped the belt toward her, showing her the unlighted LED.

"We'll put ours on when we're closer," she said. "I want to have a full charge going in. Don't want to risk damaging them either . . . or being seen bouncing around like Neil Armstrong."

She gave him a look, and he said, "I've been careful. Besides, the tourist traffic is down by half, if not more. The monastery's closed, and the check-point guards on the Valley of Gazelles road to St. C's are discouraging travel here."

"But Beth is still there, you're sure?"

"Saw her this morning, after Jagger left. She and her boy wandered around in the gardens, then it looked like Gheronda called them inside the compound. The monks were locking down."

"No extra security?"

"Egyptian cops this morning. They left before Jagger did. Didn't seem too interested. You know how they are about the monastery."

She smiled at him, patted his arm. "Good job." She turned and headed back to the copter.

"Hey," he said. "Did you bring food?"

She tossed an energy bar over her shoulder to him. "There's more where that came from," she called without looking. Then she clapped her hands and yelled at the others, "Move it, guys! Let's get this show on the road!"

[38]

Beth had looked for Tyler in all his favorite spots: the burning bush, the tunnel that ran diagonally under half the compound—formed by storerooms, monk cells, and chapels built helter-skelter around and above it—a cave-like recess in the east wall, said to have once been lived in by a monk who'd claimed the spartan cells were too luxurious. Now she stood in the court between the basilica and mosque, squinting up at the top bell tower, five stories high, calling his name. He knew not to go there, but he'd left the apartment in a funk, and she thought maybe his need to get away by himself would override the prohibition.

Father Leo stepped up beside her, peering up. "Want me to go up and check?" he asked.

She shook her head. "He'd answer if he heard me."

He nodded toward a bowl she held. "Lunch?"

She looked down at the *um aly*—raisin cake soaked in milk. Its edges bore evidence of her nibbling at it as she'd looked for her son. "A snack," she said. "Tyler loves it. More upstairs if you'd like . . ."

"Thank you, but I'm not very hungry today." He scanned the tops of the buildings south of them. Beyond them the Southwest Range Building loomed, and behind it, Mount Sinai. "Have you checked the terraces?"

"Not yet," she said. "I thought maybe the library, but I guess not." Leo was the monastery's librarian, and it was a rare occasion when it was open without him. He was also something like Gheronda's right-hand man, running interference on problems heading the old man's way, passing orders to the other monks on his behalf. Beth wasn't sure what his official role in the order was, but he seemed efficient and had always been pleasant to her family. He was young, about thirty, same age as Beth and Jagger—well, the age Jagger appeared and pretended to be. Leo's baby face and wispy, best-I-can-do beard made him look younger, but his confidence and cool affability pulled impressions the other direction, so she figured thirty was a good guess.

She was about to say, *Do you mind my asking* . . . when he waved his finger toward the roofs and said, "Why don't you head up there from the west? I'll come around from the north. Between the two of us, I'm sure we'll find him."

She agreed and carried the *um aly* up the steps leading to the first level of rooftop terraces. She remembered finding Tyler several times on the bench in front of Father Jerome's cell and ascended another flight to the topmost jumble of roofs. Crossing a bridge, she stepped onto a flat, gravelly rooftop. A flue rose six feet high from its center, and terra-cotta roof tiles lined the edge, token reminders that it was a roof first, a makeshift terrace second. A rickety chair leaned empty against a whitewashed half wall along the edge closest to the Southwest Range Building. *Southwest Range Building*—what a blah name for such a pretty building. It was a shame someone hadn't thought up something more picturesque. Tyler called it the Colosseum because of its levels of columned arches and its imposing presence over the rest of the compound. She should start doing that too, get Jagger to join in; maybe it would catch on.

She reached the next roof-terrace, two feet lower, no steps to it. She hopped down, now on a four-foot strip of roof between Jerome's cell and a drop-off to the roof a floor below. How could she let Tyler scramble around this dangerous place? He was a ten-year-old boy, that's how, agile and curious. He'd told her he'd reached places that made the hair on the back of her neck stand up: on top of the Southwest . . . the Colosseum and a little wooden deck fifty feet up on the outside of the wall overlooking the archaeological dig. Accessed through a small door and tunnel through the wall, the deck had once been used for meditation. Now it looked rotten and ready to fall. She'd made these places—as well as the bell tower and the machicolation box, which at one time was the monastery's only entrance and now clung like the world's most poorly located outhouse to the wall forty feet over the current gate—off limits to him. The rest was fair game, and he'd never been hurt outside the sort of cuts and bruises any active boy would get doing almost anything.

She rounded Jerome's cell and saw that the bench in front of it was empty. She started toward the next roof and stopped. She'd heard someone whisper her name. She looked beyond the bench into a shadowy corner, and there was Leo, crouched in front of her son. Somehow the monk had arrived here first, despite having to cross at least twice the distance.

Tyler was sitting on the ground, legs pulled up in front of him.

She walked up to him and stopped beside Leo. She held the bowl out to Tyler. *"Um aly?"*

Without looking, he shook his head. He sniffed and ran the back of his hand under his nose.

She sat cross-legged next to him, facing him, and gave him a sad look. Leo stood and wandered away, disappearing around a corner.

"Are those tears for the monks?" Beth asked.

Tyler touched a drop on his chin. "This one's for Father Luca." He pointed to a spot on his T-shirt that a tear had darkened. "That was for Father Bardas . . . and this one for Father Corban." He rubbed the wetness under his eye. "These are for Dad."

She put her hand on his knee. "Dad loves us very much. He's doing everything he can to get home fast."

"Why'd he have to go?"

"Owen needs his help."

"You mean John."

"He goes by Owen now."

He nodded and looked at her. "What about Dad? He's not really Jagger?"

"I think he's had many names. But you know what, Jagger is the only one he remembers, so let's not ask him about it. Besides, no matter his name, he's still Dad. He's still the good man I married."

"A rose by any other name smells just as sweet."

"You remembered," she said. They'd covered *Romeo and Juliet* a few months ago as part of their homeschooling program.

Tyler smiled. "Can I change my name?"

"I like Tyler."

He thought about it, nodded. "So do I." He looked into her eyes and asked, "When will Dad be home?"

She knew he wanted more than a time; he wanted assurance that Jagger *would* come home.

"Soon, I—" She almost said *promise*, but she stopped herself. "I think. But he *will* come home. Look at him, he's a superhero."

"He can't die, right?" Tyler said.

"He's stronger than other people."

"And he can't die. You said he was immortal. That means he can't die."

"I meant he doesn't age. He can die, but it would take a lot to kill him."

"Like what?"

She wasn't going to use the word *decapitation*. "Just . . . a lot more than it would take to kill someone else."

Tyler wasn't satisfied, but she could tell he realized that was the best he was going to get. He said, "He hasn't died yet. Three thousand, five hundred years."

"Right," she said. "He's too stubborn to die, and he loves us too much." It constantly amazed her, the dynamic between parent and child. It wasn't merely about the older nurturing, protecting, and teaching the younger. It went both ways: from Tyler she remembered her youthful wonderment of the world, and in remembering, regained it. By instilling hope in him, she felt it herself.

Leo appeared again and crouched in front of Tyler, his cassock piling up on the gravel as though he were melting. "What's that you have there?" He pointed at an item Tyler was turning over and over in his fingers.

Tyler showed him: a spent bullet cartridge.

Leo nodded, frowning. He said, "The other monks are preparing a memorial service in the basilica. We need someone to put charcoal in the thuribles. Could you do that for us?"

Tyler cocked an eye at him. "Thurible?"

Leo grinned. "It sounds like the way Elmer Fudd would say *terrible*, doesn't it? 'That cwazy wabbit is thurible!'"

Tyler laughed, and it warmed Beth's heart.

"Actually," Leo went on, "they're those round metal balls the monks walk around with, swinging at the end of a chain."

"They smoke and smell like flowers," Tyler said.

"That's them. Well, they smoke because there's charcoal inside, and incense on top of the charcoal. Dried rose petals, stuff like that. Could you fill them for us?"

"Swing them around too?"

Leo made a face. "Not that, I'm afraid. It takes practice to keep from hitting people with them. That's why they won't let me do it. I knocked out three monks last time I tried." He winked.

Tyler laughed again.

"Whaddaya say?" He stood and extended a hand to Tyler.

Tyler took it and stood. Beth slapped at his rump, brushing off the gravel. Leo helped her up and said, "We can find things for you to do too."

She nodded. "Yeah, I'd like that." Thankful for the opportunity to turn her mind away from grief and worry. "Sound good, Ty?" But he was already running ahead toward the stairs.

[39]

They'd been in the air two and a half hours, flying over the Black Sea now. Owen had set the autopilot and watched Jagger at the computer researching Bronson Radcliff for twenty minutes before heading back to the bathroom. Jagger knew more than he ever wanted to about the billionaire head of Ice Temple Enterprises: he'd had four wives, each one younger than the last; he'd made his first few million developing what only the most naïve or forgiving person would call what it called itself: "an online dating service." An online brothel was closer to the truth, as far as Jagger could tell. The man had parlayed that into a fortune through investments in real estate, oil derivatives, and biotech companies. Most disturbing: he'd been accused of child molestation, rape, and kidnapping, using his household staff to procure young girls for him. The news agencies that reported the allegations had followed up with news of the prosecutor's case falling apart as one by one the witnesses recanted their statements and moved away—more than a few into nice new homes in tropical locales. The man had bought his way out of jail in plain view of everyone, and there was nothing anyone could do about it.

Where were the Tribe when you needed them?

This wasn't a guy who funded archaeological digs for altruistic or religious reasons. Either he suspected that relics held power, power that he could use to advance or mask his hedonistic lifestyle, or he thought they could be used to expand his empire. Or he was merely a front for someone else. Jagger's money was on that one.

He was mapping the quickest routes from the Stockholm-Bromma Airport to Ice Temple's headquarters in Stureplan, the city's financial district, and to Radcliff's private residence in the affluent suburb of

Östermalm, when an alarm sounded. He jumped and looked toward the cockpit, expecting smoke or a view of the ocean as the jet plunged toward it.

Owen came hustling out of the bathroom, zipping his fly and adding to Jagger's anxiety. "What is it?" Owen asked.

"You're asking me?" But then he realized the blaring tones came from the computer under the desk, and the second screen was flashing a red banner with the words *Match Found*. "I think your scanner found a match."

Owen sat beside him. "It only sounds an alarm when more than sixty percent of the search terms match. Otherwise it only beeps."

"It's beeped a few times since we left Sharm."

Owen nodded. "I ignore those, or I'd be running back here every ten minutes. This is something, though." He slid the keyboard in front of him and began typing. The alarm stopped, and the banner was replaced by lines of text, most in a language Jagger didn't understand.

Owen said, "Varna, Bulgaria." He turned toward Jagger's screen, clicking keys, and the map of Stockholm disappeared. A different map appeared, showing an icon of a plane over a field of blue. Owen zoomed out until land appeared on the left. "We'd have passed it in twenty minutes."

"Passed what? What's the match?"

Owen's gaze went back to the other screen. "Homicide. Multiple suspects, one with black makeup or a tattoo streaked over his eyes. Did you add that to the keyword list?"

"Yeah, I just thought—"

"Good job." He laughed. "I see some others you added."

"Which ones?"

"Somebody encountered the suspects at the harbor. They think he's unreliable, though. He was rambling about seeing demons." Owen kept reading.

"Why would someone other than the Clan see demons?" Jagger said. "I thought—?"

"Here," Owen interrupted. "A couple, tourists, called the cops.

They saw the man—he was panhandling, had approached them first, then he went to a group of people. 'Creepy bunch' is the term they used. Two or three women, three or four men. One of them looked like a wrestler and had black eye makeup. One of the men—dark hair, black clothes, a fedora—"

"Bale had on a fedora last night."

"It looked like this guy punched the beggar, and that's when the beggar went crazy. That's what the witnesses said—'went crazy.' He started running, screaming. They thought the guy injected him with something, that's why they called the police." He continued scanning the screen, scrolling it down. "The cops started searching for this group and found a nightclub door with what looked like blood on it. Someone had apparently done a shoddy job cleaning it up. Inside they found a massacre."

"Massacre?"

"Twelve bodies."

Jagger felt sick, and a bit of the doubt he had about traipsing off with Owen fell away.

Owen scrolled back to the top, said, "This is a transcript of police communications. The scanner began monitoring it fifteen minutes ago. It reached enough matches to set off the alarm six minutes ago." He stood and brushed past him, heading for the cockpit. "We can be at the crime scene in forty, fifty minutes."

"We're going there?"

"The Clan was there less than an hour ago."

"What if it's not them?"

Owen turned to give a look that said, *you're kidding, right?* "Massacre. Eye makeup. Fedora. *Demons.*"

"I'm just saying if it's not, we'll miss them in Stockholm."

"I'm willing to risk it," Owen said, ducking into the cockpit.

Jagger called, "They're obviously not there anymore, not at the crime scene. Shouldn't we stake out the airport?"

"Now you're thinking," Owen said. "But if we don't see their plane, it doesn't mean they're not there. They usually rent private hangar space, keep it locked up. Besides, Varna has . . ." He paused and through the cockpit door Jagger saw him pick up the iPad from the copilot seat. Fifteen seconds later he said, "Varna has two airports and at least another half dozen nearby. I think our best bet is to go to where we know they are . . . or were recently."

Jagger watched the little plane on the monitor. It stayed in the center, aimed northwest now, as a mass of land slid in from the left edge of the screen toward it. A label for Varna appeared over a large city situated at the apex of a natural harbor. A series of canals linked the Black Sea to a lake. Varna appeared nestled in the crook where they all converged.

"Come up here, would you, please?" Owen said. When Jagger got to the cockpit, Owen said, "You have the Stone, the fragment Ollie gave you?"

"Yeah, it's in my pocket. Why?"

"I want you to have a look." He nodded toward the city through the windshield.

"You want me to touch the fragment?"

"See what you can see—in the spiritual realm."

"But it lets you see angels and demons, blue beams of light—from pray-ers, I think. How will it help us find the Clan?"

Owen rolled his head, threw a smile at Jagger. "I don't know. Neither do you. If it can show us something, now's the time to try."

Jagger let out a heavy breath, not sure he wanted to peel back the veil, afraid—*okay, yes, afraid*—of what he might see. But he pulled the cloth from his pants pocket and sat in the copilot seat. Holding the cloth in his real hand, he lifted the layers off with his hook. Then he touched the hook to the Stone, just a tap. When nothing happened he clamped it with the twin hooks and put the cloth on the wide armrest next to him. He stood and leaned close to the windshield and touched the Stone.

After a blinding flash, the first things he saw were angels. They were flying with the jet, in front of it, on the sides. Their embers like wings, but not flapping; they were splayed out from the angels' shoulder blades back past their heels. They reminded Jagger of jet engines spewing out flames, and he almost laughed.

"What do you see?" Owen said.

"Angels. Five of them are with us, flying outside the plane."

"Ha ha!" Owen said, delighted. "What else?"

Jagger looked past the angels to the approaching city. "More angels," he said. "And demons. They're flying all around the city, over it. Hundreds of them, if not thousands. Blue lights everywhere, coming out of rooftops, ships, looks like a couple parks." Most of the beams were thread-thin, a few were a bit thicker. One appeared to be a lot more substantial, a rope to the others' threads. As they drew closer, he saw it was coming out of a steeply pitched roof from which rose a steeple.

Good for you, he thought.

"Nothing that indicates where the Clan is," he said. Despite his objections to Owen, he'd half expected something to flag the Clan for them: a gathering of angels or demons—if there was a concentration of either down there, he couldn't detect it; a red instead of blue light, maybe, or darkness, shadows where there shouldn't be any. Why wouldn't such concentrated evil be reflected in the spiritual world?

"Wait a minute," he said. Away from the city, on the other side of the big river, a blue beam thick as two or three entwined ropes shot into the sky—or down from it, he still wasn't sure. Not the Clan, surely, but if the blue light signified what he thought it did . . . "There's some heavy spiritual activity over there." Pointing at it. "Something *good*. It's not in the city. Looks kind of far away, a small town or village. Owen, you hear me?"

He turned to see Owen and screamed. Owen was praying, his lips moving silently. From not just his head, but his shoulders and chest as well, flowed the brightest beam he'd seen yet—the far-off cord of light coming from the village, factoring in the distance, was possibly thicker and brighter, but not by much. Standing behind him, in a space too small to accommodate him, was an angel. His head was bowed and his hands rested on Owen's shoulders. The embers flowed lightning fast around the angel and Owen, staying a few inches from their bodies. They swirled around Owen's torso, down and up his legs, over his arms, reminding Jagger of documentaries that showed the circulatory system, the constant flow of blood through the body. The overall effect was that the two of them were glowing and sparking, and more: that the two were one, connected through prayer, joined by the angel's glowing cocoon.

Owen's eyes snapped open. "What? I only closed my eyes for a few seconds. I got it covered, Jag. Right on course."

The beam faded and disappeared. The angel raised his head, smiling down on Owen. The embers streamed off of Owen and gathered behind the angel, who seemed to step back through the plane. Before vanishing into the air beyond the cockpit's wall, he smiled at Jagger.

"Jag?"

Jagger could only stare at the spot where the angel had been. Finally he told Owen what he'd seen.

Owen said, "Good to know"—a little simply for Jagger's taste, given how extraordinary the sight had been. But then, maybe it wasn't so extraordinary. The vision of it, yes, but not the fact of it. Not to Owen. "Do you *feel* it?" Jagger asked.

"I always feel God's presence, but never so much as when I pray." He nodded toward the city. "Nothing?"

Jagger turned back to the windshield. "Oh, I wouldn't say nothing. A lot. But nothing that gives away the Clan's location."

"Then we'll do it the hard way." He grinned at Jagger's puzzled expression. "Footwork," he said. "We get to play detective."

[40]

The Tribe sat in the clearing behind the outcropping Toby used to surveil the monastery, putting on their Austin boots. They faced each other in a circle, each with an open black suitcase beside him or her. The pieces of the Future Warrior System exoskeleton fit into recesses molded into the suitcases' polyurethane interiors: the hip clamps, battery, belt, wiring, leg braces, knee joints, and the boots themselves.

It was late afternoon, the sun heading for a false dusk behind a range of mountains. But it was still light out, the sky above them the color of denim. An empty candy bar wrapper tumbled on a soft breeze into Nevaeh's leg. She picked it up, saw more spilling out of the little cave Toby had been living in, and held it up to him, one eyebrow raised.

He smiled, shrugged.

"I can't wait," Jordan said, pulling a boot over a red water bootie on his foot.

"For what?" Toby said, leaning against a cliff wall. He hadn't taken his boots off since arriving on the mountain. "You're just the lookout."

"But Nevaeh said—"

She held up her hand to stop him. "Toby, I need you to take his place in that role today."

"What?" he said, pushing off the wall. "I've been here four days. You *said* I could go in."

"I know, but I think Jordan can help with Tyler."

"The kid? I thought you were just going to knock him out and take his mom."

"Do you know where he is now? Is he with Beth?"

"Now? I don't know. I've been with you."

Nevaeh nodded. "He explores the monastery a lot, right? On his own?"

"Yeah."

"If we can't get to Beth right away, we may need him to draw her out. If he's on his own, wandering, he's more likely to trust another kid about his age than one of us, than you."

"Any kid down there after closing's going to be suspicious."

"Jordan less so. If a monk approaches him, he got separated from his parents."

"I can be separated from my parents." Toby bent his knees, jumped, and landed on a rock five feet high.

"Look," Nevaeh said, "I'll make it up to you. But every mission needs to be evaluated to determine which resources are best to ensure success."

"You sound like Ben."

"I'm trying to fill his shoes. You know that."

"This is garbage," Toby said, jumping off the rock. "Don't you think, Phin? You're going to inject the kid and be done with him, right?"

Phin clamped a lower leg brace into a boot. He said, "If he's where I can get him. If not"—he shrugged—"Jordan's the man for the job."

"Ah!" Toby said, and spat on the ground. "Elias?"

Elias squinted up at him through smoke drifting off the end of his cigarette. "Next time, kid." He had finished getting on the Austin boots and now sat there with a duffel bag resting on his lap. He drew on the cig, plucked it out of his mouth to blow out a stream of smoke, and returned it to his lips. He unzipped the duffel and began fishing out machined-metal parts: a long barrel with a flanged and ported end, a trigger assembly, tubing . . .

"You brought *Betsy*?" Nevaeh said. His favorite flamethrower.

Elias didn't say anything, just continued pulling out pieces: a valve, a flat plastic backpack with straps.

"We're in and out, you know?" Nevaeh said. She should have known he'd bring it; he'd bring it grocery shopping if he could.

"I think Elias is going to hell," Phin said, tossing a balled-up sock at him. "That's why he likes fire so much."

Elias swatted away the sock and glared. "Not funny, Phin." He struggled to free something big, and Nevaeh realized it was a tank—two tanks. One contained propane, the other homemade napalm—gasoline and a polymeric thickening agent. Ash from the cigarette fell on a tank. It was no good mentioning the health hazards of assembling a flamethrower while smoking. He'd been doing it for decades and hadn't blown up. Yet.

Nevaeh stood, flexing her legs, watching the way the braces moved with her. She picked up a long case made of soft black material and started unzipping it. "Come here, Toby. I have a present for you." She handed him a black rifle.

"No!" he said, grinning now. "It's a Barrett M82"—looking puzzled—"isn't it?"

"Barrett XM500," she said. "Prototype. Same as the M82 but with a bullpup design."

The M82 was a .50-cal sniper rifle; the "bullpup" meant its firing and cartridge-ejection action was behind the trigger mechanism, essentially in the stock, making it forty-seven inches long instead of the M82's fifty-nine inches. It was lighter, more accurate, and easier to handle than the standard M82.

Toby ran his fingers over it, caressing it. He pulled one of the spare bullets from an elastic holder around the stock, examined it, and put it back.

Nevaeh tapped a contraption mounted over the barrel. "Day/night optics," she said.

Toby raised it to his shoulder, sighted along the barrel. "Oh yeah." He effected a passable imitation of Dirty Harry and said, "This thing can take your head *cleeeeeeean* off."

"Just in case things go wrong," she said, raising an eyebrow. "Only just in case."

When they all had their Austin boots on—bending their knees, striding around the clearing, getting used to them—Nevaeh produced two syringes, their needles covered with plastic caps. Amber liquid in both. "Chloral hydrate," she said. "Fast-acting knockout drug." She checked them both and handed one to Phin, saying, "Fifteen cc's for the boy. I have 20 cc's for Beth." She slipped it into a breast pocket. "Phin, forget your history with the kid."

Toby laughed. "You let him take the microchip, couldn't catch him, then got your face blown off."

"It was Jagger who shot me," Phin said, glaring at Toby.

"Phin," Nevaeh said, waving her hand to get his attention. "Let it go. Just inject him and leave him alone. No extra punches or kicks. And don't shoot him."

"What if it's an accident?"

"No accidents." She didn't like the way he didn't meet her eyes. "Phin, you hear me? We can put Toby on it."

"Yeah!" Toby said, holding the rifle at port arms. "You can't trust Phin. He's got it out for Tyler."

"I have it out for his father," Phin said, glaring again at Toby. To Nevaeh he said, "I hear you."

Nevaeh reached into a canvas sack and began handing out walkie-talkie-style radios.

Phin stared at his, as though she had spat in his palm. "What's this?" he asked. "Where are the earbuds, the throat mics?"

Handing one to Elias, she didn't look at Phin when she answered. "Incinerated, like most of our other gear. I'm working on getting them replaced. Until then . . ." She turned toward Phin, held the radio up to her mouth. "Click the red button to talk."

"I know how to use it," he grumbled.

"Okay, so," Nevaeh said. "Phin, Jordan, and I will go to the apartment. I'll get Beth; Phin, you take care of—" She decided to reword that. "You inject the boy. Jordan, you keep watch. We'll let you know if we need you."

Jordan, bouncing, going eight feet in the air, nodded.

"Elias, stay undercover unless something happens. Make sure the monks and anyone else who might be there stay out of our hair."

Elias was cinching the tanks to his back, making sure the gun-like barrel assembly was securely attached to it and readily accessible over his shoulder, the way Nevaeh stored her long-swords when she carried them.

"Toby, you said you found an easy entry point?"

"Follow me. I'll take you in."

"We need you here, watching. Just show me."

They stepped to the downhill breach in the rocks around the clearing, and he pointed to the far end of the Southwest Range Building. The ground was highest there, closest to the top of the wall.

Nevaeh nodded appreciatively. "That's right where the apartment building starts."

"Just watch that jump," Toby said. "It's a doozie. See that big boulder at the base of the wall? You want to hit it straight up and down, feet flat."

"Got it." She turned to the others. "Let's go."

[41]

Jagger and Owen weren't able to get close to the nightclub entrance. Blue-and-white Opel Astra cruisers, light bars flashing blue and red, blocked it, and uniformed cops chased them away. Jagger saw a forensic team in white coveralls crouched around an open door halfway down the alley, men and women in plainclothes watching them. At the far end, more cops and cruisers blocked that way.

Now he and Owen stood on a plaza of flat-rock pavers between a row of shops and a concrete barrier, which lined the edge of the harbor. Several cops were gathered nearby, comparing notes. Another one spoke to people sitting at the outdoor tables of cafés or strolling past. He'd point in the direction of the nightclub, get a shake of the head, and move on to someone else.

"This is pointless," Jagger said, watching the demons and angels in the harbor, some on ships, others in or on the water, a few in the air. For the past fifteen minutes, they had both repeatedly touched the fragment in Jagger's pocket, hoping to spot a visual clue. "They're long gone."

Owen turned in a slow circle, gazing at everything. He scratched his beard. "I thought the Clan would leave something for us to follow."

"If we could get to the crime scene . . ."

"That's not going to happen."

Jagger was disappointed, not only in their futile attempt to locate the Clan, but also in Owen. He said, "I thought you had connections, people who could get us in there."

"I don't know everybody everywhere. I could probably find an angle in, maybe through the *Sledovateli*, the National Investigative Service, but it'll take time. And I'm wondering now what help it would be, getting into the nightclub."

Jagger watched the cop question a couple coming out of a bakery, then raised his attention to the sky. That brilliant blue beam was still there, sputtering now, growing dimmer and smaller. Hmmm. He looked over his shoulder at the harbor's angels and demons. They were more translucent than thirty seconds ago, but sputtering or disappearing. He turned back to the light. It was gone.

"Hey, hey." Owen reached back to tap him on the chest. "Look over there."

He nodded toward an old bum sitting against the wall near the corner of the strip of shops and cafés. The man's legs were bent up in front of him, and his forehead rested against his knees. His arms were wrapped around his legs, hands clasped in front. A blue thread of light came out of him, and two angels were crouched beside him, a hand from each resting on his head.

"The beggar," Owen said.

"The one who saw the Clan?"

"I'll bet he is." Owen started for him.

"Wait a minute," Jagger said, catching his arm. "What about the angels?"

"What about them? Just ignore them. Our business is with the old man."

Ignore them. Sure.

One angel turned his head to watch them approach. The beggar lifted his face toward them. His stubbly chin quivered. Owen knelt before him, spoke gently in Bulgarian, and placed a hand on the man's knee. They conversed, the man's voice trembly and growing louder.

Jagger was puzzled and reached into his pocket, past the folds of the cloth, to touch the fragment. The angels sprang into more solid form, like dialing up the brightness of a television monitor.

Jagger said, "Is he actually talking to you . . . or praying?"

Owen glanced up. "He's talking. Said he saw the Clan over there, about where we were standing. One of them—who looked like a model, he says—pressed a rock to his face and . . . well, you know."

"But the blue thread's still coming out of him, and both angels are with him. I thought it was a prayer thing." He pointed. "You too. I figured it was . . . I don't know, left over from your prayer in the plane, but now . . ."

"We don't know enough about what kind of vision the Stone imparts," Owen said. "But I do think you're right—the threads represent direct connectedness to God."

"You just said he's talking to *you*, not God."

Owen shifted to face Jagger more directly. "Do you know the difference between *continually* and *constantly*?"

Jagger scowled at him. "Continually is intermittent, with breaks in between. Constantly means never stopping."

"'Never ceasing' is the way Luke put it, and Paul wrote, 'pray constantly' in several of his letters. You don't think God would ask you to do something impossible, do you? Or expect you never to talk or eat or read? We can do both because God's doing it with us."

"I was never too good at rubbing my tummy and patting my head at the same time." It's something Tyler would say when he thought too much was being asked of him.

"It does take practice"—Owen looked at the old man—"or a big scare. I'll bet Beth prayed ceaselessly after Tyler got shot, even while talking to you and crying."

"If not all the time," Jagger said. Beth was an amazing woman. He couldn't remember—if he even noticed—if there was a thread flowing from her last night, when they'd seen the angel fighting the demon in their apartment, before she started praying.

Owen began speaking again to the beggar.

Jagger reached out to touch one of the angels. His fingers disappeared into its shoulder. As though he'd moved his hand into a shadow, he felt nothing.

Jagger yelled, "Look at me!"

And the angel did.

[42]

"You *can* hear me," Jagger said to the angel. "Help us, please. Where are the Clan? Help us stop them. Why won't you answer?"

"They're servants of God," Owen said, not turning from the old man. "Unlike humans, they're clear in their duties, unflagging in staying true to them. They aren't often distracted."

"I'm not trying to distract him. I just want him to help."

Listening to the beggar, nodding as the old man mumbled, Owen said, "I don't think our being able to see the spiritual world is going to change the way God does things."

"The angel can't even say hi—or 'get out of my face'?"

Owen finally looked up at him. "They're around us all the time, Jag. Since when have you heard an angel talk to you, with your physical ears?"

"But I can see them now. I'm looking right at him."

"*You* can see *him*. He's always been able to see you. The God Stone doesn't replace your need for faith. That you think it does may be a good reason why it's been buried for so long, and why we should get it back from the Clan."

Jagger made a face at the angel. "I don't understand why he can't just talk to us, give us a hint."

"If he has hints to give. He's a created being. He's not omniscient; he knows what he's seen and what God tells him. Even if he knew what we needed to catch up to the Clan, he's not going to tell us unless God instructs him to."

Round and round.

Jagger said, "So why doesn't God do that?"

"He is," Owen said, "in His own way."

"'His ways are higher than our ways,'" Jagger quoted. Sometimes it felt like a way of excusing God's capriciousness, His not doing everything He could to help, whatever the situation. Then again, He could snap His holy fingers and make evil go away, make all sadness and grief evaporate. Jagger had accepted that it didn't work that way in this fallen world. So why couldn't he accept that God was leading him now, despite Jagger's being able to glimpse a bit of the spiritual realm? Going back to what Beth had said, he guessed: he could see it, which made it more real to him—though his not seeing it didn't make it any less real, not really, not in truth. Being able to see it made him expect more . . . maybe not *more*, but something different. That was his fault, not God's. Still . . .

"It's frustrating," he said.

"It can be," Owen said, turning back to the old man, "with the wrong perspective."

Owen spoke, and the man jabbered back. He pointed toward where he'd seen the Clan, then drew a line in the air with his finger, stopping at the roofline above.

"What's he saying?" Jagger asked, thinking he knew.

"Bale was pointing into the sky, saying something about going there, out of the city."

Jagger leaned over and grabbed the man's hand, pulling him up. "Where, exactly?"

Owen raised his hand to stop him. "What are you doing?" he asked.

The man was tugging his arm away, trying to stay seated.

Jagger said, "Tell him to show us where they were pointing!" He realized he was going about it all wrong. He released the man and rubbed the old guy's bony shoulder. "Tell him I'm sorry."

Owen spoke to him, then helped him up. Together they walked into the courtyard and stopped before reaching the breaker wall. The beggar turned toward the shops and pointed over the roofs.

"That's where I saw the big blue beam," Jagger said. "Remember, I told you about it from the plane. Thicker and brighter than anything in the city, than anywhere."

"Is it still there?" Owen asked.

"It's gone. I saw it flickering before we went over to the old guy. I looked away, then it was gone."

Owen nodded. He dug into his pocket, pulled out a wad of cash, and handed it to the beggar. The man took it and bowed his head. His fingers flipped through it, and he held it back to Owen. *"Ne. Kolko struva tova."*

Owen pushed his hand away. *"Ne se trevoji."*

The man smiled and nodded. *"Mnogo blagodaria!"*

"Ti si dobre doshal," Owen said, and watched the man shuffle off. "How much was that?"

Owen said, "He'll be able to feed his family for a couple months. I wish it were more." He flipped open the flap on the satchel he wore over his shoulder and pulled out his iPad. He started walking toward a café, saying, "You know the direction of the big beam you saw, southwest. You saw it from the air. Think you can pinpoint it on the map? I can call up a satellite photo and get it to display almost the same altitude and perspective as when you saw it from the plane."

"Maybe," Jagger said. "I described the location to you; it was past some other villages, in the woods."

Owen sat at a table under an umbrella with beer logos, none of which Jagger recognized. Jagger scooted his chair around to be closer and sat. While Owen tapped and slid his finger around the screen, Jagger asked, "You think that's where they went?"

"The old man seemed to think so. It also aligns with what I believe they're using the God Stone for, at least until other opportunities present themselves. I pray I'm wrong, but I don't think so."

"What—?" Jagger started, before a waiter stepped up to the table, pulling a notepad from his apron. The guy needed a shave, a change of clothes, and a new attitude; Jagger thought he should have been moving cargo containers to and from the ships rather than serving appetizers to tourists.

Owen ordered two coffees, and the waiter grumbled something at him.

Owen told him, *"Niama nikakav problem."* He went back to the screen, saying, "They serve only what we would call espresso, in shots. I told him that was fine."

Jagger scooted closer. "What is it you think they're using the Stone to do?"

Owen handed him the tablet computer. "See if you can find it, the place where you saw the lights." Jagger took it and waited. Owen sighed. "I'm not superstitious, but sometimes saying something out loud makes it seem more real than just thinking it." He closed his eyes. "They want to grieve God."

"Right."

"I believe they're using it to identify the people who are the closest to Him."

"Closest?"

"The ones most connected to God. Spiritual warriors, or those who have the most spiritual purity."

"To do what?"

Owen opened his eyes, pinning Jagger with his gaze. "To kill them."

[43]

They'd stolen a van, Cillian being proficient at such things. Following the lights, which all of them now saw, the Clan wound south and west through the city and crossed the Asparuhov Bridge over three canals that linked Lake Varna to the sea. Wide roads narrowed into two lanes of blacktop in dire need of repair. Convenience stores, gas stations, souvenir shops, restaurants, and bars slowly dropped away, yielding to fields and intermittent forests.

"Pretty out here," Hester said.

They crested a hill, revealing more of the same.

"Boring," came Artimus's opinion.

From the front seat, Bale watched him fiddling with his sub-machine gun, pulling the magazine out and pushing it back in, chambering a round, tightening the sound suppresser, which lengthened the gun's short barrel by eight inches.

Bale said, "Did everyone bring suppressors? I don't know what we're walking into, but with what we left back in the city, let's fly under the radar."

Cillian was a knife guy, usually carried three SOG Seal knives on him; Hester had her crossbow; and he'd already seen Artimus's weapon fitted with a suppressor. So he looked at Lilit, who liked pistols—she held up a Beretta semiauto, suppressor attached—and Therion. Never knew what he'd use. He showed Bale a machete.

They turned onto an even narrower asphalt road and rolled into a wooded area with dense trees, heavy shrubs; the area looked medieval. Several vehicle trails—showing dirt in tires ruts, grass between them—branched off the road into the woods. Bale leaned forward to look into the sky above the trees. Close now. He told Cillian, "Pull off onto the next side trail. We'll walk the rest of the way."

Out of the van, they followed the asphalt road on foot. Bale could see buildings up ahead—low-slung houses, a smattering of nicer ones—probably vacation villas—and the lights streaming into the sky. They rounded a bend and faced a short main street, businesses on both sides, ending in trees where the road bent again. They passed a wooden sign with the name of a village carved into it: *Zdravets*.

"Here we go," Bale said.

They walked through the village, keeping to one side of the road, trying not to look like thugs. All of their weapons were concealed; still, Bale knew there was no way people wouldn't notice them or forget having seen them. If there were any people to notice.

"Ghost town," Therion said, voicing Bale's thoughts. They passed houses first, then small shops: a barber, a general store, a livery, but nothing seemed open and no people walked the street or peered out at them from windows. He assumed the men were in the fields, the kids in school, probably bused to a larger nearby town, and the women were doing whatever village women did when their homes were empty.

Finally they saw an old lady on all fours, planting flowers in a garden outside a small house. She raised her head as they walked by and lowered it again.

The lights were coming from just around the bend, and Bale started to get excited. He picked up his pace, the others a step behind on both sides. They rounded the bend, and he saw that the heavy beam that had drawn his attention from thirty miles away was comprised of fifteen or twenty individual strands; they came together directly over a barn that looked like something John Wayne could have built in one of his Westerns. A rust-patched car and three or four bicycles sat outside. An angel stood on the peak of the roof, already poised in a posture of defense, a sword in one hand, its spinning sparks congealed into a shield in front of it.

The big demon who'd been hanging around Therion and the human-shaped one sailed over Bale's head. Ashes rained down on him, then spiraled up as if caught in a whirlwind and trailed after the demons. The demons attacked the angel from different directions, hacking it with their weapons. The three of them rolled off the rear of the building.

"It's a barn," Lilit said.

"Exactly," said Bale. "Who'da thunk? Out here in the boonies, more spiritual life than any of the city churches."

"How do you know?" Therion said.

Bale looked at him. "What do you think the blue lights are? We're not looking for specials at Kmart."

Therion's gaze followed the beam into the sky, the significance of it only now seeming to dawn on him. "From people praying," he said. "Why are so many here, now?"

"Midafternoon service," Bale said. "Not uncommon in these parts," and he wondered why they'd ignored the region for so long, choosing to focus their attention on the countries that got all the credit: Italy, Spain, the US. It was the Eastern Europeans who knew how to pray.

Therion whistled. "This is going to tick someone off."

"That's the point." Bale continued toward the barn.

The two big front doors were mostly closed, opened just enough to admit a person turned sideways. He slipped through, moving out of the way for the others. Flowery incense couldn't quite mask the odor of the place's former bovine residents or the sweet, earthen smell of hay that covered the ground like shag carpeting. Rows of roughly cobbled pews lined both sides of a central aisle, at the end of which a cross hung from a hayloft. Below the cross a man stood facing them, his head back, giving Bale a view of the underside of his chin and nostrils. His arms were splayed out, hands cupped as if catching rain.

Men and women stood between the pews, some mimicking their leader's posture of worship, others with their heads bent low, their hands clasped in front of them. Angels stood with them, their sparks forming pod-like encasements around them. Bale remembered the Eastern Europeans' tradition of standing to pray, which they would do for hours at a time. And their children and teens always stood in prayer.

There they were, in the space behind the pews, directly even with where the Clan was gathered. Their angels stood around them, their swirling sparks a shield around the lot of them. One angel glared suspiciously at Bale, who winked at it. Several of the young people had beams the width of their heads shooting through the roof, and every one of their beams was bright, brighter than all but two of the adults'. Collectively, their brightness outshone the adults' by double, even though there were fewer of them.

It was one of the ways God cheated: making kids believe so readily, so earnestly in unseen things: Santa Claus, love . . . God. Just as they learned foreign languages quickly, before their minds started solidifying around their native tongues, they grasped God's language, His world, before becoming so reliant on their eyes and what others said of the world. Stacking the deck in His favor was so very much like God.

Bale knew why the Clan had not previously targeted kids—except as collateral damage or as tools to break the spirit of adults; their slaughter caused the sort of outrage that drew unwanted attention to the Clan, nationally, internationally. It wasn't conducive to staying free to continue their assault on the things God held dear. Had he *known* and not merely suspected that these little ones were indeed closest to God, he would have focused on them long ago.

He nudged and tapped the others, making sure they saw the kids. Weapons appeared in their hands: knives, guns, a crossbow, a machete. Angels turned their way, drawing their own swords, congealing glittering orange shields. The Clan's demons rushed them.

Bale said, "Let's get this party started!"

[44]

After reaching the roof of the Southwest Range Building, Elias turned right, heading for the opposite corner. From there he would make his way down to a lower level and conceal himself among the shadows, ready to spring if necessary. Toby crouched behind the concrete wall along the front edge of the building, binocs in one hand, pistol in the other. Jordan, Phin, and Nevaeh dropped from the corner onto the pitched roof of the apartments, which extended along the compound's west wall, perpendicular to the Southwest Range Building.

The Austin boots' rubber soles gripped well, while their pistons adjusted to the slope, making Nevaeh feel she was walking on a flat surface. She remembered from previous visits to the monastery ages ago that the rooms beneath her had no attic, only plastered planks and roofing material, nothing to muffle their footsteps. So they walked on the outside edge of the roof, over the foot-wide eaves. To their left the ground lay sixty feet below, and she would never have risked walking so close to the edge without the boots.

She looked over her shoulder to see Phin's maniacal eyes and insane grin as he wiggled his hips and bobbed his head to the music only he could hear. Farther back—too far—Jordan walked as though he were on a tightrope, carefully laying one foot in front of the other, arms extended out on both sides, wavering up and down. He was staring down at his feet.

"Jordan," she whispered.

He stopped and looked up.

"Trust the boots," she said. "Walk normally."

He nodded, and continued walking his imaginary tightrope.

Well before reaching the end—the family's apartment was last in line—she turned, stepped softly to the peak and down to the inside edge. She glanced over the compound, saw no one looking at her—in fact, saw only two monks, one sweeping the basilica steps, the other rushing through a courtyard toward the basilica, holding a big box. Over the opposite wall, she saw in the distance a stream of tourists coming down the mountain. She believed they would be too intent on not tumbling to pay the monastery any mind, and if they happened to see them on the roof, so what? The monastery was closed, and considering last night's attack, the monks wouldn't let anyone in no matter what they might shout from the outside.

Still, doing this in broad daylight—especially standing on a roof as if daring people to challenge her presence—was a bit nerve-racking. She was a nocturnal creature, unaccustomed to daytime missions.

She turned, dropped to her stomach, and slid over the edge, swinging to jump onto the portico outside the third-floor apartment doors. Phin came next, and together they helped Jordan down. Heading for Beth's door, Nevaeh withdrew the syringe of chloral hydrate and flicked off the cap with her thumbnail. She showed it to Phin, reminding him to get his ready for the boy.

She thought about her entry. Kicking the door in would be the most satisfying. But that would make noise, draw attention. Beth or Tyler would answer a knock; why wouldn't they? If the boy answered, maybe she'd say, *Nice to see you've recovered. Sorry I shot you.* Or simply, *Is your mommy home?* She hoped Beth wouldn't see them from deep inside the room. But then, what could she do, her kid standing right there? If Beth answered, she'd say, *Bet you didn't expect me.* No, something wittier, like, *Surprise!*

But then she heard someone coming up the wooden stairs at the end, pounding up them in a hurry. She gripped the syringe in her fist, using her other hand to pull a short sword—a *suwaiya*—from a pocket on the outside of her thigh. She was ready. In the Austin boots she'd be like a nightmare, running at him in fast-motion.

The footfalls didn't continue to the third floor, but clomped along on the portico below them. Nevaeh held up her hand, telling the others, *Stay cool.* A door down there opened. She waited for it to shut. When it didn't she held up one finger: *Wait.* A few moments later the shoes were back on the portico, the door slammed, and the person rushed away, down the stairs, and onto the stones of the court-yard at the bottom. She caught a glimpse of a monk hurrying toward the basilica, carrying a five-foot-long gold crucifix.

She sheathed her sword and continued toward the door.

[45]

Tyler came out of the bathroom, a towel around his waist, hair plastered down and dripping. He went into his room and shut the door. A few moments later he came out in his underwear, drying his hair with the towel. "Where are my clothes?"

"Right there, hanging over the chair," Beth said, trying to fix her hair in the reflection of the toaster and realizing she could do it in the bathroom mirror now that Tyler was out. "I ironed them."

"Ahhh," he whined. "Not *these*."

"Ty, don't give me a hard time. The memorial is honoring people you loved. You dress up for that."

The monastery allowed them to wear street clothes to the services, and Tyler probably hadn't dressed up in a year. Twenty months, she corrected herself, remembering the last time: the funeral of the Bransfords, the family who died in the crash that had taken Jagger's arm. Robby Bransford had been Tyler's best friend, just as his father, Mark, had been Jagger's, and his mother, Cyndi, had been hers. Everyone had loved the baby, Brianna.

"But, Mom, a tie?"

She watched him slip into the trousers and knew what was coming next.

He said, "These don't even fit!"

Of course they didn't. They were the ones he'd had for the funeral. When they'd moved here from Virginia they'd packed meagerly, and that outfit was the only nice clothes she'd brought for him.

"What'd you wear for Christmas service, and Easter?"

"My khakis and a button shirt. Dad said."

That's right. Jagger would go to church in ripped, dirty work clothes if it weren't for her disapproving eye. Clean work clothes was about all he could muster, and his son was following suit. As spiritual as St. Catherine's was, and as reverent and ritualistic as the services were, the monks put little value in the clothes attendees wore.

Gheronda had once told her, "God doesn't care; why should we?"

"Okay," she said. "Wear them." He skipped into the bedroom. "But we're getting you some nice clothes. And you're going to wear them. You hear me?"

"Yes, ma'am." Polite now that he'd gotten his way.

No, that wasn't fair, she thought. Tyler was usually polite and well-mannered. She was just on edge. Last night's attack, the demon in their apartment—the very idea of a rock that peeled back the spiritual veil!—Jagger taking off so suddenly, the monks . . . She really wasn't up to the memorial service. Death was the last thing she wanted to think about, with Jagger chasing the Clan.

She was standing with her hands on her hips, looking at the shirt, tie, and jacket—the crumpled pants on the floor—wondering if she should donate them, unable to picture a little Bedouin boy in them, when a knock came from the door.

Leo coming to escort them, she thought. "Hurry, Ty. We're late."

She opened the door and Nevaeh stood there, dressed all in black, long dark hair hanging behind her, taller than Beth remembered. She seemed ready to say something else, but said only, "Hi, Beth."

Beth stepped back, swung the door closed. Nevaeh's foot stopped it and it rebounded open, its handle smacking the wall. She saw two more members of the Tribe behind Nevaeh: Phin, that crazy goon Jagger had shot in the face; and the little boy, Jordan. They seemed eager to get in, pushing up against Nevaeh's back.

Beth spun around. "Tyler!" she yelled, and felt Nevaeh grab her collar. She turned, the material ripping, and punched Nevaeh in the jaw, causing her to lose her smile and stagger back into the others.

"Tyler!" He stepped into his bedroom doorway. "The room! The panic room! Now!"

Tyler swung around into the master bedroom and was opening

the panic room door when Beth's shoulder hit the bedroom door-jamb. Sounds behind her, stomps. Tyler was in! Yes, at least that. She nearly yelled for him to shut it, shut yourself inside, but she knew he wouldn't and she was almost there.

She felt a pinprick of pain at her neck, kept moving. Nails brushing over her hair and back, fingers grabbing at her arm.

Tyler was holding the door open for her, just wide enough to slip through. His body leaned out of the darkness along the door, to pull it shut as soon as she was in, but trying to stay out of her way.

Nevaeh was right on her, inches away. No way to slip in and shut the door.

Beth stopped suddenly, turned sideways, and dropped to all fours. Nevaeh barreled over her, the woman's legs knocking her down. Beth sprung up, kicking at the hands trying to grab her ankles. Nevaeh's head was at the base of the door, looked like she'd struck it. Beth kicked her in the head, to get it away from the door. She kicked, jumped, and danced past the flailing arms and hands into the closet, turning to grab the handle, yelling, "Shut it! Shut it!" Tyler did, and Beth threw the first bolt, then the one above it and the next one and the one closer to the floor.

Banging from the outside, pounding. Fists, something metal. Echoing in the panic room. Sounding like they were standing inside a drum, Ringo Starr beating it for all he was worth.

Tyler started crying, and Beth took her palms off the metal surface of the door—as though they could quiet the sounds, calm the people making them—and hugged him tight, stroking his head, hair still damp. "It's okay, Ty, it's okay."

"Who are they?" he said through sobs. "What do they want?"

"Shhhh," she said. *Lord, You are our refuge. Keep us safe from these enemies. Send Your angels*—she pictured the one she'd seen: strong, glorious, reflective of the One who sent him—*send them to protect us.*

The pounding stopped. Then one more loud *bang!* Rattling the door. Low. Someone had kicked it. Then nothing. Quiet. And that may have been worse.

[46]

Beth comforted Tyler, feeling him tremble under her arms, against her. Feeling his tears wetting her skin under the material of her dress. She reached over, felt the wall, patted it until she found the battery-powered light, and pulled the chain. She stepped back from Tyler, holding his face in her hands. She leaned to look him in the eyes, nose to nose. His whole face was wet. "Remember, Tyler. Be strong and courageous. What's the rest?"

"Do not"—he choked back a sob, his breath hitching—"be afraid."

Beth said, "Do not be discouraged."

He pulled in a stuttering breath. "For the Lord your God . . . will be . . . with you wherever you go."

"Do you believe it?"

He nodded and pushed his head into her.

"That's my boy."

Their attackers were arguing outside the door . . .

Phin: "You couldn't *grab* her?"

Nevaeh: "Shut up. She was fast."

Phin: "She was standing right in front of you. Where's the chloral hydrate? Here's what you do. See? Like that. Nothing to it."

Jordan: "She was *fast*."

Chloral hydrate. Beth reached to the back of her neck, rubbed where it hurt, brought back fingers that weren't bloody, but had blood on them. A little. She didn't know what chloral hydrate was. Something to drug her. She hoped only to knock her out. If they wanted to kill her, wouldn't they use a knife or a gun?

She eased Tyler away. "Sit, honey. Relax. Take a deep breath."

He sat on the floor, same place he'd been last night when the

Clan had attacked. She pushed her back against the wall behind her and slid down it until she was sitting across from him. He was wearing only his khakis, and he was absently fiddling with the bullet on a chain over his bare chest. "You know," she said, "no shoes, no shirt, no service. Hope you don't get hungry."

He smiled, and she saw the wheels turning in his head, thinking of some smart comeback, which he found: "You better hope I don't have to go to the bathroom."

She nodded appreciatively. "Well, here we are again."

He lost his smile. "Do you know who they are?"

"The Tribe."

His face moved through several different expressions, settling on puzzlement. "The ones who shot me?"

"That woman who almost got me," Beth said. "That's Nevaeh."

He knew her name. He had talked about carving it in the bullet that hung around his neck. She rubbed the pinprick on her neck again. No new blood. Besides her heart beating a thousand times a minute, trying to ratchet it down, she wasn't feeling any weird effects, no drowsiness or nausea. If it had been a needle that had poked her, she doubted Nevaeh'd had a chance to plunge any drugs into her. Beth had been moving away too fast.

"What does she want?" His eyes were huge.

"I don't know, sweetheart." If they'd intended on drugging her, they wanted her out . . . Why? Keep her quiet, maybe, while they waited for Jagger to return. Did they know he was gone? Phin and Nevaeh together: perhaps they'd expected to find both Beth and Jagger in the apartment. If they were waiting for Jagger, what did they want with him? Retaliation for their last encounter?

She processed the possibilities like flipping through recipe cards. Why else would they want her unconscious? To take her . . . or Tyler. Easier to kidnap someone who's not struggling and yelling. But again, why? Her mind kept coming back around to the same answer: they wanted Jagger. They must have targeted him for one of their vigilante hits, their twisted minds thinking him evil for having stopped them.

Owen. He had shown up this morning. Could they be after him . . . or both men? If they wanted revenge, it made sense.

She got to her feet—Tyler asking, "Mom?" to which she whispered, "The gun"—and pressed her thumb to the biometric reader on the box above his head. The door popped open an inch. She opened it fully and pulled out the big revolver, a .44 magnum, dull steel with a molded black grip. She sat again, both of them staring at the gun. She cracked open the cylinder, saw the backs of six bullets, and snapped it shut.

A knock at the panic room door. Incredibly, Tyler's eyes grew wider.

"Beth?" Nevaeh said. "I just want to talk, really."

"It's true," Jordan called.

"Who's that?" Tyler whispered.

"Remember I told you about Jordan? He became immortal when he was eleven."

"And he still acts like a kid?"

Beth nodded. Why would they bring him? With their numbers down, maybe they'd promoted him to more serious duties.

"Go away!" Beth yelled through gritted teeth at the steel-covered door.

"I want to talk about Ben, what you said to him."

"You could have called," Beth said.

"It's not the same. I don't think it was your words that did it, it was you."

Her eyebrows came together. "What are you talking about?" She looked at Tyler, eyes more normal now, calming down.

"God forgave him. He called him home."

"That's between him and God."

"I think you had something to do with it."

Beth leaned her head back against the wall. "I just told him to stop seeking God in his head and look for Him in his heart."

Silence, then: "There has to be more to it."

"I don't know what to tell you."

"Let's talk about it," Nevaeh said. "Face-to-face."

"That's not going to happen."

"We can tear down this door."

Beth raised the barrel of the gun, pointing it at the door. She shifted to put her back against the rear wall, holding the gun between her bent knees.

Tyler shook his head. "Don't try to shoot through it. Dad got metal that bullets can't go through."

She nodded, thinking, *Then I'll wait until they rip off the door, shoot them in their faces*. Hoping she wouldn't have to.

[47]

Jagger and Owen drove their rented BMW into the countryside southwest of Varna, Owen behind the wheel, driving fast. Except for the rock walls, which partitioned fields, and the tiny whitewashed houses, it reminded Jagger of rural Virginia: rolling hills, splotches of woods. It was serene, and Jagger had a hard time reconciling the locale with the evil he knew roamed it. It was a lot easier picturing the Clan loose in a city, plying their blood trade in filthy alleyways and the back rooms of opium dens. Imagining them here made him think of them as animals—except that animals killed for food or to protect their territory. The Clan was here with worse than malicious intent, not only to cause harm to man, but in doing so to strike out at God.

Jagger had hated God after the crash, but the way that had played out was his turning his back on God. He hadn't cared or even thought about it then, but he thought now that his response was pretty typical of people who'd felt God had done them wrong. He'd never, not even in a fleeting fancy, considered attempting to *hurt* God by hurting the things He loved. What Bale and the Clan were doing was almost beyond comprehension.

Almost. Now that he knew their objective, it made weird, terrible sense. If you truly believed in God and truly hated Him—and had an evil disposition and a sociopath's lack of regard for others—then, okay, you're going to go after Him. And since you can't actually reach God, you were left hurting the things He loved. Jagger had once read of a man who'd been rejected and ridiculed by a girl in high school. He went on to court her, marry her, and father her baby. He then killed the child and told his wife, "That's how much I've hated you all these years." Incomprehensible. Insane.

But it was exactly what the Clan was doing to God.

"It's coming up," Owen said. He'd entered the coordinates of the place Jagger had identified into the car's GPS; the screen now said their arrival time was four minutes away. They were winding through a forest, no village in sight. Jagger reached into his pocket, touched the fragment. The beam appeared over Owen's head and went through the car's ceiling. He looked in the backseat, expecting an angel, then scanned out the windows. Nothing. He rolled down his window and stuck his head out. High above, two angels soared with them, glowing embers visible on either side and jutting out past their feet. Without appearing to slow, they shifted into a horizontal position and looked down at him.

Jagger pulled his head in and rolled up the window. He said, "There are some blue threads here and there over the trees. Nothing like the big one I saw."

Owen nodded. He was frowning, and Jagger knew he expected the worst.

"Whoever was making the big beam," Jagger said, "they could have just stopped praying. You know, service over, let's go home."

"If it was a worship service of some kind," Owen said, "I hope they broke up and dispersed before the Clan found them."

Jagger pulled a duffel bag from the back seat and placed it on his lap. Owen had carried it through customs as though it contained stuffed teddy bears—the security guy in the private-plane terminal was more interested in a TV game show than them. He pulled out a revolver, a semiauto, and a three-foot sword. "These are going to stop them?" he asked, and thought, *Only if we catch them sleeping*.

"Not in a direct firefight," Owen said. "We'll have to follow them, try to get each one alone."

"The way lions pick off stragglers."

"Something like that."

"Is that likely?

Owen shrugged. "They have to go to the bathroom sometime. I don't think they'll do that in a group."

"As soon as we get one that way, they will."

"As soon as we get one, they'll hunt for us. Probably separate to find us."

"And we'll ambush each one before they get us?" It didn't sound like such a good idea. Now that they were two minutes from confronting the things that had seemed so far away when Owen described them, Jagger realized how stupid this was. What made Owen think they could take on the Clan?

This is the guy who flew his jet into a mobile home, he thought, and shook his head.

Owen glanced over. "Look," he said, "we only have to get the Stone back. Bale probably has it. They don't know we're after them, so he's not going to have his guard up. We find them, trail them, and as soon as Bale goes some place alone, we spring." He made it sound easy.

Jagger said, "And what if we find them about to kill some people? Are you going to hold back and watch, follow through with your plan?"

"No, we'll have to try and save their victims."

Jagger waited for more. When Owen remained silent, he said, "And?"

"Let's play it by ear."

"What? Get ourselves killed . . . for nothing?"

Owen didn't respond. Jagger rummaged in the duffel again. Another handgun and a lot of ammo. He got his hand around something and pulled it out. "Is this what I think it is?"

Owen looked. "If you think it's a hand grenade, then yeah. Should be four of them in there."

Well, okay then. If they were going to go down fighting, at least the grenades evened things up a bit. As long as the Clan didn't have a few of their own.

"The only advantage we have," Owen said, "is the element of surprise." He pulled out of his breast pocket a pair of aviator sunglasses and slipped them on. He smiled at Jagger, his crazy hair and beard fanning out from the glasses as though each hair was trying to get away.

"Is that supposed to be a disguise?" Jagger said.

"Just something to break up my features. They haven't seen me in a while. You, on the other hand . . ."

"Steampunk . . . Hester got a good look at me." He thought of Bale smiling up at him from his observation point on the rocks across from St. Catherine's gate. "Bale too. Probably the others."

"They know you. That handsome face of yours hasn't changed in centuries. I haven't always had so much hair."

Jagger couldn't imagine Owen clean-shaven, nattily coifed.

Owen said, "If we see them, duck down. I'll look away, like a tourist trying to find something."

Jagger felt like half of a bumbling duo in a mismatched-cops comedy. But if they messed up, they weren't going to get a mere chewing out from their boss. He tried not to think about Beth and Tyler opening the box containing his head.

They rounded a bend and drove through a small village. Two old guys sitting on chairs in front of a store. A woman carrying a wicker basket of something up the street. They slowed to let a dog pass. Past the businesses, they hit a stretch of road lined with houses. Two little kids were kicking a ball to each other across three front lawns—if hard earth and weeds could be called lawns.

"See anything?" Owen asked.

Jagger shook his head. "Few side streets, more like rutted dirt roads. Maybe we should try them."

"Look at the map again," Owen suggested. "See if this still looks right." He made a U-turn and headed back into the village.

Jagger put the weapons away, pushed the duffel into the foot well, and retrieved the iPad from Owen's satchel in the back. He studied the map, then closed his eyes to picture the sight from the cockpit windows. Angels and demons over the city. The column of light catching his eye; when he was looking at it, it was through the windshield in front of Owen. He'd followed it down to the ground. Villages, trees, roads like varicose veins. He snapped his eyes open and immediately saw the problem.

"We're one village over from it," he said. "I'm sure of it. We didn't go far enough."

Owen pulled to the side of the road. "Let me see."

Jagger held up the display and tapped the village just west of their current position. A pop-up box displayed the place's longitude and latitude.

"Hold it there," Owen said, looking from it to the GPS and back, punching in the new coordinates. "These rural areas," he said. "The roads go around fields; some look like roads but are really mile-long driveways. We'll let the GPS tell us how to get there."

"If it does, then backwoods Bulgaria has better maps than the US."

"Lots of tourists, places to see out here. Ten minutes ago we passed a road leading to the ancient stone baths where they say a Roman soldier, on orders from Nero, drowned Marcus Tullius."

"Never heard of him."

"That's because he drowned. Rumor was he was going to attempt a coup."

"And you know this how?"

Owen shrugged. "Trivia."

"There's that terrible memory again."

"Point is, Bulgaria has all sorts of sights interesting to history buffs. If everyone gets lost, half their tourism income goes with them. Places like this are fanatic about their maps, GPS and otherwise."

"Good to know. Now, you ready to go?"

Owen got the car moving and honked and waved as he passed the kids with the ball. Just another leisurely drive through Bulgaria. Jagger half expected him to stop for a game of checkers with the old guys in front of the store.

[48]

Nevaeh had stopped talking. Beth suspected she didn't really want to know what she'd told Ben, at least that wasn't all she wanted. It was a ruse to get to her, to use her to get to Jagger.

She heard mumbling out there, in the bedroom. Then: "Hey, Tyler?" It was Jordan. "Tyler, can you hear me?"

"What?" Tyler said. Beth shook her head, gestured for him to stay quiet.

"I know things about your dad. I knew him before you did. Want me to tell you?" He paused. When Tyler didn't respond, he said, "We can play in the monastery. I know hidden places I bet even you haven't found yet." Trying everything. "I know something about *you*, a secret. If you come out, I'll tell you."

Tyler looked puzzled.

Beth whispered, "He doesn't know we already told you about Dad being an Immortal. That's all."

Silence.

Someone kicked the door again, and they both jumped, Tyler letting out a little scream.

"They're just mad they can't get us," Beth said to him. "Daddy did a good job."

Right outside the door, Phin said, "Come out here right now! If I have to come in and get you, I'll hurt the kid. I mean it."

Tyler propelled himself into Beth's arms. He squeezed her hard. She comforted him, then turned her face toward the door.

"What's the knockout drug for?"

"You," Nevaeh said, "and Tyler."

That got Tyler whimpering, pushing his face into her shoulder.

"Look," Nevaeh said, "if we'd wanted to kill you, we wouldn't have brought drugs to put you out. I'll be honest with you, Beth. I want to take you with us. Just for a little bit. I need to know what happened with Ben, how he found forgiveness."

"Why?"

"Because I want it for myself. I need it."

"This is how you go about looking for God's grace?" Beth said, surprised to hear the words coming out of her mouth. The Tribe's quest for grace—by killing sinners—was insane, utterly against the word of God and the word *grace* itself. But in a twisted way, it made sense. All you had to do was forget about Jesus Christ. The Tribe claimed to be Christians, but other than their reading about faith and Christ, paying them lip service, and possessing a few religious icons, Beth didn't see it. No fruit. An unsummoned thought danced into her head: *Boy, does that describe half the Christians I know, or what?* At least they weren't going around killing people. Except themselves.

So, yeah, the Tribe was starting off on the level marked *Out of Your Mind*—and jumping deeper into the loony hole from there. Beth thought she understood what was happening here: Nevaeh didn't want to talk to her, she wanted *her*, her body, her presence, as though Beth were a talisman, a magic something that could confer grace, or through which God conferred His grace. Subtle but huge difference.

"Taking me won't end well," she called through the door.

"If I thought that, I wouldn't be here."

"Think about it," Beth said. "If you don't get what you want from me—and you won't, because I don't have what you're looking for—what then? Are you going to just let me go?"

"Moot point," Nevaeh said. "Ben got it from you; so will I."

"He didn't 'get it' from me! That's your problem! You're looking everywhere but where you should be. Look to God, Nevaeh, not to me!"

"I have been," she said more quietly. "For thirty-five centuries."

"So now you're looking anywhere, everywhere. And when you don't get it from me?"

"I will."

Talking to a brick wall.

"How long will you try?"

"As long as it takes."

Beth closed her eyes. Nevaeh intended on keeping her. Gone from her family forever. She had no illusions about Nevaeh finally tiring of her, letting her go. What were the fifty or sixty years Beth had left to an Immortal? A blink of an eye. A notation in her journal.

"What about Jagger?" Beth said. "You think he'll just let you take me? Haven't we played this game already?"

"Let me worry about that."

"No!" Beth screamed, really screamed.

Tyler's muscles tightened. He squirmed in her arms. "Mommy."

She was done trying to reason with a person who'd lost her mind. Jagger would go after them, as he had before, and Beth wasn't so naive to believe the outcome would be the same. This time he could be killed—if the Clan didn't kill him first, but she pushed that thought out of her head. Any way you cut Nevaeh's plan, you got a big stinking plate of rot.

She lifted Tyler, said, "Go sit down again, Ty."

"Don't go with them."

"I won't."

"Don't let them scare you into going. What the man said about hurting me—"

"He won't. I won't let him. And I won't go with them. Okay?"

He nodded, backed off of her, and sat.

Beth cocked the gun.

"What are you doing?"

"Calling for help. Plug your ears."

[49]

She pointed the revolver at the ceiling and began firing, her muscles straining to keep the recoil in check. The shots were loud and deafening. She squeezed the trigger over and over until the hammer fell on spent shells. Plaster rained down on them, chunks and dust. They lowered their heads against it. Beth looked up, past the high shelf loaded with supplies. She'd blasted away an area in the sloping ceiling the size of a large pizza, revealing planks of wood chipped away by the bullets. Through one broken chunk she saw the aluminum-colored sky.

"Tyler," she whispered, excited. She didn't wait for him to look up, his head covered in white plaster dust. She rose up, opened the gun safe, and retrieved the only other item in it: a box of shells. Reloading, she heard the Tribe yelling on the other side of the door. Gunshots sounded, and little bumps appeared in the metal skin of the door. More yelling. Everything was muffled—their voices, the gunshots— and she realized her own shooting had caused a ringing in her ears.

She raised the gun again, aiming this time. "Plug your ears," she said again. Six quick shots, each chipping at the planks, putting holes in them. Plaster chipped off around the hole she'd already made. Wood splinters fell down on them, Beth squinting to see through the debris. She opened the cylinder, dumped the shells, slipped new bullets into each chamber, her hand working like a machine: box to gun to box to gun . . . She closed the cylinder and fired again.

On the third shot, something else reached her ears—loud if she could hear it through the shots and tinnitus. She emptied the handgun, looked around. Tyler was pulling at her dress, calling her name. He looked and pointed: the wall opposite the door was shaking, cracks appearing. Something thudded against it from the other side, and the plaster pushed in, the shape of a foot.

"They're breaking through the other side, from my bedroom." Jagger had said he wanted to line all the walls as well as the door in metal, but he hadn't got around to it yet. Who'd have thought the need would come so soon—or ever?

She reloaded, put two rounds through the back wall—just to let them know she could—and the rest into the ceiling. Looking pretty good up there, shattered and broken. She picked up the aluminum baseball bat Jagger had leaned into the back corner and stood.

She handed Tyler the gun and whispered, "You remember how to be safe with this?"

He nodded, taking it with both hands and pointing it at the floor.

"When I say *go*, shoot through the back wall where they were kicking. All six rounds and count to five between each round."

"But they stopped trying to—"

The back wall rattled with a heavy blow. A new crack appeared, a piece of plaster fell away. Tyler yelled and put a bullet hole in it.

"Not yet," Beth whispered. "I don't want them to hear me breaking through the roof. Get it?"

Tyler nodded, grinning despite his fear, and for a second Beth felt really cool because that's what she was in his eyes.

"Go," she said.

He fired and she rammed the bat up against a plank. It lifted but fell down again. Another shot, another ram. The plank lifted, canted, and fell off to the side. *Bang!* She shoved the bat through a splinted board. Two more of each and she had a hole almost large enough for Tyler to squeeze through.

She crouched to reload, saying, "I can't reach the highest splintered boards. I'm going to lift you to that shelf. Wait for my shots, then use the bat to break them, okay?"

He nodded.

"As soon as you can fit through, go. Run to the Colosseum. You can go up or down from there, depending on what's happening."

"But you—"

"I'll be right behind you."

Another kick to the wall, and a socked foot appeared. She shot at it, but it was gone nearly as quickly as it'd appeared.

She stood and pulled supplies off the shelf: the plastic barrel of water, the first-aid kit . . . stuff falling to the floor. A kick and the hole got bigger. It would be easier for the Tribe to break through now that they'd knocked out a hole. She resisted the urge to fire again, wanting to save the remaining five rounds for Tyler's assault on the ceiling in case he needed them.

"Come on." She lifted him up, aiming to get his rump on the shelf. He stopped rising halfway up, and she felt his arms around her neck. He said, "I love you."

She turned to kiss his cheek. "I love you too. Now get out of here. Go."

On the shelf, he got both knees under him. He could easily reach the planks she couldn't. She handed him the bat. "Wait for me to fire."

Keeping one hand on him, making sure he didn't fall off, she pointed the gun and waited for the foot. The wall rattled, plaster flew, and the foot appeared. She fired, missed . . . Tyler smashed a section of roof away. She saw him going for another punch and fired. Perfect timing.

A face appeared in the hole. Grinning . . . crazy . . . Phin. "Yoo-hoo," he said, then pulled away just as she fired. Wood shards dropped onto her head. She glanced up. "That's big enough," she whispered, emphatic. "You can get through. Go!"

She didn't think Phin had seen what they were doing—the shelf would have blocked his view of the hole—or noticed that Tyler was not on the floor. But she didn't want to take any chances. Tyler had to go now before it was too late. She fired into the back wall and looked up. Only his back side and legs extended down from the hole. He kicked and wiggled, rising up. Then he stopped. His necklace was caught on a splintered board. He thrashed, and the chain broke, dropping the bullet onto her forehead. She heard it hit the floor beneath her as Tyler's feet kicked up and out of the hole.

A hand grabbed her ankle. She screamed and looked down. Phin had thrust his entire arm through the breach in the back wall. She shot at it, grazing his forearm. He released her ankle, but didn't retract his arm.

Stupid, she scolded herself. Shoot at the hole—more of him there: shoulder, bicep. She aimed and fired. *Click*. Out . . . and he knew it.

He began searching for her. His hand swept back and forth, slapped at the floor. She backed into a corner, slid down, reached for the box of shells. He found it first, seized it, pulled it out through the hole. He started kicking at the edges again, more enthusiastically, making it wider and wider.

She jumped at the shelf, fell back down. Tried again, pressing her bare toes against the door. She couldn't quite get up.

"Mom." A hoarse whisper. Tyler was leaning back into the hole, his hand reaching for her. She raised her hand quickly, before she lost her balance. He had her, turning his hand into a vise around her wrist. He tugged, grunting.

Below, the smashing sounds stopped.

She got one leg on the shelf. Tyler pulled. Her other foot hopped up the door.

"They're going through the roof!" Phin yelled.

"Unlock the door!" Nevaeh yelled. "Phin! The door!"

Beth glanced down, past her hip. He was coming through, glaring and smiling a tight-lipped smile, a snake slithering to dinner. She pushed hard off the door, got her other leg onto the shelf. She rose, her arm going through the hole, Tyler backing up to pull her. Her head popped through.

Tyler let go so she could get her hands on the roof on opposite sides of the hole. He rose onto his knees, sat back on his heels, smiled. His face snapped up, looking at something behind her, his face becoming terrified. Footsteps on the roof, loud: *clomp, clomp, clomp* . . .

A body sailed over her, tackled Tyler. Jordan—rolling with Tyler down the slope of the roof. The two boys disappeared over the edge.

Beth screamed.

[50]

The boy Immortal—Jordan—broke Tyler's fall. They landed on the wide wall of the compound eight feet below the roof of the apartments. Jordan landed on his back; Tyler landed on Jordan. Jordan's eyes flashed wide as he tried to pull in a breath that wouldn't come.

Tyler had knocked the wind out of himself once, falling off a monk cell and landing on his stomach. It was scary, needing air and not getting it. He imagined that's what drowning was like.

Jordan looked scared, staring at Tyler as if he wanted help.

Yeah, right.

Tyler climbed off him, pain in his knee. He must have hit it on the wall. He limped away from Jordan so the kid couldn't grab him. He only had a few more seconds before Jordan recovered. He saw the weird boots Jordan wore, six-inch soles, attached to black leg braces that went all the way to his hips. A round disk connected a lower brace to an upper brace on the side of his knees.

That must be how he crossed the roof so fast.

While he was looking at Mom, so happy to see her coming out through the hole, he'd caught movement with his eyes, and the boy was already on the roof, bounding toward him.

Stupid Tribe and their gadgets. First invisibility suits, now these things. So not fair. Cheaters.

He thought about taking the boots, using them for himself, but they looked clamped on in a lot of places. He'd never get even part of one off before Jordan recovered enough to fight him.

He looked up at the edge of the roof. "Mom!"

"Tyler!" Just her voice. "Run, Ty! Now!"

"But—!"

"Obey me! Run! I'll find you!"

He had to go past Jordan to get to the Colosseum. *He's going to get up any second and come after me, him and those boots.* Tyler ran without looking back. Surprised to make it to the corner, he stopped at the rear wall—higher than the one he was on, a lot lower than the Colosseum.

Only then did he glance back. Jordan was rolling over, pushing himself up onto his hands and knees, looking at him.

Tyler looked at the roof of the apartments. Given time, he could probably climb up that exposed beam, get his hands on the edge, and pull himself up. But he didn't have time. Jordan was trying to stand, bracing himself with one hand against the back wall of the apartment building.

Tyler looked up to the top edge of the Colosseum. Twelve feet, at least. Only one way to go. He climbed onto the top of the rear wall and ran toward the next corner, putting the Colosseum between him and Jordan . . . at least until the boot boy caught up with him.

[51]

Beth had almost cried when she heard Tyler call her. An image flashed in her mind: an angel—bright and glowing, millions of sparks seeming to come out of his body, swirling around it, trailing after it—moving fast to catch her son. It was just a thought, spawned from the prayer she'd instinctively prayed as he went over the edge. Her mind's way of seeing God's hand. But she wondered if it was something left over from the vision the Stone had given her. One of the side effects Jagger had talked about? Her imagination . . . or God?

She remembered the wall. They would have had to roll eight feet to go over *that*. Not impossible considering how fast they were moving when they went over the edge. Maybe Jordan had taken the big plunge: Tyler had not sounded encumbered by the boy when he was calling.

She had just wiggled her shoulders through the hole, scraping them against splintered planks, when a hand grabbed her ankle. She yanked and kicked, trying desperately to pull herself through. She felt nails bite into her skin and realized it was Nevaeh who had hold of her.

What was Phin doing? He would have come through the fissure he'd made in the closet wall and unlocked the door for Nevaeh. Then what? Watch Nevaeh? Help her? Or come out onto the roof? She bet it would be the roof. And he'd be moving fast.

Instead of yanking at her leg, fighting both Nevaeh and the too-small hole, she dipped down, into the closet—hard to think of it as a panic room now. She ducked her head in enough to see Nevaeh's glaring eyes. Giving the woman more of her leg had put Nevaeh's arm in an awkward position. Beth twisted it and pulled free. She kicked Nevaeh in the face, and as she was falling back, Beth dropped lower, stretched, and kicked it again. But Nevaeh was tough. She would bounce off the wall like a fighter off ropes and grab Beth again.

Beth shot up through the hole, feeling the broken planks tear at her dress and her flesh. She got her feet directly below her on the shelf, jumped and—

An image in her head, not the focus of her thoughts, but like someone in the distance: an angel lifting her.

—she pushed with her hands on either side of the hole, coming out and rolling at the same time. She felt Nevaeh's claws graze a foot. A second later Beth was on the roof, getting to her feet.

No time to think, but she did: Tyler should be gone, climbing down into the compound from the wall by the Colosseum. They would expect her to go for the nearest point of escape, the edge of the roof where Tyler and Jordan had gone over. Beth expected Phin and Nevaeh to come from the other side, the front edge of the roof, so that was out. The Colosseum was at the far end of the apartments; she'd still be running for it when they spotted her.

She went the other way, to the steep, sloping roof at the near end of the building. Their living room was directly below it, and thinking how the ceiling looked from the couch, it seemed impossible that she'd be able to get down it without tumbling. She heard a noise—a lot of noises—behind her, on the other side of the roof's peak. Two seconds to move.

She scrambled onto the slope, and sure enough she couldn't stay on it. She leaned back, sat, slid over the tiles on her butt. She went over the edge, starting to twist sideways. She sailed through the air, her tailbone heading for the stone top of the wall, which jogged in here—probably the reason the apartment building started where it did. She tried lowering her feet and hands to cushion the impact and hit the wall a foot from its inside edge. She heard a *snap*—and her arm flared with molten steel pouring through her bones into her shoulder, back, and chest. The momentum of her fall tossed her over the wall and she fell again—to the narrow roof of a storage room. She rolled off that and plunged eight feet to a terrace. She landed on her feet and backside, sparing the already injured arm, until jolting back and landing on it as well.

She wanted to cry out in pain but somehow bit it back. Among the psychedelic flashes of purple and black her reeling brain displayed, she imagined an angel holding his hand to her mouth, holding a finger to his lips—*shhhh*—looking up, as if at the apartment roof above.

Where've you been! she demanded in her head, and the image vaporized.

She gulped air, gulped it to keep from screaming, gulped it because she didn't know what else to do. Lying on her back on the terrace, she could see the peak of the apartment roof, the edge she'd jumped over to reach the slope. Voices streaming over it like air currents, growing louder.

She rolled onto her side and pushed and dragged herself to the storage room door. Reached up and turned the handle. She pulled it open, sat upright to get past the door, and slid inside.

She pulled the door closed.

[52]

Tyler peered along the length of the back wall, hiding around the corner of the Colosseum, at the opposite end from the apartments. He'd run along the top of the wall, thinking, *How can I get to a safe place?* Where could he drop down from the wall, into the compound, into one of hundreds of nooks and crannies and forgotten places in the monastery? Jordan had said he knew St. Catherine's better than he did. If that was true, was there anyplace he could hide that Jordan wouldn't find him?

Well, Tyler wasn't going to make it easy for him.

He pulled his head back from the corner, scanned the wall that lay perpendicular to him: the east wall that faced the archeological dig. It would be rough going at first, the wall here crumbling, its top shaped like the squiggly lines of the EKG printout Mom had let him keep from his stay in the hospital. At the center of its length, the wall became a building, like a castle. It was where the original monk cells were located, built into the wall. If he could get there, he could drop down to the walkway outside the top row of cells and keep going lower until he reached the roof of the Chapel of Martyrs. From there it was an easy jump to the ground.

He turned, slid his face out from the wall enough to see around it, and felt his stomach tighten. Jordan was on the wall, running toward him fast, taking bounding leaps. Those boots! Then the boy stopped to inspect the area outside the wall.

Keep looking, Tyler thought, and pushed away from the Colosseum. He jumped down the first trench-like dip in the wall, feeling the crumbled stone bite into his bare feet. He scrambled up the other side, down again and up . . . onto the flat, undamaged wall. He sprinted toward the wall's wide center, the monk cells, then stopped. He could hear Jordan coming, close to the corner behind him. There was no time to drop to the walkway and move off it without being seen.

He considered hiding behind the parapet wall, which lined the top outside edge of the monk-cell structure on three sides. But that was no hiding place. He peered over the edge at hard dirt and rocks sixty feet below . . . and something else: the little meditation deck, so small Tyler couldn't lie on it without his feet hanging over. A railing lined its perimeter, with a door leading to a monk cell on its wall side. It was about a dozen feet below the top of the wall. A beam for hanging banners and lanterns in the old days jutted out from the wall four feet down. He lay on his stomach, pushed his legs over the edge, and glanced toward the corner. Jordan came into view, swinging his gaze from the archeological site to the ruts of the crumbling wall. Tyler slid over, felt his feet on the beam, and let go of the wall. His feet slipped off, his stomach hit the beam, draping his body over it like a wet towel, and he fell to the deck. It shuddered and thunked down a few inches, a space appearing between it and the wall.

He lay there on his back, feeling the texture of the weathered boards pressing against his bare skin. He was afraid to move, afraid the deck would either come away from the wall completely or crumble or make noise that would give him away. So he stayed motionless, looking up at the beam and the edge of the wall beyond it, waiting for Jordan to peek over it.

[53]

Even with the Austin boots, Nevaeh felt as though she was about to pitch forward and go over the far end of the apartment building. If Beth had come this way, she'd be a bloody mess somewhere below. She reached the edge and leaned over, arms waving behind her for balance, acting like Jordan. Wall directly below. Even farther down, a terrace.

She turned and started back up to the peak, where Phin stood watching. "She's not here," Nevaeh said.

"I thought I heard something."

"How can you hear anything over your music?" She reached the peak and straddled it.

He used the tip of his dagger to lift a wire off his chest, showing her he'd taken the earbuds out.

"She's still not there," she said. "If she did go over and survive, I'd have seen her getting away." She pointed at him. "She'd better not be dead."

"What I'd do?" Phin said. "I got us into that closet."

"And drove them out." She rubbed the side of her face where Beth had kicked her twice.

"Then she went over there." He pointed at the outside edge of the roof, below which lay the compound's wall.

"And our looking for your imagined sounds gave her time to get away." She pulled the radio out of her pocket and held it to her mouth. "Toby? Did you see where she went? Toby?" She looked up at the outcropping and didn't spot him. "Where is he? I swear, that kid." She scanned the compound. "There's Jordan. What's he doing?"

The boy had just emerged from behind the far end of the

Southwest Range Building, running on top of the wall that faced the excavation. He looked like a cartoon character, zipping faster than humanly possible.

She spoke into the radio: "Jordan. Jordan!" The boy stopped in the center of the wall where it widened into a structure that supported the thinner, eight-foot-wide walls that winged out from it and once contained monk cells. He reached into a pocket, then two more before finding his radio transceiver. "I'm here."

"I know. I see you."

He looked around, spotted her and Phin on the roof, and waved.

"What are you doing? Where's Tyler?"

"I'm . . . he . . ."

She sighed. "Did he get away?"

She thought she saw him nod.

"Find him. Elias, you there?"

A fountain of flames shot into the sky in front of the basilica. The mosque blocked her view of the entrance. She noticed wisps of black smoke floating through the air from various spots around the compound.

She said, "What are you doing?"

His voice came through, as clear as if he were standing next to her. "When the gunfire started, all these monks streamed out of the church. I chased them back in." Another fountain of fire.

"They're *all* in there?" It was too early for vespers.

"As far as I can tell. Three bodies on tables near the altar. I think they were bodies. They were covered with white sheets. Looked like a memorial service."

She told Phin, "They would all have been there." She took it as a divine sign that their mission was blessed. Beth and Tyler hadn't gotten the memo.

"Nev," came Elias's voice.

"Yeah?"

"This church doesn't have other exits, do you know? I strolled around, didn't see any."

"Wish I were recording this," Phin said. "That's more words I've heard him say at one time in years."

She frowned at him, spoke into the radio: "If I remember right, no, just the one."

Flames streamed up, disappeared, leaving a drifting black snake of smoke.

"Try not to burn the doors," she said. "I knew the guys who made them."

"They're nice," he said.

Carved by Byzantine artists in the fourth century, the doors contained reliefs of animals, birds, flowers, and leaves. Her friend had been one of the engravers, an ornery cuss, but what talent he possessed.

The radio squawked with Toby's voice: "What's up?"

Nevaeh saw him standing on the outcropping, a small figure almost lost among the complicated textures of the rocks. "Where were you? Did you see where Beth went?"

"You don't have her?"

Nevaeh dropped her hand, said to Phin, "He was goofing off. Still ticked about having to be lookout." She raised the radio. "What about Tyler? Did you see where he went?"

"You lost him *too*?"

"Just watch for them. Don't leave your post." She dropped the radio into a pocket and headed for the edge of the roof where Beth must have gone over. She could feel the boots' pistons moving up and down to compensate for the roof's pitch. Without looking, she leaped over the edge. Her boots and braces prepared for impact and she landed on her feet. Above her, Phin jittered around on the edge of the roof.

"Come on," she said. "Let's find her and get out of here."

[54]

Jordan had clomped past, kicking dirt down onto Tyler's face. Tyler didn't even spit it out of his mouth or wipe it from his eye. He simply closed that eye and pressed his lips together. His heart pounded, feeling like it was strong enough to beat the deck from the wall, loud enough to draw Jordan's attention. He tried not to breathe, but that didn't work so well; he wound up pulling in air louder than he would have had he kept a regular rhythm. Dirt went down his throat.

Someone else was up there with Jordan: the woman he'd heard through the panic room door, Nevaeh. Right there, saying, "Jordan! Jordan!"

The boy stopped, only a few feet away, said, "I'm here."

"I know. I see you."

And Tyler realized they were talking on radios.

Nevaeh spoke to someone else, but Jordan stood up there listening in. Someone named Elias had apparently kept the monks from coming to their rescue when Mom fired the gun. Then another person said, "What's up?" Sounded young, a teenager. He'd been away from his post, and Nevaeh wasn't pleased. Tyler learned two important things from this conversation: the teen was up in the mountains, watching the compound, and Mom had gotten away. Tyler felt like he did on Christmas morning, hearing that. The talk ended and Jordan moved off, toward the front wall.

Tyler lifted his head to look at the mountain rising to the south. Lots of places from which to watch St. Catherine's. He finally wiped the dirt away from his face, his eye watering to wash out what he couldn't get with his fingers. He kept looking at the mountain, slowly scanning back and forth. The spy wasn't anywhere he could see, so the spy couldn't see *him* either. When he got back into the compound, he'd have to be careful—and warn Mom.

He dropped his head to the deck and wished she were with him now. And Dad. If Dad were here, he'd wipe the monastery floors with their backsides.

But he wasn't here.

Tyler wiggled, seeing if the deck would shift. Then he rolled onto his stomach and stood. The platform creaked but didn't move. He grabbed the door, operated the thumb-latch, and pushed. The door didn't budge. He put his shoulder into it, and still the door pretended to be a wall.

Oh, come on!

It was unlocked last time. He had tried to get Mom to come see, told her they could surprise Dad by tossing breakfast rolls at him while he stood surveying the dig—his favorite spot was near the wall within roll-shot of the deck. It would be funny. But she hadn't thought so. He'd bet any money Mom had mentioned it to Gheronda, who had boarded it up or locked it or otherwise rendered it no longer a door. Just to make sure, he rattled the handle, pushed at the door with his palm, chest, knees.

The deck creaked and shifted, ratcheting away from the wall another inch. Tyler grabbed the handle and turned his feet sideways to get them on the sliver of floor that protruded from under the door. He stood there, cheek pressed against the splintery door, trying to make his entire body cling to it like paint. He couldn't stay like this; even the minimal expansion of his chest as he breathed threatened to knock him back onto the deck.

He pressed the toes of one foot to the deck, then lowered his heel, gradually shifting weight onto it. The deck made a low groaning sound, but it didn't move. He put both feet on it, watching the gap between the deck's rear edge and the wall.

Maybe if he didn't move, he could wait out whatever was happening with the Tribe in the monastery, without the deck collapsing and without being spotted. But then Mom wouldn't know about the spy. She'd sneak around, looking for Tyler, and sooner or later the teenager in the mountains would see her and tell the people inside where she was. Then they'd take her away. And Dad would go after them. And Tyler would become an orphan. Saying it like that—being an orphan—wasn't so bad, but what it meant—Mom and Dad gone, dead—was the worst thing he could imagine. Just the thought of it brought tears to his eyes and made his guts ache. He couldn't stand here and let that happen.

He looked up to the top of the wall, way overhead. The beam was closer, and if he could get on that, he could reach the top.

He tested the railing. It wobbled but seemed sturdy. Gripping with his fingertips the little edge of wall available on his side of the door and the railing itself with his other hand, he stretched his leg up to get his foot on the top railing. He hopped up, rising fast, sliding his fingertips up with him. The railing teetered out, creaked. Tyler wavered, moving his hips back and forth, trying to keep from falling. The railing wobbled with him. The railing and he settled into a slight back-and-forth motion, something he could live with. Now he had to turn around. He rotated his head, then his shoulders, then his hips. He lifted one foot, turned it around, and placed it on the opposite side of the other foot. He lifted that one, turned it around, and he was done: standing on the railing, gripping the wall, facing the deck and more important, the beam, which was above him and a little ahead.

He stretched to reach it, touched it with his fingers, couldn't get his hands around it. Shifting his feet back on the railing, he rose onto his tiptoes. His fingers were almost . . . over . . . the . . . post . . .

The railing snapped backward, collapsed.

And Tyler fell.

[55]

Jagger knew they had the right place as soon as they drove into Zdravets. A man came toward them from the far end of the street, his face wracked with grief, tears streaming down his face, mouth open in a wail Jagger couldn't hear. In his arms was draped the body of a child, his head and feet bouncing as the man ran.

"Oh, dear God," Owen said, speaking, Jagger knew, to his Lord. "Please say we're not too late. Please."

But the evidence to the contrary was bobbing and flopping toward them in what was surely his father's arms. Jagger's stomach turned into a tight fist. He thought of Tyler, how recently he'd carried him like that, Tyler bleeding from a hole in his back, blood everywhere. And now Jagger could see the blood coming toward them, smeared on the father's face, turning the boy's arm into a grotesque barbershop pole.

As they drove nearer, the man made no attempt to avoid them. "Stop!" Jagger said.

Owen slammed on the brakes, and they both jumped out. Owen reached the two, quickly examined the boy, holding his fingers to his neck. He looked at Jagger, shook his head. He spoke to the man, who sobbed out a few words, then took off running again, wailing. Jagger watched him run past the car and continue up the road, as though hoping to catch his son's spirit before it left town.

But for the grace of God, Jagger thought and felt like an utter fool still questioning God, for not embracing Him after he and Tyler could have so easily been that man and boy. *Lord,* he prayed, *thank You for saving Tyler . . . I'm sorry I've been so stupid.* Clinging to his words like a shadow, he remembered praying something to the same effect when Steampunk was standing over him. What had he done since to show he was truly sorry? *Please take away the poison that's keeping me from loving You the way I should* . . .

Owen grabbed his arm. "He was tending his crops and was late getting to a church service in a barn around the bend. He found the boy when he arrived, others too. Get in the car."

They drove a hundred yards and followed the road as it curved. They saw the barn, and Owen punched the accelerator, bounding over the curb and sliding to a stop behind an old sedan. Owen's door burst open and he swung his feet out.

Jagger caught the back of his shirt with RoboHand. "The guns," he said. "They might still be in there."

Owen pulled free, saying, "Do you think they would have let the father leave with his boy if they were?"

Rounding the hood of the Beamer, watching Owen disappear into the barn, Jagger saw the bicycles and froze. Only for a second, long enough to imagine the children riding them here, dropping them in the dirt to rush inside. *No, no* . . .

The scene inside was worse than he'd imagined, worse than he ever could imagine. Bodies everywhere. Sliced and severed and leaking blood into the hay floor. A woman wailed, a choking sob that jabbed at his heart, as she mourned over the body of a girl, twelve or thirteen years old. Owen knelt a few yards away, checking for a pulse on another child. He scrambled on his hands and knees to another, then another.

Jagger dropped his head into his hand. He rubbed his hook over his temple, down his cheek, hard. He needed the pain, used it to cut through the chaos in his head. He wanted to scream.

Owen was yelling at him. "Jagger!" He was pointing up the central aisle. "Check them!"

Bodies, strewn between the pews, draped over them. Jagger ran to the nearest, a woman in her thirties. Eyes staring at the dark ceiling overhead. He pressed his fingers to her neck. He moved to the next person, an elderly man, his fingers clawing at a gaping wound in his chest. He snaked through the pews, checking, checking. He crawled to a man who was crumpled in the central aisle, missing an arm. Jagger had to roll him over, unfolding him to get to his neck. They were all dead, every one.

He started weeping, overwhelmed by death, the smell of blood, the soft flesh of the bodies. He felt a hand on his back, but he didn't look, just kept weeping.

"We just missed them, Jagger," Owen said over him. "Maybe by an hour." It was about that long ago that Jagger had seen the lights flicker and disappear. "We have to go. There's still a chance we can catch them. And we don't want to be here when the cops show up. Foreigners at the scene of . . . of . . . even *massacre* doesn't cut it this time. We have blood all over us. They'll hold us if for no other reason than to have *somebody* in jail. Jag . . . ?"

Jagger pushed up from the body. He was shaking, felt his muscles quivering on his arms, down his legs. He spun toward Owen. "How could this have happened? How could God have let it?"

Owen reached out; Jagger backed away. He pushed his hand into his pocket and pulled out the cloth. The fragment flew up and landed in the hay. He dropped and crawled to it, grabbed it and squeezed.

When he looked up he saw an angel to the right of the door. He was on his knees, one hand over his chest, the other resting on the head of a dead child. Some embers swirled around him slowly, but most seemed pooled in his lap, flowing out to move over the child, like a blanket unfurling to cover the body. His head was lowered and he was weeping.

"There you are!" Jagger yelled. He snapped his head toward another, bent over the body of the first woman whose pulse he'd checked. "And you!" A third was at the far end of a pew, his fingers moving gently over the head of a man. "You!" Pointing. "Where were you when this happened? What did you do to stop it?"

Owen put his arm around Jagger's shoulder. Jagger turned and pulled, but Owen held on. "Jag, I know."

Jagger looked at him. "They're right here! They were here, when this . . . this atrocity went down. What good are they if they can't stop this?"

"They're here to comfort."

"And protect, I thought. Aren't they supposed to protect?"

"When they can, if it's God's will."

"So God *willed* this?"

"It's the result of a fallen world, Jag. A sinful world."

"That God allows."

"Yes."

Jagger didn't want to hear Owen's answers. Not standing here in the stench of blood, the bodies of men and women and children all around, people who had been *praying* when they'd been cut down. He waved his hand around, taking in each angel. "They did nothing."

"We don't know that," Owen said. "Maybe they fought, were overwhelmed. Maybe they comforted the dying, made them feel less fear. I think of angels as restrainers, mitigators of the evil that permeates the earth. We look at the bad things that happen and say, *Hey, where were you?* And all the while they're holding back the flood, making it less bad than it would be without them."

"They didn't restrain evil here."

"It doesn't look that way to us."

"How could it have been worse?"

"I don't know, Jagger, but God was here, His angels were here. Something good will come of this."

"Not for them, not for those kids who'll never grow up to love a spouse, have children, grow old . . ."

"I think they might disagree with you," Owen said. "My guess is they're pretty happy now."

"If dying like this isn't so bad . . ."

"I didn't say that."

"If God makes everything all right, why are *they* crying? Owen, the *angels* are weeping over these people!"

"Jesus wept."

And that just made Jagger sad and confused. So many contradictions.

He walked out of Owen's embrace and knelt beside the angel. He reached out and brushed his hand over the child's cheek. Hearing of the Clan's massacre in the nightclub, he had felt his doubt about Owen's determination to get the God Stone away from the Tribe loosen, a little bit of it fall away. Witnessing this, this slaughter of innocents, his doubt crumbled like a cracker under the boots of an army. But he didn't want to just get the Stone back, he wanted to stop the Clan altogether. He wanted to kill them.

He rose and left the barn, Owen following. He kept thinking about the big bright light he'd seen shooting into the sky from this place, from the people whose blood he had all over him. Bale had seen it too; that's what had drawn him here. At the car, before opening the door, he said, "All those people dead. The Clan used something God made to murder them."

"Humans always do," Owen said and climbed into the car.

[56]

Thinking the police would approach the village from the same direction they had, Owen went the other way, ending up on a winding dirt road. He punched the airport into the GPS and saw that they could reach it the way they were heading, losing only about ten minutes over trekking back the way they'd come.

Neither spoke, each caught up in his own thoughts. Owen started praying, and Jagger was glad the fragment's effect had worn off. There was no way to look at the beam of light or the angels or the way the sky rippled with color without feeling a bit of God's glory; it was calming and awesome and . . . sublime. Jagger already had enough in his head, feeling like all of it was peeling away layers of his brain. He didn't want to add anything to it, even if it was sublime.

He looked down at his bloody hand, open in his lap. Even his hook bore smears and globs of the stuff. He rubbed them on his khakis, but the blood had already dried. "Stop up here."

"Where?"

"Right here."

"There's nothing here."

"Will you stop? Please?"

Owen pulled over. Jagger got out, walked a few feet to a drainage ditch through which water trickled over a bed of pebbles. He got on the ground and washed his real hand, then RoboHand. Scooped water for his arms and face. It felt good, ice cold and cleansing. He wished he could wash the images in his head away as easily. He sat back on his heels, leaned his head back, and just breathed, trying to think of nothing. Owen washed as well, and they both got back in the car.

After a time, while they were still in the countryside, Jagger said, "What now?"

"We try to catch them at the airport," Owen said. "Hope they used the same airport we did, and hope we get there before they do. Maybe God will throw us a bone, and the Clan will get stopped by the cops."

"And if we miss them? What then?"

Owen glanced at him, didn't answer.

"We can't keep chasing them this way," Jagger said. "Showing up at their crime scenes, the Clan long gone."

"Look how close we were this time," Owen said. "We missed them by an hour."

"Might as well have been a year."

"Hey, we just got started. We left St. Cath's only this morning, and look, we traveled over four countries and we almost got them. I say that's pretty good."

"They slaughtered two groups of people. How many did you say in the nightclub, twelve? Nineteen or twenty in the barn. That's at least thirty-one people, something like two an hour since they got their hands on the God Stone. I wouldn't call that 'pretty good.'"

"Not what they're doing—what we're doing. It's all we can do."

Jagger nodded. He saw his future and it was tragic: traveling from country to country, witnessing the aftermath of the Clan's passing, painting his skin with the blood of children, darkening his soul with their staring faces.

"We can't just keep chasing them," he said again.

"What are you saying? Give up?"

"Absolutely not. We have to get them, and I hope we can do more damage than simply taking away their toy. I just don't always want to be behind."

"Do you have any other ideas?"

He shook his head, and they drove in silence. Upon leaving the barn, Jagger had dropped the fragment loosely into his pocket. Now he reached in, trying to get his fingers between the cloth and fragment.

He did, but he couldn't grip the piece of Stone with the cloth; it was like trying to pick up a quarter with mittens on. He pulled the cloth out and reached across with RoboHand, pushing the hook in his pocket. He worked it around, clamping and unclamping. He exhaled a deep breath and rolled his head toward Owen, who was attempting to watch the road and Jagger's performance at the same time.

"I'm just going to grab the thing and put it in the cloth," Jagger said. "Five minutes of angels isn't so bad." It was actually beautiful, wonderful . . . but not now. He kept thinking about that weeping angel.

"Want me to do it?" Owen asked.

"I don't think so." He reached in, got his fingers around the fragment, and closed his eyes when the flash appeared. He pulled the Stone out, tucked it into the cloth, and returned it to his pocket. With another little sigh, he looked up. The car was climbing a hill, and the membrane of undulating colors in the sky filled the windshield. Owen crested the hill, about to dip back down into a stretch of low flatland, when Jagger said, "Stop!"

Owen hit the brakes.

Jagger stared.

"What is it?"

"A blue beam." He looked at Owen. "I feel like they should be called prayer beams, but I have a feeling they're more than that. You said they represented a connectedness to God, and I think that's right. They're umbilical cords to our Creator."

Owen turned from Jagger to stare out the windshield. "What do you see?"

"The biggest umbilical cord yet, the brightest and widest beam I've seen."

"Where?"

"Far away, it seems, really far. But it's bright and . . . stunning."

Owen wiggled his fingers at him. "Let me touch the fragment."

Jagger fished it out, pressed it to Owen's fingers, and replaced it. Owen was nodding, smiling. "Wow."

"If Bale saw that, he'd go for it," Jagger said.

"How could he not see it?"

"Could've just started. The Stone's effect on him may have worn off before whoever's causing that got to praying."

"He sees it," Owen said. "I know it."

"Like . . . a feeling?" Jagger ducked to see more of the angel that was standing outside Owen's window. "Did an angel tell you?" Yesterday those words would have been sarcastic; today they weren't.

"I don't know. I just do."

"So where is it? How do we get to it?"

"That's flying distance," Owen said, squinting out the windshield. He looked at the GPS. "Northeast. You drive."

"To the light?

"The airport."

"I haven't driven a car since the crash."

"You'll be fine."

Owen walked around the hood of the car, and before settling into the passenger seat he reached behind it for the iPad. While Jagger followed the GPS toward the airport, Owen worked on the tablet. About five minutes later he spoke. "Okay, okay. Let me just cross-reference this . . ."

"What?"

"Hold on." They were winding through Varna, close to the airport, when Owen said, looking at the screen, "I think I know where it's coming from. Listen to this—from a blog called *Heaven on Earth, A Quest for the Holy Among the Profane*. It's in German. It says, 'Never in my life have I found a community so in tune with God. They pray ceaselessly'"—Owen looked up at Jagger, eyebrows raised—"'but calling it prayer seems to diminish what it really is: communion. God is with them and they with him. Spend even the shortest time with them, and this fact becomes apparent. But they don't walk on sandaled feet, carrying candles, chanting. They live their lives as I imagine God intended them to: They read John Grisham novels and watch Steven Spielberg movies, laugh and joke—but no teasing, they respect each other and the differences God puts into everyone too much for that. They watch and play sports. One I met collects stamps, another football cards, yet another has an incredible Lionel train set on a diorama that would make the most avid collector jealous—but then if the collector told the owner of the train set that, he might just find himself with the diorama; these people are that generous and sensitive to others' feelings. These are humans experiencing all this temporal plane has to offer, and they do it with a constant companion, Jesus Christ.' It goes on and on about how they've melded human existence with holy living."

"What is this community?" Jagger said. "A monastery?"

Owen smiled. "An orphanage."

[57]

"Romania?" Jagger said. They had turned in their rental and were carrying their bags—the duffel of weapons and Jagger's backpack with medical supplies Owen had insisted on bringing—across the tarmac toward the jet.

"Outside a town called Zărneşti, in the foothills of the Transylvanian Alps."

"Transylvania?"

Owen looked at him from the corner of his eye. "Don't get all superstitious on me, now."

"I've faced worse than Dracula."

Owen nodded. "We're facing worse now. Believe me, you want monsters, you don't have to read fiction. The real world's full of them."

"How far away?"

"Two hundred and twenty-eight miles, due northwest. Forty-three degrees west of due north."

"Two hundred twenty-eight miles," Jagger repeated. "You think we saw the beam from that far away?"

"I think if we got used to the vision, we'd be seeing beams a lot farther off than that. We can see stars billions of miles away. The curvature of the earth is the only thing keeping us from seeing the whole world's prayers."

"That and not having our God-eyes."

Owen smiled at that. "Or the big Stone."

On one hand the conversation was perfectly ridiculous, akin to: *The only thing keeping me from flying is not having wings . . . and being too heavy . . . and not being a bird . . . and gravity . . .* But with their visions of the spiritual realm, they weren't talking about the impossible, only degrees of limitation. To Jagger, it helped put the power of the Stone into perspective. Seeing prayer, seeing someone's connectedness to God. Even forgetting about the Clan's using it to target their victims, the ways in which that power could be abused was terrifying. He imagined some fanatical religion—or a traditional religion that became fanatical because of the Stone—sending people into exile or actually killing them because of their lack of connectedness to God as revealed by the Stone. It would end in a world war, the bright-enough believers against everyone else. A whole new kind of persecution on a global scale. Maybe this is how the apocalypse would start.

"Jagger!"

Owen's voice jarred him out of his thoughts.

Owen was pointing at a plane on the runway. "That's it! That's the Clan's Bombardier!"

It was black with silver stripes. Sleek as a bullet, like Owen's, but three times larger. It was zipping along a runway two hundred yards away, building the velocity required to take off.

"Don't point," Jagger said.

"Turn away."

Glancing over their shoulders at the plane, Jagger said. "Is it too late to prevent them from taking off?"

"What? Jump in a service vehicle, chase it down, and crash into it?" As he spoke, the jet's nose lifted and its fuselage followed. It climbed like an eagle after catching its supper. Owen said, "Yeah, it's too late. It was too late as soon as they started taxiing."

"Just thinking of every option," Jagger said.

"Try to keep your eye on it. See which direction it goes."

"Can we catch it in the air?"

Owen shook his head. "*Boanerges's* top speed is four hundred sixty-five miles per hour. Theirs is close to six hundred." He began jogging toward his jet.

Keeping up, Jagger calculated and said, "So it'll take them about twenty minutes and us thirty. That's only a ten-minute difference."

Nice that they were traveling only two hundred and thirty miles. If they were going across a continent, the faster jet could get hours ahead.

"Add another twenty for us to get clearance and take off."

"Half hour behind. That's enough time to do a lot of damage." An orphanage . . . full of godly kids . . . He thought of the scene at the barn.

They reached the jet and Owen opened the door. Pulling down the steps, he looked back at Jagger. "But they don't know we're after them."

"So they might dawdle at the airport, stop for a bite."

"The Clan? I doubt it. If they're hungry, they're probably eating now." He helped Jagger up, then turned to enter the cockpit. "Shut the door," he said, then: "Besides, it's not food they're hungry for."

Just what Jagger wanted to hear. He said, "Is there anything else we can do?"

"Pray."

He retracted the steps, but before closing the door he leaned out and looked for the Bombardier. Twilight had breathed a uniform grayness into the sky, making anything up there all but invisible. But he'd tracked it up until he'd turned to enter the jet, so he knew its general vicinity. Something caught a ray of sunshine and glinted. There it was, over the Black Sea. It made an arc in the sky and headed northwest.

[58]

Jagger sat in the copilot's seat with the jet's satphone and attempted to reach the Mondragon Home for Boys and Girls. An answering machine allowed him to choose his preferred language, and a pleasant female voice informed him that the staff and students were attending services and would be available for emergency calls at nine thirty p.m. Regular office hours were between eight a.m. and five p.m. Please call back then.

"Nine thirty's too late," Owen said. "The Clan will be there by then. Try the police in Zărneşti. I think it's about twenty miles away from the orphanage."

Jagger found a number for a constable. He dialed, but no one answered. He disconnected after more than a dozen rings. "They must not have much crime in the area."

"The Clan is about to send the whole country's violent crime stats through the roof."

Jagger called the monastery's satphone. His call went to voice mail—Gheronda's creaky voice telling him someone would return his call and God bless. He remembered Gheronda had been making plans for an evening *Trisagion*, an abbreviated memorial service for the fallen monks. A full-blown service, called *First Panikhida*—which included the washing and dressing of the bodies and the Divine Liturgy—would take place three days after their deaths, this Friday. He imagined Beth and Tyler were attending the *Trisagion*. He left Owen's satphone number and requested that someone ask Beth to give him a call.

Not sure what else to do, Jagger picked up the iPad and began reading about the home—named after Octavian Mondragon, a philanthropist railroad tycoon who converted an old royal estate into the orphanage in 1911. He'd believed that there was a unnecessary polarity between secular and Christian living, that Christians too often wore their faith like clothes instead of *being* their faith in everything they do. "Faith should be a part of every molecule that composes their bodies," was the way he'd put it. He believed followers of Christ could and should permeate every aspect of society: politics, banking, medicine, geology, education, music, exploration—a glamorized profession at the time—theater, literature, religion. A footnote listed eighty-eight broad categories necessary for a civilized society.

The key to infiltrating society with the Good Word of the gospels, according to Mondragon, was a broad education, cursory exposure to—scanning the list, Jagger decided *everything* pretty much covered it, from fencing to midwifery, equestrianism to fishing and not a Christian education, but a "Christ-centered upbringing." To Mondragon, that meant showing the children how to pray and communicate with God "without ceasing." The goal was to open a channel to God and keep it open, through triumph and tragedy, riches and poverty. It sounded to Jagger like marriage vows.

He found a web site with the complete text of a book about Mondragon, published in 1928, the year he—oh, get this—the year he disappeared on a mission trip to the jungles of Ecuador.

"His head's probably the size of an apple now," Jagger said, "glaring out of a glass case in some museum."

The book quoted the man: "A human being—child or adult—should communicate with his Creator as naturally and automatically as he breathes, as his heart beats in his chest. He eats, sleeps, puts on his stockings. Communication with God should come as easily, it should come as readily. Not communicating with God should be as shocking and disruptive to his system as being denied breath."

What seemed to set Mondragon apart from the stern Catholic boarding schools of his day—from any of the supposed Christ-centered boarding schools or orphanages throughout time—was his belief that the only way to instill such godliness was not through militaristic discipline but through sincerely understanding love.

Recalcitrant children were not beaten or denied benefits; they were loved through their attitude problems, allowed to act out, as long as their behavior didn't harm others. When it did, they were separated from others but were housed in comfortable quarters and slowly reintegrated back into the community at large as their behavior improved, which it inevitably did "once they realized their demeanor did not confer upon them special attention, but the same agape love they receive anyway."

Jagger looked up. He said, "Are you getting the picture of choir boys in white robes, carrying candles, quoting Scripture, and asking if they can do anything for you?"

Owen glanced over. "What's wrong with that?"

"All the time?" He shook his head. "These kids don't sound nauseating to you?"

"I'm sure they're just kids," Owen said. "God made them to be curious and mischievous and full of energy. If he wanted robots, that's what He would have made. And the Bible never says children are the 'before' picture and adults are the 'after.' The reverse, in fact."

"Yeah, but 'every molecule'? They're oozing faith."

"I repeat, what's wrong with that?"

"I just keep seeing these little popes in mitre hats, washing each other's feet."

"Well, if they wash each other's feet," Owen said, smiling, "that would be cool. But why can't they be filthy, with clothes made out of brambles like the hermit-monks? Or hacking their way through a jungle in army boots and khakis, like some of the missionaries I know?"

Jagger nodded.

"Or like Tyler?" Owen continued. "He's probably not 'oozing' faith, but he loves God, doesn't he?"

"All right, all right," Jagger said.

"I met a street kid in old London once," Owen said. "Shabby little girl, stole bread from the carts in West Chepe, a chicken on good days. She'd share her plunder with the other homeless kids." He shook his head. "That kid oozed faith."

"But she stole."

Owen smiled. "We always want to put God in a box, turn His will for us into definitive rules so we don't have to actually *think* about what's right and wrong."

"But not stealing is a commandment."

"Everything in the Bible is a commandment, Jag. What about Proverbs 6:30: 'Men do not despise a thief if he steals to satisfy his hunger when he is starving'? The point is, you have to know *all* of Scripture to know any of it. Otherwise, it's like saying, 'Jagger shoots at people. He must be a killer.'"

"I get it." After thinking for a moment, he said, "Knowing *all* of Scripture . . . really?"

"How many believers can tell you more about Harry Potter than they can Jesus? It's a matter of priority." Owen stared out the window, checked his gauges, made an adjustment on a computer touch screen set in the dash.

Jagger noticed Owen's frown. "What is it?" he said.

Owen shook his head. "It's just . . . what we were talking about . . . What does a godly person look like?"

"I heard you," Jagger said. "Who knows, right? It's like—who said it, 'People look at the outward appearance, but God looks at the heart'?"

"God said it to Samuel. Tell me, who are the people you know who are the most in touch with God?"

"The monks," Jagger said, thinking of their hours spent in prayer and worship. "Pastors, missionaries, theologians . . ."

"Because they're wearing their faith on their sleeves," Owen said. "Not a bad thing, but do you think they have the *strongest* relationships with God, the best communication with Him?"

Jagger said, "I'll bet Beth could give them a run for their money. So to speak."

"Exactly. Think about it."

Jagger waited for Owen to continue, then realized he wanted him to really think about it. He said, "You're saying there's no way of knowing. Could be the plumber come to clean the hair out of your pipes." He thought. "The grocery store clerk. The little girl stealing food from a baker's cart."

Owen nodded. "It's the 'no way of knowing' part that's got me worried."

"Why would that worry—" Jagger remembered the beggar in Varna. The blue light coming out of his head, the angel. "The God Stone," he said. "That's how you'd know. That's how *Bale* would know." He needed a Tums, a whole bottle of them. "He wants to grieve God."

Owen looked at him. "What better way than to go after the people closest to Him? Not the ones who *seem* closest, but those who truly have a heart for God."

"Bale's using the Stone to target his victims," Jagger said. "He's using it to put crosshairs on the most godly people on earth."

[59]

"That's how he found the barn full of worshipers in the middle of Nowhere, Bulgaria," Jagger said.

"And why he slaughtered them," Owen said. "He's not going to keep hitting mass targets like the barn or the orphanage. They're too high profile. It's the very thing he's avoided all these years to keep from getting caught."

"So why now," Jagger said, "other than he can *see* these godly people?"

"He's like a kid who just got himself a huge bag of candy. He's indulging." Owen paused a moment. "He's still figuring it out, how to use the Stone. It won't be long before we start hearing about the puzzling deaths of a shoemaker in Paris, a housewife in Bristol, a Boy Scout in Des Moines. Maybe he'll be more ambitious: a dozen in Spain, fifty in the US, a hundred scattered across Brazil . . . whatever he thinks he can get away with." He looked at Jagger. "If we don't get it back."

"Wish he *were* just a kid with a big bag of candy."

Owen gave him a wry smile. "Think of him that way. It'll be easier."

"Except this kid's got a ream of ruthless killers around him, and machine guns and swords and crossbows."

"And he would do anything not to lose his candy," Owen added.

"I think I'd rather try to get a bone away from a pack of wolves."

"Don't dwell on it."

Jagger returned his attention to the screen, forcing himself to think of something else. He suspected raising kids in a group environment but with individual care and an emphasis on love was a lot more work and more expensive than it appeared in writing.

Bale's going to use the Stone to find them.

It would require a large staff of well-trained and vetted personnel who themselves were treated well by Mondragon and his organization.

Kill them.

But it was a philosophy and program that apparently worked. A good number of "Mondragon children," as they were called throughout their lives, went on to graduate from the country's finest universities—as well as Oxford, Cambridge, the Ivy Leagues, University of Edinburgh, École Normale Supérieure de Paris. They became leaders in politics, the military, medicine, education, the arts . . . nearly every field Mondragon had listed. They'd advised presidents, prime ministers, kings, and popes. They ran conglomerates, powerful trading firms, nonprofit foundations—*Why couldn't the Sinai dig have been funded by one of their conglomerates, instead of Ice Temple?*

Through it all, each one had a reputation for high moral values, and when asked attributed his or her success—indeed, everything—to Jesus Christ, apparently doing it without coming off as holier-than-thou.

Wolves.

He cursed under his breath and squinted hard at the screen.

Jagger gleaned most of the information about the Mondragon Home from articles and online annual corporate reports. The alumni section of the orphanage's web site contained about a hundred mini-articles and interviews with former residents, dating back to its founding. None of them covered the most elite, powerful members, but blacksmiths, accountants, nurses, construction workers . . . ordinary people leading ordinary lives. It seemed the Mondragon orphanage was just as proud of these people, as they had a right to be, of the ones who went into more prestigious circumstances.

Owen listened to Jagger describe the work of the orphanage and said, "It's no coincidence that the home works with children, has had extraordinary success to instill love for God, and that they're doing it in this location. God has redeemed a tragedy and thrown it back in Bale's face."

"What are you talking about?"

"I have experience with Bale in this region," Owen said. "In 1212, he showed up in the village of Hamelin, claiming to be recruiting for the German shepherd Nicholas. Nicholas was gathering children to go preach the gospel to Muslims in the Holy Land."

"The Children's Crusade," Jagger said.

"That's what it was eventually called. But Bale wasn't recruiting for Nicholas, at least not in Hamelin. He took the village's children, one hundred and thirty-four of them, and disappeared. When I heard of this, I came to help. I tracked him to a cave just north of Miclosoara, not far from here." He fell silent.

"And?"

"And he'd murdered them all," Owen said. "Left them in the cave."

"He killed them? Why?"

"Besides to hurt God?" Owen said. "I believe he wanted to cast Nicholas in the worst light possible. Nicholas had claimed to receive his marching orders directly from God. He was charismatic, and people believed him. Now here's an entire village's children murdered in his name. Hamelin grieved for centuries. The town's earliest written records go back to 1385 and start with the line, 'It is a hundred years since our children left.' One hundred and seventy-two years, actually, but I think the chronicler used 'a hundred years' to mean a long time. Point is, after nearly two centuries, the tragedy was still on the townspeople's minds."

"Wait a minute," Jagger said. "Hamelin . . . that rings a bell."

"It's the story of the pied piper."

"Bale was the pied piper?"

Owen nodded. "In the story, he lures away the village's rats using a magic musical pipe, and then does the same with the children when the village reneges on paying him. That's not what happened. It had nothing to do with rats, and he lured them away by telling them it was God's will. The villagers were so ashamed to have allowed a stranger to take their children and kill them, they made up the story of his having a magic pipe."

Jagger was dazed. "And the 'pied' part?"

"Means 'multicolored.' Bale was into flamboyant fashions back then. They told me he was dressed like a count, in scarlet, purple, and gold."

Jagger stared out at the darkness. Every time he learned something about Bale, the same thought crossed his mind: how could anyone be so evil?

"I chased him for eighteen years," Owen said, "trying to convince myself it was to prevent him from killing more innocents." He glanced at Jagger. "But it wasn't true, not completely. My heart had turned dark. I wanted to avenge those children's deaths. I'd seen their bodies." He closed his eyes, anguish cutting into his features, seeing them again after all this time. He continued: "Finally, I heard what God had been telling me all along. I was chasing Bale with the wrong motive. I'd become a vigilante, no better than the Tribe. I stopped the hunt and returned to my purpose: helping people."

"Wouldn't stopping Bale be helping people?"

"It would, but as you said, man looks on the outside, God looks in your heart. When it comes to Bale, my heart is conflicted."

"Then what are we doing chasing him now?"

"I keep telling you, we have to take back the God Stone."

"Well," Jagger said, "I want to kill him."

"If you remembered your time with the Tribe, as a member, you'd reconsider."

Jagger shook his head, thinking about the people in the barn, the children. "No, I wouldn't. I can't believe it would be a sin to kill someone like Bale."

Owen looked at him and tapped his finger against his chest, over his heart.

Jagger looked away.

"We're here," Owen said.

[60]

Jagger lifted his rump off the copilot chair to look down through the windshield. Lights sparkled in a sea of blackness. It could have been a cruise ship in the middle of the Atlantic. His eyes adjusted, and he saw the moon catching the tips of trees—a vast forest of what looked like pines, the tips pointed and swaying, appearing wavelike, which reinforced Jagger's first impression.

"Those lights down there?" Owen said. "That's the manor, the orphanage."

"Are you sure?" The night didn't afford him a comprehensive view, but lights from the structures' own windows showed a massive compound centered around a building with towers and spires. The front was dominated by a square tower similar to the clock towers that he'd seen at large railroad terminals. Walls, walks, and bridges connected this main structure to outbuildings the size of mansions. "It looks more like a castle," Jagger said.

"Why don't you confirm we're in the right spot?"

"How—" He caught the look on Owen's face. "The fragment?"

"We need to see what Bale sees, but I'm sure he's already locked in on the place and researched it the way you did. Even if they've stopped praying—which, from what you found out about these kids, they haven't—but if they have, Bale's still coming. The blood's already in the water."

"They haven't stopped praying," Jagger said, the tips of his fingers touching the fragment in his pocket. Ropes of blue light rose from the manor's roof, spiraling into a single beam, blindingly bright and thick as the manor itself. Golden light pulsed through it, like the flashes of paparazzi covering a red carpet event. The blue glow itself waxed and waned, seeming alive. He thought he caught glimpses of the angels' embers sparking out of the beam here and there.

Owen's blue thread was back. Praying while he talked, planned, flew the jet. Jagger's heart skipped a beat when he saw an angel looking in at him from the window beside Owen. Embers swirled into the cockpit through the wall, swirled back out. The sight gave him hope, but he didn't know why, not after the barn.

He said, "Where's the airport?"

"Almost an hour's drive away, in Sibiu."

Jagger's heart sank. "The Clan must have landed a half hour ago. If it takes thirty minutes to secure their jet, go through customs, find a vehicle—which we'll have to do too—they've probably just left the airport."

"Most likely."

"They're an hour ahead of us. We'll never catch them."

Owen banked sharply—Jagger gripping the seat's arms to keep from tumbling out—and when the jet straightened, the orphanage appeared in their windshield again.

"What are you doing?"

"Beating the Clan. See that road down there?"

Jagger strained. "I think so. To the left of the lights?" It could have been a gray pencil line on black paper.

"That's it," Owen said. "It's curvy in both directions, but straightens out as it passes the orphanage. Take a look. Does it look at least a half mile long, the straight part?"

"There's nothing to compare it to. I guess so."

"That's what I thought. The Clan's Bombardier may be faster and more comfortable, but it's bigger, almost twice the wingspan of this one."

"Yeah?"

"It could never land on that road."

"You're going to land *there*?"

"Gonna try."

"Try? Have you ever done anything like this before?"

"Once."

"What happened?"

Owen frowned at him, shook his head. "It wasn't pretty." He made another sharp bank. "I'll circle back around, give it go."

Jagger snapped into the seat's shoulder harness. "What if a car comes along?"

"This is pretty isolated territory," Owen said. "But if one does drive up, it'll have to get out of the way, because we won't be able to." As he came out of the turn, he pushed in the control wheel and flicked toggles. Jagger watched the "basic T" instruments—named for their standardized arrangement on the instrument panel—showing attitude, airspeed, altitude, and heading. Every one changing dramatically. Below Jagger's feet something vibrated, clunked, and hummed. The landing gear, he guessed. They were dropping, heading for a spot where the narrow road below and ahead of them came out of a bend and cut through the trees in a somewhat straight line. Okay, it did look a bit like a runway—one designed by a drunk or a preschooler.

"Lights would be nice," he said.

"The landing lights will pick it up when I get close."

"Is it wide enough for the wings?" The trees on either side looked like a Super Mario challenge, drawing closer and closer together as they approached.

"It'll be close," Owen said.

"Don't feel you have to be honest," Jagger said. "A lie will make me feel a lot better about now."

"We'll be fine," Owen said and flashed him a big grin.

Jagger gripped the armrests. His legs stiffened, pushing him hard into the seat back.

The jet edged over the road and dropped suddenly. The wheels bounced, then gripped the road. Jagger's head jerked forward . . . again . . . then the plane roared like a weightlifter pushing more than he could handle. Trees zipped by on either side, branches slapping at the wings. As promised, lights on the jet's nose and wings illuminated the road, branches of trees encroaching into their path. They sped past the gates to the orphanage, indicating that they'd eaten up half the "runway."

Jagger's eyelids and mouth sprang open. An angel was holding the nose of the jet, head down and tilted in apparent effort. Its embers had formed wings, which beat behind him. Jagger looked out his side window. Another angel there, in front of the wing, holding the edge. This one appeared to be getting pulled back under the jet's wing, but the angel's ember-wings were out front, over his head, flapping, flapping.

"We're going to make it," Owen said. But the far bend in the road, where trees rose up like a wall, was approaching fast. The entire plane roared and shuddered under the effort to reverse its forward momentum. Slowing, slowing . . . the trees ahead loomed, growing brighter in the landing lights. The nose of the jet pushed the angel into a branch. The angel fluttered up, his embers turning into a whirlwind around him. In a flash he zipped away, sparks trailing after him.

"Told you," Owen said. He fiddled with the controls, and an image of a road, lighted by a single bulb, appeared on the GPS screen. Owen backed the jet up.

"You going to back us up all the way to the orphanage's gate?"

"I'm going to get this rig around the bend here," Owen said. "The Clan will reach the orphanage from the other way. I don't want them seeing *Boanerges*. I just pray some car doesn't crash into it." As he said it, his blue thread thickened and grew brighter. Guess he really meant it.

Owen unsnapped his seat harness, spun out of the chair, and left the cockpit. "Let's go," he said.

Jagger let out a deep breath and looked out at the wing. The angel wasn't there. When he entered the cockpit, Owen was loading the duffel bag with weapons.

[61]

Beth had passed out. Curled on the storeroom floor, a mop bucket pressing into the back of her head, her broken left arm cradled in the right one against her chest. She felt the throbbing in her arm, the pain still shooting into her shoulder, before she opened her eyes. She groaned and started to rise. Her arm protested, sending a lightning bolt to her brain. She touched it delicately with her fingertips, which had apparently turned into white-hot soldering irons for all the pain they caused. Her forearm was swollen, huge, and something hard pushed the skin up. Had to be the bone.

"Tyler," she whispered. He must be frightened out of his mind.

Comfort him, Lord. Let him feel Your peace, which transcends all understanding. Let him be okay.

She rose to her knees, felt around. Boxes, bundled rags, gallon jugs of some kind of cleaning chemical. She had no idea how long she'd been out—ten, fifteen minutes. She found the handle and cracked the door open an inch. She blinked, not understanding. It was night. She walked on her knees and stuck her head out. Deep purple smeared the sky over the mountain, fighting as it did every evening with a starry blackness. An hour and a half at least—could she really have been unconscious so long?

She had to find Tyler.

She pulled the door shut, found a bundle of rags, and began tearing them with her teeth. She tied three around her arm, cinching them as tightly as she could bear. Her molars grated against each other, and tears streamed down her face. She wondered if she could make it to her apartment, where she could do this right, find some kind of splint, a butter knife, maybe; tape; aspirin, lots of aspirin. She thought of other reasons to get to the apartment. Number one on the list: Tyler. It was where he would go, was taught to go if anything bad went down in the monastery. Number two: the gun might still be there, and Phin most likely tossed the box of bullets aside after depriving her of them.

The apartment wasn't far, right next door. The terrace onto which she'd fallen was one floor below her own.

She shook her head. She wasn't thinking clearly. The Tribe would be watching the apartment above all things, if they weren't camped out in it. She hoped Tyler would know that too.

She started fashioning a sling out of the rags, tearing them into strips and tying them together.

Certainly they hadn't caught him. If they had, they would be yelling for her—*Come out, we have your son!* What if they had been yelling and she was too unconscious to hear? Measuring the sling and deciding she needed to add another rag, she wondered, could you be *too* unconscious, or were you either conscious or unconscious, no degrees?

Beth! Stay focused!

She thought the pain would keep her sharp, she'd heard it did. But hers muddled her mind, made her want to lie down and sleep it off.

Think of Tyler, then. He needs you.

She put the circle of rags around her neck and slipped her arm into it, wincing at the needles each little move sent coursing through her veins. She stood, found the mop, and pulled it out of the bucket. It was dry, but it wouldn't have mattered either way. She pushed the head into the floor, angled the handle, and stomped on it. It took three stomps, but it finally snapped. She felt the broken edge, sharp, like a serrated chisel. They might laugh as they shot her or cut her down with their swords, but it was better than swinging at them with her one good hand.

She was thinking about the gun again . . . and aspirin. Tyler was smart enough to stay clear of the apartment; she didn't expect to find him there, but she was weighing the risk-to-reward of going there for the gun and aspirins.

Sounded like a cheesy gangster movie: *Guns and Aspirins.*
Focus!

She opened the door, slipped onto the terrace, and found herself looking up at the apartment. She couldn't see the window, but
the roof over the portico wasn't reflecting the glow of a light inside.
Didn't mean anything. Of course they wouldn't turn on the light if
they were waiting for her.

Tyler first, she told herself. But her arm throbbed and her head
pounded. And she felt sick—yes, mostly with worry for her boy, but
how much of her nausea was the result of pain?

Forget the apartment. Find Tyler. Period. No negotiating. Done
deal.

Where would he go? She needed intel: He was small, could fit
where adults can't. He knew every inch of the monastery. He was
being chased. He was scared. He wanted his mommy. That made him
sound helpless, but he wasn't. Besides everything else, he was smart
and brave.

He liked heights, from where he could look down on things, the
compound, people. She looked up at the dome in the center of the
Colosseum. Could you get inside it? She didn't know, but Tyler would.

He liked low places, into which he could scurry and hide. The tunnels, the wells. She had never been in the monastery's catacombs, but
Tyler had said Gheronda told him about them. Had he also shown him?

Too many places . . . good . . . and bad. If it kept him safe from
the Tribe, it was good, great, praise God! Even if it meant she couldn't
find him either. The bad part was she wasn't going to *not* look, and
that meant moving around the compound, exposing herself.

Do something!

She looked at the dome again, decided to start there. At mini-
mum, the high vantage point would let her spot things she couldn't
from here: Tyler or the Tribe members. She went to the stone steps
leading down to the courtyard. She'd have to cross it to the stairs
by the apartments and take them up to a walkway. She changed her
mind. She went to the opposite side of the terrace, stepped onto a

two-foot-high wall, and holding her broken arm high, jumped across a gap to the railing outside the second-floor apartments. She grabbed the railing with her good hand, swung a leg over, then the other one.

That felt good: she'd saved herself a few minutes and a hundred paces, every one fraught with the threat of being caught. Thinking, *I can do this*, she hurried along the second-floor walkway toward the Colosseum.

[62]

"I got eyes on her," Toby said into the radio, binocs at his eyes.

"Where?" Nevaeh said. She was in the Chapel of the Burning Bush, inspecting the altar to see if it had stairs under it, as so many did. She started for the door.

"I think it's her," Toby said. "Might be the kid. I only caught a glimpse."

"Okay, doesn't matter. We get the kid, we get her. Where?"

"Second floor of the apartments, heading toward the Southwest Range Building. She's out of sight now."

"Got that, guys?" Nevaeh said, running past the burning bush now, behind the basilica, moving fast, using the boots. Before anyone answered she was already halfway up the alley beside the basilica.

"I'm on it," Phin said, and she heard the door of the family's apartment, where he was waiting, slam open.

Elias said, "I'll circle the compound toward the back corner."

"Wait," Nevaeh said, running past Elias. He was on the stairs leading down from the basilica's front doors. Leaving him behind now, moving past the mosque. The boots were exhilarating. "Stay where you are, Elias. Keep the monks in the church. They get out, I don't want to think of the damage they could cause."

The truth was, the mission would be over once they spread out into the compound. The monks had weapons, communications gear, knowledge of where to set up ambushes. The Tribe wouldn't stand a chance.

"Staying in front of the basilica," he confirmed.

"Jordan, where are you?" She reached the front of the apartments and jumped. She sailed over the stairs, landed outside the railing on the second floor, and rolled over it.

Phin was at the far end, where stairs wound down to tunnels and up to the second and third floors of the Southwest Range Building. He turned when he heard her, shook his head.

Jordan's voice came through the radio: "I'm on the wall over the front gate."

"Go around the wall and get on the roof of the Southwest Range Building," Nevaeh instructed.

"Ten-four."

"There!" Phin said, pointing.

Beth was running away from them, along the Southwest Range Building's third-floor portico, her dark shape flashing past the columns, almost to the center.

Phin raised his other hand, gripping a pistol, aiming it at Beth. He fired, just as Nevaeh shoved a shoulder into his side. The bullet shattered a lamp mounted to the wall five feet in front of Beth. She stopped abruptly, turned to stare. Started running again.

"What are you doing?" Nevaeh yelled into Phin's face. "I want her alive!"

Phin's glare could have devoured her. He snarled and disappeared into the stairwell, moving fast.

Nevaeh leaped over the railing, dropped twenty feet, and landed on the ground floor. She ran in front of the Southwest Range Building, bounding over a flight of stairs. She was almost even with Beth, who'd passed the two wide central columns and was making tracks to the building's far end—stairs there, an entrance to the administrative offices, a labyrinth of monk cells.

A building blocked Nevaeh's path. She pulled her feet together in midleap and came down flat on both soles. The boots' pistons blasted down, propelling her onto the building's roof. Two bounding strides, and she sailed over a gap and landed on the roof of the next building. She arced out, then swung in, running toward the Southwest Range Building. She leaped onto another roof, coming down on her soles, and shot toward the third-floor portico at a forty-five degree angle.

And Beth was right there, her trajectory perfect for a collision.

[63]

When the railing collapsed under him and Tyler fell, he landed on the deck, smashing his face. The deck had jarred out, one side farther than the other. Now he sat in the corner nearest the wall, away from the missing railing. The platform canted away from the wall, the outside corner opposite him a foot lower. If he didn't hold on to the railing here, he'd slide off.

His entire face hurt, especially his nose, which had gushed blood over his lips, chin, and chest. He'd wiped at it, but knew all he'd accomplished was to smear it across his cheeks. It had stopped bleeding a half hour ago.

He'd been thinking about how to get down, figuring a way that didn't involve riding the deck to the rocks below. He'd rather jump than crash down with the deck, its boards exploding and splintering around him, becoming as lethal as the fall itself.

Directly below him was a buttress—a wedged-shape projection of stones built against the compound's wall to support it. The top of the buttress was about twenty feet below him. If he hung from one of the deck supports, which ran from each outside corner diagonally to the wall, he could cut another ten feet from his fall. He'd tumble down its slope, but that was better than falling all the way to the ground. So it boiled down to a ten-foot drop onto a stone slope.

If only he could build up the courage to do it.

A gunshot sounded, startling him. He scrambled to his feet, never letting go of the railing, and looked up. The gunfire had come from somewhere inside the compound. He prayed no one was shooting at his mother, and if they were that they were terrible shots. She was looking for him, he knew it. And because of that, the Tribe had seen her . . . and shot at her. It was his fault she was in danger. He should have found a way back in a long time ago. Instead he'd sat there feeling sorry for himself, thinking that getting off the platform alive was hopeless.

He tried the door again, rattled the handle. He lifted himself over the railing—

Don't break. Don't break.

—and put his feet between the balusters to stand outside the railing. He lowered himself, feeling with one foot for the support beam. He was nearly hanging from the deck when his toes touched it. He'd have to let go of the deck and grab the support as he fell.

One . . . two . . .

He squeezed his eyes closed.

You can do it! Come on!

One . . . two . . . three!

[64]

Running toward the end of the Colosseum's portico, Beth saw Nevaeh coming, flying at her from below—made all the more frightening by how her black form and determined face were caught in the glow of lights mounted to the outside columns, which switched on automatically at dusk. She would reach the railing in seconds, probably flip over it and be standing right in front of her. Beth could hear Phin behind her, closing the gap fast, clomping like a robot.

Instead of trying to run faster—as if she could—past Nevaeh or spinning to face Phin, she darted toward Nevaeh, leaning out over the railing and pointing the business end of the mop handle at her, going for a center-mass impalement. Nevaeh's eyes flashed wide, too late to do anything. Beth steadied herself, gripped the makeshift spear with her one good hand as though it were a lifeline, and braced the blunt end against her shoulder.

Nevaeh sailed right for it—right *into* it. At the last moment, the point inches from her chest, she clenched it in both hands, ramming it into Beth's shoulder, making her stagger back.

If Nevaeh let go she could grab the railing, flip herself over. But Beth didn't let that happen. She pushed forward, walking with the spear between them, shoved out with it, and let go.

Nevaeh dropped, her body becoming horizontal, legs kicking, arms pinwheeling.

Observing the speed at which Nevaeh had moved on the ground, bounded onto the buildings, and leaped to the Colosseum's third floor, Beth figured the noisy boots she wore gave her legs super abilities. If they allowed such high jumps, they'd surely cushion a long fall—but they wouldn't do Nevaeh any good unless she could get them under her.

Nevaeh slammed back-first onto the roof of a building two floors below. A millisecond later her head and limbs struck down, all of them bouncing a little, as if to release the spray of gravel and dust that accompanied her impact. Her head sideways, showing Beth her profile, Nevaeh didn't move.

Phin's clomping stopped. Sixty feet away, he was leaning over the railing, staring down at Nevaeh. The stunned look on his face put a brief smile to Beth's lips. Very brief. He pulled back to glare at her, his hand flapping over a pocket on his hip, and she remembered the gun—not that he needed it with those boots, with Beth having nowhere to go he couldn't reach in seconds.

The building beside the one Nevaeh was sprawled on rose a floor higher and had been constructed closer to the Colosseum. Beth ran fifteen feet farther toward the end, climbed over the railing, and jumped. The roof was only six feet away and as many feet down. She hit and rolled, yelling at the pain in her arm, a Ninja's throwing star spinning back and forth between her wrist and shoulder.

She expected Phin to zip to her launching point and make his own leap to the roof. Watching as she got to her feet and scrambled toward the roof's ledge, she was surprised to see him jumping the railing where he was. He disappeared levels below her and sprang back into view, rising almost what must have been thirty feet straight in the air, grinning. At the apex of his rebound he said, "I seeeeeeee you!" Then he dropped out of view.

She knew this section of jumbled buildings. In fact, it was right over there that she'd found Tyler crying in the corner outside Father Jerome's quarters only a few hours ago. The rooftops were of varying heights, stair-stepping down to the ground, if you knew the zigzaggy route to take. She dropped to her rump at the ledge and slid off, landing on the next roof-terrace four feet below. She started for the next ledge and stopped. She heard Phin land on the chapel roof behind her. She backed up into the recess of a doorway. Phin landed on the roof twenty feet in front of her, shifting his head around as he immediately bounced up onto the adjacent roof. The clomping noises of his landings came back at her after he was gone. The speed and jumping abilities of his boots were working against him: he was moving too fast to take a careful look at anything—or maybe he figured she wouldn't pause to hide and he'd spot her climbing off the roofs, running.

She ran to the ledge, slid over, and pressed herself to the shadowy wall as Phin leaped over her and kept going. She made her way to the ground and then the tunnel that went under many of the buildings, cutting diagonally toward the courtyard by the mosque. As she moved through the tunnel she considered her options. It was a short list: get out of the tunnel and move along the buildings, out of the lights, to the tourist information center in the compound's northwest corner . . . it was always unlocked and contained closets and cabinets she could hide in until she could collect her thoughts and formulate another course of action. Or she could . . .

Nope, that was it. She could not think of anything else to do, any other place to go.

She saw the lighter gray of the tunnel exit ahead of her and slowed. She peered out: mosque straight ahead, basilica to her right. She was two steps out of the tunnel, heading for the mosque, when Elias—the old country singer-looking guy who chain-smoked and had made shrimp curry when she was the Tribe's prisoner in the Paris catacombs—came walking toward her from between the mosque and the basilica. He must have been patrolling by the bell tower.

She froze, not sure he'd seen her. He was in the light of the basilica's external lamps, but she was beyond it . . . she hoped. He plucked the cigarette out of his mouth, tossed it down, and began swinging the barrel of a weapon toward her—odd shaped, long and thin with a canister at the end, tubes trailing around his side to his back, scuba tanks peeking up over his shoulders. She remembered: Elias was the guy Jagger had said used a flamethrower to stop him and Owen in the catacombs. She spun and darted back into the tunnel.

Elias's voice reached her before she hit the first junction: "She's in the central tunnel." He was obviously using a radio. She heard a *whooooooosh*, and the tunnel behind her around a lazy curve lighted up.

Heat washed over her back. She rushed through the light at the first junction, into the right-hand tunnel, and stopped. No, the other tunnel was longer, darker, more serpentine. It offered less of a chance for Elias to fix a fiery bead on her. She backtracked and went the other way, hearing Elias almost to the junction, thankful for the silence of her bare feet.

She brushed her fingers against the rough stone walls, feeling the changing textures as she went from one of the buildings that formed the tunnel to the next. Almost there, a plan already in mind—she'd work her way around Elias and end up where he'd spotted her. Up ahead she heard clomping. Someone coming into the tunnel. She stopped, started back. The smell of cigarette smoke and gasoline reached her before the quiet steps Elias was taking—not as noisy as the person coming at her from the other way. She pushed herself against the wall, nowhere to go. It was the darkest part of the tunnel, utter blackness, but that wouldn't matter when they converged on her.

She had to run toward one of them, thinking at first she'd rather face Elias than that freak Phin. Then she imagined Elias getting off a stream of fire before she reached him, her body becoming a rolling mass of flames and stopping as a smoldering ash pile at his feet. Phin it was.

She took three quick breaths—*Run, as fast as you ever have, run . . . right past him . . . or into him . . . knock him over . . .*

Another sound, close: a click. The scuff of a shoe on the stone floor.

She gasped, louder than she intended.

A light flashed on, blinding her.

[65]

A few feet to her right a penlight flashed on, wavering in someone's hand, pointed away from her, then panning quickly. It shined on her and snapped off. Feet rushed at her, arms wrapped around her, turning her, binding her to a body pressed against her back now. A hand covered her mouth. All of it before she could take a breath, let alone scream. Minty breath blew over her ear. "Shhh."

The man—his size and strength making him a man in her mind—pulled her in the darkness, walking backward. They bumped into a wall, slid along it, and plunged back quickly. He swung her around. She felt a breeze and heard another click.

The man released her, said again, "Shhh. It's Leo."

"Leo? I—"

"Shhh."

"They're coming," she said, barely louder than a breath. "From both sides."

"Shhh."

The clomping grew louder. A muffled voice said, "Elias?"

"Yeah."

"You said she came this way."

Elias said something too muffled to understand. The clomping faded, along with Phin's complaining voice.

Leo said, "The tunnels have doorways few people know about. They're painted to look like the walls."

"Why?"

"Never know when you're going to need them. Come with me."

He brushed past her in the darkness. She followed his sounds around a corner. A click, similar to the ones before, and she felt the air pressure around her change. "Come on," he said, pulling her arm, leading her past him. She heard a gentle creak and a light came on, dull, but hurting her eyes after the Stygian darkness. She blinked, looked around. They were in a room, an old monk cell built into a corner. Everything was dirty and dusty. Lumber was stacked against a wall and a big rusty toolbox sat in one corner. Opposite the door through which they'd entered was another.

"At one time or another of its long history, the monastery housed many more monks than it does now," Leo said. "As many as a hundred or more. There are monk cells and extra rooms everywhere."

Beth nodded. It didn't take wandering too far off the tourists' route to see how superfluous most of the buildings were.

His mouth fell open when he saw her arm. "Are you all right?"

"Nothing a bottle of aspirin won't fix. It doesn't feel as bad as it did, or I'm getting used to the pain. Where are the other monks?"

"The Tribe has them in the Church of St. Catherine," Leo said, meaning the basilica. He was that way, using the proper names of things even after they'd become familiar and routine. "We were all in there for the memorial service. We heard gunshots and ran out, but that man, Elias, chased us back in—with a flamethrower."

"That was me firing the gun," she said. "They tried to drug Tyler and me. Nevaeh said she wanted to take me to find out what I said or did that made God forgive Ben. I told her it wasn't me. Whatever happened was between Ben and God."

"Of course." Leo rubbed his scant beard, thinking. "Nevaeh's been frustrated for a long time. I think Ben's passing turned that into desperation. She's a seeker. She knows she needs God but doesn't know how to find Him. So she's grabbing at anything and everything."

Despite the pain and danger Nevaeh's wayward quest had caused her family, Beth felt sorry for her. The answer was simple, but Nevaeh was convinced that nothing as profound as eternal life with God could be easy or simple.

"If you were in the basilica for the service," she said, "how'd you get here?"

Leo grinned. "The rear windows look like stained-glass panels mortared to the building, but they're hinged."

She remembered the two small windows above the roof of the Chapel of the Burning Bush, whose altar protruded into a round addition at the back of the basilica. Or rather, the basilica was the addition: the chapel had been there first. Helena, the mother of Constantine the Great, had ordered it built upon finding the bush. Two hundred years later Emperor Justinian I ordered the construction of the walls, and all the other buildings had sprouted like mushrooms over the next fifteen hundred years.

"You climbed out onto the chapel room and dropped down?"

Leo nodded. "Into the courtyard of the burning bush, me and Gheronda."

"Gheronda?" She couldn't imagine the old man performing such a feat.

He smiled. "I gave him a hand. He insisted, said he knew the place better than anyone and could get around without getting caught."

"Where is he?"

"Should be back soon." He gave her a concerned look. "I hope."

"What about the others?"

"Still in the church. If too many of us disappeared, Elias would have noticed. He pokes his head in now and again." He walked to the other door, cracked it open, peered out. He turned his ear to the opening and listened.

"Are they coming? Can you hear them?" she said.

He closed the door. "I wasn't checking for the Tribe. The connecting rooms lead through several buildings, all the way into the Chapel of Martyrs. Gheronda left to see if he could go from there to his office."

That was on the Colosseum's third floor.

"The monastery's satellite telephone is there, and a gun." Leo looked at her, his brow furled. "Where's Tyler?"

"I don't know. He escaped through the roof of the panic room Jagger built in our apartment. That little Tribe boy, Jordan, was chasing him, but I think something happened to him. When I got out, I couldn't find Tyler." Why hadn't that been the first thing she told Leo? It was the most important. But with everything happening so suddenly, she'd gotten caught up in the story of how Leo had come to be here, to save her. "We have to find him," she said. "That's what I was trying to do when they spotted me. How did you know I was in the tunnel?"

"I didn't," he said. "I've been watching for Gheronda to come back. If the way he went gets cut off, he'd try to get back here another way. I've been checking periodically, in case he was injured or needed help. I knew I'd hear the Tribe if they were coming through. They have these boots—"

"Tell me about it," Beth said. "Those things let them run like cheetahs and jump like . . . well, nothing I've ever seen. Forty feet straight up."

Something banged in the other room, and the door flew open. Gheronda rushed in, out of breath. His crinkly old face smiled when he saw Beth, and he said her name like a father welcoming his prodigal daughter home. He moved in to give her a hug, then paused, frowning at her arm.

"It's broken, but it's not what bothers me now. Tyler's out there somewhere." She told him what had happened.

Gheronda said, "I saw Jordan. He's walking on top of the walls." He rubbed her good shoulder, smiled—sort of—and said, "If they found Tyler, they probably put him in the basilica with the others."

"If they found him," she said, "they'd parade him around the compound, calling for me to come out." Or . . . she didn't want to think about it, but her mind kept pulling it into her consciousness: what if they'd found him and hurt him? Nevaeh had said they wanted only to put him under. She had also said she wanted to take Beth with her. If that was true, why had Phin shot at her? Why had Elias blasted the tunnel with fire? Either the others had not gotten the message about not hurting them, or now that Nevaeh was out of commission—probably not for long and certainly not dead—all bets were off.

She said, "Help me find Tyler. Please."

"We may soon get some help," he said, pulling the satphone from under his cassock. "I called the police from the office."

Leo stepped forward. "They're coming?"

"They weren't very enthusiastic, but I believe I convinced them. And look . . ." He flipped a switch, turned a dial on the phone. Voices came through.

". . . she all right?" Elias.

Phin: "She's coming to now."

"They're talking about Nevaeh," Beth said, and told them what happened.

Leo said, "Fall like that would have killed anyone else." He turned to Gheronda. "We can hear them. Can they hear us?"

"Only if we want them to. The phone uses radio signals to communicate with a satellite transmitter in the office," Gheronda said. "The transmitter is connected to a dish on the roof. It lets us use it anywhere in the compound, even under all these buildings." He looked at the ceiling as if seeing through it. "It's a regular 2 meter/440 band radio. I scanned for communications outside the wall, even though it doesn't have much range. That's when I picked up the Tribe's chatter."

Nevaeh's voice came through the tiny speaker. "Toby, tell me you saw where she went." She didn't sound so good.

Toby: "I saw her while she was on the roofs. Phin was right there. I thought he was going to get her."

"Nothing since?"

"Negative."

"What about the kid? Tyler?"

Beth tensed.

"I haven't seen him at all. He's holed up somewhere."

That's my boy.

"Lot of good you're doing up there."

The three of them tilted their heads toward the phone. Finally they heard Nevaeh speak again.

"Get down here, and bring the Barrett. We're going to tear this place apart."

[66]

Tyler held on. The deck threatened to fall with or without him, and he couldn't bring himself to let go. He believed any shift or change to the deck now would be the thing that brought it down. But he couldn't hold on forever. He looked down at the stone buttress—a black wedge in the darkness, but he could tell it was a lot farther below his feet than he thought it would be, and he decided maybe this wasn't such a good idea.

The support post from which he hung creaked, moaned, and shuddered.

He lifted himself and hooked an arm over the support post to relieve his muscles, which had begun to feel like Silly Putty. He hung like that for another few minutes, then reached to get his other hand onto the platform.

That's when the platform released its hold on the wall and fell.

Tyler couldn't help it: he screamed. He dropped to the top of the buttress, not feeling anything at first. In a blur of motion and fear, he hit, collapsed, and started to tumble.

The deck, weighted by its front edge, fell away from the wall, striking the buttress halfway along its slope to the rocky ground— exploding into its pre-deck form of loose planks, supports, nails.

Tyler toppled after it, instinctively protecting his head with his arms while attempting to grab at the stones of the buttress whenever his hands slapped against them. He somersaulted, rolled, smacking his head, his arms. He twisted and rolled toward the shattered deck, which had abruptly settled as a pile of wood at the bottom. He crashed into the debris, feeling pain now.

He felt dizzy, sleepy. He wondered if he was hurt more than his mind detected, in more places, more severely. He thought about moving to find out, but partly he didn't want to know and partly he was too achy and tired. He lay sprawled among the wood, staring through a cloud of dust and a fog of pain at the edge of the wall and the night sky beyond it. The stars grew bright and began to swirl, leaving tiny comet trails behind them. *Wow.* The edges of his vision became blurry, as though heavy smoke were seeping in from all sides. He blinked, blinked, and upon the third closing of his lids, they stayed that way.

[67]

Jordan bounded over the crumbling section of wall and ran along its top toward the crashing sound and scream that had come from near the monk-cell structure in the center. He stopped before reaching the parapet and turned his flashlight beam toward the ground on the outside of the wall. He raised his radio.

"I see him!" he said, his beam holding on the wreckage below. Floating dust and dirt obscured the scene like a smudge on a photograph. "It's Tyler! He's outside the wall, on the east side by the dig." The kid must have been hiding on the platform. Jordan had passed it at least half a dozen times, even looking out at the dig. If he'd angled his eyes closer to the wall, he would have spotted him.

Tyler wasn't moving, only lying there, forming an X with his arms and legs, one knee bent, the foot tucked back under his thigh. His head was downhill—rather, down-buttress—from his feet. It was tilted up as though resting on a pillow, but what propped it up was rotten, broken wood.

Tyler appeared dead, and Jordan was surprised to feel an aching sadness about that, felt it in his stomach as hollowness and in his heart as heaviness. He'd experienced the sensation before, whenever he'd heard about one of the Tribe's offspring dying. He'd talked to Elias about it a long time ago. Elias had nodded slowly, the way he did, and said he felt the same way. He'd said it had something to do with what the Tribe did, always taking away things from the world, taking away lives—wasted lives, for sure, people who'd used their time on earth for evil. But people nonetheless. That made them takers, and over time it made their existence small, growing tighter and more compact with each life they took, like a collapsing star that sucked in everything around it and gave back nothing.

Ben had argued this point, saying they were not takers, but givers, giving to the survivors of the evil people's bad deeds the closure they needed, and to their would-be victims life without the pain they would have caused.

Jordan didn't know on which side of the argument he came down—both, he guessed—but he did know that any time one of them married and bore a child—something he would never experience and sometimes regretted, but usually didn't ponder much—he felt wonderful. It was like a loosening of that tight knot they'd become, a relaxing of a bind around his chest so he could breathe: they were giving back, putting something into the world. And when that child died, the knot tightened again.

"Get him," came Nevaeh's voice over the radio.

"I think he's dead," Jordan said. "No, *wait*—"

Tyler was moving, pulling his leg out from under him, blinking and squinting against Jordan's flashlight beam. "He's alive," Jordan reported.

Tyler turned, his bottom half sliding around, down off the buttress. He rolled onto his stomach and rose to his hands and knees, then up onto his feet, glancing into the beam now and then. He went around the pieces of the platform and limped away, heading into the archaeological site. He picked up a round length of wood, using it as a crutch. Glancing over his shoulder into the light, he hobbled away.

"Hey!" Jordan called. "Wait!" He panned down to the ground below him. It was a long way down. He'd never tested the boots' ability to cushion a jump from this height, let alone onto such uneven, rocky ground.

"What's going on?" Nevaeh said.

"He's walking away, limping."

"Elias, where are you?" Nevaeh said. No answer. She said, "Jordan, Phin's coming. Make sure Tyler doesn't get away."

Jordan swept the beam up to Tyler, heading for one of the two big excavation holes, each looking like an Olympic-size swimming pool in progress. He brought the light back to the ground below. If he weren't at least down there when Phin arrived, he would be in serious trouble. Phin would push him or throw him over the edge, at the very least. If Tyler got away . . . he didn't even want to think about that.

He bent and straightened his knees, feeling the magneto-something fluid ripple under his feet, reading his movements, interpreting his intentions. The disks on the outsides of his knees hummed quietly. Better to jump than face Phin. He took a deep breath and leaped. The hip clamps tightened; the braces forced him to bend his knees. He concentrated on landing flat, not immediately straightening when he did—which would cause the boots to propel him into the air—and not tumbling forward.

He landed, stumbled forward, tripped over a rock, and fell. Not too bad. He rolled onto his back and shined the light up at the top of the wall, way, way up there. Totally sick. He rose and realized he'd dropped the radio. He scanned the ground with light and saw it in pieces among the stones. He picked up the largest piece, most of the rectangle that made up its body. The digital screen that was supposed to show the channel it was on and the signal strength was shattered. He depressed the Talk button. "Nevaeh? Phin?" Nothing.

He dropped it and raised the flashlight, looking for Tyler. His stomach rolled when he couldn't find him. Then he saw him: his head just dropping over the edge of the nearest hole. Jordan took long, sailing strides over the rough terrain to the leveled-out smooth ground around the hole and jumped in. He shined the light into the darker-than-night hole stretched out before him. At the far end it sank down, and he couldn't see the bottom. He was about to move forward when he heard the crunch of rubble on rubble behind him, breathing. He spun and caught Tyler in the light—swinging a piece of wood at his head.

[68]

Gheronda had held the phone up in his hand, Leo and Beth facing him, when Beth heard Jordan say he found Tyler, say he was dead. Emotions pounded her brain like waves on a beach, and she felt faint. Tears instantly filled her eyes and her hand shot to her mouth, slapping back a scream, not wanting to give voice to her grief, not wanting to make it real. Then Jordan had said, *"No, wait,"* then he said *"He's alive."* Beth blinked.

Please say I heard that right. Please let him be alive.

She realized Leo had stepped to her side, had his arm around her back, was holding her broken arm, pulling her tight against his side. They'd listened to Jordan's description of Tyler limping away, Nevaeh's order to make sure he didn't get away, that Phin was on his way.

Now Beth said, "It's Tyler! Tyler." She stepped out of Leo's embrace and started for the door to the adjoining monk cell.

Leo grabbed her arm. "Wait. We have to—"

She yanked her arm from his hand. "We have to get him. That's all we have to do." She turned toward the door, clicked it open.

"Beth," Leo said. "We have to think this through."

"There's no time!" Glaring at him. "You heard Jordan. He's outside the walls. He's hurt. They're going for him."

"I'm just saying—"

Gheronda stepped between them. "Calm down now, both of you." He looked at Beth. "Hysteria's not going to get Tyler back."

She could have slapped him. *"Hysteria?* You haven't seen—"

"Dear," he said, "I shouldn't have said that." He held the phone to her. "At least call your husband, tell him we need him and Owen back here now. Owen will know what to do."

She had the sense that he was stalling, trying to keep her from rushing out to save her son, give himself and Leo time to come up with a plan. But there was only one course of action: get Tyler.

She pushed the phone away. "You call him. I'm going to get my son."

"He needs to hear it from you," Gheronda said. "He won't need explanation, just a word from you: 'Get back here now.' At least do that, in case . . ."

In case I don't make it back, she thought. Maybe he was trying to save himself a call to Jagger telling him the Tribe had murdered her or taken her. And on one level, he was right: one word from her would bring Jagger running, no matter what he was caught up in trying to track down the Clan.

But seriously . . . he wanted her to make a phone call when her son was hurt and in danger?

Stalling.

"Fifteen seconds," Gheronda said, lifting the phone at her again. "Call the cavalry."

"Do you have Owen's number?"

He turned the phone toward himself, punched buttons, handed it to her.

She held it to her ear. Beeping and clicking came through the speaker. She wiped a tear off her cheek. Somewhere in the world, a satphone started ringing.

"Hello?"

"Jagger!" Beth said in a rush. "The Tribe's attacking the monastery. They're here now. Tyler—"

Gheronda held up his hand, stopping her. "Shhh, shhh." He tilted his head. "What was that?"

The door leading to the tunnel burst open and Elias stepped in, flamethrower in hand, a small flame in front of the muzzle hissing. He said, "If you're going to hide, hide. Don't talk."

Flame shot out in a stream, just left of the tight group, panning toward them.

Leo raised his hands, ducked his head, as though intending on blessing Gheronda and Beth. He threw his body into them, shoving the old man into Beth and pushing her back into the door. She crashed through it and fell. The men fell on top of her, and she saw Leo bend his leg, stretch it out. He hooked the door with his foot and swung it around, kicking it closed. He rolled off them onto his back, rocking back and forth. He was on fire, flames and sparks coming up from under him. He could have been employing an unusual method of putting out a campfire. Gheronda scrambled off Beth, reaching for Leo. He ripped at Leo's collar, pulled the flaps of the cassock back.

"Slip out!" he yelled. "Get out of the robe!"

As Leo yanked his arms out, rolling back and forth, Beth jumped to the door, pressed her palms against it. She could already feel the heat on the other side coming through. The door was equipped with a crude locking mechanism, a piece of wood that slid into a U-shaped bracket mounted to the wall beside it. She slammed her palm into the back of the wood, engaging the lock. The door thumped, rattled—Elias trying to get in. Kicking in, probably; the door at his side was still on fire, and she remembered from her conversations with Jagger that one of the awful things about the flamethrowers was the fuel it used: it was like glue, sticking to whatever it hit and burning until it had completely consumed itself. It was an agonizing, terrible way to die.

She turned away from the door. A streak of burning fuel ran across the floor, lighting the room. Leo was hopping up, away from the burning cassock. Sparks fell away from Leo as he brushed at his shoulders, his pant legs. Gheronda walked around him, slapping out little fires.

The door thumped again. Flame and smoke came in from the crack under it.

Beth looked at her empty hand. She spun around, scanning the floor. "The phone," she said. "I lost it. It must have gotten knocked out of my hand!"

Now Gheronda approached her, patting the air with his hands. "You got word to Jagger. That's good enough."

She looked at the door, heard another thump, watched it shake. She found the door opposite it and headed for it. "I have to go to Tyler."

Leo stepped in front of her. His clothes were still smoking. He said, "I'll go," and raised his hand when she started to protest. He looked at Gheronda. "Take her someplace safe, back in the cells on the other side of the tunnel. I'll find you."

Beth said, "But if we all go—"

"Then we'll all be caught," he said. "One person has a better chance at slipping past them. I can move faster alone, faster than you. I'll get him back."

She looked at Gheronda, whose contoured face was twisted into an expression of sadness and concern. But he closed his eyes and nodded. She turned in time to see Leo slipping out the door, closing it behind him.

She ran, tugged it open. "Leo!" The room beyond was empty.

[69]

"Beth! Beth!" Jagger yelled into the satphone. He hit the redial button, looked up at Owen as he listened to it ring.

Owen had stopped on the third step leading to the manor's front doors. The light coming out of his head had faded away; the angels who'd walked up the road with them, through the gates, and along the long drive to a courtyard anchored by a fountain—they were gone too.

Not gone, Jagger remembered. He hoped not gone, simply invisible.

"What is it?" Owen said. "What's happening?"

The call rolled into voice mail, Gheronda saying in Egyptian, "You've reached—"

Jagger disconnected, ran to the first step, grabbed Owen's wrist, and tugged him off the steps. "We have to get back to St. Catherine's," he said.

"Now? Why?"

"The Tribe's there. They're after Beth . . . something about Tyler! We have to leave, now!"

"What's the Tribe want with—"

"It doesn't matter. She got cut off. Something happened."

Owen's hand clamped over his own mouth, squeezing down the beard on his cheeks.

"Owen! We have to go back, we have to go!" Jagger tugged on his wrist, forcing him to take a step.

Owen looked over his shoulder at the manor doors, then back to Jagger. He began shaking his head. "We can't, Jag. You know that. We have to warn the orphanage."

"My family!" Jagger pleaded. But he knew Owen was right. They were there because the Clan was coming, and if they left now, the blood of the children and their adult guardians would be on his hands. Whatever was happening at the monastery, he couldn't stop it, not from twenty-five hundred miles away. But what if Beth and the monks could hold them off . . . for a time . . . and then he and Owen got there moments too late?

"What are they after?" Owen said again.

Jagger shook his head, resigned to having to wait. But that didn't mean they could dawdle. He brushed past Owen, started up the stairs. "Come on, let's do this and get out of here." Even then, he had to fight the urge to argue with Owen that they had to leave that very moment . . . or climb into the pilot's seat himself and try to get back to the monastery, if that's what it took.

And he did turn and descend the stairs. "I can't do this," he said, torn, knowing his anguish was showing on his face. "I can't think of anything but—"

A boy and girl had just emerged from the woods encircling the courtyard. The boy, about thirteen, carried a flashlight in need of new batteries; the girl, whose hand he held, was no older than six. He was dressed in slacks and a button shirt. She had on a pink dress with an embroidered hem. She was clutching a handful of small white flowers. They saw Jagger and Owen and smiled.

They came into the light, and the boy switched off his flashlight. The boy spoke in what Jagger guessed was Romanian. Owen replied in the same language, said to Jagger, "The boy is Aleksandar and the girl is Rayna. He says she slipped out to get the flowers."

The boy spoke again.

Owen said, "She has a habit of doing that. One of the other children has to fetch her."

Jagger couldn't take his eyes off her little face. She was cherubic. Pursed doll lips, dark liquid eyes, cheeks that looked like she'd stuffed her mouth with gumballs. A scar, pink and thick, ran from her temple to the corner of her mouth, looking to Jagger like a worm was stuck there. "What happened to her?" he said.

Owen knelt, spoke gently to her, touched her head. He stood, leaned close to the boy—Aleksandar—and whispered. He listened to the boy's hushed words and turned to Jagger. "She came to Mondragon with an injury suffered at the hands of her father, a drunk."

It broke Jagger's heart to think of her with her face sliced open, bleeding, crying. He wondered if the injury was worse for her because it was inflicted by someone who was supposed to love her.

He said, "Owen, we're in a hurry. The Clan—"

Owen spoke quickly to Aleksandar. He put his hand on the boy's shoulder and pulled him forward a step, pointing to the front door.

"*Nu,*" Aleksandar said, shaking his head. He gestured toward a corner of the manor and began walking that way, pulling Rayna along.

Owen clapped Jagger on the back, urging him to walk with him as he followed the children. "He says the front door's locked. He's taking us to a side entrance."

As they hurried behind Aleksandar and Rayna, Jagger said, "You acted like we had all the time in the world back there, chatting with the kids."

Owen didn't say anything. Jagger caught a slight smile bending the man's mouth. He said, "There's nothing funny about this."

"Not funny, no," Owen said. "Just amazing."

"What?"

"I suppose you think Aleksandar and Rayna showing up like that was a coincidence?"

"No, it was God," Jagger said flatly, sorry it came out that way as soon as it did.

"Seeing them," Owen said, "their faces, the living, breathing, human side of what we're doing here . . . Tell me you're not more committed to saving them."

"We still have to hurry, for their sake, and Beth and Tyler's." But Owen was right: Jagger couldn't just leave now anymore than he could kill these kids himself. Something occurred to him. "Are you saying you stalled back there so I could get a good look at them?"

"Maybe just a little."

They followed the kids around the corner, onto a large stone patio. Beyond a waist-high wall on the right, ancient pines blocked the moon. Through them Jagger could see another building, one of the mansion-like structures he'd viewed from the plane. On the left they passed rows of French doors.

"Want to bet there's more to these two showing up than giving your heart a thump?" Owen said.

"Like what?"

He raised his voice and spoke in Romanian. Aleksandar replied over his shoulder, gesturing toward the house.

Owen told Jagger, "The staff doesn't answer the front door after seven."

"We would have found an open door or pounded on different ones until someone inside came to find out what we wanted."

"After wasting how much time?"

"You're convinced God's guiding us?" Jagger said.

"At least helping."

"Then He should make the Clan's jet crash."

Owen smiled at him. So comfortable with the way he believed things worked. Jagger wished he possessed a small fragment of Owen's confidence. He said, "How do you know it's not just . . . I don't know, the world turning, things happening just because they happen? Does it always have to be God?"

"Or those working against Him or man's own decisions catching up with him."

"See?" Jagger said. "Maybe it wasn't God helping us."

"Why are you so insistent that it isn't?"

Because a helpful God isn't the God I know, Jagger thought. He still struggled with a God who allowed bad things to happen, only to help with things that maybe/kinda/sorta lessened the severity of the blow. It seemed fickle. It was easier to accept that things simply happened, for good or for bad, than that the world was guided by a Supreme Being who either changed His mind with abrupt and stunning frequency or was altogether arbitrary.

The boy had stopped near the back corner of the manor, past the glass doors. He opened a wooden door, and the girl rushed in. He said something to Owen.

Owen translated as they entered a long hallway, the boy shutting and locking the door behind them and hurrying past to lead the way. "The headmaster's name is Mr. Stanga. He's with the rest of the children and staff in the chapel."

Up ahead, Rayna pulled open a heavy door and disappeared inside. Aleksandar caught it before it closed and called into the room. He stood there holding the door, looking in, obviously waiting for someone.

Owen turned in front of Jagger, stopping him. He said, "Quick, get the fragment."

[70]

Evidence of Owen's theory of divine guidance sprang into view as soon as Jagger touched the fragment. Angels everywhere, filling the halls, towering over Aleksandar, whose beam of light pierced the ceiling over his head even while he was saying something to Owen.

Owen's light was thicker and brighter than the boy's, but come on, he was John the Apostle.

Jagger reached his real hand to the wall, steadying himself. The shift from normal vision to what he'd started thinking of as God's-eye vision was dizzying. Forget the millions of swirling embers, which were somehow part of the angels and seemed to be forming images as they moved, like secret messages he was meant to decipher; forget the melodic chorus of voices, dim but insistent, and the sense that there was so much more right in front of him he should be seeing, a sort of shifting of vague colors, like putting on 3-D glasses outside of a theater. The mere instant appearance of angels was enough to knock you back and make your head do cartwheels.

A man came through the door Aleksandar held. He was a head shorter than Owen, wavy black hair down to his shoulders, salt-and-pepper mustache drooping to the bottom of his chin—and thick sideburns. He reminded Jagger of half the leading men in movies from the 1970s—Al Pacino, James Caan. Not the dapper, buttoned-down English sort of gentleman he'd expected. A blue beam rose from his head.

He and Owen spoke, and the two stepped into the room. Owen leaned out through the door to wave Jagger in. The chapel appeared to be a converted ballroom. It was about half the size of a football field with a wooden floor and round, ornamental medallions spaced evenly over the ceiling where Jagger guessed chandeliers used to hang. The long wall opposite the doors was a huge grid of paned glass, starting at a sill three feet high and rising twenty or more feet to the ceiling. It was too dark outside to make out the view, but he caught the hints of trees, needles and branches swaying in the wind.

Candelabras bearing tall white candles, each capped by a flickering flame, lined the walls and appeared to be the room's only source of light . . . if you didn't count the pulsing blue beams extending from the heads of at least two hundred children and a dozen or so adults. He squinted against their brightness and noticed that they were as varied in appearance as were the faces turned toward him and Owen. Some were as thin as spider's silk, others as heavy as industrial extension cords. Gold flakes sparked in some, while in others the gold looked more liquid, spiraling around the beams. The hues of blue ranged from the color of a washed-out summer sky to stunning sapphire.

As far as Jagger could tell, none of the people were praying, not in the classical sense of focused and exclusive communication with God. If they produced beams this vivid when they weren't praying, he thought, what a stunning display they must send to heaven when they all bowed their heads in communal worship. No wonder they'd drawn the Clan's attention.

There were no pews or chairs in the room. All the children— ranging in age from toddlers to teens—knelt on colorful woven mats. It called to mind Muslim prayer rugs, but these were round. They were in rows, facing a freestanding wooden cross at the front of the room to Jagger's right; he'd entered on the side at roughly the midpoint of the rows. The children appeared to be organized by age, with the youngest in front.

Rayna headed toward an empty mat in the third row. Aleksandar walked straight ahead and sat cross-legged on a mat in the center.

The adults were stationed around the kids. As soon as they saw Owen and Jagger, they came toward them.

A boy about Tyler's age waved at him, and Jagger waved back.

That started a flock of fluttering hands, and Jagger felt like a politician, waving at everyone at once. Light laughter rippled among them.

They looked like ordinary kids, the boys dressed in jeans, slacks, or shorts and button shirts or colored tees; most of the girls were in dresses or skirts, though a few wore slacks and blouses. They could have been the student body of any small K–12 school. That made him realize what he had half expected: starched uniforms—black, buttoned to the neck—Quaker hats, creepy smiles, glazed eyes. He'd read too many Stephen King books.

Angels stood or knelt by some of the kids. More angels hovered near the roof, and Jagger remembered reading somewhere that churches were originally designed with high ceilings to accommodate the congregant's guardian angels. Those architects were onto something, though Jagger doubted low ceilings would keep the angels out.

Owen was conversing quietly with Mr. Stanga, his waving arms at odds with the volume of his voice. As each new adult joined in, the tight group grew more animated. Jagger wanted to say, *Enough! Everybody hide!*

He set the duffel bag down and stepped over and put his hand on Owen's back. "What's going on? We don't have time for a discussion." He leaned his lips close to Owen's ear, whispered, "Look, this is life or death. Let's whip out the guns and force them to hide. We can apologize later." He thought about how quickly he wanted to be gone and added, "By phone."

Owen turned away from the group, took Jagger by the arm, and walked toward the back of the room with him. Keeping his head down and his voice low, he said, "I convinced them of the danger. Told them we've been tracking a very dangerous group of serial killers, and we know they're coming to the home within the hour."

"They just believed you?"

Owen lifted one shoulder. "I had to impress them a bit first."

"Impressed them? With what?"

"My credentials as a doctor, a theologian, a criminal investigator . . ."

"All those things? That would make me suspicious."

"I didn't just *say* them. I rambled a bit. You know, a quick run-down of the pros and cons of *finitum capax infiniti* versus *finitum non capax infinitum*, stuff like that. So they're willingness to believe us isn't the problem."

"What is?"

Owen smiled. "I'll show you."

[71]

"You still have the vision?" Owen asked.

Jagger showed him the fragment in his palm.

"Stay here," Owen said. "Tell me what you see when I come back." He looked around the back of the room: a museum-quality desk, bookcases, stacks of hymnals and Bibles, flags on poles in stands . . . He headed for three heavy wood armoires in a row.

"What am I looking for?" Jagger said.

"Me."

Jagger looked back at the children, their faces turned toward him. He smiled and nodded, and a few waved.

Owen opened the first armoire. It had been fitted with shelves, standing books and reams of paper on them. He closed it and moved to the next one. Black and white robes hung inside. He slid them to one side and stepped inside.

The children laughed.

Owen smiled out at them, reached for the doors, and closed them. His God-beam extended out of the top and rose into the ceiling high above. An angel grabbed hold of it and followed it down, feet up. His head and shoulders disappeared into the top of the armoire, and he stayed that way, half in, half out, as though satisfying a curiosity. Then he dropped into the armoire just as Owen was opening the doors again. Owen stepped out and walked quickly to Jagger, who nodded.

"Isn't there anything that will block the beams?" Jagger said.

"Like what? Lead? Kryptonite? Wherever they go, their lights will give them away." He held out his hand. "May I hold it, the fragment? It might give me an idea."

Jagger dropped it into his hand. "Those lights are going to get them killed. The beams go straight up. If we can get them into a locked room, the Clan won't see them once they're inside."

Owen shook his head. "All Bale would have to do is station someone outside to tell them where to go."

"What are we supposed to do, let the Clan get them?" He looked at the kids and thought of the slaughterhouse the Clan made out of the barn. *God, no, not these children.*

"We have enough weapons to arm the adults," Owen said.

"Take a stand?" Jagger pictured a firefight, the Clan picking them off one by one until no one was left to defend the children.

"I can't think of anything else."

"Then let's take a stand," Jagger said, trying to keep his thoughts from entering a pitch-black mental shadow where whispers said he would never again see his wife or son. "Because we have to do something, and we're out of options." He turned, already thinking which weapons he'd disburse and which he'd keep for himself.

"Wait," Owen said. His gaze drifted over the sitting kids. He looked straight up, the blue beam now appearing to flow from his face. "It's far from ideal . . . and it may blow up in our faces, but . . ." He grinned. "I have an idea."

[72]

When the deck support struck Jordan's temple—Tyler putting everything he had into it—the older boy flew sideways, hit the wall of the
excavation hole, and crumpled. His flashlight rolled out of his hand.
Tyler picked it up and switched it off, tilting his ear up to listen.
Nothing at first, then: "Jordan!" It was Phin.

A light, diffused by distance, spilled into the hole, panned across
it, slipped out. Phin was up on the wall where Jordan had been. The
angle prevented him from seeing into the first ten feet of the hole.

Tyler grabbed Jordan's booted feet and tugged, quietly dragging
him closer to the wall nearest Phin. He heard a loud stomp, then the
clattering of wood and stones. Phin had jumped off the wall and was
scattering the deck pieces, making sure no one was hiding underneath.

Tyler stepped over Jordan and rolled him so that he lay in the
corner formed by the hole's wall and floor. He crouched at the boy's
feet and waited, setting the flashlight on the ground and holding the
deck support in front of him. He rubbed his throbbing knee.

"Jordan!" Phin called, closer. His boots clomped over rocks, making a clicking-hissing sound that reminded Tyler of movies about robots
taking over the world. The light flashed into the hole again. It was
brighter and lingered longer. Phin jumped diagonally over the hole,
landing on the ground that ran between the two holes. Tyler could see
the back of his head as he scoped out the other hole. If Phin turned, he
could shine his light right at him. Tyler crouched lower, pushed himself
against the dirt wall, wishing he could press himself right into it.

Phin raised his hand to his cheek. "They're not here."

Nevaeh's voice over the radio: "What do you mean, they're not
there?"

"Jordan and Tyler, they're both gone."

"Jordan must be chasing Tyler."

Phin said, "I found Jordan's radio on the rocks by the wall, smashed." He turned in a circle, passing his gaze over Tyler, and stopped when he was facing the monastery.

"Well," Nevaeh said, "find them."

Phin's head rotated toward Tyler, then the other way, up the mountain. He seemed to hop, then went flying high and arcing out of Tyler's view, jumping over the upper hole. He called, "Jordan!" And again half a minute later, farther away. Tyler pictured him heading up the Siket El Basha trail toward the peak.

He shifted to face Jordan. He set the length of wood down and felt the boots. Hard, with buckles, like ski boots. Their soles were at least four inches thick. He stood, looking in the direction Phin went, and ran his gaze over the top of the wall. Seeing no one, he picked up the flashlight, covered its lens with one hand, and turned it on. The leg braces attached to the ankles, went up to disks at the knees, and disappeared under Jordan's T-shirt.

He switched the light off and used both hands to unsnap one of the buckles. As he felt for the second buckle, Jordan's foot moved, turning and pulling away. The boy groaned, his head rotating left, then right. His hand went to his head and rubbed.

Tyler picked up the wood with both hands, raised it over his head, angled back to keep it from poking out of the hole. Jordan looked at him, sat up, scooted back until he was pressed against the wall of the slope that allowed the archaeologists to walk into the hole without jumping. He rubbed his temple.

"You clobbered me."

"Be quiet or I'll do it again." He didn't like not being able to see Jordan very well. Dad had taught him to watch people's eyes; you could tell what they were thinking, what they might do, by the things they looked at and the things they didn't want you noticing they were looking at. Keeping the wood raised with one hand, straining to do it, he felt for the flashlight. He turned it on and set it upright on its lens, letting a pebble tilt it up slightly. Another Dad trick. It provided enough light for Tyler to see Jordan's eyes, but he thought it was too dim to shine out of the hole.

Jordan said, "You're not going to hit me again."

"I will if I have to. Take off your boots."

"They won't do you any good," Jordan said. "You don't know how to use them."

"At least they'll be off you."

"See? You're not going to hit me."

Tyler swung the support beam down at Jordan's leg. Jordan gasped and pulled his legs up, but not far enough. The wood stopped before making contact. Tyler raised it again. "I'll pound them to smithereens with you wearing them if you don't take them off."

Jordan thought for a moment, then finished unbuckling the boot Tyler had started on. Without looking up he said, "Nevaeh only wants to talk to your mom."

"She can do that without taking her."

"You don't know Nevaeh." He turned something on the ankle and the brace sprung free. He tugged the boot off, tossed it at Tyler's feet.

"The braces too," Tyler said.

Jordan sighed and unclamped two metal loops attached to the brace, over and under his knee. He started fiddling with something under his shirt, reached his hand around back.

"Stop!" Tyler said in a harsh whisper, threatening to bring the wood down on Jordan's head.

"There's a belt," Jordan said. "And two clamps around my hips."

"What else?"

"What, 'what else'?"

"A gun?"

Jordan shook his head. "I can't put a gun back there. Not with the belt and battery pack." He leaned back against the wall. "Anyway, I wouldn't shoot you."

"Why not?"

"Same reason you're not going to hit me. You might kill me. You don't want to do that."

"You're immortal," Tyler said.

Jordan looked surprised. "You know?"

"My father told me everything."

"Everything?"

Tyler nodded.

"Then you know I'm not going to hurt you and you're not going to hurt me."

"I hit you once already."

Jordan shrugged, rubbed his head. "You were scared. I was after you. This is different, you looking me right in the face, the two of us talking like this. Besides . . ." He smiled. "It's not what brothers do to each other."

[73]

Lilit waggled her hand at Bale. "Let me touch it again," she said.

He slapped her hand away. "You just did."

"I need to get charged up for the assault."

"You're fine. We're almost there. When the vision starts to fade, let me know."

They were riding in the back of a commercial minivan—no side windows behind the driver and passenger seats, no rear seats, just a black rectangle of space. It was the only vehicle available at the sorry excuse for a rental car agency in the airport. But what did he expect? Aeroportul International Sibiu displayed a cheery banner proclaiming 176,000 passengers served last year—about the number that passed through JFK in New York in a single day.

The rental agency hadn't had any GPS units—and they lost cell coverage a few miles outside sibiu—so Hester was sitting in the passenger seat with a crumpled paper map, giving Cillian directions. Simple enough, except the deeper they went into the foothills of the Transylvanian Alps, the more little roads branched into the forest and the fewer road signs there were. Despite continually checking the map and the lights in the sky, they'd found a number of dead ends, and Hester and Cillian had exchanged more than a few choice words in the ninety minutes they'd been on the road.

Bale sat behind the driver's seat, his back to the bare metal side of the cargo area. He had his Salvatore Ferragamos propped on a bag of weapons and his fedora tipped over his eyes, arms crossed. Lilit sat beside him, getting on his nerves. Artimus sat on her other side, nearest the rear doors, growling and huffing at Therion, seated across from him. It was their ritual, getting into combat mode. It wasn't nearly as irritating as Lilit's constant nagging to hold the Stone and breathy descriptions of the demons riding with them.

Early on, one thing had interested Bale: the demons Lilit saw looked different to her than they did to him. She'd admitted there was something attractive about them but described one as "an ugly little cuss, isn't it?" And another as being "frightening, in a vampire sort of way, the fangs." None of the ones Bale saw had fangs, except the cute monkey, but that was Lilit's ugly cuss, not her vampire. Bale had tucked the information into his memory and settled back to get some rest before the festivities.

Hester had other plans. She said, "Hey, hey," and tapped the brim of his hat. He pushed it up. She was turned in her seat, smiling at him. "It should be just up here. Look." She pointed through the windshield, but he didn't see anything. Then the van started around a curve, and the light slid into view. A thick, throbbing conduit, like the universe's largest gem sculpted into a column.

"Wait," she said. "What's it doing?"

As he watched, moving to kneel between the front seats, strands of light broke off from it and moved away. It was coming apart.

"Hurry," he told Cillian, elbowing him in the ribs.

They turned again, and the column of light was up ahead on the right. They drove on a straight road, and Cillian slowed as they approached the entrance to the Mondragon Home for Boys and Girls. A sign mounted to a wall beside the drive announced it in several languages. Tall iron gates could block the entrance, but they were open.

The column of light had narrowed by half. Strands, most looking like fine bright threads, moved away in all directions, except toward the road on which the Clan was stopped. There must have been over a hundred of these glowing threads fanning out from the larger central one.

"What does it mean?" Hester asked.

"The children were all together," Bale said, guessing. "Now they're not."

"What do we do?"

He watched the threads sliding away through the night sky, thought about the children walking in the forest, scattered all over. What were they doing? Some kind of exercise: Hey, kids! This Wednesday, join us for our semi-annual moonlight prayer hike! (BYOFL—bring your own flashlights. Ha ha!)

They could hunt them down one at a time, but what a pain. The alpine forest was rough terrain. It would take them all night. He said, "That central column looks mighty mouthwatering to me. Must be a good number of Bible brats are still in one place. Let's get them."

Cillian drove up the driveway and parked in front of the stairs leading to the big main doors. Therion, Artimus, and Lilit poured out the rear; Bale followed Hester out the passenger door. They dropped two bags on the ground and geared up: weapons, ammo, flashlights . . .

Artimus unzipped another bag, tugged out a bulky black vest, and held it up. "Who wants body armor?" he said.

"For kids?" Therion said, turning back to the shotgun he was loading.

"The web page said they employ a full-time staff," Cillian said.

"Armed?" Hester said, pulling on her leather mask, zipping it up tight. Through the canister hanging down from her mouth, she said, "These guys haven't seen a gun their whole lives."

Artimus waited another moment for someone to speak up, then pushed the vest back into the bag and zipped it closed.

The front doors were locked. Therion pushed through the small group, cleared them away, and kicked it. Like kicking a stone wall. He tried again, bellowing out a guttural roar. The doors rattled, nothing more.

"I thought that roar was going to do it," Lilit said.

"Back away," Artimus said, hitching his .50-cal machine gun into position. Therion grumbled, stepped off to the side. The gun showed him what a real roar sounded like. Artimus could have been operating a jackhammer, he shook so much, using the weapon to tear a splintery seam along the line where two doors met. Shells flew through the air and tinked down on the stone patio like metal raindrops. The blasting stopped, and Artimus stepped through a haze of nostril-stinging smoke. He pushed the doors with his palm. They creaked open.

He stepped back, bowed, and addressed Therion: "After you, m'lady."

Therion shoved him and went inside. The others joined him in a marble-floored entry hall. Before them, two arching staircases rose to the second floor. An oak-paneled wall stretched between them, a settee and round table with flowers in a vase in front of it. A wide hallway to the left, and one to the right.

Hester's gas-mask canister said, "Did you see where the lights were coming from?"

"About in the middle," Cillian said. "Maybe a bit toward the back."

Bale pulled the Stone from his jacket pocket and held it out in his palm. The others touched it, each immediately stepping back, looking around, gaping at the beings that had popped into view. Bale pointed. "Lilit, Artimus, Cillian, that way. Therion, Hester, come with me." He lead them into the right hallway, once again wondering about those threads breaking away from the central column of light and fanning away.

[74]

Aleksandar heard the sound of the machine gun and stopped to look back. The manor was barely visible through the trees. Another minute and it would be lost from sight altogether. He'd been holding Rayna's hand, and now the two exchanged frightened glances.

He said, *"Haide"*—*Come on*—and they continued their trek over the untamed terrain. A rock rolled under his foot and he stumbled, pulling her with him. She let out a quiet yelp and braced herself against a tree.

"Scuzati," he said. *Sorry.*

They continued down a gentle slope, heading away from the home. All the children were to go alone into the forest except the youngest, the ones who could get lost or hurt; they went with someone older. Mr. Stanga had explained that bad people were heading to the home, and everyone had to leave until they heard the school's hand-cranked air-raid siren, left over from World War II. As each child filed out of a rear door, Mr. Stanga would point using his entire hand, giving him or her a small compass—used in their wilderness training—and issue a true north compass bearing: 070 . . . 267 . . . 135 . . . Aleksandar heard a few of the others' bearings and understood that Mr. Stanga determined them based on each student's ability to navigate various terrains. Aleksandar's direction was fairly mild because of his hiking with Rayna. The worst of it would be crossing a five-foot-wide stream, nothing, really. All the students were familiar with the surrounding woods; small groups of them, eight years old and up, camped monthly within five kilometers of the manor.

He considered his last few thoughts and made a correction: the worst of it wasn't the stream. It was how scared they were. Even the older kids had flashed round saucer eyes as they waited in line for their compasses and directions. Despite the number of kids—211—they felt like family. Their morning prayer service consisted of praying out loud for the others. You were expected to talk to the kid whose name you'd drawn the day before to find out what you should bring before God. Then for weeks afterward, you'd check with him to see if God had answered your prayers.

All of it had seemed like a big pain in the rump when Aleksandar had first come to Mondragon five years ago. But he had done it because he was so thankful to be away from the abuse he'd suffered at his previous orphanage. And he'd soon found that praying for other people, cooking for them, taking care of them when they were sick did something strange inside him: instead of being jealous and suspicious of others, not wanting to share his food or his feelings, he grew to trust the others and didn't mind sharing or helping. He found himself hurting when they hurt, smiling when they were happy.

Now he was scared, for himself and for all the others.

He helped Rayna over a fallen tree, and they continued on their 243-degree course. He squinted into the darkness, trying to make out obstacles on the ground and the spindly branches that threatened to scratch his face and snag his hair, communicating the dangers back to Rayna. Whispering in his own tongue, he prayed, "Lord Almighty God the Father, Lord Jesus Christ the Son, Lord Holy Spirit, everything You have given me is enough, but if it is Your will, see me through this night. Walk with the other kids, hold their hands, keep them safe, guide their paths. Blind the bad people who've come to hurt us. Make the men who came to help us strong. Give them sharp eyes and let them shoot straight."

Behind him, something exploded.

[75]

Bale, Therion, and Hester had navigated the hallway, working their way toward the back and center of the manor. They peeked into each room they passed, finding no one. They turned a corner and faced a hallway that stretched all the way to the opposite side of the building—Artimus, Cillian, and Lilit at the far end, making their way toward them. Halfway down, a set of double doors was cracked open in the center, blue light spilling out. Angels had congregated in front of it, swords out, sparkles forming shields and odd-shaped projections arching over their shoulders. Bale didn't know what these shapes were but assumed they were piercing weapons of some sort.

You could drive a tractor-trailer down the hallway without clipping any of the decorative tables or chairs that lined the walls. It allowed them room to progress shoulder to shoulder, and Bale couldn't help but feel he was back in the Wild West, striding with his gang into town for a showdown. Oh, those were good times.

Too bad this one was going to be more like picking off gophers from a rocker on the front porch. He wondered what the children would do when the Clan started in on them: run screaming . . . pray in quiet acceptance . . . fight? Wouldn't that be something?

The Clan's demons bounded down the hall to engage their enemies. Bale smiled at the futility of the angels' efforts and continued toward the doors. He stopped after ten paces. The angels had dispatched the demons within seconds, slicing them with their swords and sparkling . . . *whatevers*, leaving piles of demon-ash on the floor or hurling them through the ceiling and back wall.

He said, "The force is strong in these little ones," and chuckled. The others didn't seem to get his allusion, and that irritated him; how could they not? The power of prayer—or at least one's connectedness to the spiritual realm—was so obviously the basis for the "force" in *Star Wars*. Bale knew it, and he was certain Satan did too, loving the way people embraced things they didn't understand. It made his job much easier.

He shook his head at their ignorance and hurried to reach the door before the other three coming toward him. He walked into the clutch of angels and suddenly felt nauseated. Chalking it up to the presence of creatures from a heaven he'd never seen, nor ever wanted to, he ignored the sensation and waited for the others to reach the doors. He gave a thumbs-up and watched as each of his team responded with the same. He turned, kicked the doors open, and stepped inside, the rest of the Clan crowding around him in the entrance.

No kids, not a one.

In the center of the big room, Owen sat cross-legged on a colorful mat. His arms were raised, palms tilted up, a posture of worship. His eyes were closed. A blue light flowed not only from his head but from his entire body. It was as wide as a thousand-year-old redwood, bursts of golden light like small explosions appearing throughout it. What looked like molten gold flowed over his head and shoulders, onto the floor, where in a blink it formed into an angel, then another. At the same time, different angels melted into the gold stuff and whisked up into the light. A continuous cycle of appearing and disappearing angels.

Owen opened his eyes, looking directly at Bale. He lowered his hands to his lap. The light narrowed, becoming the size of a rope extended from the top of his head. Bale could have sworn he felt a change in the atmosphere, a drop in air pressure, the way huge fires pull and consume oxygen from the air, but in reverse.

He felt a momentary twinge of doubt, maybe even fear. The others must have felt it as well, because beside him Therion tensed. He sensed the others edge back ever so slightly. But in Bale the feeling was gone as quickly as it came. He reminded himself that the Stone showed him the invisible, but when it came down to it, the room was empty—save for a single man, a fool waiting to die.

A few feet from Owen, a heavy desk rested on its front, showing Bale its top, scarred with repaired gouges from countless slips of pens and letter openers over the years.

Bale thought, *Now why would that be there, in that position?* He doubted the kids, in their rush to leave, had knocked over such a substantial piece of furniture. So it had been situated like that, and for only one reason: someone was hiding behind it. He scanned the rest of the room, which he realized was a large chapel: a cross at the front. On a wall, a framed picture of Jesus praying, holy light washing over His face. He spotted a couple armoires in the back where more people could hide.

He slapped his palms together, again and again, clapping slowly. "Bravo," he said. "You got us. How fervent your prayers must be to replace those of so many children, and we know how bright a child's light can be. I'm impressed, Owen—and why did you change your name again? Not ashamed of who you are, are you? But I *am* impressed. Not only did you not lose your faith over time, as so many do, but apparently yours has gotten stronger and stronger. And yet here you still are, cursed with the rest of us, stuck here on earth instead of lounging around the pool up in heaven. You must be so frustrated."

Owen simply stared. Something dawned on Bale, and he turned his head slightly to look at Owen out of the corner of his eyes. "How did you ever find us? *I* didn't even know I was coming here until hours ago." He rubbed the trimmed goatee on his chin. "Extraordinary luck? Divine guidance, perhaps?" He held up an index finger. "Ah . . . I remember now." He grinned. "You sly devil. You figured out what I was doing with the Stone, didn't you? Did that archaeologist . . ." He snapped his fingers a few times, thinking. "Oliver—did he tell you what it revealed? And once you knew that, it wouldn't have taken you long to figure out how I'd use it. Of course, you'd think of this place, wouldn't you? Such a beacon of godliness. Thanks to you . . . Mr. Mondragon."

Slowly Owen smiled. His hands came out of his lap, and he tossed an object along the floor toward Bale. Clattering over the polished wood planks, rolling, spinning.

Bale squinted at it.

A grenade.

He jumped back—catching a glimpse of Owen rolling behind the desk. Bale scrambled against the others to get out of the doorway, away from the open doors. He saw a figure at the far end of the hall lobbing what had to be more grenades. They landed short and rolled to the Clan's feet. Bale spun, grabbing hold of Therion's massive shoulders, and turned the big man with him back into the chapel. He wrapped a leg across Therion's lower shins and shoved from behind. Therion dropped onto the grenade Owen had tossed. Bale jumped on his back, crouching. The explosion, its sound muffled, lifted Therion, and Bale jumped off before he fell.

Another explosion from the hall—Bale watched a body tumbling in the air, sailing past the open doors. Lilit, he thought. More explosions, mingled with screams and yells. Artimus's machine gun began firing.

A clattering sound behind him, familiar. He spun to see a grenade dancing across the floor toward him. He considered picking it up, tossing it back, but knowing Owen—not a stupid man, old enough to have done this sort of thing before—he would have certainly held the grenade a few seconds after pulling the pin, specifically to avoid having it returned to him. Bale leaped over it and ran all out for the desk. Before he reached it, the grenade exploded. Heat washed over him, shrapnel peppered his back, and the blast sent him tumbling over the desk.

[76]

The blasts in the corridor tore away wallboard and plaster, sent bits of carpet runner into the air, shattered a door on the opposite side from the chapel, and left plumes of smoke pressing against the confines of the physical space. Jagger couldn't see a thing. Shadows shifted in the cloud. He debated between throwing another grenade and firing a mini-Uzi into the swirling gray haze.

A loud rattling kicked up, and things around him began rupturing in a spray of tiny explosions. In front of him the carpet and floor beneath it popped and churned, as though an invisible madman were using a tiller on them. The tilling approached him, and he dived behind a wall, into the corridor that ran perpendicular to the hallway, toward the front of the manor. The wall behind where he'd been standing began to disintegrate. He thought of the commando guy with the massive .50-caliber machine gun and felt disappointed that he of all of them hadn't tasted the bite of his grenades.

He pulled another grenade from the pocket of a vest specially designed for grenadiers. He pulled the pin, counted to five, and tossed it around the corner without looking. The explosion shook the floor, and another billow of smoke rolled down the hall and around the corner.

Jagger peered along the side corridor. He could run to the front of the manor, cross to the opposite side, and come at the Clan from behind. But it was a pretty sure bet that they'd already thought of that and were heading for him from around the front.

The machine gun had stopped. They were waiting down past the smoke or coming around. He glanced around the corner. The smoke was clearing, blowing apart and away from the double doors at the center of the hallway. A chilly breeze skimmed over his skin, and he realized one of the blasts in the chapel must have shattered a window. He could see the wall at the far end, but no Clan.

The Uzi hung from a strap around his neck. He wished RoboHand were capable of holding and firing the Uzi without assistance from the other hand. That would have allowed him to carry both a grenade and the Uzi in a firing position. He'd have to look into an Uzi-holding-and-firing attachment for the prosthetic. He gripped a grenade in his hooks, slipped a finger through the pull ring, and rolled around the corner. Crouching low, staying close to the inside wall, he ran through the smoke—hovering over the floor now like mist—and stopped by the open double doors.

The grenades' destruction to the hall here was massive: charred-rimmed craters in the floor and walls, splintered furniture and doors.

He listened. Something was happening in the chapel. Banging around, huffs and grunts. People fighting. One of them had to be Owen. He pulled the grenade's pin and tossed it the rest of the way down the corridor. If anyone was around the far corner, it would chase them off or kill them. It exploded without flushing out any of the Clan. Jagger lifted the Uzi off his belly, gripped the front stock with RoboHand, and got his other hand around the grip and trigger.

He looked through the chapel's entrance, pulled his head back. Owen and Bale were struggling on the floor near the desk. He hadn't seen anyone else. He stepped into the room and over Muscle Man's body—Therion, he remembered from Gheronda's scrapbook. He rushed toward the two men. They were rolling, Bale on top, then Owen; Bale's hand gripped Owen's throat, and Owen had a fistful of Bale's hair, pulling it back and away from him. Bale held a pistol in his other hand, and Owen was gripping the wrist under it.

Jagger raised the Uzi, waiting for Bale to roll back around. He heard a squeak behind him, spun, caught movement in his peripheral vision before he was all the way around, and raised RoboHand protectively across his face. An arrow thunked into the prosthetic forearm.

Steampunk was running directly at him from where she'd been hiding when he'd entered: just inside the door against the wall. He swung the Uzi around and fired. Too late: she kicked the gun as he pulled the trigger. The bullets stitched a dotted line up the wall and across the ceiling. She kicked again, this time a power thrust into his stomach. He'd seen it coming and pulled his belly away, minimizing the impact. It still knocked most of the wind out of him. He pushed aside the pain and panic, ducked a haymaker she was throwing at him, spun with a roundhouse kick, and planted his heel in her sternum, thinking, *Commotio cordis!*—a blow to the chest that causes cardiac failure. One in a million chance, but a guy could hope.

Steampunk staggered back. As she did—ever the 3,500-year-old pro—she pulled a sword from a sheath mounted with brass studs to the outside of her thigh. She halted her backward momentum and charged him, sword high over her head. A tinny radio-scream issued from the gas-mask canister bobbing below her chin.

Jagger used his real hand to grab the Uzi's grip, slipping his finger over the trigger. He backpedaled away from her, swung the gun up, and pulled the trigger. A single round punched into her chest. She froze, a grisly figure from a horror movie: stitched and zippered leather mask, black-glassed goggles, sword in ready mode. He pulled the trigger again. Nothing happened. She staggered toward him. The sword came down, and he ducked and spun away from it. He yanked the arrow out of his fake arm and plunged it into her shoulder. She fell, straight back onto the floor.

Jagger checked the Uzi's magazine: empty. The duffel bag contained at least six more, but it was back at the junction of the hallways. He slipped the weapon's strap over his head and dropped it. He hurried past Steampunk's body and picked up her sword.

Owen and Bale remained locked in a tussle that would have exhausted professional wrestlers. They rolled and flipped, kneeing and head-butting each other. Owen's forehead looked as though it had been skinned. Bale rolled on top. "Do something," Owen said to Jagger through clenched teeth.

Jagger raised the sword. Bale rolled away from him, putting Owen between them. Owen released his grip on Bale's hair and punched his jaw. Bale's head snapped sideways, came back grinning, teeth bloody. Owen began a series of rabbit punches to Bale's chest. Bale threw him off. As Owen tumbled away—keeping his grip on Bale's gun hand— he grabbed at Bale's jacket. His fingers snagged a pocket and ripped it off. The God Stone hit the floor.

Jagger moved in, reaching. Owen's hand shot out. Bale grabbed the Stone first, his arm extended along the floor. Owen clawed at Bale's clenched fist.

"Owen!" Jagger yelled. "Pull in!"

Without looking or hesitating, Owen pulled his arm back.

The sword thunked into the wood floor, severing Bale's hand.

[77]

Jagger stared at the sword stuck into the floor.

For a moment it looked like a magic trick: an arm stopped at the wrist by a gleaming wide blade, a hand on the other side. Then Bale screamed and lifted his arm, blood pumping from the stump, flying everywhere.

Owen scrambled up, and while Bale was momentarily distracted by pain and shock, Owen kicked the man's gun hand, sending the weapon spinning away on the floor. Then he shifted and kicked Bale in the head. The man's head snapped sideways again, but this time it stayed that way. He was out. Owen picked up Bale's hand, peeled the fingers back from the Stone, and dropped it into his breast pocket, buttoning the flap. He dropped the hand to the floor.

He was breathing hard, bleeding from his lips, nose, cheek, eyebrow, forehead. His beard looked like roadkill. He ran his open palm over his face, smearing it all into a film of glistening red. He held out his hand. "Give me the sword."

Jagger looked at the bodies on the floor—Bale, Steampunk, and Therion—and imagined their heads severed from their bodies, their miserable lives snuffed out . . . finally. "I'll do it," he said, stepping toward Bale.

Owen stopped him. "My hands are already bloody. You're a family man. Don't taint that with this."

Jagger hesitated.

Owen said, "It's not an action any sane man can forget."

Jagger nodded. He held the sword out to Owen.

Something clattered in the room. Jagger turned, saw a grenade rolling toward them. "Down!" he said. He dropped the sword and tackled Owen, who tripped over Bale, and they fell behind the desk. Jagger felt the blast's concussion in his skull.

From around the entrance in the hallway, Artimus's machine gun began screaming, spitting out half-inch-diameter bullets at a rate of 850 per minute. The right-hand doorjamb began flying apart, splinters and chunks of wood exploding out from it. The door itself tilted, then fell.

The machine gun's fire angled into the room, away from the jamb, and walked along the wall, turning everything in its path into dust and confetti. Artimus would soon be at the entrance, panning his firepower across everything inside.

Jagger patted his hand over his vest. He was out of grenades. "Come on," he said, lifting Owen by the arm.

"The sword! Bale!" Owen yelled.

"No time!" Jagger tugged Owen over Bale's body and shoved him toward the broken windows. He raked RoboHand over the fang-like shards of glass jutting up from the sill. The ground was twenty feet below, bushes and lawn to land on. He pushed Owen into the sill. "Go. I'm right behind you."

Owen climbed up, rolled onto his stomach, hung, and dropped.

Jagger swung his legs over the sill, turned, and dropped onto his belly. He had to look: the muzzle of the machine gun was poking into the chapel doorway, flames sputtering out of it. Two more steps would give Artimus the entire room as a target.

He slid over the sill, thinking, *Lord, just get me home, please . . .* and stopped abruptly, caught on something.

Glass shattered to his right . . . more and more of it as Artimus panned toward him. The gunner wasn't visible yet, but he would be in seconds.

Jagger found the thing hanging him up: a grenade. It was in a pocket high up by his shoulder, easy to miss. He yanked it out, pulled the pin, and tossed it across the room. It rolled into the hallway. The machine-gun fire stopped and the barrel flashed away.

The grenade exploded, and the last thing Jagger saw as he

slipped over the sill was the sword on the floor. Leaving it behind—
not having used it—pained his soul. He felt a heavy weight descend
upon him, the burden and guilt of all the people Bale was yet to
murder.

[78]

"Hurry! Hurry!"

"Calm down, Jag," Owen said, slowly maneuvering the jet around the bend in the road. "This isn't a dune buggy."

Jagger was constantly moving, looking out the windshield, the side cockpit windows, rushing back to peer through the cabin windows. He was sure the Clan would pursue them. Bale had been conscious when Jagger went out the window. Certainly he'd send at least the machine-gun-packing commando after them.

"Come on!" he yelled from the cabin.

The jet's nose angled around the bend, and they were facing the long, almost-straight road on which they'd landed. Sound from the engines rose in pitch, becoming the soundtrack of a thriller movie. The plane began moving, eating blacktop faster and faster.

Standing, Jagger leaned close to the windshield, one knee on the copilot's seat. He watched for the driveway into the home, guessing its position until the jet's lights swept over it. As they passed he followed it with his eyes. His heart skipped a beat. Someone—a silhouette against the house lights—was jogging toward the road.

"Someone's coming," he said. "I think he's got that big machine gun."

"How close?"

"Halfway to the road from the manor."

Owen blew out a raspberry. "We'll be in the air before he reaches it. That gun can bring us down, though, so I'll fly straight off the road for a while before turning."

He said something else, but it was lost to a thought that Jagger should have had earlier. "What about the children? We can't just leave them with Bale still there."

Owen turned his eyes away from the makeshift airstrip for a second to smile at Jagger. "The kids?" Owen said. "They're all safe in the woods, and they won't return until they're sure it's safe. Bale doesn't have the Stone to find them, and I think he's got more important things to concern himself with, like healing and tending to his wounded."

"Then what?" Jagger asked.

Owen shrugged. "Never know with Bale. He might go on his merry way, stirring up as much trouble as he can." He paused. "He might come after the Stone."

"When?"

"A few weeks, a few years."

Jagger nodded, thinking, *Let him come. I'll be ready next time.* He remained standing until the nose lifted, then the whole plane, its lights flashing on treetops as they flew over them, close. The ascent was steeper than he expected, and he staggered back. He pulled on the back of the copilot's chair and climbed in over the armrest, like trying to board a moving swing. He leaned into the corner of the seat and twisted toward Owen.

Owen's face was a study in horror. Bloody, beard matted with the stuff, scrapes and cuts—all of it masking a grim face that could have been carved from granite.

"Are you all right?" Jagger asked.

Owen paused before answering. He looked at Jagger. "We had a chance to rid the world of Bale."

"No, we didn't. If we had tried, right now we'd be the ones without our heads."

Owen glared out the windshield, shook his head. After half a minute, he said, "When we're at altitude, I'll set the autopilot and wash up, grab a few winks. I can use a painkiller. You?"

Jagger ached all over. "Yeah."

"In the medical bag near the bed," Owen said.

But first Jagger fished into his pocket for the satphone. He hit redial and wanted to throw the phone when he got Gheronda's voice mail again. He retrieved Owen's doctor's bag and returned to the cockpit seat. Owen's idea of a painkiller was over-the-counter Tylenol. "Nothing stronger?" Jagger said.

"Take two." Owen grinned. "Bet Bale needs a lot more."

"Put me and Bale together, and we could clap."

They looked at each other and began laughing. The relief Jagger felt at surviving their encounter with the Clan, getting the God Stone back, was like waking from a nightmare. But it only took a few moments for Jagger to remember his nightmare wasn't over. Thinking of Beth and Tyler, the Tribe after them, his stomach felt like twisted ropes. But for the next few hours there was nothing he could do. Best not to let speculation and worry gnaw at him; he'd be exhausted by the time they arrived at St. Catherine's, a less effective fighter—and all he wanted to do was go all warrior on the Tribe.

"Any more grenades?" he asked.

Owen shook his head. "I'm wondering if there's even a handgun onboard."

That didn't bother Jagger as much as it should have. He was so angry and so psyched up from the action at the orphanage, he felt *he* was the best weapon he could possess anyway. A walking, talking nuke. He'd focus his fury and rage and protective-daddy instincts and become a Tasmanian devil of leave-my-family-alone destruction. The plan: get to one Tribe member and use his or her weapons—and his own rage—on the rest.

That made him feel better, having a plan of action, no matter how vague.

Now take your mind off it. An hour out, you can get into warrior mode. For now, rest and relax. Yeah, right.

He leaned over and shook Owen's shoulder. He said, "You did it. You wanted the Stone back and you got it. Honestly, I had my doubts."

"O ye of little faith."

Jagger looked out at the darkness through the windshield. He didn't think Owen was being witty; the man was assessing Jagger's spiritual condition. And it was true. He saw God as a presence, maybe benign, maybe not, but it didn't matter because for the most part He was hands-off. Yeah, maybe His angels milled around humans, but more as witnesses than helpers. The irony of Jagger's actually *seeing* angels, of being *saved* by them, and still doubting God's active, loving involvement with man was not lost on him. Maybe it was that he was truly cursed—not just with immortality but with stubbornness when it came to faith. Or maybe it was seeing the barn full of brutally murdered men, women, and children: what had God or His angels done for them?

As if reading Jagger's mind, Owen said, "I know retrieving the God Stone will ultimately save thousands of people, but right now I'm more elated that there are two hundred and eleven children, plus their guardians, alive now who wouldn't be if God hadn't used us to intervene."

Jagger smiled. All those faces staring at him, their little hands waving. What he'd felt at the time, but didn't want to admit, was that they were waving good-bye.

He was nicely settled into the copilot seat, angled against the cabin wall, almost facing Owen. He stretched a leg out and gave Owen's arm a kick. "Did I hear Bale call you Mr. Mondragon?"

Owen glanced at him, didn't say anything.

"Why didn't you tell me?"

Owen shrugged. "It wouldn't have helped. My involvement was a long time ago."

"Involvement? You started it. You established the philosophy. Even a century later, it's churning out kids who are changing the world."

"That's God's work, not mine."

"Still, did you have to be so coy?"

"It becomes habit, Jag, doing things and burying them in the past."

"You're being humble."

"Doing things like that is no different from tithing. It's giving back to God. I can only do it because God gave me the resources in the first place. The credit goes to Him, not me."

"It wouldn't have been bragging if you told me."

"I didn't mean to be deceptive."

Jagger looked at the GPS. They were over Bulgaria now, west of Varna. Below them a smattering of lights in a landscape of blackness.

"How long to the monastery?"

"Fourteen hundred miles, give or take. Three and a half hours to Sharm. But we'll need to refuel, that'll take at least an hour."

"Refuel?"

"Boanerges's range is only fifteen hundred miles, and we've already gone from Varna to here. If we had the Clan's plane . . . that thing's range is almost six thousand miles. Then, from Sharm, it'll take an hour, hour and a half to secure a helicopter and fly there."

"How long if you bypass Sharm El Sheikh?"

"Bypass?" He flashed Jagger a puzzled look. "What are you think-ing? Parachute again?"

"If need be, but . . . you landed on *that* road." Gesturing behind him with his head.

Owen didn't say anything, just stared out the windshield. Finally: "That road that runs up the valley *is* pretty straight."

"It is."

"It's long enough."

"Longer than the road in front of the orphanage."

Owen glanced at him. "Egyptian P.D. will freak out."

"It's Beth and Tyler, Owen."

"I'm just saying." He nodded. "Sharm is south of St. Cath's, so we won't be bypassing it."

"Okay." Waiting.

"Landing at the monastery will cut our ETA by at least an hour, probably more like ninety minutes." He paused. "All right, let's do it. Besides, Egyptian prisons aren't as bad as they say."

Pushing his luck, Jagger said, "And you're sure about having to refuel?"

"Unless you want to crash before we get there."

"How close would we get?"

"Jagger."

[79]

Bale rested his backside on the overturned desk, checking that his tourniquet was adequately preventing more blood loss. He felt weak and lethargic, a condition he hadn't experienced in a very long time. His stump was throbbing and so was his head.

Lilit had survived getting tossed the length of the hallway by a grenade, with only a few lacerations on her legs, back, and arms, and a patch of missing hair on the side of her head. Now she was crouched beside Hester, tugging off the leather mask. She kept touching her bald spot and pulling at the hair around it. She stood and dropped the mask onto Hester's chest.

"She'll be up and around within a week," she said. "Him . . . I don't know." She looked at Therion, sprawled facedown in a pool of blood by the door. "Couple months, at least."

Pointing, Bale said, "Hand me that, will you?"

Lilit picked up his hand and gave it to him.

"Find something to hold it in place, will you?" Bale said. "Get the healing started."

She moved off toward the back of the room. Bale stood up and lifted a drawer out of the desk, looking down into the hole at the supplies that had fallen out.

He was half sitting on the desk again, holding his hand to the stump while Lilit unrolled a spool of duct tape around the gap, when Cillian walked in. Bale asked him, "Where've you been?"

"Gathering weapons, putting them in the car."

"Jet's all fueled?"

Cillian nodded. "Topped off in Varna."

"All right," Bale said, pushing up off the desk, pulling his arm away from Lilit. "We gotta get going, fast. Help Artimus put these two in the car." He indicated Hester and Therion. The circle of cardboard from the tape clung to his wrist. He scowled at it, held it up to Lilit, who tore it off.

"Where we going?" Cillian asked.

Bale gave him the same look he'd given the cardboard circle. "To get the Stone back."

[80]

Having ascended all the way to the peak without sighting Jordan or the woman's son, Phin bounced and leaped down the trail. He recognized where he was and decided to take a quick detour. He moved off the trail and moved horizontally across the mountain. A few minutes later he reached the clearing where they'd launched their attack, where they'd put on their Future Warrior Systems. He hopped up, landed flat on his feet, and bounced onto the outcropping where Toby had kept an eye on the monastery. He could look into the entire compound, but most of the lower levels were blocked by rooftops. The gardens were the farthest away and least visible, especially in the dark. He panned his gaze to the archaeological dig, all but the area nearest the wall in plain view. Two big rectangles of blackness against the grayer terrain marked the excavation holes. He turned to jump down, then turned back. The faintest of light—a candle?—glowed against the wall of the lower hole.

"Gotcha," he said, and leaped off the outcropping.

[81]

Gheronda had led Beth through a maze of rooms and passages. They had climbed rungs nailed to a wall and gone through a hatch in a ceiling into a dark room that filled her nostrils with a dank odor, with a subtle smell of decay. She felt a bit like a wine connoisseur, sniffing the air, trying to determine the composition of an underlying scent. Gheronda struck a match and lighted a candle. Beth gasped quietly. In the corner of the small room lay a dead cat, its eyes sunken in, lips pulled back from its fangs. Gheronda pulled a blanket off a cot, kicking up a cloud of dust, and tossed it over the animal.

Now Beth sat on the edge of the cot, praying that Leo would find Tyler and they would be safe.

Gheronda crossed the room and sat beside her. He wrapped spindly fingers over her clasped hands and said, "Tyler will be fine."

She tried to bend her trembling lips into a smile and couldn't. She said, "Bad things happen to good people," and let a sharp laugh ride out on a single breath at her use of the cliché. "I . . . uh . . ." She pushed hair off of her face and hung her head. A teardrop fell onto Gheronda's hand. She whispered, "I think I caught a little of Jagger's skepticism."

Gheronda squeezed her hands. "About what, dear?"

She watched two more tears fall onto the old man's hand, then said, "God's intentions." She glanced at him. "I know the Bible says that God works for the good of those who love Him, but . . ." She sniffed, looked into the monk's eyes. *"I want my son. With me. Safe."* The tears poured out; she had trouble catching her breath. "You can't tell me he's going to be fine. You don't know that. Look who's after him! Killers!" She dropped her head again. "If Tyler dies, how is that good?"

Gheronda started, "Dear—"

"I know, I know." Her words rolled over his. "Evil is man's doing, not God's, but He allows it, doesn't He? How can He *do* that?"

"Because He loves us."

She turned an incredulous looked to him. "Bad things happen *because* He loves us?"

"Evil stems from love."

"*What?*"

"God *is* love. All creation is an expression of that love. He desires that all creatures reflect the love with which they were created."

She said, "He wants us to love Him back. What does that have to do with—"

"Shhh," he said, patting her hands. "Love can't be forced, can it? It can't be coerced. For love to be genuine, it must be freely given, freely chosen."

"Free will," she said. "The freedom to choose love . . . or not."

"So for humans to love—love others and love God—there must be the possibility of choosing against it."

"Of choosing evil."

He nodded. "People do, and we bear the consequences of that, the consequences of our own bad choices and those of others. You and Tyler are suffering because of the Tribe's decision to choose evil."

Beth said, "Is that supposed to make me feel better?"

"As much as you hate it, if they didn't have the ability to harm us with evil, you wouldn't have the ability to love Tyler, to love Jagger, as much as you do."

She looked at Gheronda, unable to prevent her feelings from showing on her face, a deep frown, eyebrows threatening to slide away. "I'm so scared."

Gheronda pulled her into his arms. "I know," he said.

She pressed her face into the material of his robe. "God is with us; I know that," she said. "I just . . . I just want Him to do *more*."

"He's helping in ways we don't see," he said. "You don't think we escaped from Elias without help, do you?"

Beth sniffed. She thought about what the fragment of the God

Stone had revealed. She believed that angels were with her son at that moment, that he wasn't alone with the Tribe after him. But did that mean he was safe? She said, "Do you think angels were in that room with us when Elias came in?"

"I do."

"Like . . . how did they help? Did they tell Leo to shield us, to shove us through the door?"

"Something like that," Gheronda said. "Maybe they pushed him into us, or made him move just a bit faster than he could without them."

She remembered how Elias had aimed away from them, panning the flame toward them, giving them the second or two they needed to get through the door. She said, "Do you think Elias aimed right at us and an angel knocked the barrel aside?" Could they *do* that?

Gheronda shrugged. "Or something even more incredible. God exists outside of time; He's everywhere, 'everywhen.' What if, when Elias was learning how to use that thing—ten years ago, *fifty* years ago—God showed him the advantages of sweeping across a target instead of aiming right at it? What if God did that only because He knew this day would come and He wanted to give us those few seconds of grace?"

God working for her benefit, for this one specific blessing, even before she was born . . .

He watched her thinking, processing. "Or it could be simply that you pray," he said. "That's one way you've exercised free will. You've *asked* God for help."

"You have not because you ask not," Beth said.

"Or you have because you do."

"Praying," she said, "is like picking up a shield."

"Too few of us think of it as being so real," he said. "But it is."

She leaned away from him and nodded. She ran her fingers across her cheeks, and Gheronda produced a white handkerchief from inside his robe. She used it to dab under her nose. "So," she said, "will you help me pick up a shield? For Tyler?"

He smiled and bowed his head.

[82]

"I guess he didn't tell you everything," Jordan said.

"What do you mean, 'brothers'?" A part of Tyler was thinking, *Yeah, we're all brothers and sisters in God's eyes.* But a larger part knew that's not what Jordan meant. He remembered Mom saying that when she woke up in the Paris catacombs, Jordan was in her cell. She had tears in her eyes and through them thought Jordan was Tyler. "He does look like you," she'd said. "But you're way cuter."

And Dad, describing his and Owen's breaking into the catacombs to get Mom—he'd said Jordan had been peeking out at them from a wall of skulls, and Dad had thought for a second that it was Tyler.

Staring at Jordan now, Tyler recognized the way the corners of the boy's mouth extended a little beyond his lips and curved up, making him look like he was smiling even when he wasn't. And the eyes, almond-shaped. They were the same features he saw when he looked into the mirror. When he looked at Dad.

But why hadn't Dad told him? Unless even Dad didn't know. He had lost his memory in the crash, all of what had happened to him before meeting Mom. Could he not *know* he had an immortal son? He would have known before the crash. Which flooded Tyler's mind with all sorts of disturbing questions: How could he have left his son to marry Mom? Did that mean he could leave Tyler as well?

Tyler felt sick.

Answering Tyler's question, Jordan said, "Kin. Siblings. Brothers. Well, half brothers. Jagger is my father too."

"You're lying," Tyler said.

"Look at us. We could practically be twins."

They weren't *that* similar, Tyler thought. "I don't believe you, but even if I did—" He stopped. Stomping, coming closer, fast. Had to be Phin—he was pounding over the hard granite and loose rocks of the foothills, coming down the mountain.

"Here!" Jordan screamed, turning his face up. "I'm here!"

Tyler jumped up, tossing away the support beam. As much as he would have liked nothing more than to give Jordan another knot on his crown, it was pointless now. He had to get out of there. He jumped up, pulled himself out of the hole, and saw Phin cross through a swath of light at the back outside corner of the monastery. He was taking ten-foot strides, rising six feet into the air with each one. Arms in a classic sprinter's pose, pivoting forward and back, forward and back—their motion obvious because of the swords he held in his hand. He was grinning.

Tyler ran toward the front of the monastery. Floodlights high on the wall illuminated the facade, the stone court and front walkway, the narrow valley floor, and the beginnings of the opposite mountain's foothills. They would turn off automatically at ten. As he ran for the lighted area, Tyler wondered why. He couldn't get in the gate. There were no guards and—tonight—not even any tourists milling around. But there were numerous outbuildings on the far side—the charnel house, where the bones of monks dating back to sixth century were stored; storehouses; way up the road, a guardhouse manned only during daylight hours—and the gardens. Yes, he could hide there, in the trees, crouched under the bushes.

He looked and realized he'd never make it. Phin had angled toward him and was approaching like a lion attacking an injured gazelle. Tyler pushed harder, forcing his hurt knee to keep up. He reached a split-rail fence and rolled over the top. Phin was almost on him. He dropped onto the path that crossed in the front of the monastery, went around the dig and up the mountain. He was under the lights now, feeling more exposed, more vulnerable.

Why'd I come this way? he admonished himself. *Stupid!* He should have gone deeper into the valley, where the rock formations would have given him cover. The answer came to him like news that a close friend had died suddenly—a feeling he knew from experience, the awful sensation that your guts, from heart down, had come loose and fallen into a pile at the bottom of your torso. The reason he'd run this way was because under normal circumstances, this is where the people were—and he didn't want to die alone. But who he really wanted was his mother. He was closer to her here than he would have been out there, in the dark, barren wilderness. Of course, she might as well be on the moon. He couldn't get to her, couldn't even see her.

Before reaching the front of the monastery, he heard Phin behind—*clomp, clomp, CLOMP*—then nothing, silence. Seconds later the man landed in front of him, facing him, backpedaling to a stop. "Ha ha!" Grinning, Phin made a beckoning gesture with both swords and said, "Come into my parlor . . ."

Said the spider to the fly, Tyler's mind finished automatically as he spun and ran the other direction.

Phin clomped behind. Tyler heard the sound, followed by silence, and looked straight up, raising his hands in defense. Phin soared overhead, turning slowly, balletically. He came down ten feet in front of Tyler. He said, "You're all eyes, Master Tyler, but I can fix that." He scraped his blades together.

Tyler turned, heading again for the monastery's front court, waiting for the clomping, the silence, the abrupt appearance of his enemy in front of him. His heart, wanting none of this, pounded on his chest to get out.

"Phin!" It was Jordan, calling from the excavation. "Stop it!"

Tyler glanced over his shoulder. Phin was still where he'd landed, looking off into the dark archaeological site. He yelled, "What you mean is 'end it.'" He bowed, twirling a sword in a flourish. "Yes, sir!"

"Phin, no!"

Phin lowered his head like a bull and charged. He ran without the high, arching strides, his legs moving at twice a normal man's speed.

Tyler realized he had slowed to watch, listen.

Stupid!

He darted past the only rounded tower in the wall, at the northeast corner, and now the front wall loomed to his left. He was approaching the wall's other tower, the odd-shaped Central Tower—a large rectangle with bulging, rounded corners—that housed the Chapel of St. George, the dragon killer. On the far side was the main gate.

Phin's clomping footsteps grew louder, quicker.

"End it," he'd said.

Thinking of the gardens, Tyler ignored the front gate—melded into place by last night's blast, anyway. He yelled, a groaning scream that he hoped would not be the last thing he heard on earth.

Phin obliged, laughing and saying, "Run, run as fast as you can . . ."

You can't catch me. I'm the Gingerbread Man!

He looked back again and stopped.

Phin was heading straight for him, his fists by his ears, swords raised, like an ad Tyler had seen in a magazine of a hungry, bibbed diner with his utensils held high, anxious to dig in. But what had made Tyler stop was what he'd seen hiding behind the main tower's curving wall.

Phin said, "You're not giving up, are—?"

Father Leo stepped out from the shadows and swung a shovel into Phin's face.

Phin's momentum sent his body sailing forward—parallel to the ground. He thudded to the stones of the courtyard in front of the gate, out cold. Blood gushed from his nostrils and from a gouge across the bridge of his nose.

"Leo!" Tyler yelled and ran for him, arms wide open.

Leo tossed the shovel down and scooped Tyler up, squeezing him tightly. Tyler pushed his face into Leo's shoulder and started to cry. Leo rubbed his back. "You're safe now. It's okay."

"What about Mom?"

"She's fine. I'll take you to her." He carried Tyler toward the gardens. Tyler realized the monk was wearing only black slacks and a white tee. He said, "Where's your robe?"

"It got a little hot, so I took it off."

Movement over Leo's shoulder drew Tyler's attention. Phin was up, wiping his forearm across his mouth.

Tyler meant to say, *"Leo, it's Phin!"* but what came out was a stuttering scream. Leo turned and they watched Phin stoop to pick up his swords. He began walking toward them, weaving the first few steps, then finding his balance, picking up speed.

Leo set Tyler down. "Run," he said.

[83]

Light high on the monastery's front wall turned the area into an arena.
Phin moved toward Leo, twin swords slicing the air in front of
him.

Tyler, crouching behind an emaciated bush, pressed his back into
the wall that separated the walkway from the valley floor. He wished
he could do something to help. He saw the shovel Leo had used to
deck Phin; it was lying back by the main gate. Leo needed *something*
to defend himself against the swords, and it didn't look like he could
get to it himself, not with Phin between him and the shovel.

At the far end of the front wall, near the round tower, Jordan
appeared. He stopped when he saw Phin and Leo.

Don't you do anything to help Phin, Tyler thought. *You do, I'll be
all over you.*

As Phin narrowed the gap between himself and his opponent,
the men edged out from the wall, centering themselves on the wide
walkway. Tyler realized he couldn't reach the shovel now either. Phin
would cut him down before he'd taken three steps.

He started to pray . . . eyes open, unable to *not* watch.

Phin and that crazy smile. He said, "Ironic, isn't it, monk? We
both do God's work. And here we are, facing off."

Leo said, "The irony is that you think you do His work."

Hunched, the men sidestepped, as if tracing the same circular
path from opposite sides. They reminded Tyler of the high school
wrestling matches his father used to bring him to in support of a
neighbor's son. Leo was steady, cool; Phin jittery, anxious to get it on.

"Don't I?" Phin asked, whipping his swords through the air. "The
wages of sin is death. I don't make the rules, brother. I just enforce

them." He leaped at Leo, the blades blender-fast. Leo jumped sideways, spun, and hit Phin in the spine with his fists clasped together. Phin stumbled forward, swung around.

Leo backed away. He said, "And here you are, trying to murder a monk and a little boy."

Phin's facial muscles tightened. It took him a moment to respond. "Those who get in the way of good are bad."

Leo gave him a sideways look. "Where in Scripture is that exactly?"

Circling. Both men tense, ready.

Leo continued: "Is that how you justified wiping out that family in Buenos Aires?"

Phin looked puzzled. He blinked a few times. "They were harboring a Nazi war criminal."

"They were his family. The children weren't even born when he committed his crimes."

Phin shook his head. "That was . . . forty years ago. How do you know—?"

"And that woman in London? Your getaway carriage ran her over. You dragged her three hundred feet."

Phin's shoulders sagged. His swords drooped until their tips clinked against the walkway's stone pavers. He whispered, "Two hundred years ago. No one knew that."

"You look for reasons to kill," Leo said. "You wear blood as cologne."

Phin seemed to swell: his chest puffed out, his shoulders came up, one sword-wielding arm rose high, the other stayed low. With an animalistic bellow, he attacked Leo. One blade arced up toward Leo's belly, the other down at his shoulder.

Tyler willed his eyes to close, but they didn't obey.

Leo stepped back, just enough to avoid the blades. They flashed past, and as Phin's hands became even with each other at chest level, Leo advanced, seizing both of his opponent's wrists. He crossed his arms, forcing Phin to cross his, and pushed one up as he pulled the other down. From Tyler's perspective, the monk was attempting to tie Phin's arms into a knot.

Something had to give, and it was Phin's wrist, which twisted backward and released a sword. Leo caught it as it fell and stepped back quickly. Phin was down on one knee, clutching a sword and glaring at his wrist as he rotated the hand attached to it. He looked up at Leo, surprise replacing his ferocious snarl.

He said, "Looks like someone else has some experience with violence."

Leo closed his eyes, opened them slowly. "Regretfully so."

Phin sprang up, spinning, slicing the sword on a plane with Leo's neck. Leo ducked and lunged. Phin twisted, and Leo's blade opened a wound in his thigh. Phin seemed to pirouette behind Leo and plunge his sword back, as though putting it into a scabbard at his ribs.

Leo gasped, jumped away. He was holding his right arm, blood seeping between his fingers. He switched the sword to his left hand.

Phin was on him: he brought his sword over his head and chopped down at Leo. Leo parried, holding his sword above his head. The blades clanged and sparked, clanged and sparked, as Phin continued to chop, raising his sword only inches before plunging down again, preventing Leo from swinging his weapon. Leo kicked Phin, who staggered back. Leo thrust at Phin's chest.

Phin hopped back, landed flat on both feet. The shoes shot him straight up. Over Leo's head, he turned. Coming down behind Leo, Phin held out his sword, slicing Leo from scalp to tailbone.

Leo opened his mouth in a silent scream, dropped his sword, and followed it to the ground.

Tyler gave voice to the scream Leo couldn't get out. He started at the monk, lying still not six feet away.

Phin stood at Leo's feet, the sword gripped tightly, his face fierce and triumphant. His gaze rose and locked on Tyler. Slowly a smile returned to his lips. He stepped over Leo and stopped in front of Tyler. He raised his sword over his head.

Tyler pushed away, sliding against the wall.

"Sorry, kid," Phin said.

Phin's back exploded, sparks flying out from behind him. Tyler caught a flash of shock and pain on Phin's face, then the man sailed over him, hurled by the blast.

But he hadn't exploded. He'd been *pushed*.

Tyler stared, more fear gripping him than when Phin had the blade poised above his head. His entire body shook. Unable to blink, tears filled the edge of his lower lids and spilled over.

Leaning forward in what Tyler thought was a martial arts pose—rear leg straight, front one bent; one arm cocked back, ready to strike, the other extended, hand flat, as though pressed against an invisible wall—a man scowled out into the valley, presumably at Phin. He was huge, tall and muscular—and he was glowing. A rippling white robe covered his body from neck to feet.

The man relaxed, pulling in his legs and arms, standing upright. From directly behind him came something like an explosion in slow motion: millions of sparks and tiny spinning orbs like orange diamonds billowed out. They curved up over the man's head, around his sides, then they came back in, forming—Tyler's mouth gaped wider—*wings*. They beat the air in a slow, smooth rhythm.

He smiled down at Tyler, extended a hand. "Tyler," he said. "Don't be afraid."

Tyler's hand rose to his chest, feeling for the bullet he'd worn around his neck for the past six months—his symbol of courage and victory. Then he remembered, it was gone.

Tyler's lips quivered, making speech difficult. He managed to say, "Who are you?"

"You knew me as Father Leo."

Tyler's heart stopped—could it do that, actually stop? It seemed everything inside him turned into something else, one big lump of boy-shaped Silly Putty. But then he recognized the man's features. The eyes were blue instead of brown, the facial hair was gone, the skin smoother, more perfectly formed than he'd ever seen. But it was Leo.

Tyler said, "Are you . . . an angel?"

The new Leo nodded. "Yes."

Tyler knew better, but he had to ask: "Because you died?"

"While you knew me, I had taken on human form. But I've always been an angel."

Tyler stood. "I knew it!" he said. "There was something strange about Leo . . . you." The meaning of what he'd said caught up to him, and he said, "Sorry. I mean, you were always vanishing. There and . . . just gone. And smiling. My mom said it was like you knew things everyone else didn't."

"I guess that's true."

Tyler took a step forward, pushing through the bush's bare branches. He realized he could see the shape of the angel's body: massive chest tapering to the hips, legs tapering to the feet. But the way he glowed so brightly with a white, pulsing light, he appeared—only appeared—to be covered in flowing material. Tyler couldn't help but smile. "Are you . . . *naked*?"

"I'm clothed in my Father's glory."

Tyler leaned to peer behind the angel at the empty walkway. "Where's your human body?"

"It's a part of me, or used to be. We don't inhabit bodies; we form into them so perfectly that we need food and rest, we bleed, feel pain, and shed tears."

"If you're so human when you're . . . human, how'd you vanish? And my dad told me something weird happened when he was with Dr. Ollie. You wiped away some blood, and his cuts disappeared. Dad said he must have imagined the cuts, but he didn't, did he?"

"Sometimes," the angel said, "I cheated."

Tyler gasped. *Angels cheat?*

Concern came over the angel's face—just a slight crease between the eyebrows. He said, "With God's blessing, of course." He winked, and any doubt that this being was truly Leo left Tyler.

"Did God send you?"

"Of course."

"It must be cool being an angel," Tyler said, thinking, *Flying and going through walls, never having to sleep or eat or go to the bathroom . . .*

"Being in constant communion with God," the angel said.

"Yeah . . . that too," Tyler said. "Did you hate it here, as a human?"

"It was a blessing, getting to meet you and your family in your world, on your terms. And someday, Tyler, you will shed your physical body and join me in the spiritual world."

"You mean when I die?"

The angel nodded. "You'll be ready. You're experiencing so much of the spiritual world now. You just don't understand yet."

Tyler realized that in the rippling brightness of the angel's body he could see galaxies of stars, swirling, appearing and disappearing. The central point from which they all came and fanned out was in the angel's chest. Looking at it, he felt good—more than just good: a warmth overcame him and . . . something familiar . . . he had to think about it, then it dawned on him. It was the feeling he had when Mom or Dad snuggled with him, hugging him, squeezing him, kissing his forehead. The feeling of being loved.

Tyler stepped closer, the warmth increasing as he did. But it wasn't coming from the angel—or it wasn't normal heat. He didn't feel it on his skin. It came from inside him. He wanted to feel it forever. To be near it forever.

"Someday you will," the angel said.

That startled Tyler. "You can read my mind?"

"We can."

The angel glanced past him, and Tyler turned. The valley's ground was formed by waves and swells of hard rock, as though in the far past it had been a boiling sea of molten stone before suddenly freezing into its current form. On one of these swells Phin lay sprawled on his back, head hanging over.

"Is he dead?" Tyler asked.

"No," the angel said. "He'll wake soon." He pointed toward the garden side of the monastery. "Go to the back of that wall. There's an iron door. I left it open."

"You're not coming?" Panic setting in.

"You won't be alone."

"You saved me," Tyler said. "Does that mean the Tribe's not going to get me? I'm not going to die?"

"No one but God knows when it's your time to come home. It could be in a hundred years, or a hundred minutes . . ."

Minutes!

The angel looked at him with so much . . . love, compassion . . . More stars filled his body, the ones in his chest becoming blindingly bright. Tyler felt that warmth inside again, burning away his fear. Whatever happened, whenever it did . . . it was okay.

The angel continued: "But your time wasn't when that Immortal wanted it to be." He said *immortal* in a way that made Tyler think the angel didn't believe it, or thought it was funny. "Watch yourself," the angel said. "Pray."

Tyler looked toward the side of the compound, so dark there. "I know the door you're talking about, the Siege Door," he said. "Right?" He turned back, and the angel was gone.

[84]

Two hundred miles outside of Antalya, Turkey, Jagger climbed out of the copilot's seat and went back into the cabin. The lights were dim and soft music was playing through ceiling-mounted speakers—an instrumental Jagger thought he recognized from a movie. Owen was in the cabin's one bed, a tangled sheet barely covering him, one arm hanging off. His mouth was open, and he was snoring to wake the dead.

Jagger said his name and shook him. The snoring stuttered, then fell back into a steady rhythm.

"Owen!" More shaking.

Owen bolted up. "I'm up!" he said. He rubbed his eyes, tugged at his beard. He blinked and finally focused on Jagger. "Hey," he said. "No alarms? No one screaming we're in restricted air space?"

"How would I know? I don't speak the languages of the countries we're flying over."

"The F-14 escorts would be your first clue," Owen said, stretching the muscles of his face. "Besides, English is the default language of aviation worldwide. You'd know."

"I didn't pick up on any trouble, but we're about twenty minutes to Antalya."

"Right." Owen threw off the sheets, stood, and stumbled back toward the bathroom. He left the door open while he splashed water on his face.

"After refueling," said Jagger, "we'll be over the Mediterranean."

"Yeah?"

"You said you wanted to throw the Stone to the bottom of the ocean."

"I said I'd rather do that than let the Clan keep it." He came into the cabin, drying his face. "I'd rather return it to the mountain."

"Sinai? Won't it just get dug up again?"

"I'll find a safe place for it."

"You don't . . . want to keep it?" Jagger said.

"What for?"

"I don't know. It just seems too special to get rid of it."

"I'm not going to get rid of it. I'm giving it back to God."

"But don't you think it can do some good for mankind? Prove to the world the spiritual world exists?"

Owen shook his head. "Those with eyes to see already know. It's about faith, Jagger. Faith is what makes us believe that God created us and loves us. Faith gives us the eyes to look back at the crucifixion and know His Son paid the price for our sins. It gives us strength in times of need because we trust He's there for us. How does seeing angels—as wonderful as it is—instill faith?"

"It confirms an invisible realm, more than our eyes can see."

"It undermines faith. People will say, 'I believe in angels because I've seen them.' All the more reason for them not to believe in God or Christ or Christ's sacrifice—"

"Wait, wait," Jagger said. "You don't think angels are proof of God?"

"Want to bet on how many people will say the angels are aliens . . . or non-spiritual beings from an alternate dimension . . . or created by God who then went away, leaving them here with us? People will always find a way to deny God. The Stone won't change that. But I can think of a hundred ways it will lead to trouble. Bale's use of it is just one example."

Jagger nodded. "Don't you think Bale will come for it?" he said.

"He might." Owen went to the cockpit entrance, turned back. "If Gheronda will have me, I'll hang around St. Catherine's for a while in case he shows up." He went into the cockpit, calling back: "If he does, I'll take his other hand. And his head."

[85]

Tyler was getting cold. The temperatures in the desert this time of year weren't like they were back in Virginia. You couldn't freeze to death. But they did dip into the fifties, and it didn't help that he didn't have a shirt or shoes.

He was in the rocks in the foothills of the mountain opposite the monastery's front wall. He'd tried to make it to the door that Leo—the angel: he didn't know how to think of him anymore—told him about. Before he'd reached the courtyard outside the side gate, he'd spotted someone on top of the wall: the teenager—Tyler had heard Nevaeh call him Toby. He was shining a bright flashlight down outside the wall, moving away from Tyler, toward the rear of the compound. Tyler was glad about that—his moving away from him—until Toby's light flashed on the small iron door, which was open a few inches. He'd jumped down, opened the door, and crawled inside. A few moments later he pulled it shut behind him.

Tyler hadn't even gone to see if it was now locked. He thought the teen would be waiting for him. He'd stood under the eave of a storage shed, wondering what to do. A few minutes later he heard someone up on the wall again. Toby dropped down into the courtyard twenty feet from Tyler, who pushed himself farther into the shadows. But the boy went into the gardens without looking Tyler's way, shining his light at the bushes and into the trees. A rifle was strapped to his back.

Tyler darted along the wall and ran out into the rocks, where he was now.

He had watched Phin—halfway between Tyler and the wall—come to. He'd rubbed his head, sat on the rock for a few minutes, looking around as though he'd forgotten where he was. Then he'd staggered away, stopped at the wall, and looked up at it for a long time. He started bouncing, going higher with each jump. He gripped the top of the protruding box—which Mom called an outhouse—and climbed on top. From there, it was an easy jump to the top of the wall.

The lights mounted on the front wall had clicked off, only to come on again about twenty minutes later. The teenager began patrolling along the top of the wall, back and forth. When he'd reach the ends, he'd head back toward the rear, but always reappeared a few minutes later. Tyler was trapped.

The lights were dim where he hid, and he was between two boulders—dark, just enough room to lie down—so he was pretty sure he was safe. Unless they came looking for him.

He lowered his forehead to the ground and tried not to cry. He wanted his mother, wanted to be sitting on the couch with her arms around him. He pictured her face, smiling, almost could feel her fingers stroking his cheek, and he did cry. Keeping it quiet, but letting himself go with it. Dad would pick him up, saying, *Come here, you. You'll never be too big to pick up.* And he'd give Tyler a bear hug. He'd tuck him into bed and sit on the edge while Tyler prayed—sometimes Dad prayed too, sometimes he didn't. But he always sang to him. One of Tyler's favorites was "Down in the Valley."

Roses love sunshine.
Violets love dew.
Angels in heaven know I love you.

The lines meant more now that he'd *seen* an angel. Wait until he told Dad!

He sniffed, tears falling from his eyes to the ground.

He heard a noise and stiffened. He rose to his hands and knees and edged around the front boulder. Toby was still up on the wall. Tyler watched him reach the end and walk away on the garden-side wall, appearing to shrink until he was gone.

Tyler backed into his hiding place, turned, and let out a yelp.

Jordan was sitting there in the shadows at the other end. He was smiling, and lifted his finger to his mouth. "Shhh."

Tyler was frozen, wanting to turn and run, knowing it was hopeless.

Jordan gestured and whispered, "Sit." Tyler settled down between the boulders, keeping his legs tense, ready to jump up. Jordan said, "You scream like a girl. Was that crazy, that angel?"

"You saw him?"

"How could I not? Who was he?"

"Leo," Tyler said, suddenly missing him. "He was one of the monks."

"Did you know he was an angel?"

Tyler shook his head.

"Man, he knocked Phin *away*. You think the other monks are angels?"

Tyler hadn't thought of that. "I don't think so," he said.

"How do you know?"

Tyler shrugged. "What are you going to do?"

"What do you mean?"

"They're looking for me, the others . . . you."

"I found you."

"What about the others?"

"They didn't."

Tyler sighed. He didn't know if Jordan was really stupid or really smart.

"Are you going to hurt me, or tell the others?"

Jordan scrunched his nose, shook his head. "Nah. I thought I'd sit with you, keep you company." He leaned back, clearing the boulder, twisting to look toward the monastery.

"Then what?" Tyler said.

Jordan smiled at him. "Let's see what happens."

[86]

Owen's jet flew low over the monastery on a southeast trajectory, through the valley of Wadi El-Deir. Sunrise was still an hour away. It was too dark to make out people, but the monastery was lit up like a Christmas tree—the external wall lights, the compound's getting-around bulbs, the lights that shone on the Southwest Range Building's columns on special occasions. Not a good sign.

"I couldn't see anyone," Jagger said.

Owen climbed and banked, nearly skimming Gebel Ed-Deir, the mountain north of St. Catherine's.

"I'm going to do another flyby," Owen said.

"That'll tip them off we're coming."

"There's no way to land without their knowing. I need to scope out the road again, but I'll tell you one thing: it's not straight."

"You can't land?" Jagger said. "Where's your parachute?"

"Hold on. I didn't say that. I'm just not sure I'm going to be able to stay on it."

"Meaning . . . ?"

Owen grinned. "Buckle your seat belt."

• • •

Nevaeh was in the refectory, studying a large map of the compound for places they'd failed to look, when the jet flew over. She looked at the ceiling, as if expecting to see through it. She took off, bursting through the door into the courtyard of the burning bush. She scanned the black sky. The jet's engines rumbled to the south. She jumped up and came down flat on her feet, making the Austin boots propel her to the roof of the refectory, then the top of the wall overlooking the archaeological dig.

She saw the plane's white taillights, meaning it was flying directly away from her. As it gained altitude, the red light on the left wingtip appeared. It was banking sharply, probably to come around again. As she watched it, she rubbed the back of her head, felt the huge knot there and the blood crusting her hair into rope-like clumps. She still ached from the fall she'd taken, but she felt better with each passing hour. By the time they were back in Palermo—with Beth, she told herself—she'd be back to normal.

But the injury had taken its toll. For hours she'd been too shaken—oh, all right, she'd been in too much pain—to do much searching or managing of the others' search. Consequently, they hadn't found either Beth or Tyler. She wondered how Ben would have handled their failure.

Ben's voice in her head: I wouldn't have gone there for the woman in the first place, you know that.

Nevaeh: But say you did.

Ben: I wouldn't have.

Nevaeh: We're here, okay? What now?

Ben: Get while the getting's good.

Nevaeh: What about salvaging the mission?

Ben: How?

Nevaeh: Do something right. Don't leave empty-handed.

Ben: What are you thinking?

Nevaeh: Certainly, there are sinners here.

Ben, stern: *Nevaeh.*

Nevaeh: It's what we do. Kill sinners. If we have to leave without Beth, at least we can settle some scores. For God.

Ben: Bad idea.

Nevaeh: Just one . . . or two. For God.

Silence.

Nevaeh: Ben?

Just like Ben to abandon a conversation when he didn't like its direction.

The jet was gone now, hidden by the mountains. She ran along the wall toward the front. As she did, she tugged her hand radio out of a breast pocket. "Elias! Phin! Toby! Jordan! We have a jet. It's buzzing us." She stopped. Her last line had echoed back at her, a second after she'd spoken it. Then she saw why: Toby was sitting on the wall atop the round tower in the corner, leaning against its parapet. He was fast asleep, the sniper rifle across his lap, his radio resting in his hand, limp on the ground beside him.

How could anyone sleep with that plane flying over? And her screaming through the radio? Beth and Tyler could have marched right by him, playing a drum and blowing a trumpet, and he wouldn't have noticed.

She picked the rifle up off his lap and kicked the bottom of his feet. The boots hummed, their soles moving in and out, trying to figure out what Toby was up to. He startled awake, saw her standing above him.

He groaned and said, "I must have dozed off."

"You think?"

He reached for the rifle. She pulled it away, taking a step back. "It's mine now," she said.

"Come on. I've been patrolling all night."

"You can have it later. I have a feeling I'm going to need it."

"What's up?" he said, using the parapet to help him stand. "Time to go?"

"A plane just flew over. I think it's coming back."

"Who?"

She shook her head, checking the gun, making sure its optics were functioning.

Toby said, "I saw Phin earlier, down in the courtyard by the mosque. I yelled at him, but he acted like he didn't hear."

"I haven't seen him for hours," she said. She held the radio to her mouth. "Phin, you there?" Silence. "Phin!"

"Yeah, what?"

"Where are you?"

"In their apartment, in case one of them comes back."

Nevaeh could see the dark window of the apartment from where she stood. "Get out here. Something's up. A plane." She didn't wait for acknowledgement. "Elias?"

A fountain of fire billowed up between the basilica and mosque.

"You hear?" she asked. "A plane."

"I saw it," he said over the radio. "Low."

"Did you recognize it?"

"Negatory." Then: "It was a Cessna Citation."

"Keep the monks in the church unless I call you."

The flames billowed up again.

"Jordan?"

Toby said, "I haven't seen him."

Remembering that Phin had found Jordan's radio smashed outside the walls, she looked out at the excavation and called his name.

· · ·

"Jordan!" came Nevaeh's voice.

"She sounds mad," Tyler said. He was on his knees, hands pressed on one of the rocks between which he and Jordan hid. They'd both been asleep when the jet flew over. The sound had been like water thrown over them.

Jordan nodded, but said, "She's all right."

Tyler returned his gaze to the last place he'd seen the jet's lights. "You know who it is?" Jordan asked.

Tyler smiled a little, hoping . . . hoping . . .

· · ·

Beth scrambled down the rungs from the attic room as fast as she could with one hand. The pain in her broken arm had settled into a dull throbbing. She went through room after room until she came out in a tunnel. She turned left and emerged in the open space between a clutter of buildings and the Colosseum. She looked to the sky just as the plane soared over again.

Jagger? she thought. *Is that you? Owen?*

What if it were the Tribe leaving? That would be just as good . . . better!

A single gunshot shattered that idea. She moved to the wall of a building, edged to the corner, and peered around. Through a gap between the jumbled structures and the monk cells on the west wall, the glow from monastery lights allowed her to see Toby and Nevaeh standing on top of the round tower. Nevaeh was aiming a rifle at the retreating jet. She fired again, stumbling back from the recoil.

Beth looked to the top of the wall nearest her, the monk cells rising almost as high. She believed she could reach the top from the cell's roof, and darted to the rickety wood stairs that serviced the cells.

[87]

On the third circle around, Owen brought the jet into a steep descent. They flew into the junction of two valleys, occupied by the village of St. Catherine's, crossed it, dipped onto the road leading to the monastery. The plane's landing lights showed asphalt much curvier than Jagger remembered; but then again, he'd never traveled so fast on it—150 miles per hour on touchdown. Owen, simultaneously slowing, engaging the reverse thrusters, and keeping the plane on the road, said, "I think we're going to end up in the desert."

"What?" Jagger said.

"Oh, crumb," Owen said, and Jagger saw why: the jet had jarred left, following the road, and its lights now illuminated the little guard shack that was more like a visitor's information center than it was anything to do with security. The plane swerved left, bounding off the road, but too late to avoid its wings from clipping the shack. The sound was like a mountain splitting in two. The entire plane canted right, settled back, trembled.

Then they were in the desert, shaking and bouncing—seeming to Jagger that they were about to take flight again. The lighted monastery grew larger in the windshield, its many walls, levels, outbuildings, and the garden's trees, which would make the prospect of actually hitting the monastery pretty slim, but Jagger wondered what would happen to the jet.

The first of the trees appeared to slide at them, and Jagger got the sensation that the jet wasn't moving, but it was the earth that was rolling toward them, bringing destruction.

The jet slowed without easing its bouncing-shaking whitewater-raft movement. Then it stopped, just like that: one last jolt and Jagger was staring at a tree twenty feet in front of the jet's nose.

He turned to look at Owen, the man's eyes huge. Jagger said, "Holy—"

The jet exploded.

Or seemed to: to the sound of crunching metal, shattering glass, wood, plastic—the *Boanerges* lurched into the tree, seeming to swallow it. It continued forward, crushing more trees, bounding up onto them, and plummeting down as they gave out under the plane's weight. Finally the encore ride stopped, the plane's front angled down, its landing lights filtered through a pile of branches and leaves.

"What was that?" Jagger said.

Owen was snapping out of his harness. "Nothing good," he said, rushing out of the cockpit, having to ascend the floor like a ramp to do it. Jagger released the harness's hold and followed. The cabin was half the length it was when they'd taken off. The rear had crumbled toward the cockpit like a tube of toothpaste. The polished mahogany that formed the bathroom and storeroom walls was shattered and splintered in midcabin. The ceiling had peeled back, showing sky.

Owen used his palm to break the glass of the door's emergency release and pulled the handle. The door *thumped!* and flew off. Owen jumped into darkness. A few seconds later, when Jagger reached the door, Owen was sidestepping away, staring toward the rear of the plane. He gestured toward Jagger. "Come on! Hurry!"

Jagger jumped, looked: the Clan's black Bombardier was canted upward, pushing and lifting the aft of the Citation—where its tail used to be. Its nose was crushed, its windshields shattered. The metal skin running under the Bombardier's side cockpit windows, as well as the entirety of the *Boanerges's* skin, was crinkled, all of it looking like crumpled and reopened chewing gum foil. The Bombardier was much larger than Owen's jet, and the wreck was akin to a semi smashing into a minivan.

Dirt and smoke filled the air around them, creating a dream-like atmosphere. Jagger had the notion that if he tried to get away, he would run in place.

But none of this changed anything: he was here to save his family from the Tribe, and the Clan wasn't going to stop him. He grabbed Owen's arm. "Let's go! We have to get into the monastery."

They scrambled over the dirt and trees the jet had plowed into a pile. Coming down the other side, they heard Bale behind them, calling: "Hey! Where you going? I came to give you a hand!" And he laughed.

[88]

When they saw the jet coming directly for the monastery and then dipping out of sight, Nevaeh and Toby sprinted across the front wall to the corner where it met the garden-side wall. They watched the jet land on the road, weave and waddle, shear the roof off the guard shack, and streak out into the desert—still heading for St. Catherine's, but on the road. Incredibly, another plane was hot on its tail. This other jet—larger, black—touched down farther back on the road, but appeared to be going faster and not slowing as quickly as the first jet.

"They're going to hit," Toby said, excited. And they did, the second jet smashing into the first, pushing it into the gardens. The first jet mowed down four or five trees. They came to rest at odd angles, one with its much-shorter rear end raised up; the other with its crumpled nose in the air, holding up the other's rear. The front plane was also canted sideways, resting on the tip of its right wing.

Someone behind them stomped up the roof of the monk cell building. Phin leaped up onto the top of the wall. "What happened?" he said.

Toby waved at him. "Com'ere, com'ere, com'ere! Two jets just crashed into each other."

"In the air?"

"They were landing," Nevaeh said.

"*Here?*" Phin said. "In the desert?"

Elias's voice, sounding small: "What was that?"

Nevaeh pulled out her radio and told him.

"They're here for us," he said.

"I realize that, Elias," she said.

Toby showed her a puzzled look. "What do you mean, here for us?"

Nevaeh dropped the radio in her pocket. She looked at Toby for a few seconds before answering. "I think Beth's white knight just arrived."

· · ·

Tyler couldn't see anything, just a big cloud of smoke. But the sounds told him the plane had crashed. He wanted to run to it, but Jordan was holding him, both arms around his chest and back.

"It's my dad!" Tyler said. "I know it. Let go!"

"It's not safe," Jordan said. "Dad or not, Nevaeh and the others are still after you."

Tyler squirmed, trying to see more. "I think there are *two* planes."

"Two?"

"Let me go!"

· · ·

Some people came out of the first plane. Two, Nevaeh thought. "Toby, I want you down there," she said.

"To do what?" Toby wanted to know.

"If they head toward the monastery," Nevaeh said, "they're coming to interfere with our mission. Make sure they don't."

"Do I get the rifle?"

"Use your pistol."

Toby looked over the edge, doing nothing.

"Well?" Nevaeh said.

"I'll jump down at the back," Toby said. "It's not so far." He ran along the wall toward the Southwest Range Building.

Phin's head moved as though he were listening to seriously rocking tunes, but the earbuds attached to his MP3 player were dangling over his chest. Whatever beat he was rocking to, it was in his head. If that's what crazy looked like, Nevaeh had a fleeting thought that she'd be hearing that melody herself soon enough.

She told him, "You know the Siege Door?" It was the small iron door near the rear of the garden-side wall, where Toby had said he'd jump down.

"You mean the one Creed used when he came here?"

"That's it. I want you to reach it from the inside. Go through the Southwest Range Building. I think Jagger and Owen are going for it. I don't want them to see you or they'll try something else. If they come that way, take care of them."

"Yeah, baby," Phin said and leaped down, straight to the courtyard in front of the mosque. He didn't land right and tumbled. Cursing, he got up and limped toward the back of the compound.

Nevaeh turned on the rifle's electronic scope and switched it to night vision. She raised the rifle and scanned through the trees and branches toward the first plane. Showing in shades of green, the scope put her right in front of the jet's windshield, obstacles scattering dark blurry blotches across her field of vision. She panned down, scanned right and left. There. Someone moving. An arm and hand—carrying something; must be a gun—swept through the scope's optics. As she moved her sight to catch the person, she realized what she'd seen: not a hand and gun, but hooks. And then he was there: Jagger.

I thought so.

She centered the crosshairs on his head, moving as he did, panning to keep him dead center.

She pulled the trigger.

[89]

Jagger stepped over a tree that the jet had apparently cut down and hurled forward, his feet coming down on defoliated branches. He reached out to a standing tree for balance, gripping it with RoboHand. He started to turn to make sure Owen was keeping up when the tree exploded. Something knocked RoboHand off it, and splinters sprayed into his face.

Then he heard the shot.

He ducked, looking first at the tree. A large-caliber bullet had taken a bite out of it, leaving a splintery semicircle cutting halfway into its eight-inch-diameter trunk. "Down!" he said.

Both men fell on their stomachs and scrambled to a foot-high wall encircling a tree. Owen was lying on top of Jagger's knees, his head at his hip.

"Was that a gunshot?" Owen asked.

"Almost took my head off," said Jagger.

Owen was looking back at the planes.

"It came from the monastery," Jagger said. "I think from the top of the wall."

Another shot rang out and a crack, like the sound of a sledgehammer on stone, sounded from the other side of the little wall, opposite his head.

"One of the Tribe?" Owen said.

"That'd be my guess." He looked back. Four people were heading toward them, their figures backlit by a white taillight on the Clan's Bombardier, their silhouettes oversized and fuzzy, bobbing up and down.

The gun—a sniper rifle by the sound of it—spat out another

round, this one going high. It pinged on the *Boanerges's* wing. The Clan scattered, diving under the plane, running behind the wreckage. With the light no longer directly behind them, Jagger could make them out: Bale; the commando—Artimus, he thought; and Lilit, the rock band girl. A few seconds later another one darted from behind a tree to a boulder. Cillian.

Thank you, Mr. Sniper, whoever you are, Jagger thought. He said, "They think the shooter is targeting them, covering for us."

"They wouldn't know that somebody inside the monastery wants us dead."

"I suppose you started praying as soon as we hit the ground."

"Long before that, my friend."

[90]

Where are they? Nevaeh thought. She was sure they'd dropped down behind a low wall after her first shot, but now she couldn't see them. *Wait a minute.* Something moved behind the wall. She centered the crosshairs on it. A tuft of hair was sticking up in all directions. Had to be Owen. Good enough.

She fired.

Directly behind the hair, a small explosion on the flat paving stones marked the bullet's point of impact. She kept her aim in the area, sweeping a little to the left, then the right. They had to pop their heads up sometime. They'd probably move together, running for the next protective obstacle closer to the monastery. She'd sniped before, the last time using a bolt-action M40A3, which required manually ejecting a spent cartridge and chambering the round. Too slow between shots for target-rich environments. She was glad for the XM500, which was a gas-operated semiautomatic, able to fire bullets as fast as she could pull the trigger. So it was quite possible, probable even, that she'd nail them both, seconds apart.

Boom. Boom. Mission salvaged.

Movement, off to the right. Oh, look, a foot. The .50-caliber round would blow it right off. In fact, a foot was nothing. Toby had been right, mimicking Dirty Harry: this thing could blow a head *cleeeeean* off. She took aim on the foot, preparing for three quick shots: the foot would cause the victim to scream and writhe, most likely revealing himself; the other man would try to help, putting himself in her sights if only for a few seconds. That's all she needed.

Footsteps approached her on the wall.

"Toby, get your butt down there," she said. "Now, *shhhh*, I got 'em."

"I don't think so," Beth said.

Nevaeh spun her head half a second before a two-by-four wood stud slammed into her face. She reeled back—catching a glimpse of Beth holding the board in one hand, one end wedged against her shoulder, rifle-like; the other arm in a sling—and the stud smacked into her face again. She heard her nose break, sucked in breath, and started gagging on blood. She reversed, stumbled, and fell onto her back.

Her mind moving, moving, moving past the pain, the panic of choking. She'd dropped the rifle, and Beth was bending to pick it up. Nevaeh arched her back, flipped up onto her feet, spun, and slammed the ball of her foot into Beth's head. Beth staggered sideways, hit the parapet, dropped the gun. Nevaeh jumped for it. Beth kicked it, hard. It slid on the top of the wall, past Nevaeh, who turned to grab it. Bent over, arms out, she ran for it, grabbed it, and spun—thinking, *Whoa, whoa . . . don't kill her . . . leg shot, shoulder shot . . .*

The top of the wall was empty. Beth would have had to flip over the edge to be gone so fast. She took a fast glance over the parapet. No, she'd splatter on the ground going that way. She looked on the other side. A roof lay six feet below. She could have dropped down, then over the edge to a balcony.

Nevaeh jumped to the roof, verified the balcony below, and jumped to that. A row of doors to the monk cells. Nevaeh spat out blood, blew blood out of her nostrils. She wiped the sleeve of her coat over her lips and kicked open the first door.

[91]

Vasco de Sousa had stopped needing alarm clocks three decades ago. His biorhythms were conditioned to wake him at 4:30 in the morning. In all that time, they had never failed him by more than a minute. This morning the clock read 4:19. He lifted it and held it close to his face. Eleven minutes! He wondered what it meant. Was this it, the start of a rapid decline ending in a grave?

Rapid? Ha!

He'd had aching joints, failing eyesight, bowel problems for years. But he'd been able to take care of himself, which was more than he could say for a lot of people thirty years his junior. He fixed his own meals, went for walks, could still make people laugh. He had his mother to thank for it. Even half her genes, however, passed through a generation, had limitations.

He'd always thought that the way he'd go was a steady, gradual decline, then a plunge: slide down the hill, go over the cliff. And that was fine by him. He wanted people to say, "What? Vasco's dead? I saw him just yesterday. He was shuffling around, telling stories—good ones too." Much better than: "Oh, what a blessing he's gone. Finally out of his misery, poor dear."

Maybe it was his mother's visit that had thrown him off. Lord knew he was excited about this morning, his morning prayers. That must have been it. Anxious to pray. He stood and turned to pull his sheet and bed cover up, making them straight. At his age, you never knew when the ticker would stop ticking, and heaven forbid he'd leave a mess for someone else to clean up. He went to the marble-topped sideboard in his room and poured water from a pitcher into a basin. His son had upgraded the bathroom when he remodeled, all the modern conveniences, but some things you couldn't let go of, and washing his face and brushing his teeth from a freestanding basin was one of them.

After his personal hygiene routine, he went to the kitchen to start a pot of coffee—percolated, not dripped. Normally he'd fry an egg, toast a slice of bread while waiting for the coffee, but he thought this morning he'd start his prayer time early. Why not? He'd woken up early for a reason, he supposed, and it wasn't to spend extra time in the kitchen.

He'd been so excited about praying today, he'd told the children about it last night. They'd smiled and nodded, their little faces saying, *Whatever, old man, where's the* pastéis de nada? But they were good kids from good homes: he'd known their parents as babies and their grandparents as babies, and even most of their great-grandparents.

He considered forgoing the fire pit on the patio and simply diving in with *My dear Father in heaven*—and everything he wanted to say. But the mornings had been chilly lately, and his body didn't insulate his bones the way it used to. Two logs would do.

He picked up the magazine from the table by the patio doors, brushed a curtain aside to get to the handle, and opened a door. He froze in place. The fire pit was blazing, and sitting around it and his favorite chair were all the children—not just the ones who came in the evenings for *pastéis*, but their siblings as well, children—teens now— who'd grown too old to listen to an old man's stories in exchange for something to eat. And their parents . . . a few grandparents as well. Every one of them held a white votive candle, all the flames illuminating a congregation of compassionate faces.

He began to weep, and a man stepped up to help him to his chair. He grinned, trying to communicate his joy to each person in turn. It wasn't unusual for most of them to be up so early in the morning; despite its newfound resort status, Sesimbra was still a fishing village, after all, and boats hitting the water by five pulled in the best hauls. But that they came to support him . . . that meant the world to him. His shaking fingers opened the magazine in his lap and picked up a card. He said, "I guess your children told you how special today is for me. I'm going to tell you some things that you won't believe, and that's okay. Just chalk it up to a senile old man."

Light laughter all around.

"My mother came to visit me the other day. Not as a vision. She is very much alive." He held up the magazine and tapped Nevaeh's face. "This is a picture of her, the only one I have. Yesterday, I picked up the magazine and this card fell out. You see, she left it for me." He looked at her handwriting, Portuguese words in a fine script: *Pray por favor para mim.* A tear leaked into his face's network of wrinkles.

When he spoke again, his voice was unsteady, quiet. Several people leaned in to hear. "You know I've always been a religious man, but some things I knew about my mother made me question her—I guess you could say, the state of her soul. That has always caused pain in my heart. So this means more to me than I can say."

He held up the card. "It says, 'Please pray for me.'"

He didn't read the rest, which meant almost as much as her request: *Mamã do amor.* Love, Mom.

"So that's what I plan to do. Thank you for joining me."

He bowed his head and began the most heartfelt prayer of his very long life.

[92]

The first monk cell was empty. Nevaeh moved to the next. She kicked in the door, and the first thing she saw was the candle on the floor, perfectly centered, its flame flickering. A man was standing at the back of the small room, caught in the candle's light. He was casually leaning against the wall, one leg bent to push the bottom of his foot against the wall. His arms were crossed over his chest. He was young, about thirty, with a wispy beard, wearing a monk's black cassock.

She brought the rifle up. "Who are you?"

"They call me Father Leo," he said.

"Well, they-call-me-Father-Leo, what are you doing here?" She scanned the room quickly. "Where's the woman? Beth?"

"I haven't seen her recently."

"Why aren't you with the others in the basilica?"

"I have other duties."

She shook the gun at him. "What are you talking about?"

"You, Arella," he said, using her birth name. "I'm talking about you."

A chill iced her veins. "How do you know that name?"

"You want to know what Beth told Ben."

"You know? What?"

"It's both simple and complex. It won't help you."

"Listen," Nevaeh said, "I don't know who you are, but—"

"She told him his faith was trapped in his head."

"He *was* a brain."

"But you, you're not thinking enough."

"Hey—"

"You have a purpose. Find it."

Below her a door slammed, someone ran across the court—the slapping of bare feet on stone. Nevaeh spun, rushed to the rail of the balcony. No one there. It had to have been Beth. She watched a dark corner near the mosque, thought she saw shadows shifting within.

She backed into the cell's doorway. "Look, buddy—"

The monk was gone, and he'd taken the candle with him.

[93]

"The shooter's gone," Owen said, peering over the wall.

Jagger popped his head up, ready to snap it back down—as if his reactions were faster than a bullet. The dark figure he'd seen on the wall wasn't there anymore. "Maybe he's moving to a better vantage point."

"You want to wait and see?" Sarcasm was so un-Owen-like, Jagger had to turn to read his face.

"All right," Jagger whispered and stood. He started through the garden.

Owen caught up. "Where?"

"Let's try the garden gate first. If that doesn't work, there's a door into the compound on the same wall, near the back."

"The Siege Door," Owen said. Added in the sixth century, it allowed the monks to escape in times of siege.

"Yeah, I was told it was sealed shut," Jagger said, still bitter that Gheronda had lied to him about it, "until they used it to sneak Creed in." It was the incident that drew the Tribe to the monastery six months ago, starting their whole adventure with them: Tyler shot, Beth kidnapped.

They hadn't gone ten paces when a figure came bounding— practically *bouncing*—along the garden-side wall from the rear of the compound. It stopped at the garden gate, turned toward them.

Jagger tackled Owen to the ground. "Someone's there," he said, a harsh whisper. He raised his head. The figure was heading back toward the rear. It jumped on top of the roof of a building used to store garden tools and vanished in the shadows.

Jagger said, "This way," and rushed, crouching, to the wall that separated the gardens from the tourist walkway to the front of

St. Catherine's. He jumped over it and dropped down. Owen plunged down behind him. The wall was tall enough to conceal them standing at full height. They followed it toward its end, where the grounds opened up around the monastery. There they would be totally exposed.

Behind them, a gun fired. A piece of wall beside Jagger's face chipped away. He turned to see the Clan coming over the wall, Lilit already over, pointing a pistol at them. She fired again.

Owen bolted, heading for the end of the wall, the open area.

"Not there," Jagger called, right behind him. "The guy on the side!" Not to mention the sniper who, hearing the siren call of the gunshots, would probably return to that side. "There! There!" He pointed and broke away from the wall, heading into the rocky, uneven ground of the valley floor in front of the monastery. The terrain's crevasses, depressions, hills, and boulders offered them an infinite number of hiding places—black shadows against the lights from the top of the monastery walls.

Jagger had his eyes on a depression that snaked back into the foothills when the gun cracked again, and his leg flared with pain and collapsed out from under him. He tumbled, hitting his chin, banging his prosthetic arm on the stone surface. Owen was on him before he rolled to a stop, grabbing him, lifting.

"Go!" Jagger said, clutching his calf, feeling his pant leg wet with blood. "Leave me here."

"Not a chance," Owen said. "I got you."

"You mean we got you," Bale said, jogging up to them, the others at his side. They circled Jagger and Owen, guns drawn. Lilit, grinning, proud of herself, stepped on Jagger's leg.

He started to scream, but bit it back, grinding his teeth together.

Bale stopped in front of them, eyeing them as he might trophy game. His teeth gleamed in the light. He said, "You make it too easy." He tilted his head, that fedora perched so suavely on top. "But I'll give you the orphanage. That was masterfully played." He rubbed silver tape that was wrapped around his wrist. The hand looked like it belonged on a mannequin. Then two fingers twitched.

Artimus moved closer to Bale, the muzzle of his big machine gun staring at Jagger. Cillian, holding a combat knife at his thigh, stepped to Bale's other side. Lilit held her ground, putting pressure on Jagger's wound with her booted foot.

Bale grinned at Owen. "This has been a long time coming, hasn't it, my friend?"

"*You* can call no one friend who loves the Lord," Owen said.

Bale threw his head back and laughed. "You think you're still writing the gospel! If not friend, then you've been a fine adversary. I only wish you appreciated me more. What was it Buddha said? 'There has to be evil so that good can prove its purity above it.' I gladly perform my part, so you may perform yours. You're welcome." He pinched the brim of his hat.

He looked down at Jagger, who was twisted at the waist to watch him, his leg still pinned. "You," Bale said, "you just confuse me. You were doing so well for so long, killing all those people. You were so cold-blooded. I thought I'd met my match in you, always upping the game, seeing who could kill more in such creative ways. Oh, but that's right: your victims were *sinners*, so that made it all right. Did you ever consider that we were always on the same team? After all, 'all have sinned and fall short of the glory of God.' That you did it 'in God's name' is just too rich! I wish I'd have thought of that. That would have *really* ticked the Big Guy off. Then I hear you left the Tribe, changed your ways. What was that about?"

Jagger simply stared.

Lilit ground her boot into Jagger's leg. He squeezed his eyes closed, tightened his facial muscles, taking the pain.

"Okay, guys," Bale said. "You know what I'm here for." He looked at Cillian, cocked his head toward Jagger and Owen.

Cillian stepped forward, crouched beside Jagger, and started patting him down.

Watching, Bale said, "I need that Stone. It makes my job so much easier. And I have unfinished business at the orphanage. Of course, I can do that nasty work without it now that I know where it is, but it's so cool watching their lights go out." He looked at the monastery. "I bet I'll find plenty of lights to snuff out here first, don't you think?"

Cillian felt the folded cloth through the material over Jagger's pants pocket and reached his fingers in. He pulled it out. Jagger heard the fragment hit the ground, but apparently the others didn't, looking for the larger Stone. Cillian tossed the cloth away and moved on to Owen. He stepped back. "It's not on them," he said.

Lilit dragged her boot to his ankle. She leaned over and pushed the barrel of her pistol into his wound, wiggling it, probing. This time Jagger did scream.

"Stop!" Coming from behind Bale, farther up in the foothills. Jagger recognized the voice and felt his insides turn to stone.

Bale turned, clearing Jagger's line-of-sight to his son, standing there, big eyes, shaking.

"Run, Tyler!" He tried to scramble up. Lilit stood on his leg, kicked the back of his head.

Owen started to run toward Tyler. Artimus swung the barrel of his machine gun into his chin. Owen staggered back, fell. He started to rise, and Artimus pushed the muzzle into his forehead. Owen stopped, perched on his knees.

Cillian darted for Tyler.

"Go, Ty! Run!" Jagger yelled.

Tyler appeared confused, moving one way, then the other. He turned toward two boulders near him, but Cillian reached him and grabbed the back of his neck. He lifted him, turned, and plunked him down on his feet, Tyler grimacing in pain.

"No!" Jagger said.

Tyler looked at him with teary eyes. "Dad?" he said.

"Dad?" Bale said, looking from Tyler to Jagger. "Oh yes," he said, drawing a dagger from inside his jacket. He began walking toward Tyler, swishing the blade around.

"No!" Jagger yelled. "Stop, please!"

He didn't.

Jagger said, "We'll give it to you. The Stone, it's yours."

Bale turned toward him. "Oh, I'm sorry, you misunderstand. I'm not *threatening* the kid to get to the Stone. I'll get that one way or another. There're only so many places it can be, right? I'm *slaughtering* him . . . just because I can. It's just too bad I'm not going to keep *you* alive longer to bask in your grief. Since your anguish will be so brief, let's see what I can do to make it *excruciating*. Maybe I should disembowel your boy first, you think? The Japanese perfected the method. They saved the heart and lungs for last, prolonging death until the very end. Or *lingchi*, you know that one? It's also called 'slow slicing'—you get the idea."

He turned and walked to Tyler.

[94]

Jagger wailed. He twisted under Lilit's foot, kicked at her leg. She dodged, stomped his wound, cracked the back of his skull with her gun.

Tyler squirmed and cried. He cast pleading, scared eyes at Jagger, then turned to stare at the dagger coming closer. Cillian had sheathed his knife and now had a grip on Tyler's hair as well as the back of his neck. The boy kicked and wiggled and fought, helpless to get away.

Owen started to rise again, and Artimus slapped him with the machine gun's barrel. He fell into Jagger and got to his knees again. He said, "Pray, Jagger, pray!"

Jagger wanted to scream at him. He needed to *act*, not pray. *Stop Bale . . . stop Bale . . .* over and over in his head . . . *stop Bale.* That was the only thing that mattered. If his life, all 3,500 years of it, meant anything, it came down to this: Stop Bale. Save Tyler.

Jagger rolled out from under Lilit. She danced around him, straddled him, cracked the butt of her gun into his head. His vision was fading, weak from the constant bashing.

No! Tyler!

Lilit sat down hard on his back. She slammed one boot down on RoboHand, the other on the wrist of his real arm. She pushed the gun barrel into his neck, gripped his hair, and pulled his head back, forcing him to watch Bale standing in front of his son. The tip of the dagger glided in the air inches from Tyler's face, down to his belly button, as though Bale was rehearsing the cuts he would make.

Owen seemed to let out a short laugh. His face turned toward the sky, and he said, "Yes, Lord, Yes!"

Jagger wailed louder, tears streaming down his face. Owen had snapped, gone totally insane, and Jagger was close to it.

Owen yelled, "Can you see, Jagger? Can you *see?*"

Bale looked over, grinning. "Yes, Jagger, can you see? This is all for you." He drew the dagger back, low behind his hip—not up over his head in some theatrical pose. The motion left Jagger no hope: the man wasn't toying around. He fully intended to plunge the blade into Tyler's stomach.

He bellowed, all the rage and pain the world has ever known. "God, no! Please!"

Owen whispered: "Oh, Lord, open his eyes so he may see."

In a flash, the valley was full of angels, wielding swords, riding horses and chariots—all of them on fire, the flames constructed of the burning orange embers Jagger had seen swirling around the angels. They were perched on the rocks and boulders, on every outcropping rising up the mountain, on the ground around them. The horses were rearing up, beating the air with their hooves. The chariots floated in midair, gently moving back and forth. The angels, flaming swords drawn, stood watching the action of the humans below them. They appeared to be waiting for something.

Jagger heard a booming sound, rhythmic.

The angels turned their heads at once, staring into the sky.

Jagger followed their gaze: a sky full of stars. They grew brighter, vibrated with movement. They grew, and he realized they were coming closer—not stars at all: angels. Millions of angels, filling the sky, each one bright as a small sun. They moved and swirled, forming . . . something. It was a face, etched in three dimensions in the sky by approaching angels. It blinked—angels moving down and up. The eyes were alive, glistening. They turned to look directly at Jagger.

He cried out, no words, just a gasp of awe. He knew the face, the face of Christ, watching through His angels.

Still, it—*the face*—they—*the angels*—approached, filling every inch of the firmament.

Jagger saw demons as well. Scampering around and on the Clan. Big ones, little one, all sorts of ugly beings. They saw the angels as well: they screeched and howled and roared; they spun in circles, cowered in a ball, arms crossed over their heads. Finally, ashy black wings formed around them and they flew off, swiping and turning, glaring back in fear.

Bale saw too: his blade stopped in midthrust. He staggered back, his head snapping all around, eyes and mouth round with shock.

The approaching sky-angels suddenly accelerated from *fast* to *light speed*. They were all there in the valley, crowded against one another, against Jagger and Owen and Tyler and Bale and the rest of the Clan.

Instead of mimicking the demons—cowering, fleeing—Bale seemed to draw strength from the presence of this heavenly host, taking them as a challenge, defying them. He laughed, said to the sky, "Oh no, no, no! Is this all you got? Bring it on!" He turned to Tyler, swung his blade.

[95]

From the top of the front wall, Nevaeh had watched Jagger take the bullet to his leg. She saw the team of gun- and knife-toting thugs converge on him and Owen. When she saw their apparent leader, she turned and slid her back down the rampart, sitting hard, resting the rifle in her lap.

Bale.

If ever there was a sinner in need of vigilante justice, it was Bale. She raised her eye to the night sky.

But, God . . . I'm so confused!

She had been thinking about the monk—obviously *not* a monk. He'd known her given name. He'd been there, then had simply vanished. The balcony in front of the monk cells was not wide enough for him to have slipped past without bumping into her. And there was no other way out of the room.

His words had been maddeningly vague, ambiguous to the point of being meaningless. *Purpose*—something in that word, but what? Yes, she was here for a reason. Is that why she hadn't been called home, after all these years? She hadn't fulfilled her purpose? She'd determined his visit wasn't about what he had said; it was the *visit* itself. God noticed her! He was *communicating* with her. The hopelessness that had been crushing her spirit, filling her mind with blackness—slowly growing, oppressing her more and more, like cancer—it left her, evaporating as surely and abruptly as a raindrop on a hot surface.

She knew that all this time she had been wrong. Killing wasn't the answer; it wouldn't draw her back into God's arms. She'd been holding the bodies of sinners out to Him, gifting them to Him, but all she'd done was fill her own arms so she could not embrace anything else. She could not embrace *Him*.

For the first time in as long as she could remember, the urge to kill was gone.

She'd come to the top of the wall to find out what was going on, to see if it was time to go home and figure out what she was going to do now. It was a daunting prospect, her future. She welcomed it, waiting for Him to see that she'd heard Him, that she'd changed. She prayed it wasn't a momentary respite from the burning frustration that drove her to kill—but it didn't feel that way. She prayed it wasn't a symptom of the insanity she'd felt clawing at her—but it didn't feel that way. This felt . . . genuine, real, *holy*.

But if it were, why was He waiting? Hadn't He taken Ben right away?

In His time.

Yes, in Your time, Lord. I can wait.

But she wanted, expected, every thought to be her last. *That was it. Okay*, that *was it.*

She'd better learn to get a handle on this. Or she'd go mad for altogether different reasons. Or backslide, pushed again by frustration.

No! That won't happen! It won't!

Then she saw Bale.

Sitting with her back to the parapet, she prayed for guidance.

Don't You want him dead, God? Him of all people? She supposed if God wanted the man dead, he would be. But then: *What if I'm the one to do it?* God's fist. No . . . that's what she thought before.

She turned and rose slowly, peering over. The boy, Tyler! Bale was approaching him with a dagger. She knew enough about Bale to be certain he meant to kill the kid. Then Jagger, then Owen.

If she did nothing, wasn't that the same as killing them—Tyler, Jagger, and Owen? Wasn't allowing evil the same as committing it yourself?

But . . .

Aaaaaaaagh!

She brought the rifle up, rested it on the wall. She nestled the stock against her shoulder and aimed. Bale was waving the dagger in front of the child, taunting him—and his father. She drew a bead on Bale's head.

This thing can take your head cleeeeeeean *off.*

Exactly what Bale needed: decapitation. So what if it was from a distance, using a modern weapon? It was only fitting that Bale would get it this way.

She pulled the trigger. Nothing happened. She yanked the magazine out: empty.

No, no, no, no, no . . . No time for this!

Bale pulled his arm back, aiming for the boy's belly. She'd seen the move before, commonly used on prisoners convicted of treason in the middle centuries: he'd plunge it in, then slice up, spilling the child's guts.

She thought, *God is going to make me watch to punish me for all the blood I've spilled. Lord, no, I'm sorry. Search my heart—I am!*

In a blink, the world became brighter. Angels and horses and chariots filled the valley before her. They stood on every possible edge and ledge and bump all the way up the mountain opposite the monastery. They stood on the wall with her, on top of the parapets. Bits of flame flashed all around them, forming wings, shields, weapons . . . *halos.*

They all turned their heads to the sky. She looked and gasped, tears instantly springing from her eyes. Millions of angels—the face of Christ!

She pried her gaze away, spotted Bale yelling at the sky, and she saw her chance, grabbed this moment of grace.

She pulled a five-cartridge stripper clip from an elastic band over the stock . . . held it to the rifle's open ejection port . . . used her thumb to slide the bullets into the magazine . . . and snapped the bolt closed, chambering the first round.

She lined up the crosshairs on Bale—turning again to Tyler, thrusting the dagger at him—and fired.

Bale's head exploded.

[96]

Jagger couldn't grasp the extent of Bale's evil. Even with God's army of angels surrounding him, the man thrust the dagger at Tyler. Jagger screamed again: "Nooooo!"

And Bale's head disappeared in an exploding mist.

The angels vanished. Like that, they were gone—no, he corrected, he just couldn't see them anymore.

Tyler had his head turned away, eyes pinched shut, waiting for the bite of Bale's steel. Jagger saw another boy emerge from the rocks behind them—Jordan, the Tribe boy. Jordan made an incredibly long leap and—as Bale's body fell to the ground—he tackled Tyler out of Cillian's clutches.

Cillian looked dazed, staring at Bale's corpse, holding a fistful of Tyler's hair. His chest exploded. He fell to his knees and toppled to his face.

Artimus lifted the machine gun over Jagger's head, aiming at the top of the wall. It rattled out bullets, his whole body shaking, trying to control it. Shells flew away from it as a belt of ammo over his shoulder was pulled into the gun. A chunk of his shoulder erupted, was gone. He took a round to his sternum and fell backward, the gun blasting at the sky for a few seconds. It stopped and toppled like a tree.

● ● ●

Nevaeh was on a roll. After taking out Bale, she shifted to Cillian, blocked by Tyler. Something flashed across the scope's optics, and Tyler was gone. She pulled the trigger, didn't wait to watch Cillian fall. She rose higher to get an angle on Artimus.

He was already firing, shredding the parapet in front of her. She fired, got him in the shoulder. Bullets ripped into her. She fired again, staggered back, and fell off the wall. She hit the edge of a roof, flipped around, and dropped thirty feet to the stone courtyard below.

She lay there, facedown, feeling more pain than she could ever remember, feeling her blood flowing out of her. She loved it.

Lord, she thought. *I'm Yours. Please forgive me.*

When Phin rolled her over, she blinked at him and smiled. "Phin," she said, blood gurgling out of her mouth. "We"—she coughed—"we were wrong." She said, "Look."

He followed her gaze to the lightening sky, a swath of orange smeared across its eastern arc.

"The sun's coming up," she said. "It's so beautiful."

He looked at her wounds. "This is nothing," he said. "You've suffered worse. You'll be fine."

She shook her head, barely moving. "Not this time. Thank God."

● ● ●

Phin lifted her top half, preparing to toss her over his shoulder. She was too limp. He leaned her back, took in her face. Her eyes were open, staring . . . at nothing. "Nev? Nevaeh!"

Toby came bounding around the mosque, taking great strides and stopping a few feet away. "Phin, pick her up," he said. "We have to go. People are dropping like flies out there. Let's go!"

Phin was looking into her eyes. "I think she's dead."

"Yeah, right. Come—" The teen must have seen his tears, his stunned expression. He said, "What?" He stepped over and dropped to his knees. *"How?"*

Phin shook his head.

Toby stuck his face right in hers. "Nevaeh! Nevaeh!" He rotated his head to look at Phin, his eyes wet now too. "Phin!" he cried.

Phin pushed him away. He lifted Nevaeh gently onto his shoulder and stood. "Let's . . ." He could hardly speak. "Go."

They started making their way toward the rear of the compound. Toby spoke into his radio. "Elias . . . Nevaeh's . . ." He lowered the radio, raised it again. "She's dead, Elias. We're leaving. Meet us on top of the Southwest Range Building. Jordan! Jordan! Where are you, man? We're leaving." He looked back at Phin, carrying Nevaeh. "Jordan, we're leaving with or without you. Get to our staging ground now. Up by the outcropping. Jordan?"

"He doesn't have his radio," Phin said.

"Then how—?"

Phin shook his head again, not caring.

Elias met up with them at the entrance of the tunnel that lead to the Southwest Range Building. He stared at Phin, at Nevaeh's body. He threw down his cigarette and led them into the darkness.

[97]

Jagger rolled to face Lilit. She wasn't there. He turned in time to see her running around the side of the monastery, by the excavation. He stood and limped toward Tyler. While he had no use of his wounded leg, he felt no pain; everything else blasting around his head pushed it out.

Jordan was lying on top of his son, saying, "I'm sorry, I'm sorry. I should have come out sooner. I was so scared."

Tyler just smiled at him. He spotted Jagger and scrambled to get out from under Jordan, then ran into Jagger's arms. His embrace was a vise on Jagger's neck and body. They kissed and cried and hugged. Jagger never wanted to let him go.

Beth's voice called their names from behind him. He turned to see her running from the garden side of St. Cath's, from the garden gate, he thought. He ran toward her, carrying Tyler. They met on the rocks, Beth throwing her one good arm around both of them.

She grimaced when he bumped her bandaged arm. "What happened?" he asked.

"Broke it playing on the roofs with Nevaeh."

She kissed Tyler, held his chin, and studied his face, smiling at what she saw. She kissed him some more, then gave Jagger the same treatment.

He set Tyler down, held his hand, and wrapped his arm around Beth's waist. He guided them to Owen, who was still on his knees, praying. They joined him, forming a circle.

Owen opened his eyes. He smiled and said, "Did you see?"

"Were they real," Jagger said, "the angels?"

Owen turned his head to give him a look. "I'm going to pretend you didn't ask me that."

"I saw them!" Tyler said. "They saved me!"

Jagger looked up at the wall, where he believed the shot that had killed Bale came from. "Yeah, I guess they did."

"You *guess?*" Tyler said.

"I mean, yes, they did." He looked at Beth. "Did you . . . see . . . ?"

She closed her eyes, smiled, and nodded.

Jagger looked past her. Jordan was standing there, watching them. Jagger raised his hand to him. "Jordan," he said, "do you want to join us?"

The boy ran up, squeezed himself between Jagger and Tyler.

They held hands, bowed their heads, and gave thanks.

[98]

Brother Ramón walked carefully on the rough stone ground of the valley floor in front of the monastery. He scoured the ground, kicked at loose rocks, brushed his sandals over gravel. He looked up at Jagger, ten yards away. "You're sure, around here?"

Jagger raised his gaze from the ground. "In this area, yeah." He made a wide circle with his hand, indicating the area in which Beth, Owen, Gheronda, and two other monks moved slowly, staring at the ground. Beth crouched, swept away pebbles. "I was lying right here when Cillian took it out of my pocket. We found the cloth it was in over there, but the wind might have blown it."

Ramón nodded, kept looking. He went as far away from the monastery as the bloody rocks. Owen had taken the bodies that had fallen here into the charnel house. Nevaeh's bullet had effectively decapitated Bale, and Owen had used a sword to permanently end Cillian and Artimus's reign of terror. He wondered what Hester, Lilit, and Therion would do now that their leader was gone.

Tourists occasionally came over to ask Ramón if the monastery was really closed. For a week or so, he'd tell them. Sorry.

Twenty minutes later he stopped. He had just kicked away some rocks and there on the ground was the fragment as Jagger had described it. He glanced around. No one was looking. He crouched and picked it up. A flash of white light blinded him for a moment, then he saw them, so beautiful: little ones with long, spindly limbs, big ones lumbering around him, grinning. Veiny, light-colored flesh. A couple were hunchbacked, others appeared to be no more than skeletons covered with tight, leathery hide. Most bore fangs, all had claws. Ashes swirled around them, some forming wing-like spiked protrusions along their backs. The little ones—like the one that leapt onto his shoulder—were cute; the bigger ones handsome beasts.

He saw other beings too: angels, strong, with glowing bodies that seemed to ripple like robes. The swirling things around them were orange. They sparkled and whipped around with much more fervor than the ashy stuff that encircled the other creatures. They were walking with Jagger, Beth, and the monks, and stood on rocks and the compound walls. All were watching him. He turned his back to them and said to the demons around him, "Shhhh."

One of them chuckled.

He slipped the fragment into his pocket. Incredibly, the vision didn't go away when he released the Stone.

"Anything?" Jagger called.

Brother Ramón wiped the smile off his face and turned to him. He said, "I'm afraid not."

[99]

Jagger, Beth, and Tyler sat on the floor of the Chapel of the Holy Trinity on the summit of Mount Sinai. Beth's left arm was set in a plaster cast—signatures and doodles from her family, Owen, and every monk at St. C's making it look like graffiti art. A sling, patterned with bright, multicolored daisies, held it against her chest.

Jagger rubbed the place were Brother Ramón had dug a bullet out of his calf. It had completely healed, and now he couldn't even prod it into aching. He saw Tyler looking at him, and Jagger pulled on a thin chain around his neck, letting the bullet attached to it fall back over his shirt. Tyler did the same with his bullet, and they shared a look only fellow combatants would understand.

On the walls around them, frescos chronicled the life of Moses. The building was small. Jagger guessed a single minivan could park in it—assuming someone found a way to get it up the mountain's 3,800 uneven steps. Its construction was unremarkable: blocks of square pink granite bound together by thick, sloppily applied concrete mortar. The peaked roof looked like tar paper.

The structure contrasted sharply with the vistas of rugged mountain peaks that seemed to go on forever. Seen at sunrise or sunset, each mountain range took on different colors: purple, pink, blue, gray, looking like the world was nothing more than layers of ripped construction paper and watercolors.

In front of the family, Owen knelt in the center of the floor, chiseling away the mortar around a piece of flat stone. He had posted barricades and Closed signs on the two trails up the mountain, Siket El Basha and Siket Sayidna Musa, to safeguard their privacy. Jordan stood guard outside the closed front doors.

"You sure this is the best place?" Jagger said.

Owen looked at him. "It's the *right* place."

Beth opened a wicker picnic basket and handed out sandwiches and soft drinks.

Taking a bite of a PB&J, Tyler looked at the roof beams and said, "You think they're here now, the angels?"

Jagger ruffled his hair. "I'm sure of it, Ty."

"You think Leo's here?"

Jagged looked up at the ceiling beams. "Could be, I guess."

"Did the monks know Leo was an angel?"

Jagger shrugged. Beth turned to him. "I don't know."

"Well, wouldn't they do a background check on him? I mean, before they let him work at the monastery?"

"If God wanted him there, disguised as a human, He could set up a good cover for him, don't you think?"

Tyler's eyes flashed wide. "Like an undercover agent!"

"The best ever. In the Bible angels eat, sleep—"

Tyler jumped in: "Dad says he saw Leo get electrocuted!" He turned to Jagger for confirmation.

"Well, shocked," Jagger said, thinking of Leo grabbing the Cobra. "He spasmed in pain. Looked real to me."

"Why didn't he just become an angel, a real one, and . . ." Tyler's big eyes narrowed as he searched for the right word. "And *smite* those robots?"

"Good question," Jagger said.

"Maybe it wasn't time to reveal himself," Beth offered.

Tyler chewed, thinking. "Why do you think God sent him here?"

"Hmm," Beth said. "Protect the monks, maybe, or the monastery."

"Or me?" Tyler smiled up at her sweetly. "Maybe he's my guardian angel."

"Then he did a very good job."

"This time," Jagger added. He raised an eyebrow at his wife and dug into the basket for a bag of chips.

Beth rubbed Tyler's back. She said, "You're full of questions today."

"Aren't *you*?"

Beth made eye contact with Jagger. "They're pouring out of my ears, Ty. But God works in mysterious ways, and I'm okay with that. There are some things we're not supposed to know."

Owen grunted and hammered a mallet into the chisel, harder than before, judging by the sound.

Tyler watched him strike a few more blows, then said, "I wish we could keep the God Stone."

"Why?"

"It's cool, seeing angels and that whole thing—what did you call it?—the spiritual realm."

"You don't need a relic to see it, honey," Beth said.

He looked over at her, one eye closed. "Huh?"

"It's in you, right here." She touched his shirt over his heart.

"That's not the same."

"Isn't it enough to know it's real, all around us, even if you can't see it?"

He shrugged. "I'd rather see it."

Owen set his tools down and started prying the stone up with his fingers. Jagger crawled over and helped. They pushed it away, and Owen shined a flashlight beam into the hole. "Wow," he said.

"What?" Tyler said, crawling over. Beth joined them around the hole, all of them gazing down.

"The stories were true," Owen said.

"What?" Tyler asked again.

Owen held the beam on a stone surface below the chapel's floor trusses. "See those round indentations in the rock? Those are the impressions of Moses's knees when he knelt here to talk to God."

"For real?"

"I believe it."

Tyler looked up at him. "You *knew* Moses. I mean, in person."

"Yep." Owen turned and picked up a wooden box he'd made in the monastery's workshop.

"Can I see it?"

Owen hinged the lid open. Resting in black velvet was the Stone.

Looking in, Tyler said, "What about Ollie?" Always thinking of others. Jagger placed his hand over the boy's shoulder, gently rubbed it. Owen had used his satphone to stay current on Ollie's condition, first letting the others know that the archaeologist had made it through the initial surgery and that doctors were optimistic. Later, reporting that he'd intermittently regained consciousness long enough to demand where the angels had gone, growing more belligerent and vigorous, getting stronger, healthier.

"What about him?" Owen asked.

Tyler tilted his head toward the Stone. "He called it his Holy Grail. He's going to want it, isn't he?"

Owen stared at the Stone, not saying anything. Finally he said, "Sometimes it's better we don't get what we want." He looked at Tyler, seeing if he understood. Tyler nodded, and Owen closed the box. He lowered it into the hole and set it over the knee prints. "I believe this is Yours," he said.

They returned the floor stone to its place, and Owen mixed mortar in a pan, coloring it to match the surrounding mortar. When he was finished, Tyler said, "That's it? Is it safe?"

Owen smiled at Jagger and said, "Things around here have a way of lasting a very long time."

Acknowledgments

While my name appears on the cover, no endeavor like this can be completed without the love and encouragement, the help and advice of family, colleagues, readers, and experts. To name but a few, my deepest thanks to . . .

My family—thank you for constantly supporting my storytelling, even when I'm too lost in it to be much more than the guy roaming around the house mumbling about angels and demons, far off places, and the dilemmas of people who live only in my imagination. Honestly, I couldn't write a word without you.

Team Nelson—especially my fabulous editors, Amanda Bostic and L.B. Norton, Becky Monds, and Allen Arnold, whose eye for story details I will sorely miss.

My agent, Joel Gotler at Intellectual Property Group. You're right, life is good.

My beta readers—my wife, Jodi, Melissa Willis, Devin Berglund, John and Sarah Bolin, and Wayne Pinkstaff. Thank you for nudging the story into place.

For helping with the Russian language—Sharon Dupree and Jennifer Rose.

And for their inspiration, friendship, and just plain coolness, my thanks to Larry Hama, Burke Allen, Frank Redman, James Byron Huggins, James Rollins, Steve and Liz Berry, David Morrell, Thomas Perry, Jerry Jenkins, Connie and Dwight Cenac, Paul and Jennifer Turner, the Ruark family, Mark and Mari Nelson, John Fornof, Mike Landon, Tom Manzer, Rel Mollet, Mark Lavallee, Dave Rhoades, Nicole Petrino-Salter, Jake Chism, Joe Cuchiara, Kim, Ben and Matthew Ford, Ted Dekker, Tosca Lee, Kevin Kaiser, Eric Wilson, Steven James, and the Ragged Blue Monkeys.

Soli Deo gloria.

READING GROUP GUIDE

1. In the story, pieces of the first Ten Commandments—the ones Moses broke upon finding the Israelites worshiping a golden calf—allow people to see through the veil that separates our world from the spiritual realm. Throughout history, there have been claims that other religious relics hold special powers, such as invincibility and resurrecting the dead. What are your thoughts about relics holding special powers? Do you believe the claims? If so, why do you think God imbues items with supernatural power?

2. Owen worries that if the world found out about the God Stone's powers, it could lead to chaos and destruction. What are some ways it could be misused? Do you think proof of a spiritual realm through something like the God Stone would lead to spiritual conversions and changed lives . . . or would most people think it was a trick or discount its significance?

3. One of the themes of *The Judgment Stone* is that there are beings all around us working for us or against us, and we should be more willing to have faith in things we cannot see. Do you believe this is true? Have you ever experienced a situation that defied logic and drew you closer to an understanding of invisible forces in your life?

4. Did the revelation about Father Leo's true identity surprise you? Did you notice some things that indicated he was something more than he appeared to be? Why do you think he was undercover at the monastery?

5. Brother Ramón touches the fragment of the God Stone and sees demons around him. What do you think is going

on with him? Could he be a man experiencing a crisis of faith . . . or does he have something more sinister going on? Do you think someone like that could have gone undetected in such a place as St. Catherine's Monastery? Have you ever known anyone who completely deceived you?

6. For you, what is the most significant aspect of *The Judgment Stone*? What was the most exciting part? The most touching?

7. *The Judgment Stone* is a complex tale told through multiple points of view and two distinct storylines—Jagger and Owen chasing the Clan, and the Tribe at the monastery. Do you enjoy reading stories structured this way, or would you prefer stories told through the eyes of a single character? What are some of the benefits to a reader of experiencing a story through various characters? What are some drawbacks?

8. Would *you* like to see the spiritual world with your physical eyes? How would it change you?

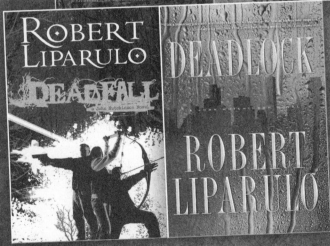

About the Author

Robert Liparulo has received rave reviews for both his adult novels (*The 13th Tribe, Comes a Horseman, Germ, Deadfall,* and *Deadlock*) and the best-selling Dreamhouse Kings series for young adults. He lives in Colorado with his wife and their four children.

Photo by Gabe Wicks